5 Worlds

BOOK 1

THE SAND WARRIOR

Mark SIEGEL **Alexis SIEGEL**

Xanthe BOUMA **Boya SUN**

Matt ROCKEFELLER

Random House 🏠 New York

"One by one the five great Beacons
went dark and the Gods were gone.
And none would ever again light the
shining Beacons, save a Warrior of
Sand, crowned with living fire. . . ."
—FROM THE HOURS OF PRINCE FELID

Chapter 1

RUNAWAY SAND

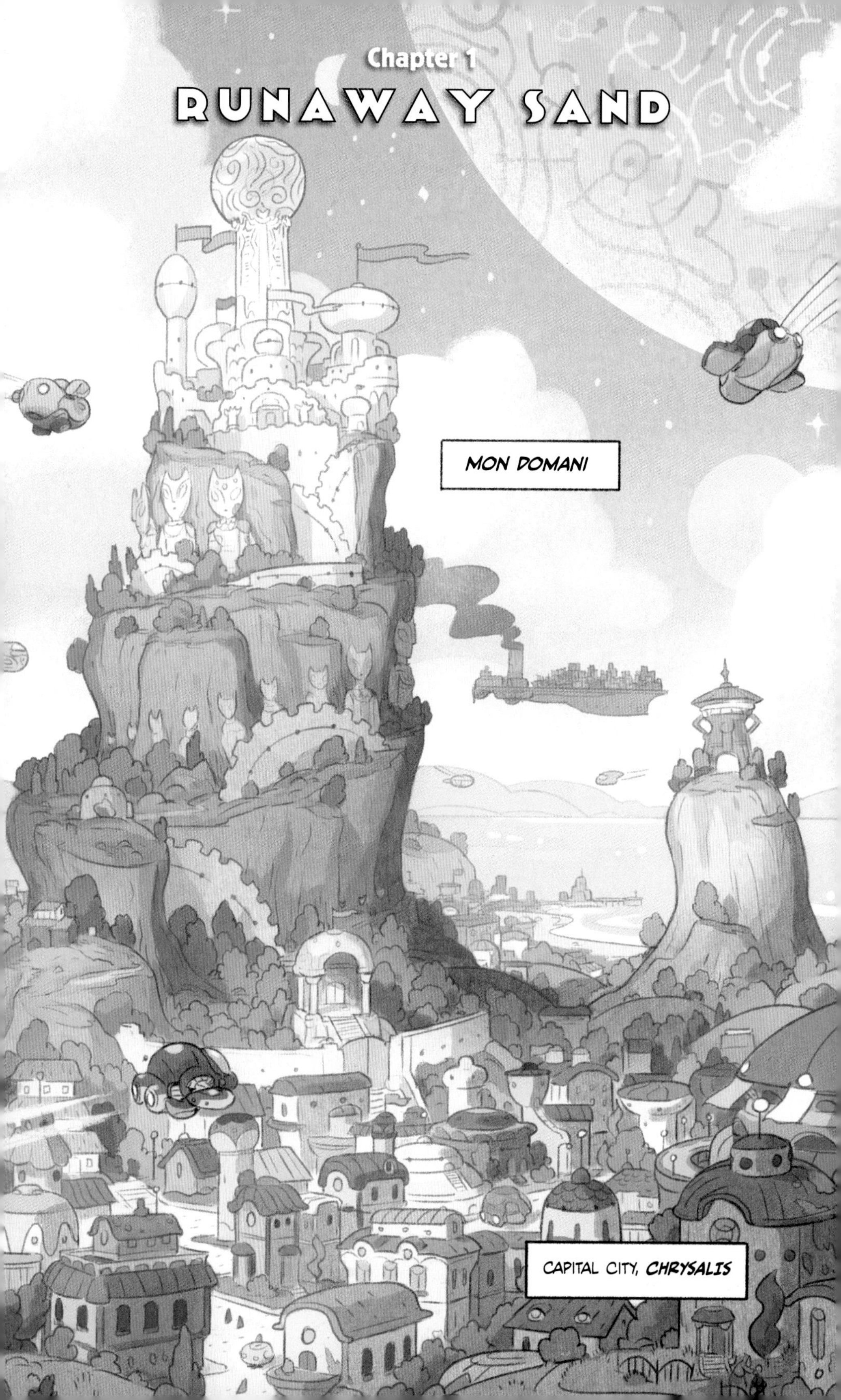
MON DOMANI
CAPITAL CITY, CHRYSALIS

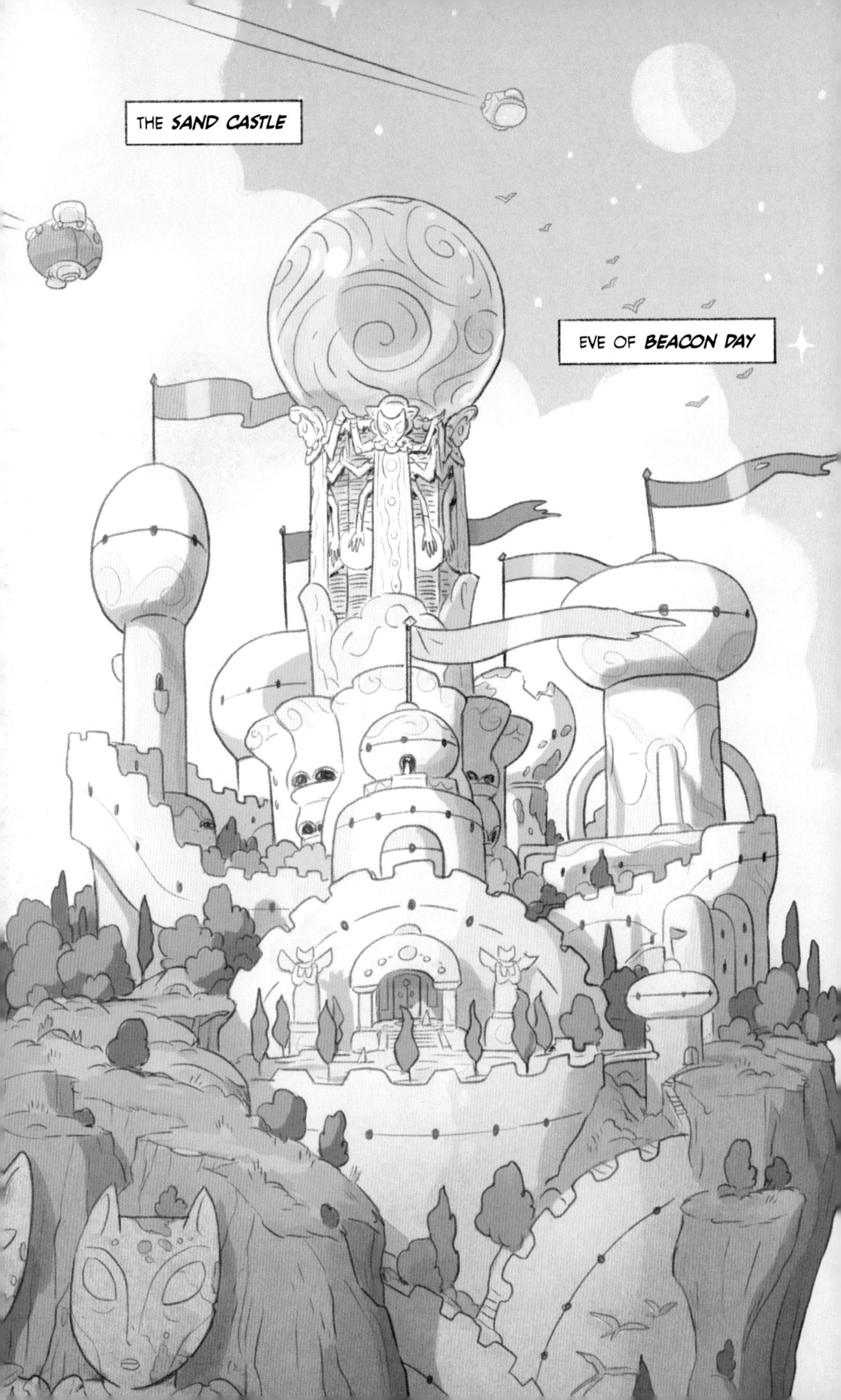
THE SAND CASTLE
EVE OF BEACON DAY

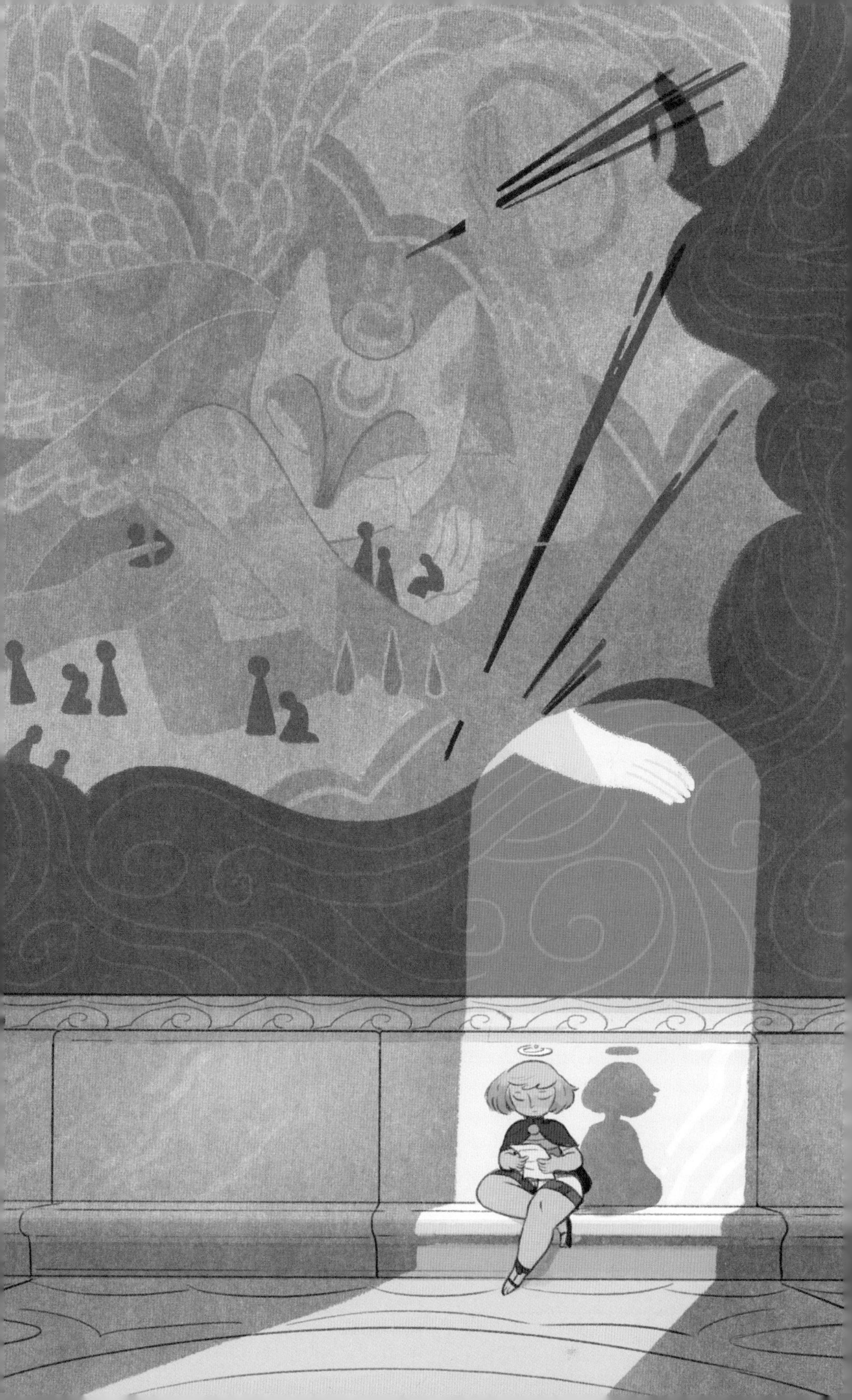

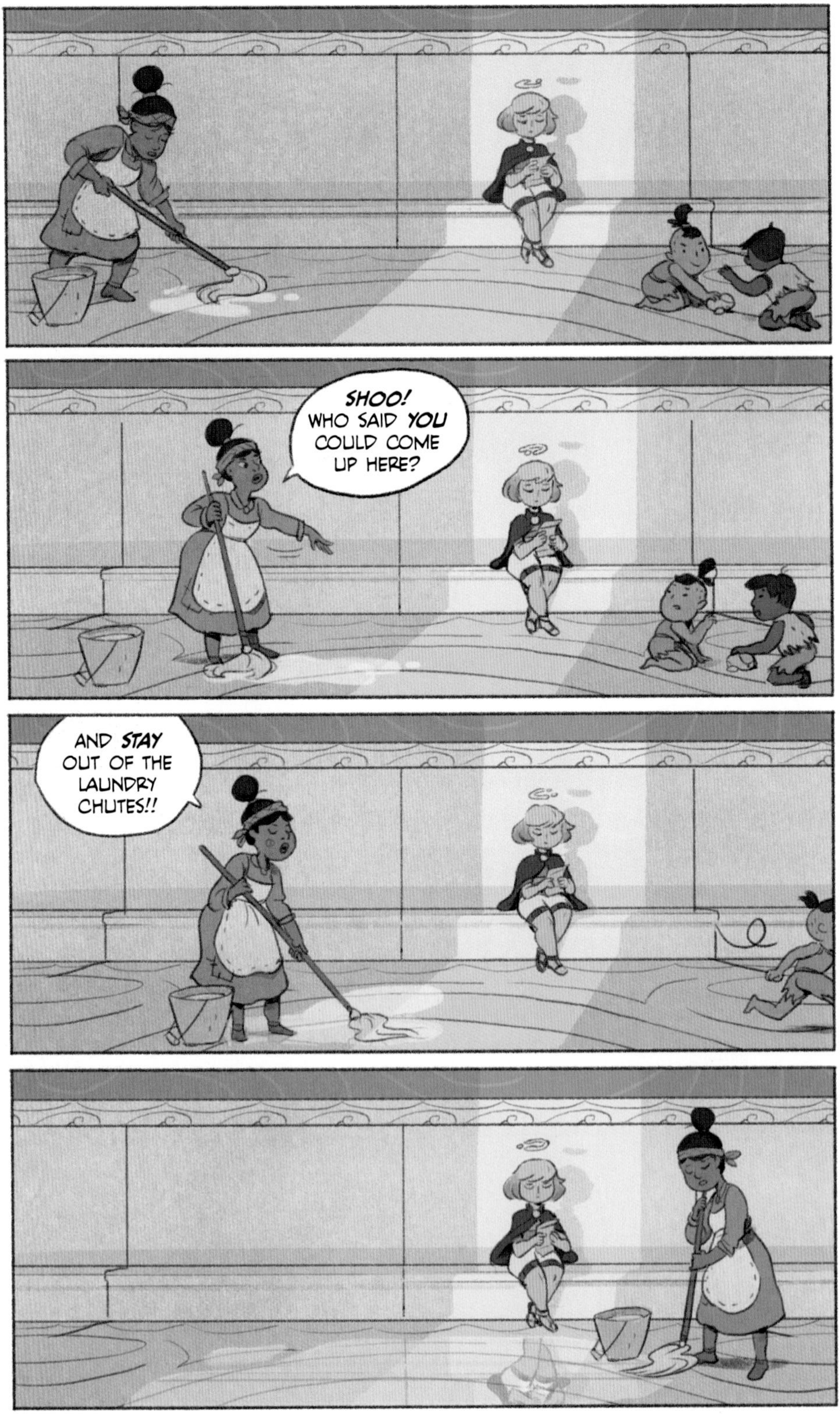
SHOO! WHO SAID YOU COULD COME UP HERE?
AND STAY OUT OF THE LAUNDRY CHUTES!!

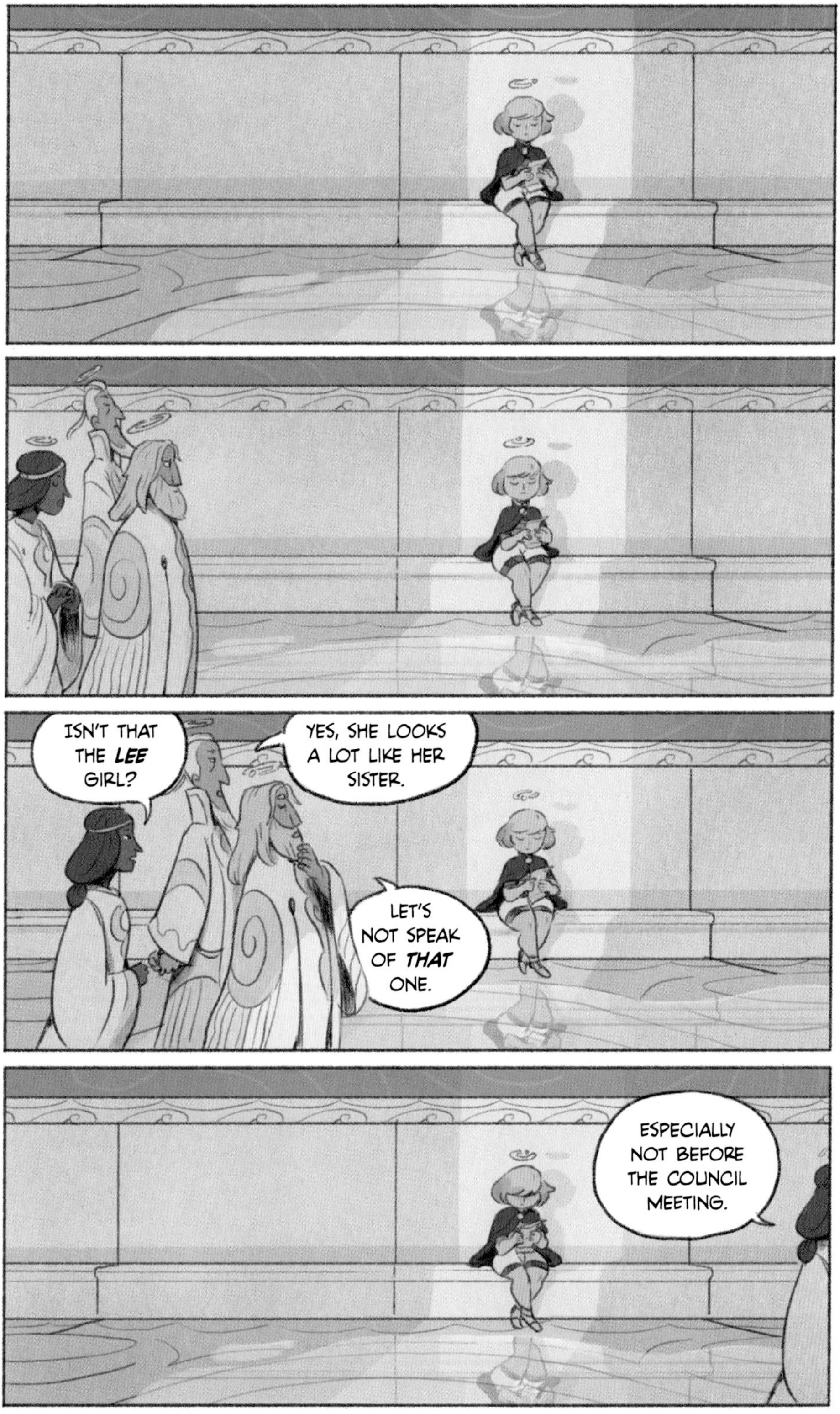
ISN'T THAT THE **LEE** GIRL?
YES, SHE LOOKS A LOT LIKE HER SISTER.
LET'S NOT SPEAK OF **THAT** ONE.
ESPECIALLY NOT BEFORE THE COUNCIL MEETING.

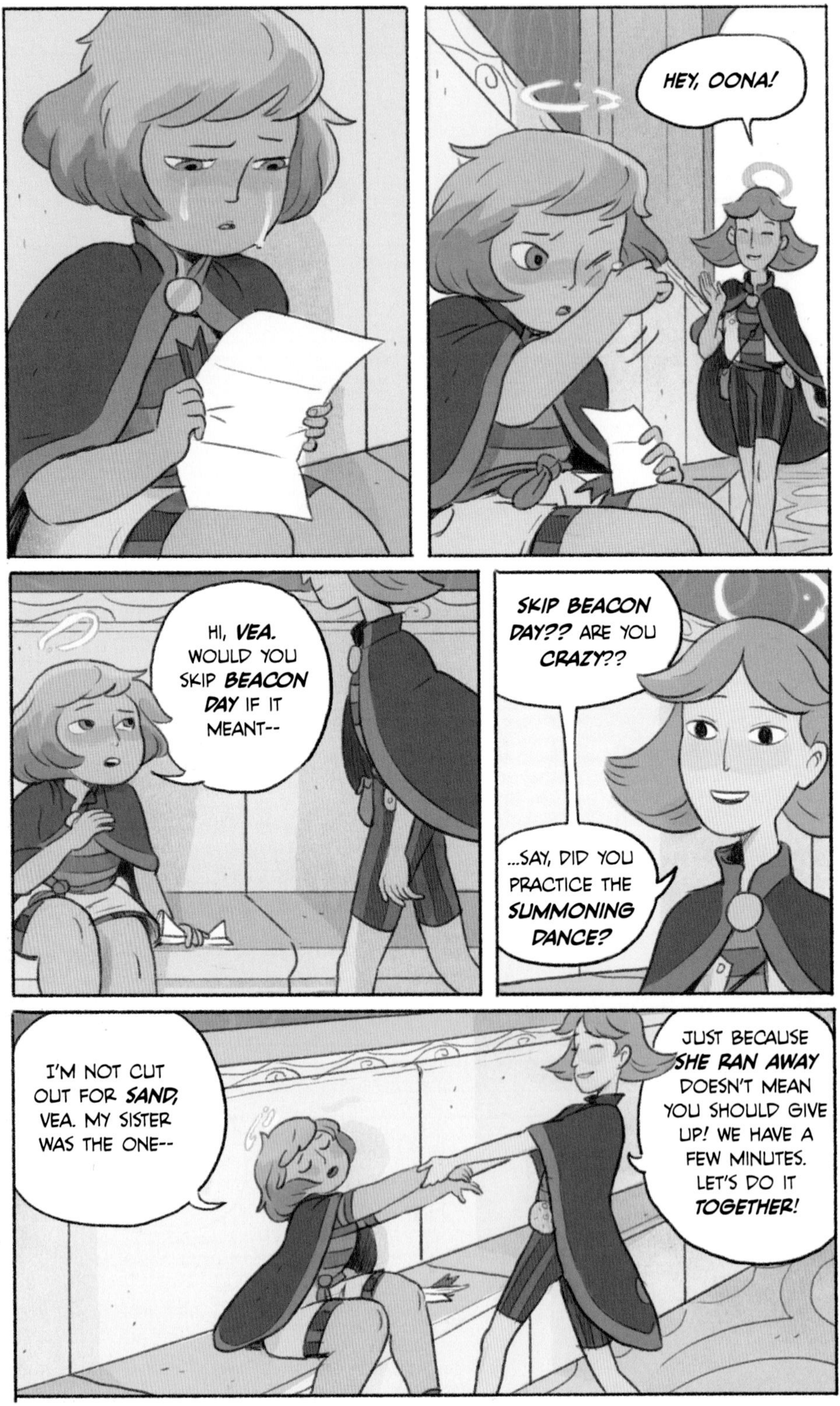
HEY, OONA!
HI, VEA. WOULD YOU SKIP BEACON DAY IF IT MEANT--
SKIP BEACON DAY?? ARE YOU CRAZY??
...SAY, DID YOU PRACTICE THE SUMMONING DANCE?
I'M NOT CUT OUT FOR SAND, VEA. MY SISTER WAS THE ONE--
JUST BECAUSE SHE RAN AWAY DOESN'T MEAN YOU SHOULD GIVE UP! WE HAVE A FEW MINUTES. LET'S DO IT TOGETHER!

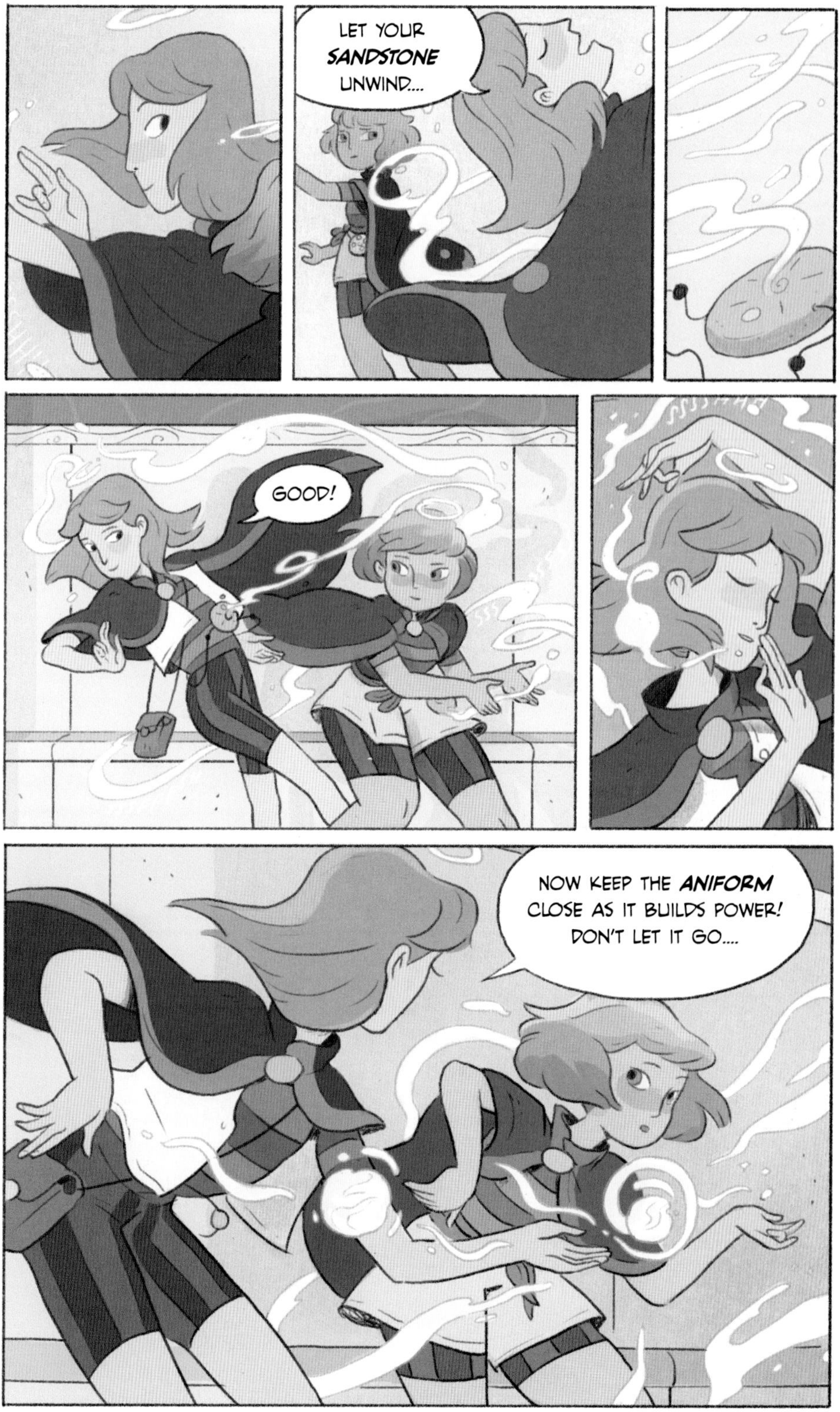
LET YOUR SANDSTONE UNWIND....
GOOD!
NOW KEEP THE ANIFORM CLOSE AS IT BUILDS POWER! DON'T LET IT GO....

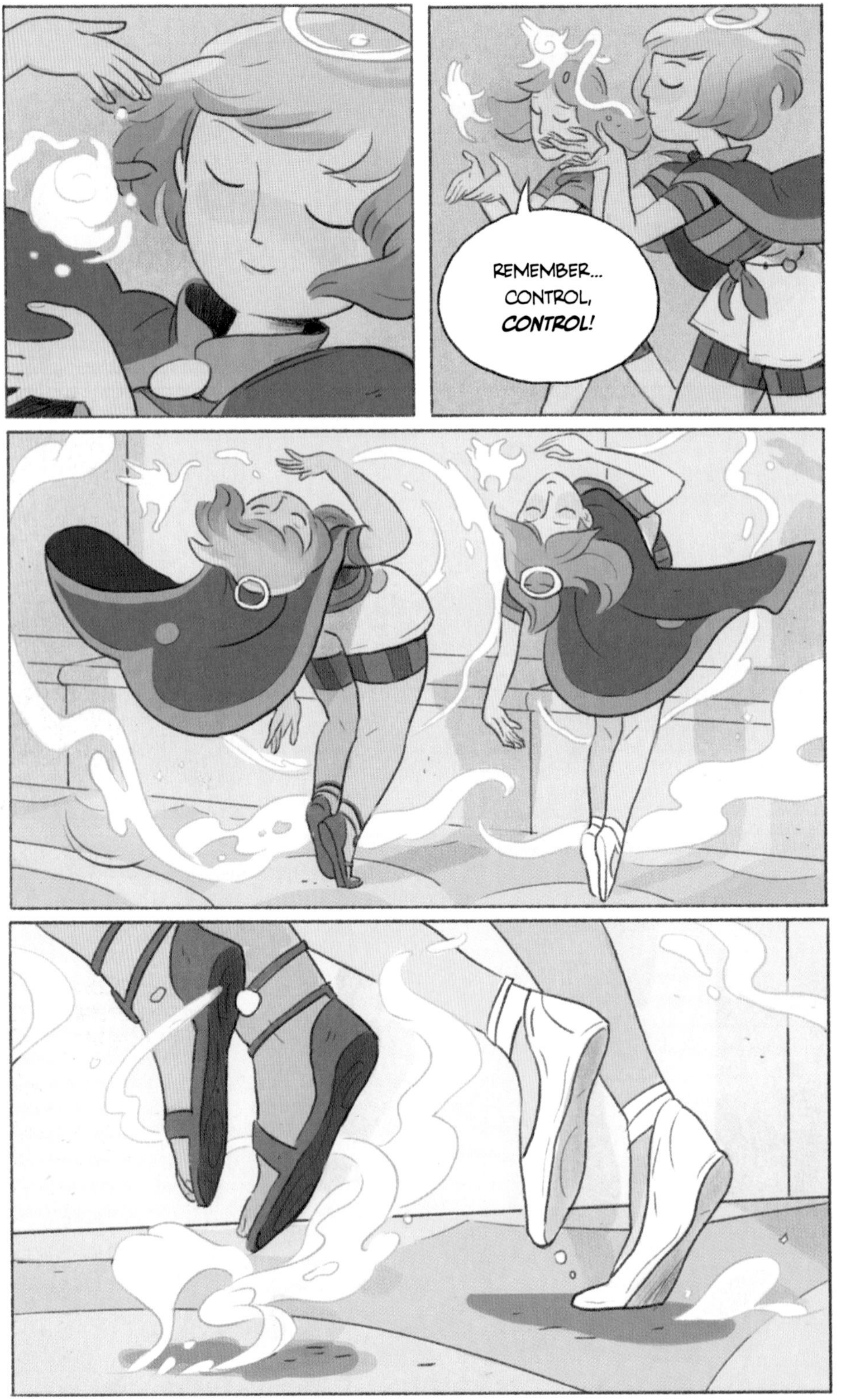
REMEMBER... CONTROL, **CONTROL!**

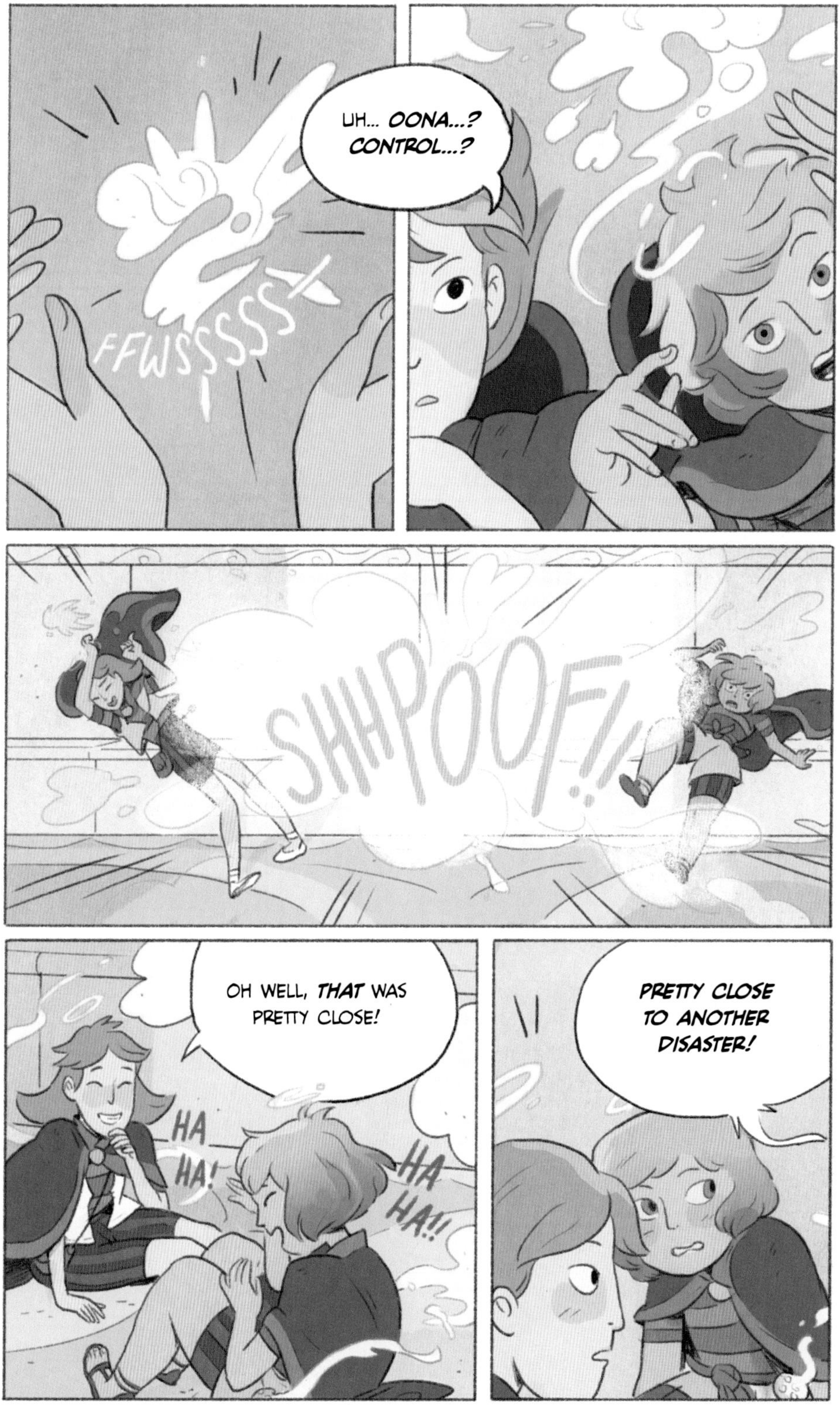
FFWSSSSS
UH... OONA...? CONTROL...?
SHHPOOF!!
OH WELL, THAT WAS PRETTY CLOSE!
HA HA!
HA HA!!
PRETTY CLOSE TO ANOTHER DISASTER!

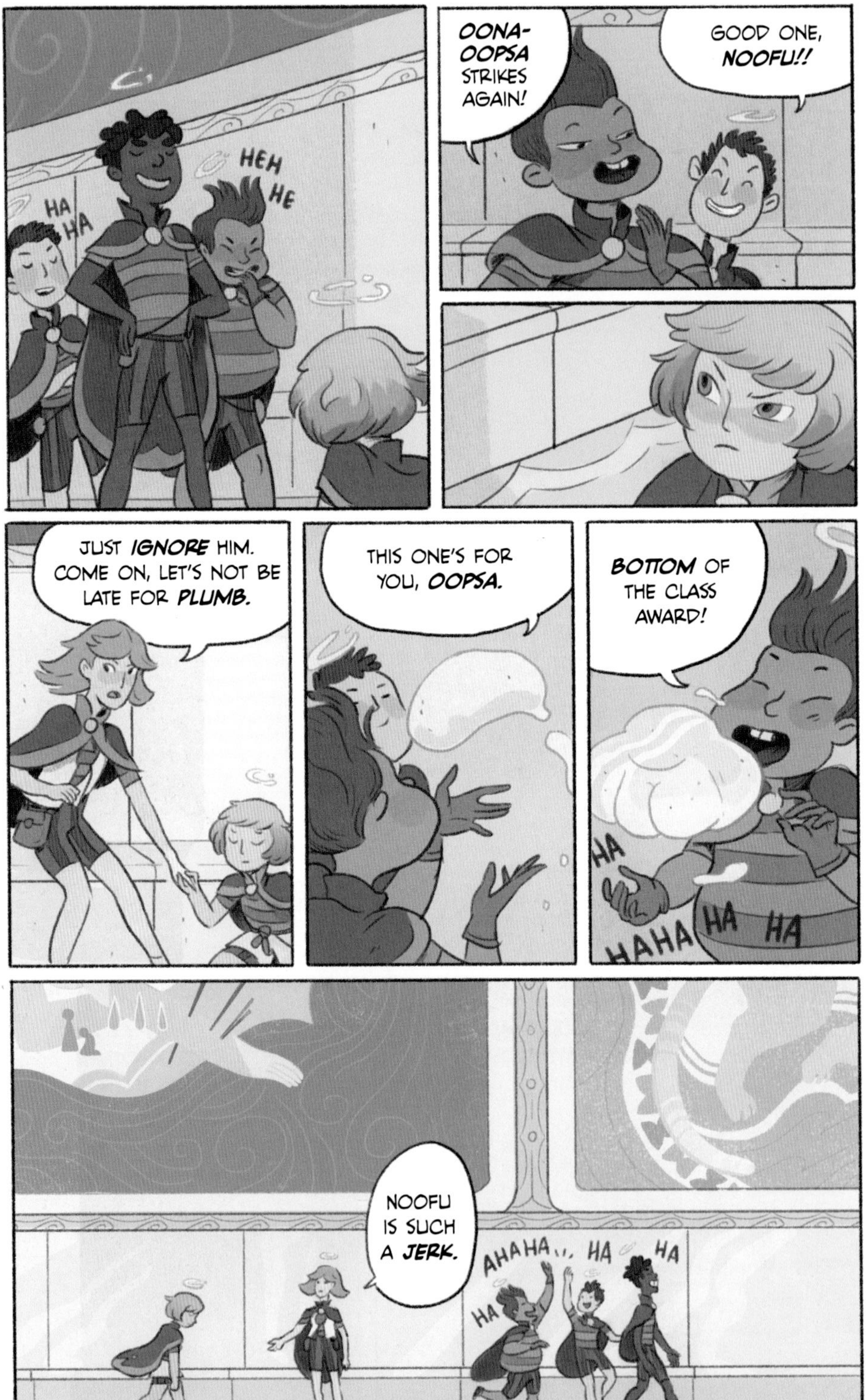
HA HA
HEH HE
OONA-OOPSA STRIKES AGAIN!
GOOD ONE, NOOFU!!
JUST IGNORE HIM. COME ON, LET'S NOT BE LATE FOR PLUMB.
THIS ONE'S FOR YOU, OOPSA.
BOTTOM OF THE CLASS AWARD!
HA HAHA HA HA
NOOFU IS SUCH A JERK.
AHAHA HA HA HA

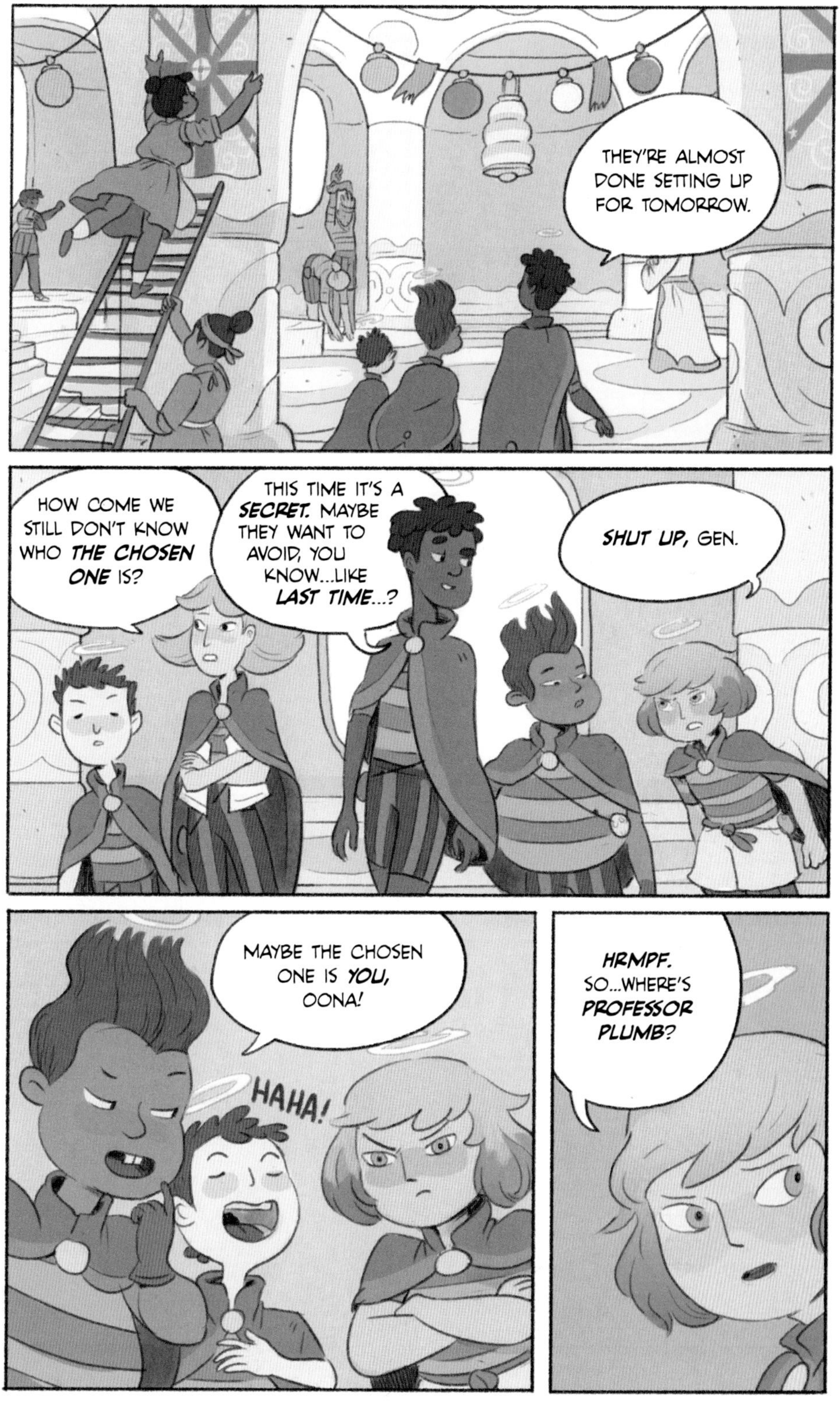
THEY'RE ALMOST DONE SETTING UP FOR TOMORROW.
HOW COME WE STILL DON'T KNOW WHO THE CHOSEN ONE IS?
THIS TIME IT'S A SECRET. MAYBE THEY WANT TO AVOID, YOU KNOW...LIKE LAST TIME...?
SHUT UP, GEN.
MAYBE THE CHOSEN ONE IS YOU, OONA!
HAHA!
HRMPF. SO...WHERE'S PROFESSOR PLUMB?

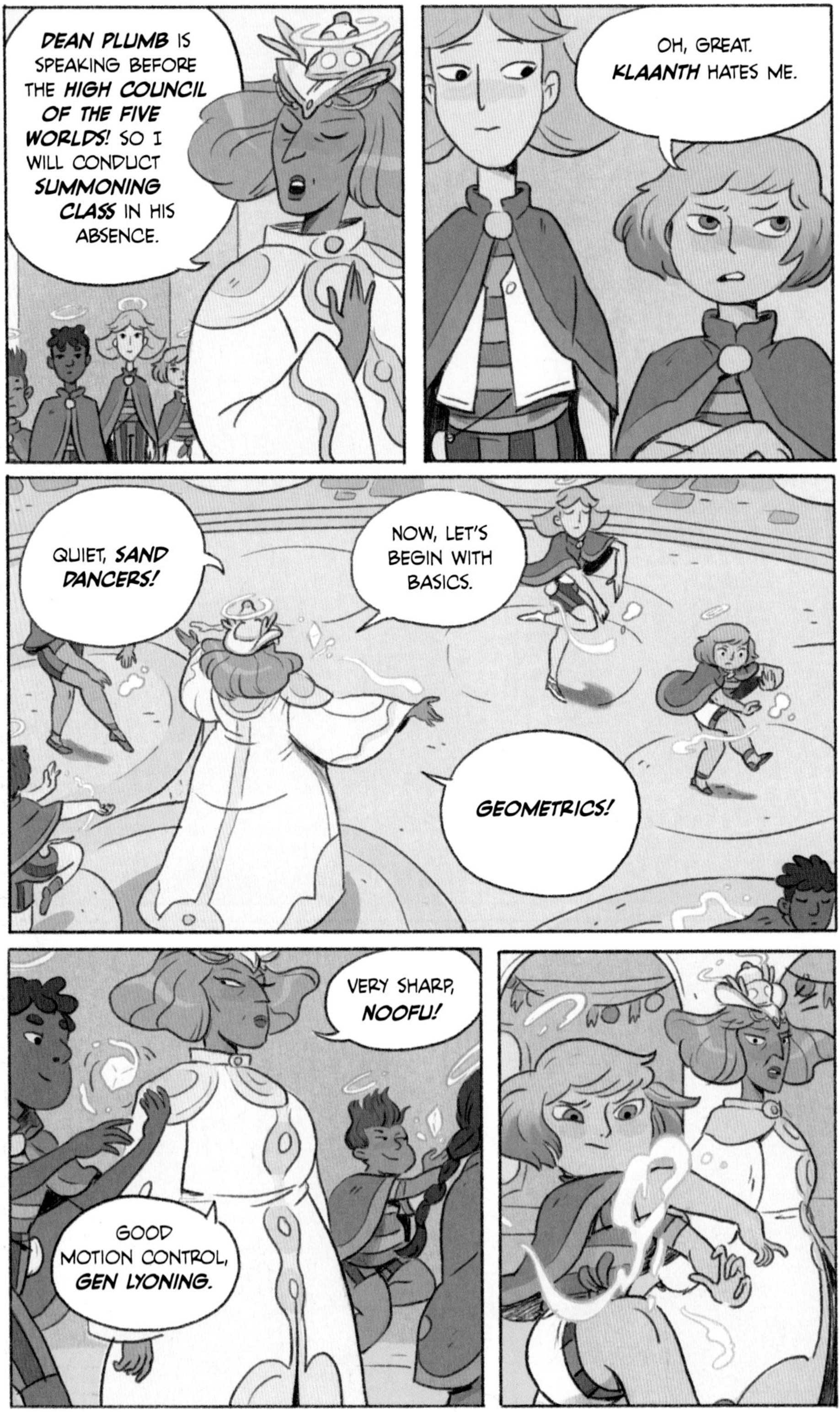
DEAN PLUMB IS SPEAKING BEFORE THE HIGH COUNCIL OF THE FIVE WORLDS! SO I WILL CONDUCT SUMMONING CLASS IN HIS ABSENCE.
OH, GREAT. KLAANTH HATES ME.
QUIET, SAND DANCERS!
NOW, LET'S BEGIN WITH BASICS.
GEOMETRICS!
VERY SHARP, NOOFU!
GOOD MOTION CONTROL, GEN LYONING.

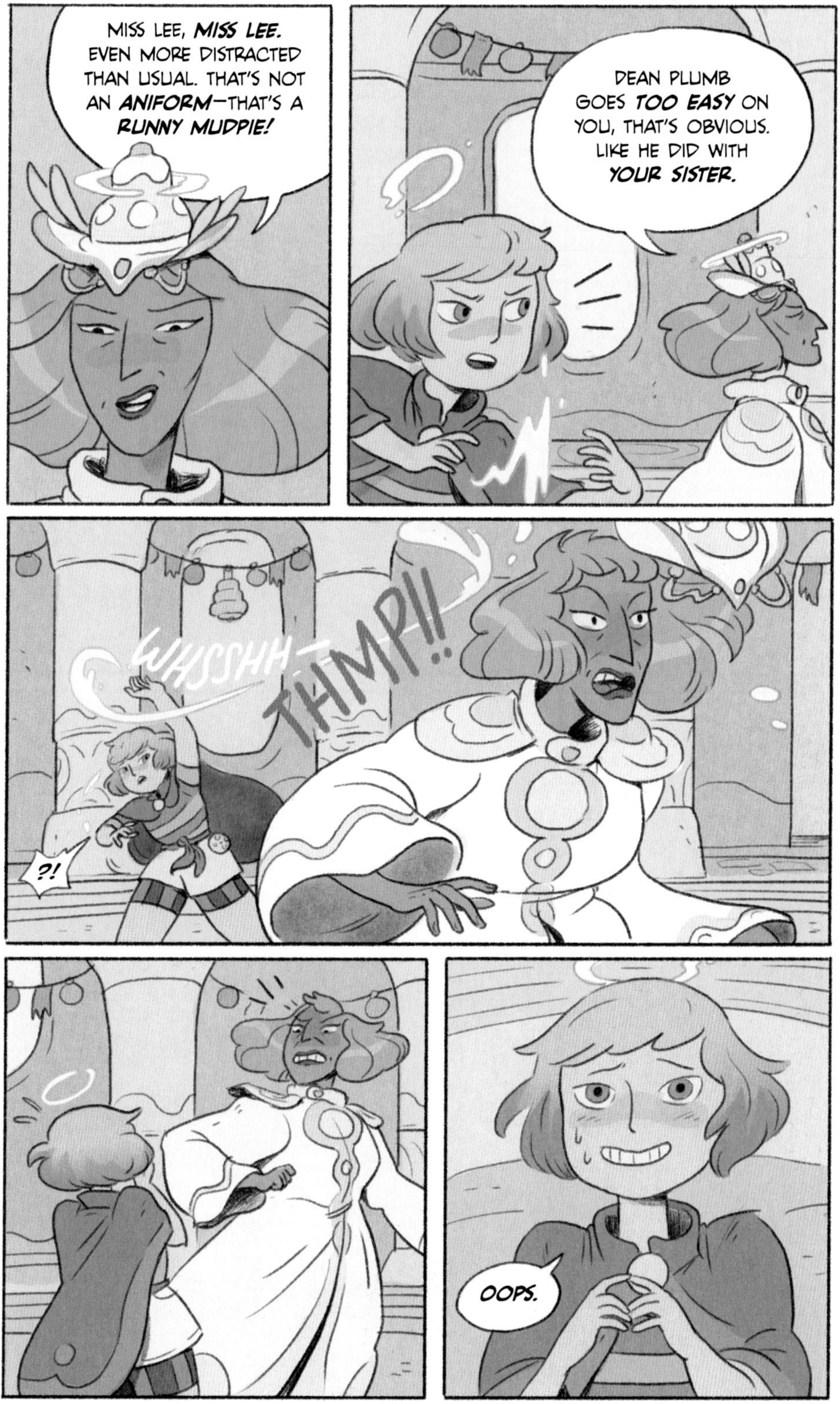
MISS LEE, MISS LEE. EVEN MORE DISTRACTED THAN USUAL. THAT'S NOT AN ANIFORM—THAT'S A RUNNY MUDPIE!
DEAN PLUMB GOES TOO EASY ON YOU, THAT'S OBVIOUS. LIKE HE DID WITH YOUR SISTER.
WHSSHH—
THMP!!
?!
OOPS.

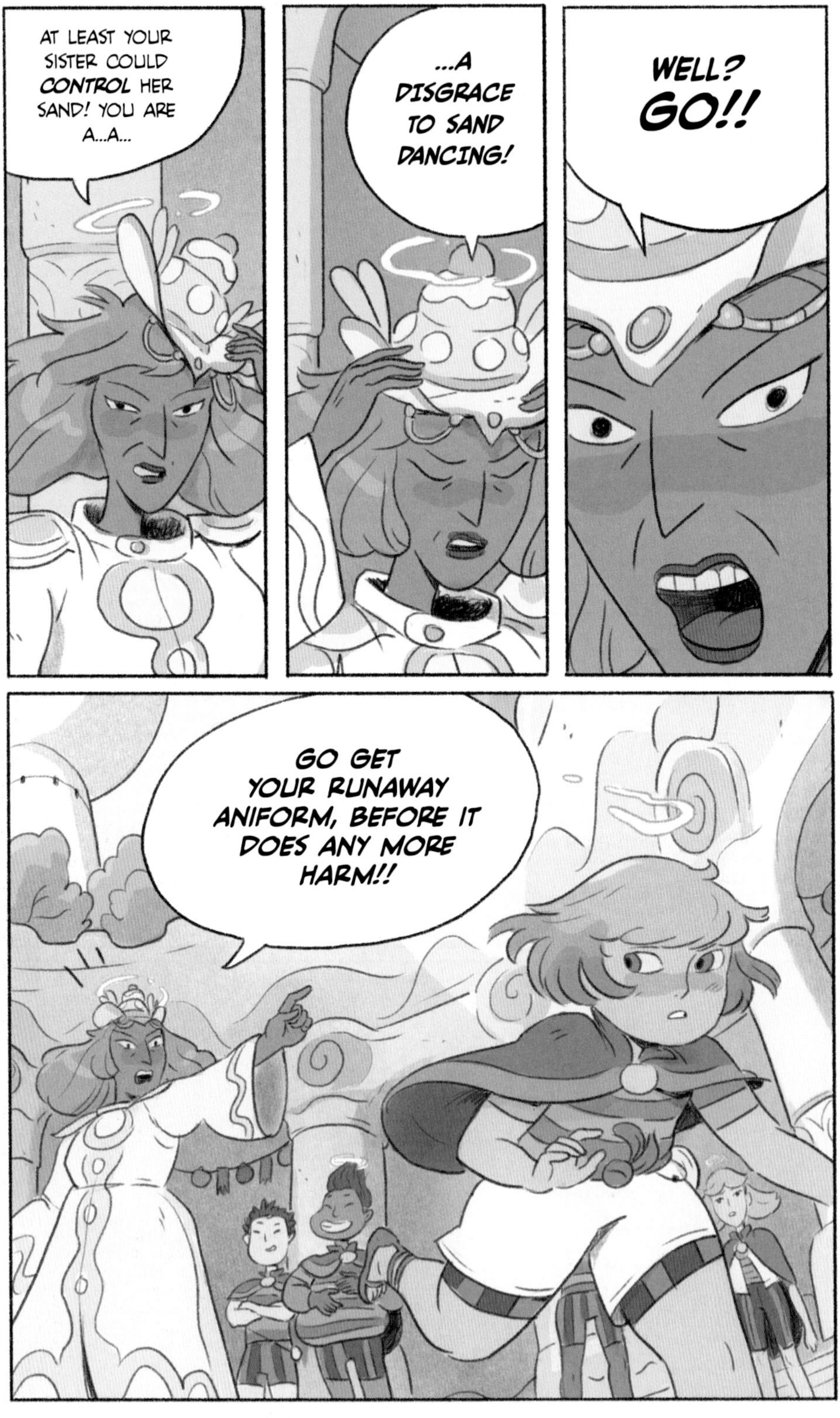
AT LEAST YOUR SISTER COULD CONTROL HER SAND! YOU ARE A...A...
...A DISGRACE TO SAND DANCING!
WELL? GO!!
GO GET YOUR RUNAWAY ANIFORM, BEFORE IT DOES ANY MORE HARM!!

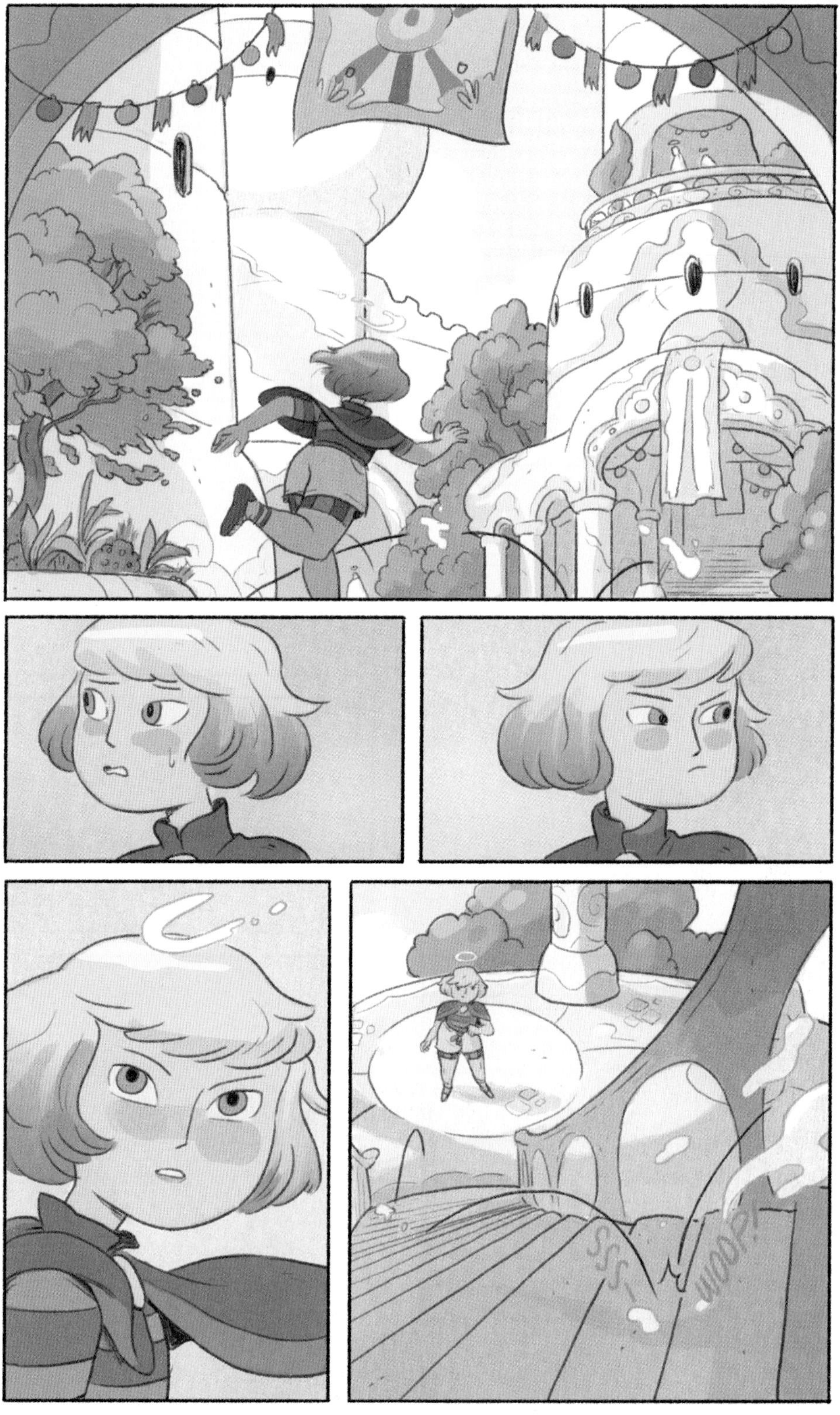
SS!
WOOP!

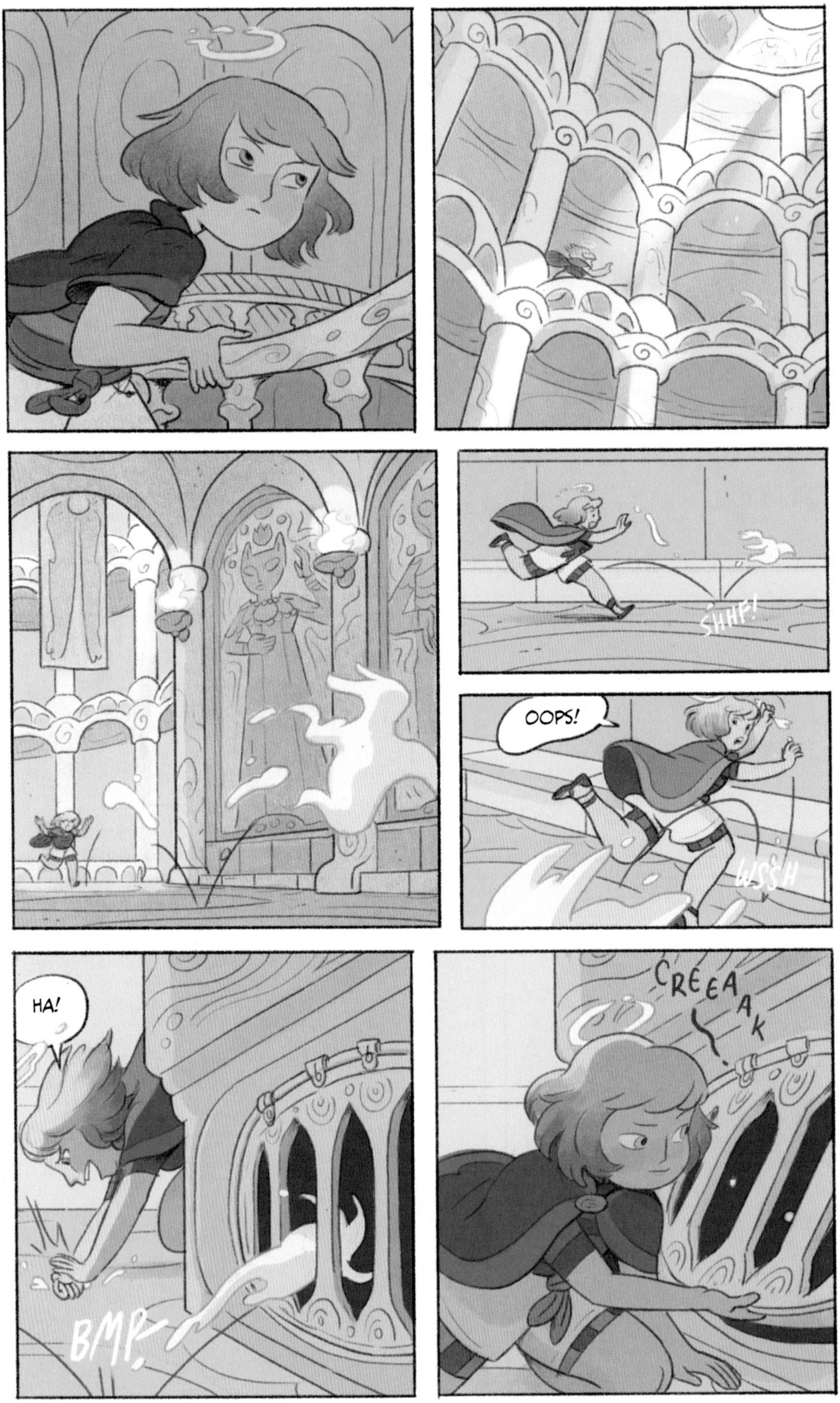
SHHF!
OOPS!
WSSH
HA!
BMP
CREEAAK

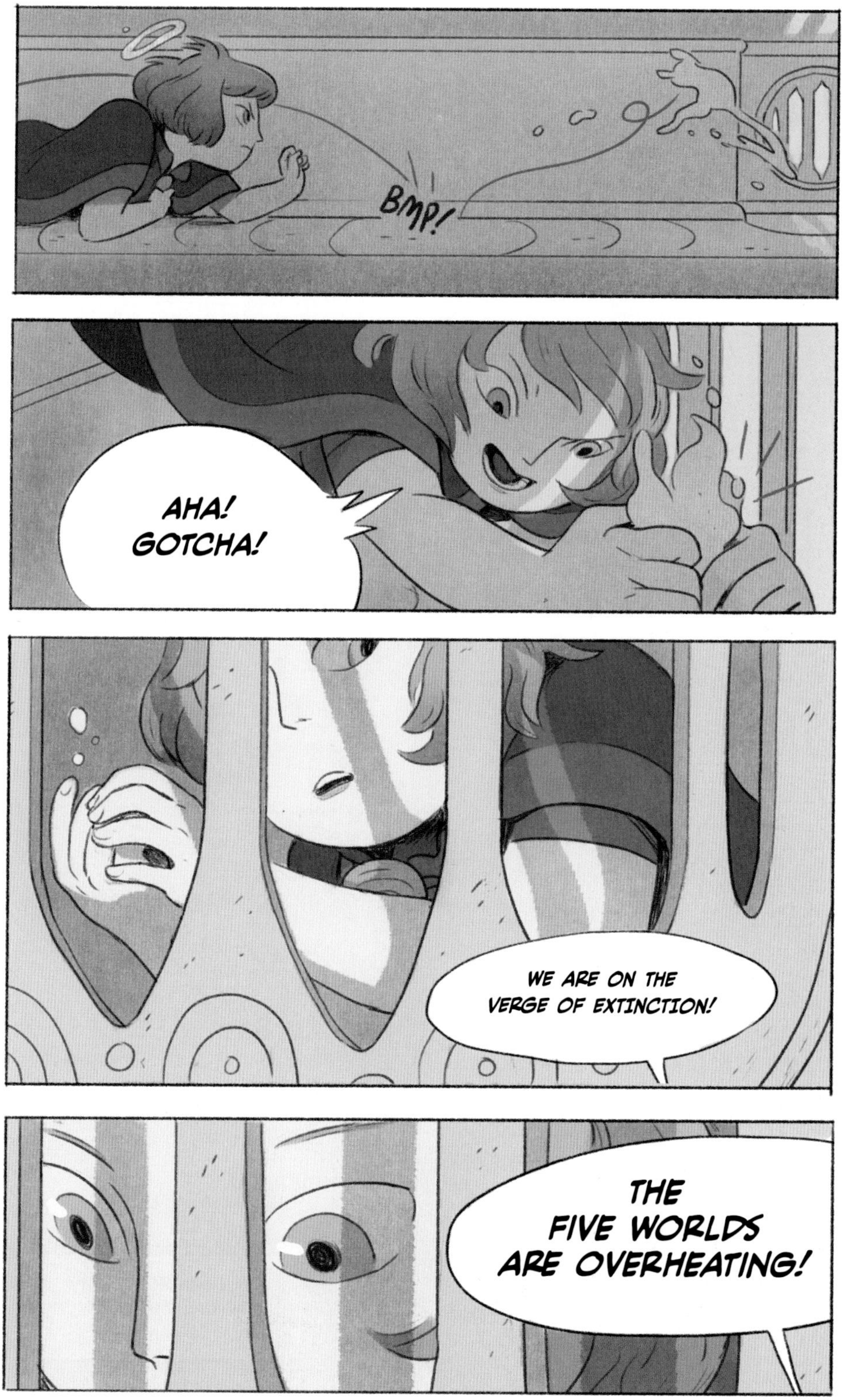
BMP!
AHA! GOTCHA!
WE ARE ON THE VERGE OF EXTINCTION!
THE FIVE WORLDS ARE OVERHEATING!

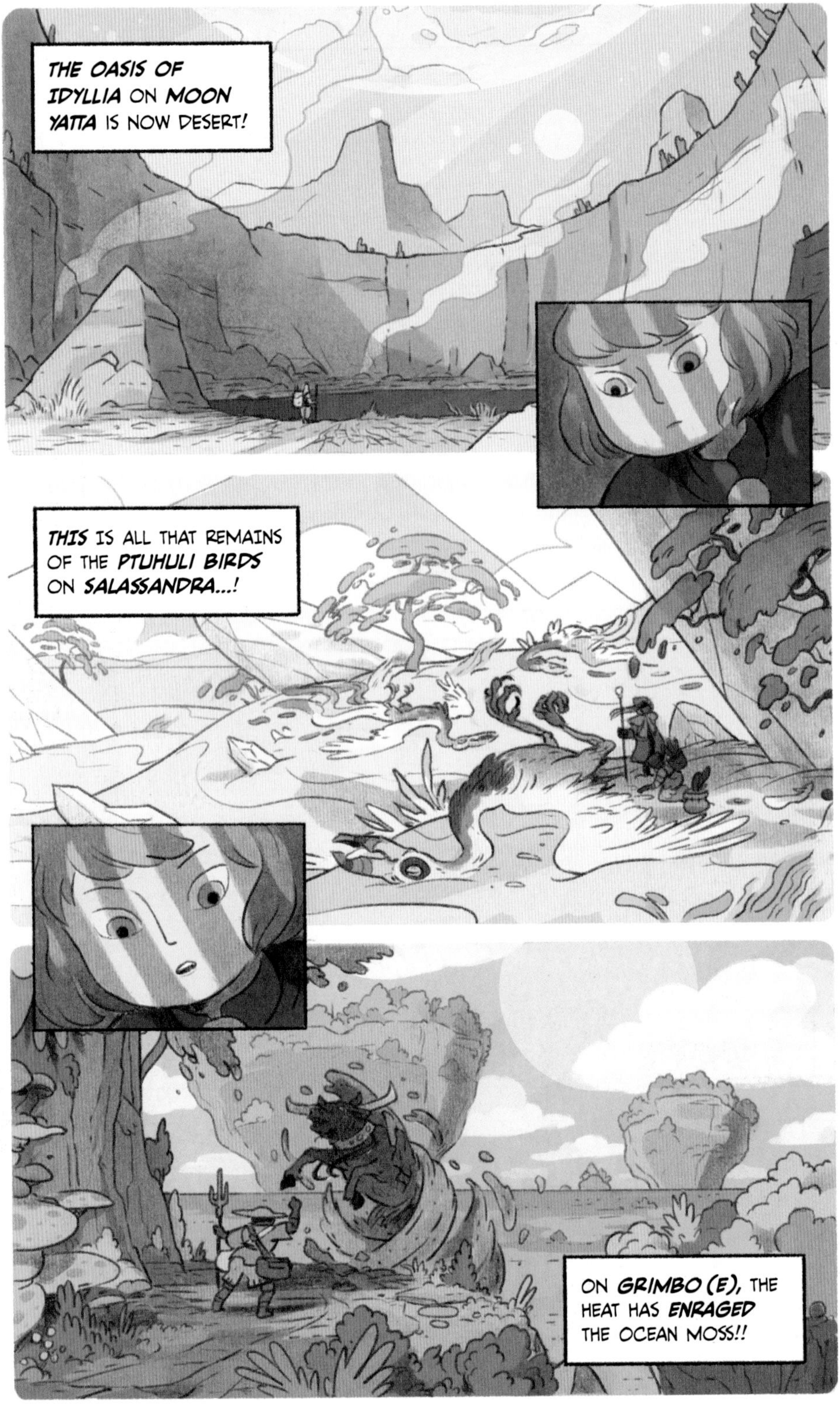
THE OASIS OF IDYLLIA ON MOON YATTA IS NOW DESERT!
THIS IS ALL THAT REMAINS OF THE PTUHULI BIRDS ON SALASSANDRA...!
ON GRIMBO (E), THE HEAT HAS ENRAGED THE OCEAN MOSS!!

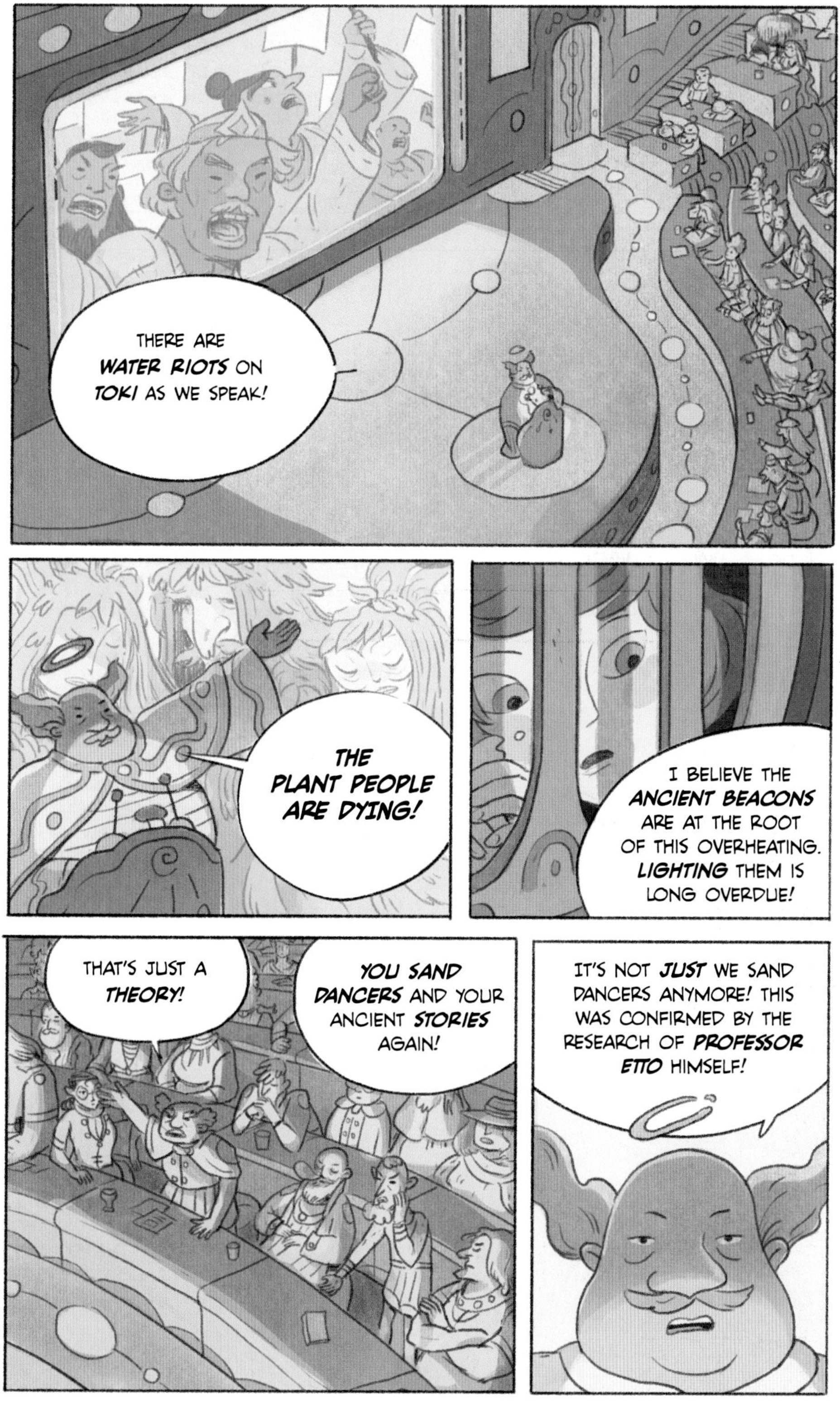
THERE ARE WATER RIOTS ON TOKI AS WE SPEAK!
THE PLANT PEOPLE ARE DYING!
I BELIEVE THE ANCIENT BEACONS ARE AT THE ROOT OF THIS OVERHEATING. LIGHTING THEM IS LONG OVERDUE!
THAT'S JUST A THEORY!
YOU SAND DANCERS AND YOUR ANCIENT STORIES AGAIN!
IT'S NOT JUST WE SAND DANCERS ANYMORE! THIS WAS CONFIRMED BY THE RESEARCH OF PROFESSOR ETTO HIMSELF!

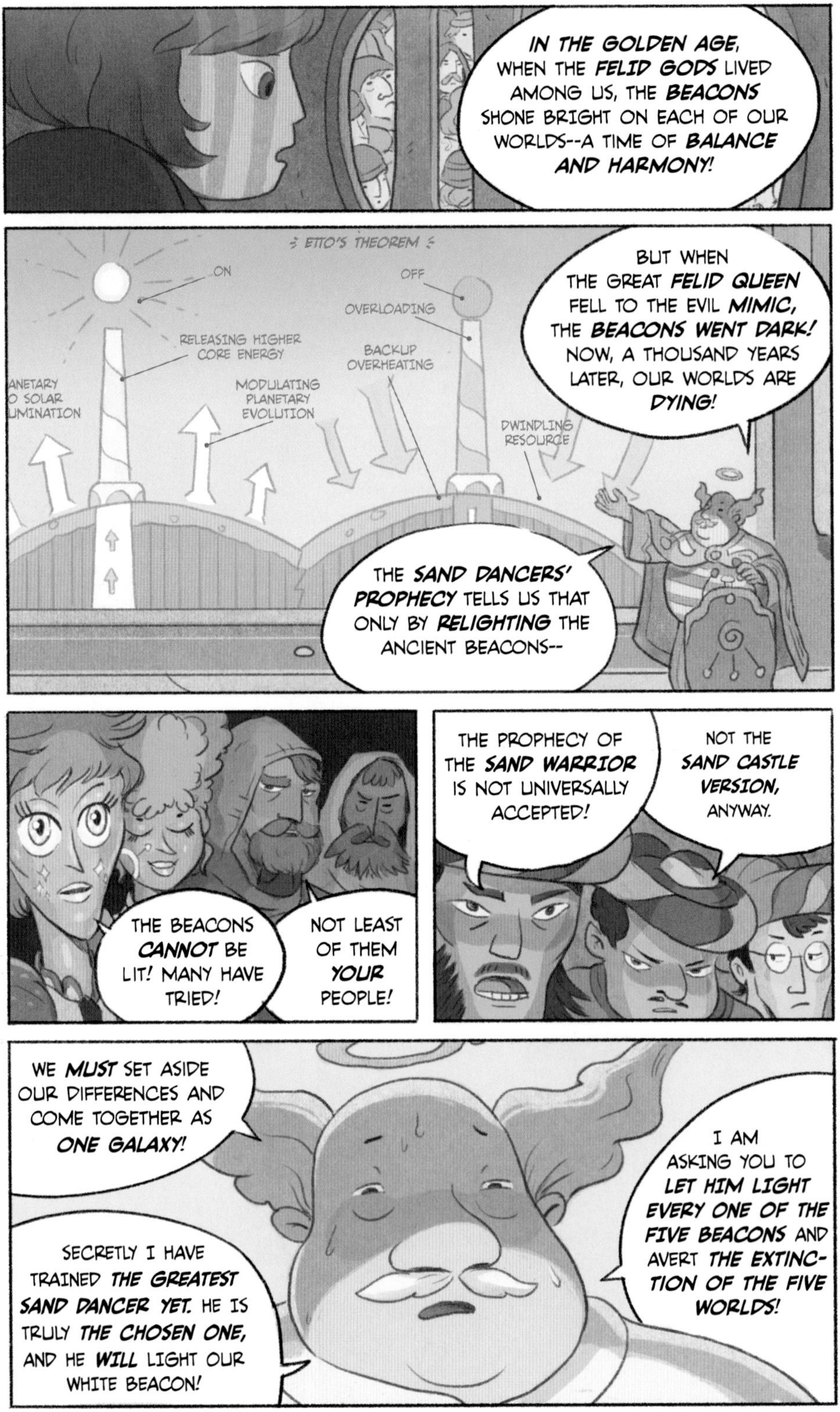
IN THE GOLDEN AGE, WHEN THE FELID GODS LIVED AMONG US, THE BEACONS SHONE BRIGHT ON EACH OF OUR WORLDS--A TIME OF BALANCE AND HARMONY!
ETTO'S THEOREM
ON
OFF
OVERLOADING
RELEASING HIGHER CORE ENERGY
BACKUP OVERHEATING
MODULATING PLANETARY EVOLUTION
DWINDLING RESOURCE
BUT WHEN THE GREAT FELID QUEEN FELL TO THE EVIL MIMIC, THE BEACONS WENT DARK! NOW, A THOUSAND YEARS LATER, OUR WORLDS ARE DYING!
THE SAND DANCERS' PROPHECY TELLS US THAT ONLY BY RELIGHTING THE ANCIENT BEACONS--
THE BEACONS CANNOT BE LIT! MANY HAVE TRIED!
NOT LEAST OF THEM YOUR PEOPLE!
THE PROPHECY OF THE SAND WARRIOR IS NOT UNIVERSALLY ACCEPTED!
NOT THE SAND CASTLE VERSION, ANYWAY.
WE MUST SET ASIDE OUR DIFFERENCES AND COME TOGETHER AS ONE GALAXY!
SECRETLY I HAVE TRAINED THE GREATEST SAND DANCER YET. HE IS TRULY THE CHOSEN ONE, AND HE WILL LIGHT OUR WHITE BEACON!
I AM ASKING YOU TO LET HIM LIGHT EVERY ONE OF THE FIVE BEACONS AND AVERT THE EXTINCTION OF THE FIVE WORLDS!

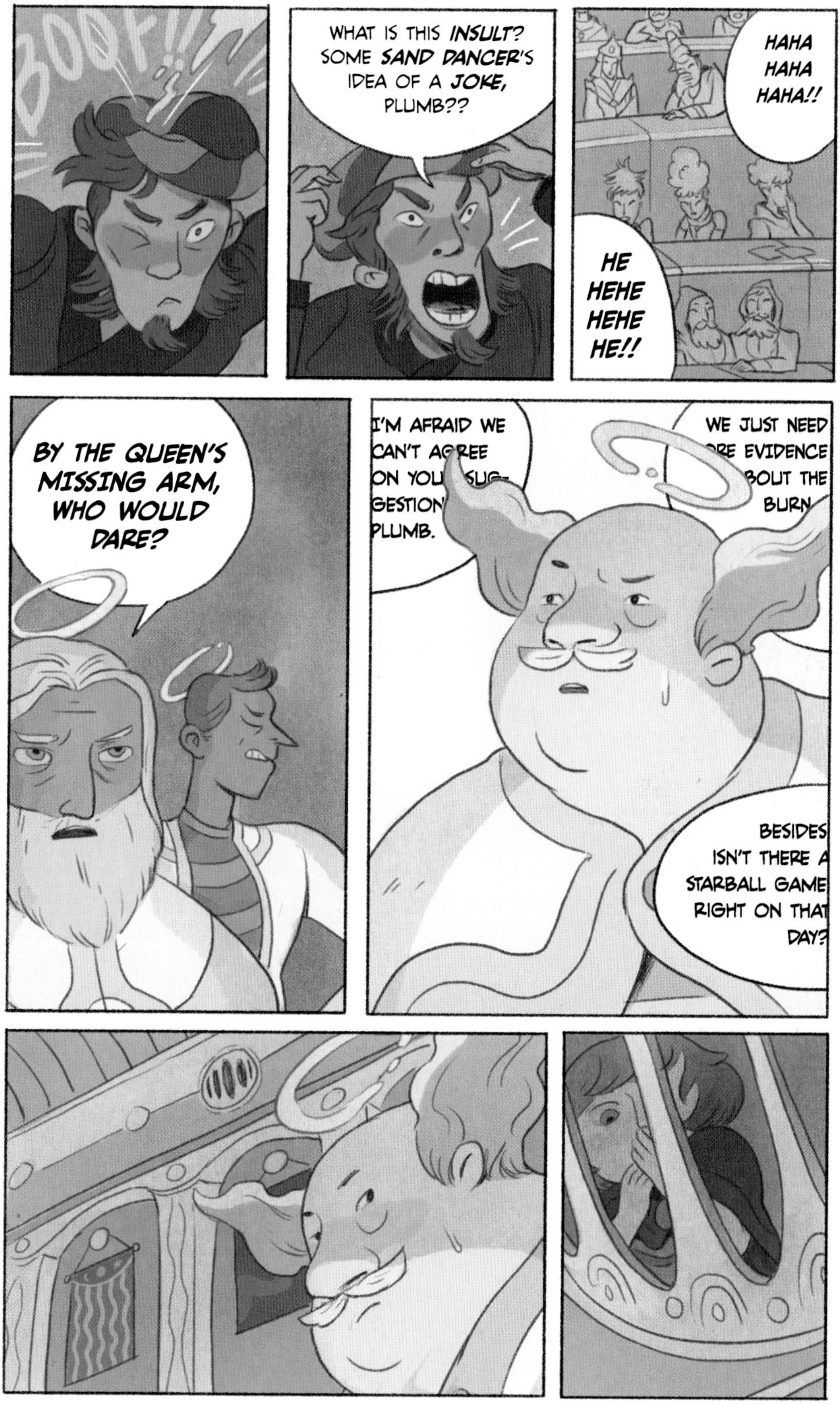
BOOF!!
WHAT IS THIS INSULT? SOME SAND DANCER'S IDEA OF A JOKE, PLUMB??
HAHA HAHA HAHA!!
HE HEHE HEHE HE!!
BY THE QUEEN'S MISSING ARM, WHO WOULD DARE?
I'M AFRAID WE CAN'T AGREE ON YOU SUG- GESTION PLUMB.
WE JUST NEED RE EVIDENCE BOUT THE BURN
BESIDES ISN'T THERE A STARBALL GAME RIGHT ON THAT DAY?

Chapter 2
THE BOY IN THE MASK

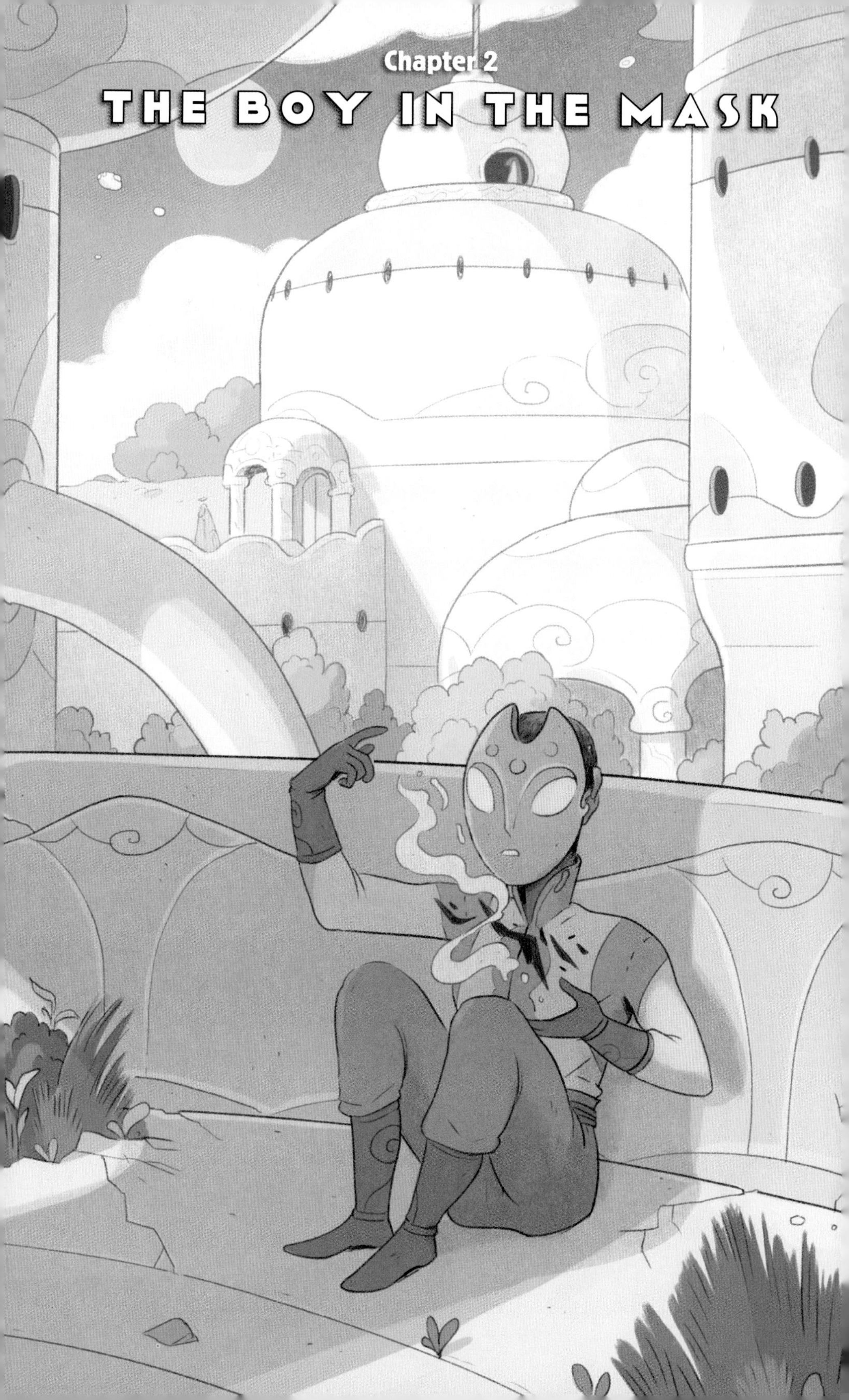

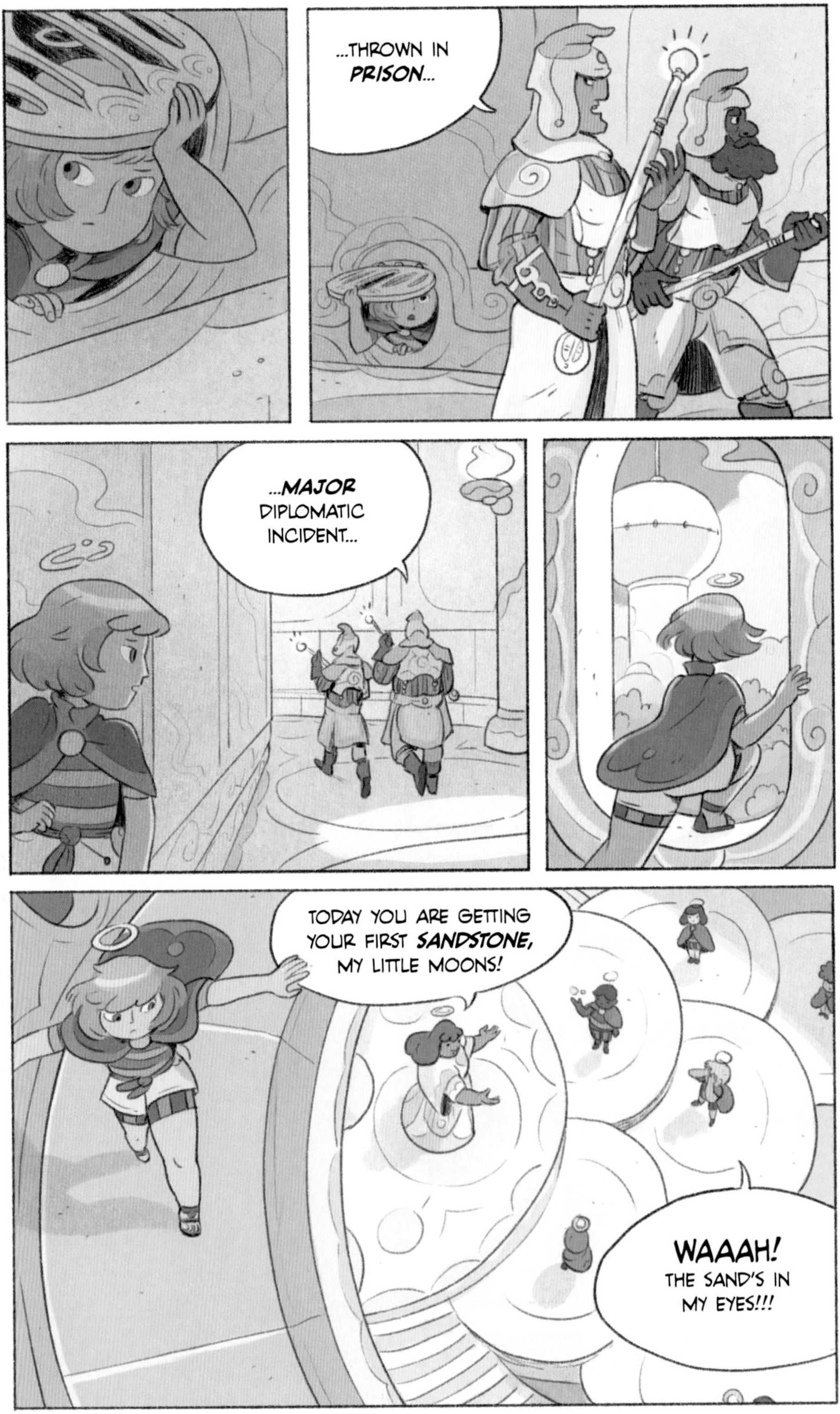
...THROWN IN PRISON...
...MAJOR DIPLOMATIC INCIDENT...
TODAY YOU ARE GETTING YOUR FIRST SANDSTONE, MY LITTLE MOONS!
WAAAH! THE SAND'S IN MY EYES!!!

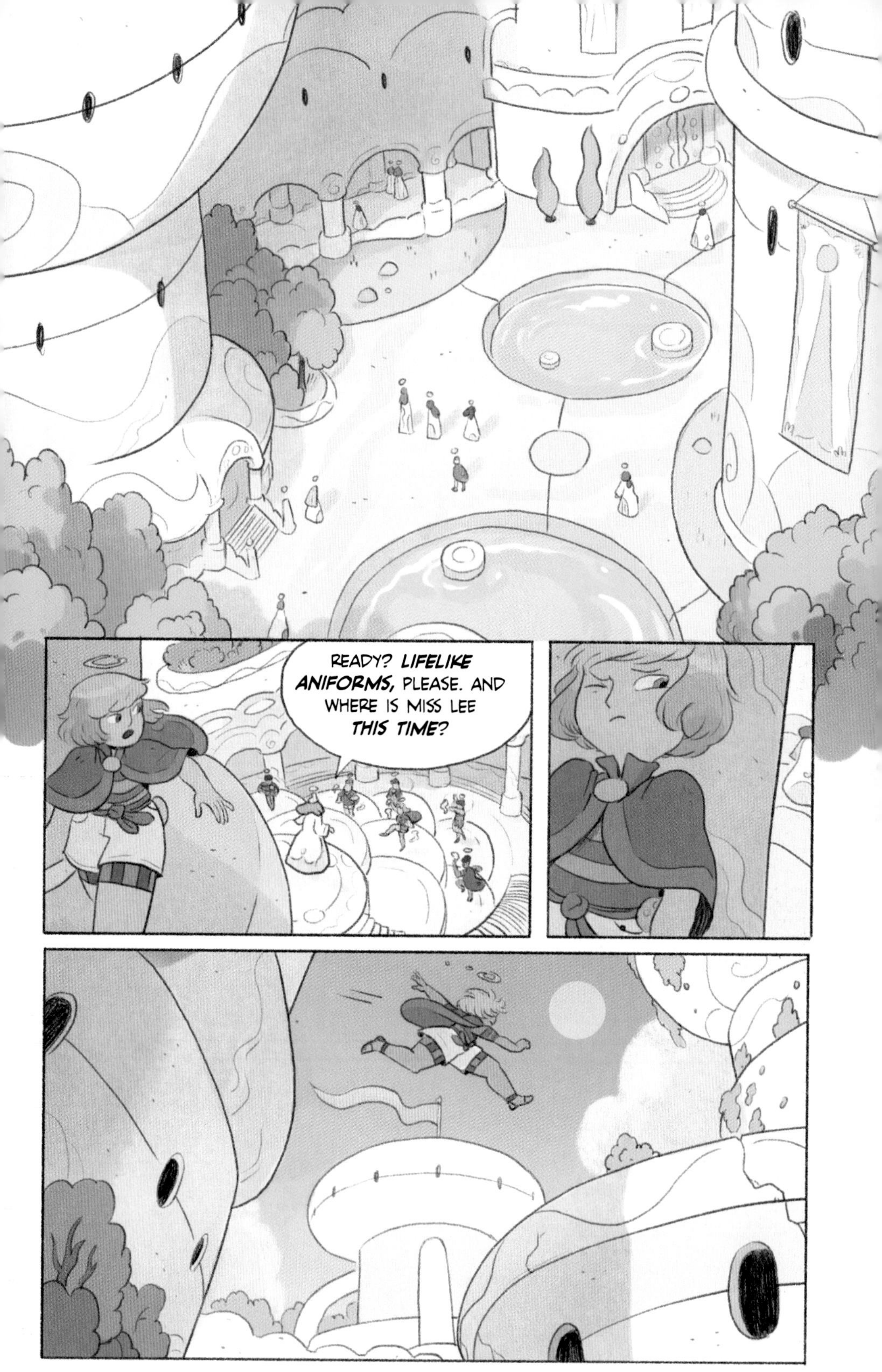
READY? LIFELIKE ANIFORMS, PLEASE. AND WHERE IS MISS LEE THIS TIME?

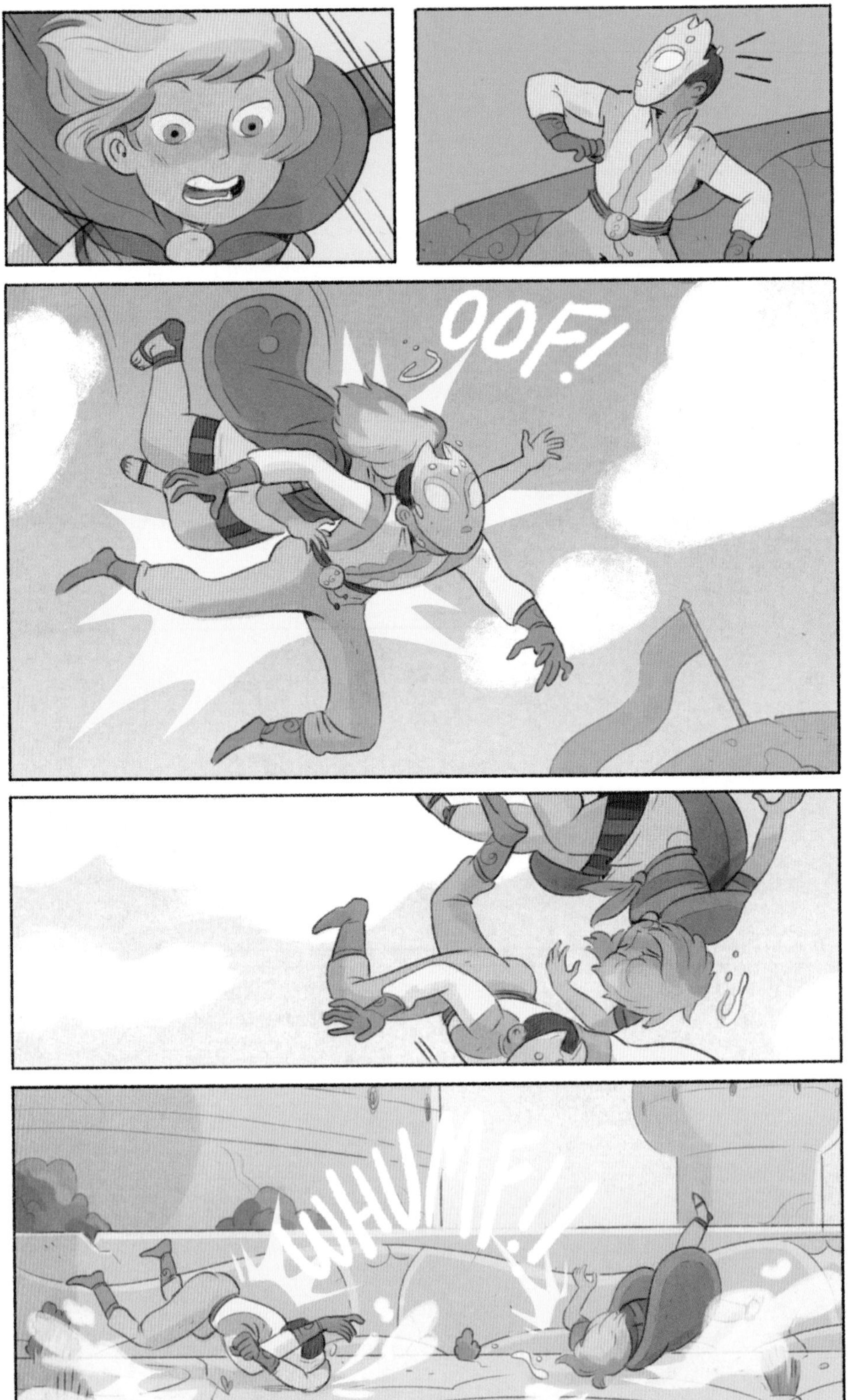
OOF!
WHUMP!!

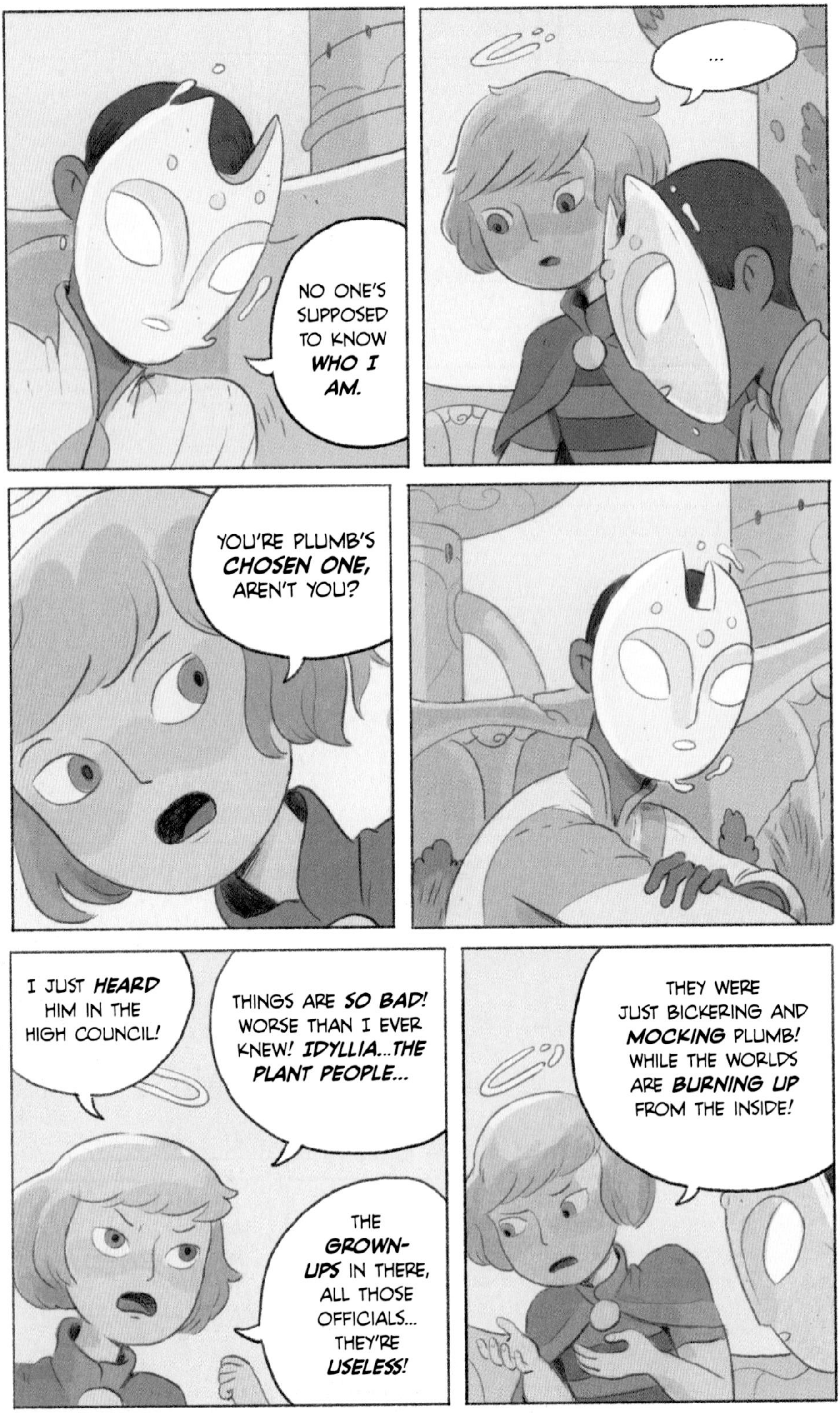
NO ONE'S SUPPOSED TO KNOW ***WHO I AM.***
...
YOU'RE PLUMB'S ***CHOSEN ONE,*** AREN'T YOU?
I JUST ***HEARD*** HIM IN THE HIGH COUNCIL!
THINGS ARE ***SO BAD!*** WORSE THAN I EVER KNEW! ***IDYLLIA...THE PLANT PEOPLE...***
THE ***GROWN-UPS*** IN THERE, ALL THOSE OFFICIALS... THEY'RE ***USELESS!***
THEY WERE JUST BICKERING AND ***MOCKING*** PLUMB! WHILE THE WORLDS ARE ***BURNING UP*** FROM THE INSIDE!

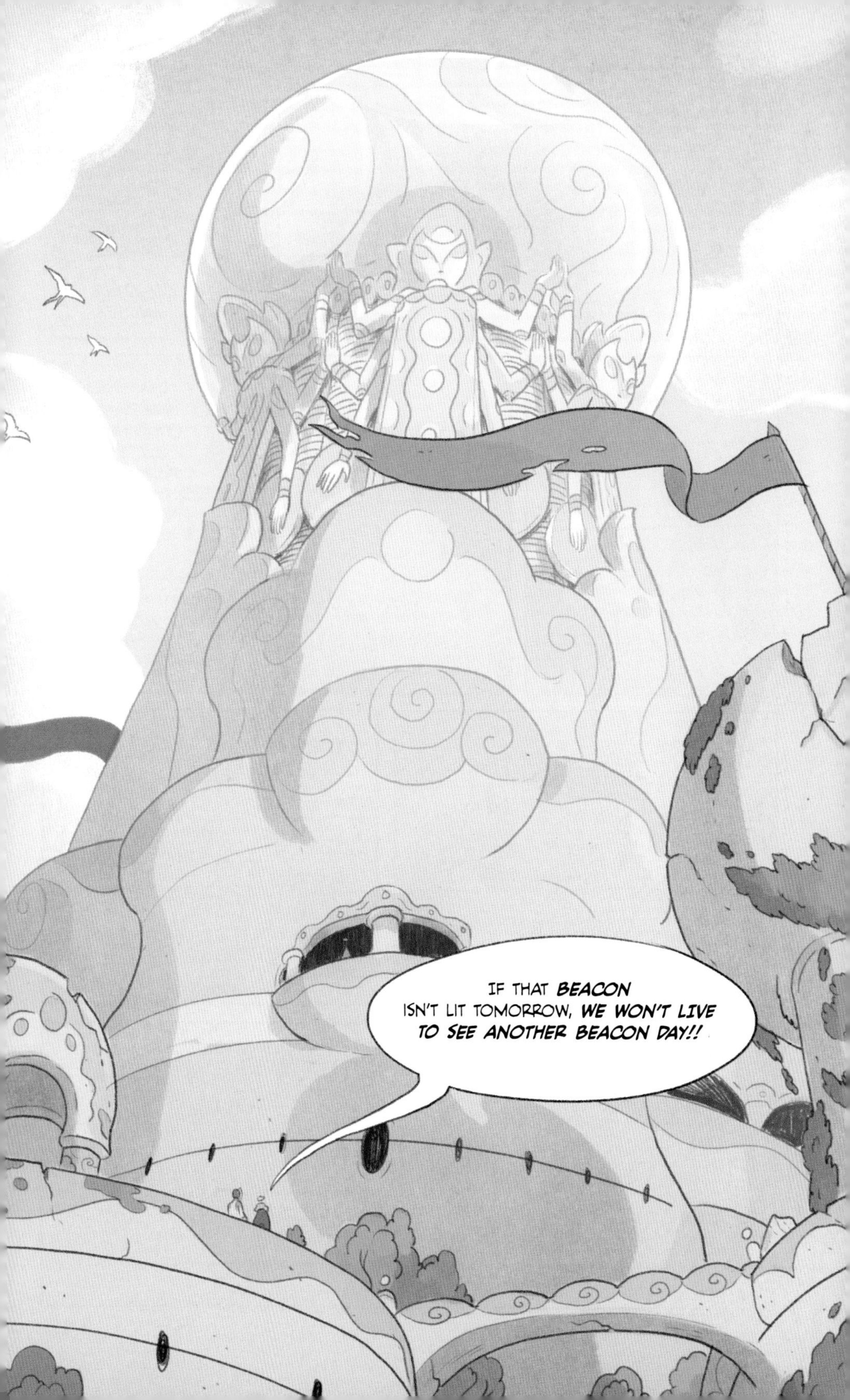
IF THAT BEACON ISN'T LIT TOMORROW, WE WON'T LIVE TO SEE ANOTHER BEACON DAY!!

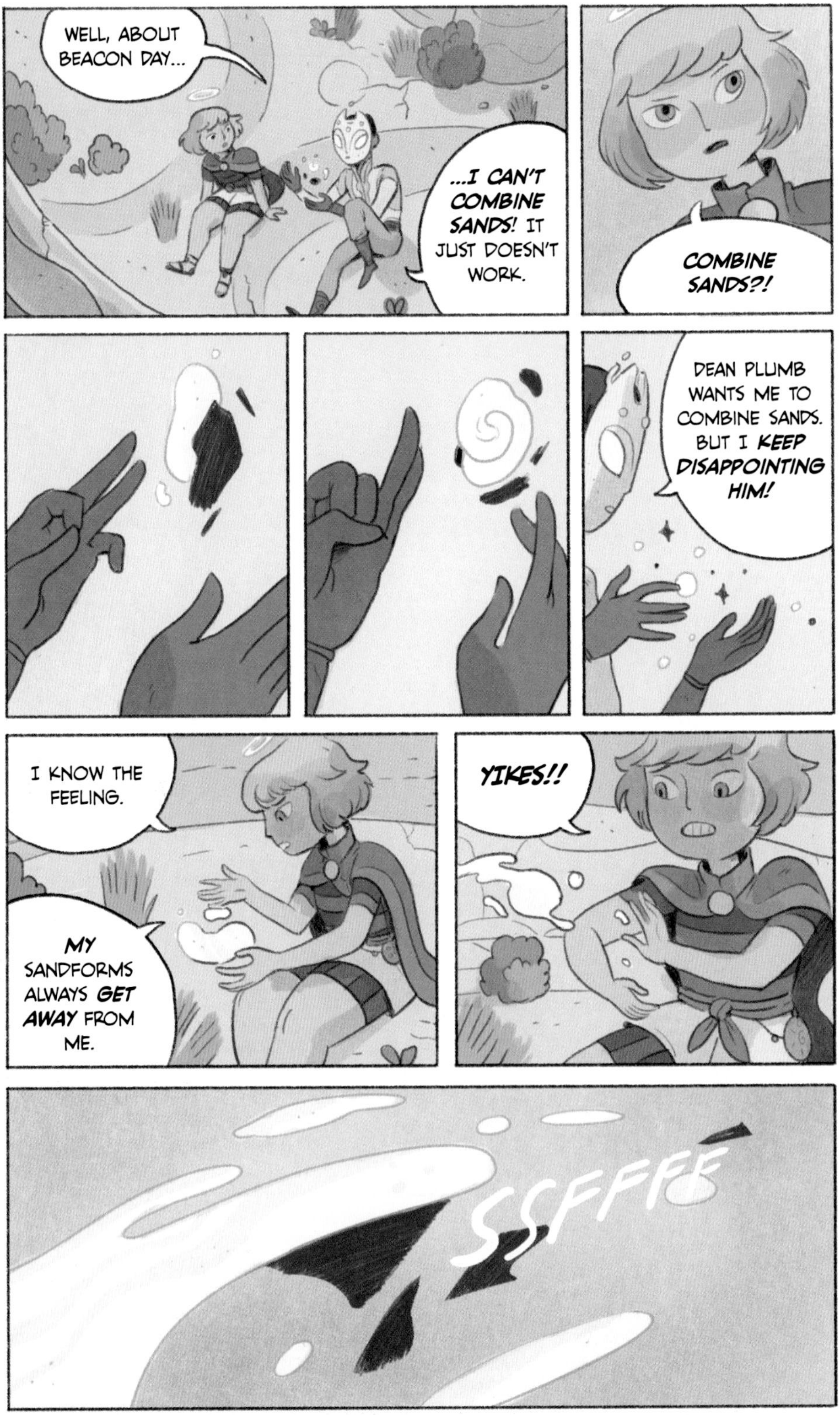
WELL, ABOUT BEACON DAY...
...I CAN'T COMBINE SANDS! IT JUST DOESN'T WORK.
COMBINE SANDS?!
DEAN PLUMB WANTS ME TO COMBINE SANDS. BUT I KEEP DISAPPOINTING HIM!
I KNOW THE FEELING.
MY SANDFORMS ALWAYS GET AWAY FROM ME.
YIKES!!
SSFFFF

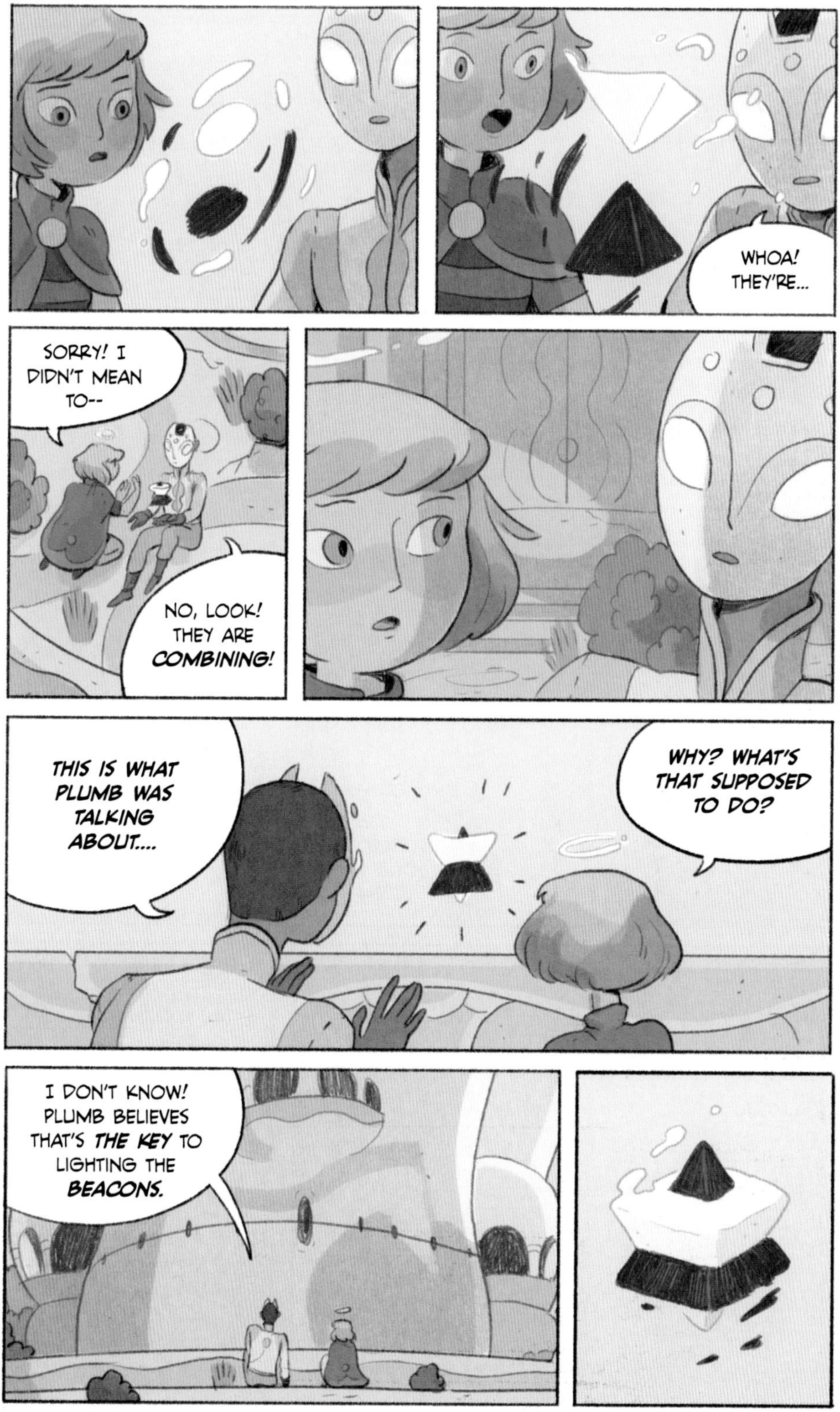
WHOA! THEY'RE...
SORRY! I DIDN'T MEAN TO--
NO, LOOK! THEY ARE *COMBINING!*
THIS IS WHAT PLUMB WAS TALKING ABOUT....
WHY? WHAT'S THAT SUPPOSED TO DO?
I DON'T KNOW! PLUMB BELIEVES THAT'S *THE KEY* TO LIGHTING THE *BEACONS.*

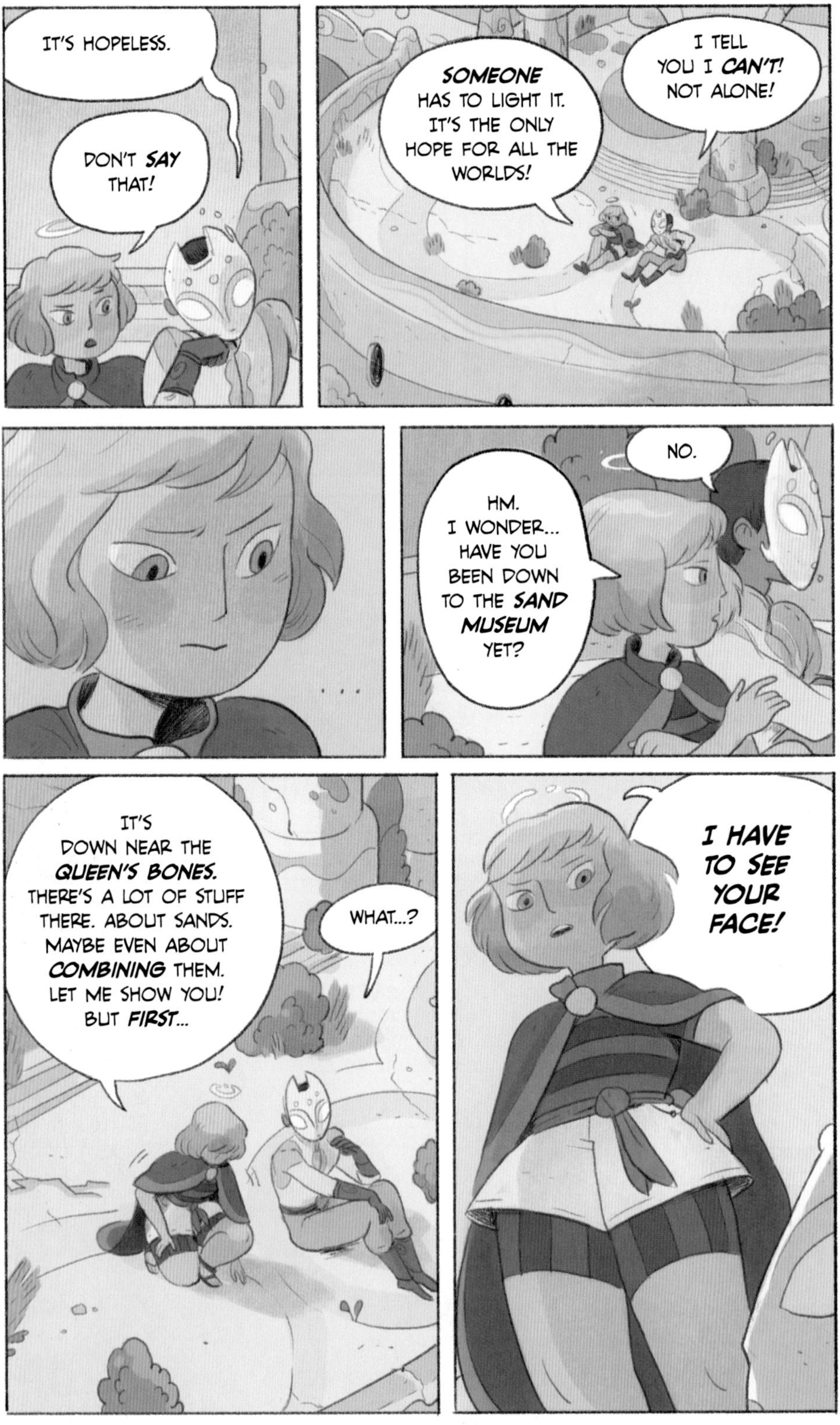
IT'S HOPELESS.
DON'T SAY THAT!
SOMEONE HAS TO LIGHT IT. IT'S THE ONLY HOPE FOR ALL THE WORLDS!
I TELL YOU I CAN'T! NOT ALONE!
...
NO.
HM. I WONDER... HAVE YOU BEEN DOWN TO THE SAND MUSEUM YET?
IT'S DOWN NEAR THE QUEEN'S BONES. THERE'S A LOT OF STUFF THERE. ABOUT SANDS. MAYBE EVEN ABOUT COMBINING THEM. LET ME SHOW YOU! BUT FIRST...
WHAT...?
I HAVE TO SEE YOUR FACE!

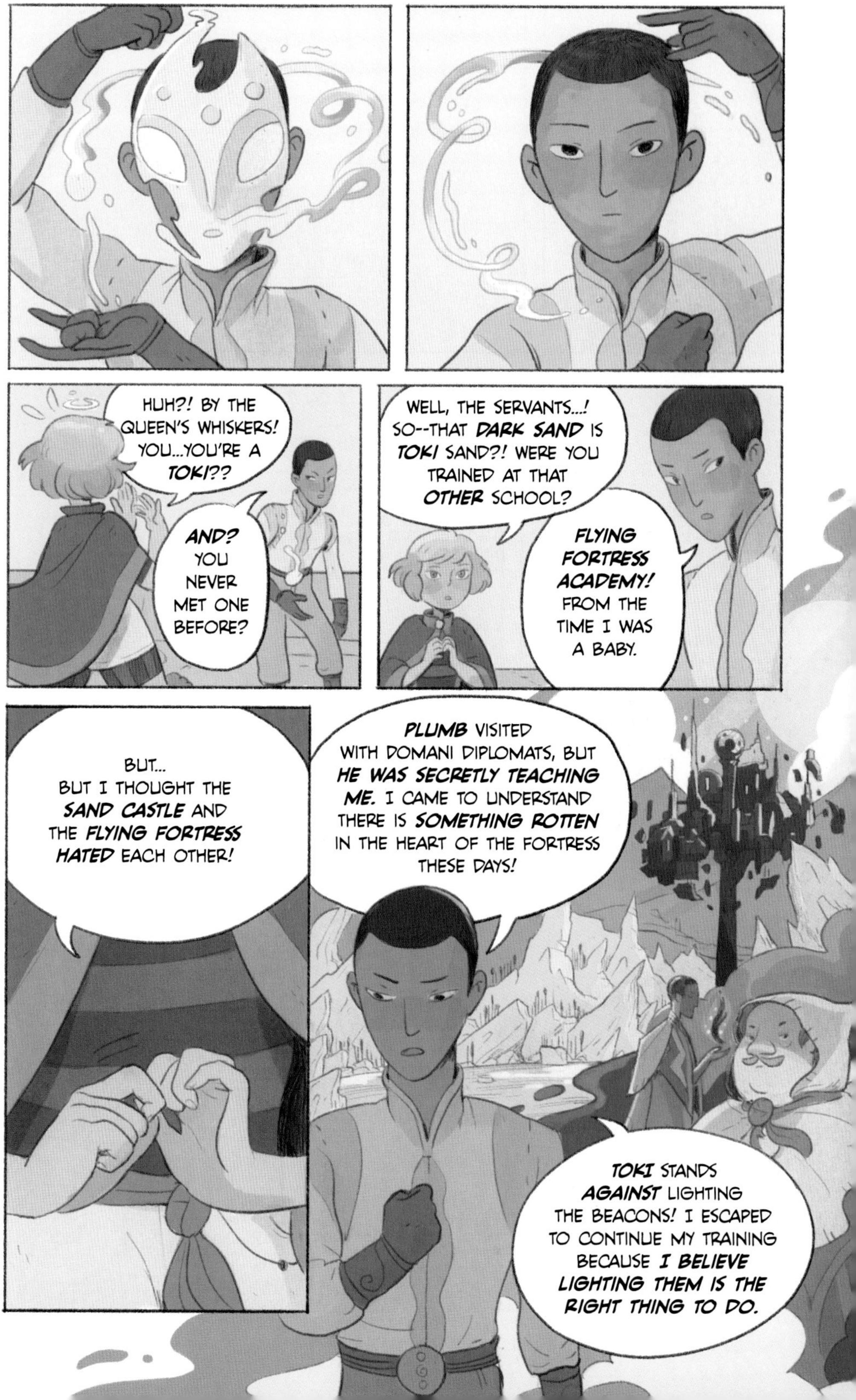
HUH?! BY THE QUEEN'S WHISKERS! YOU...YOU'RE A TOKI??
AND? YOU NEVER MET ONE BEFORE?
WELL, THE SERVANTS...! SO--THAT DARK SAND IS TOKI SAND?! WERE YOU TRAINED AT THAT OTHER SCHOOL?
FLYING FORTRESS ACADEMY! FROM THE TIME I WAS A BABY.
BUT... BUT I THOUGHT THE SAND CASTLE AND THE FLYING FORTRESS HATED EACH OTHER!
PLUMB VISITED WITH DOMANI DIPLOMATS, BUT HE WAS SECRETLY TEACHING ME. I CAME TO UNDERSTAND THERE IS SOMETHING ROTTEN IN THE HEART OF THE FORTRESS THESE DAYS!
TOKI STANDS AGAINST LIGHTING THE BEACONS! I ESCAPED TO CONTINUE MY TRAINING BECAUSE I BELIEVE LIGHTING THEM IS THE RIGHT THING TO DO.

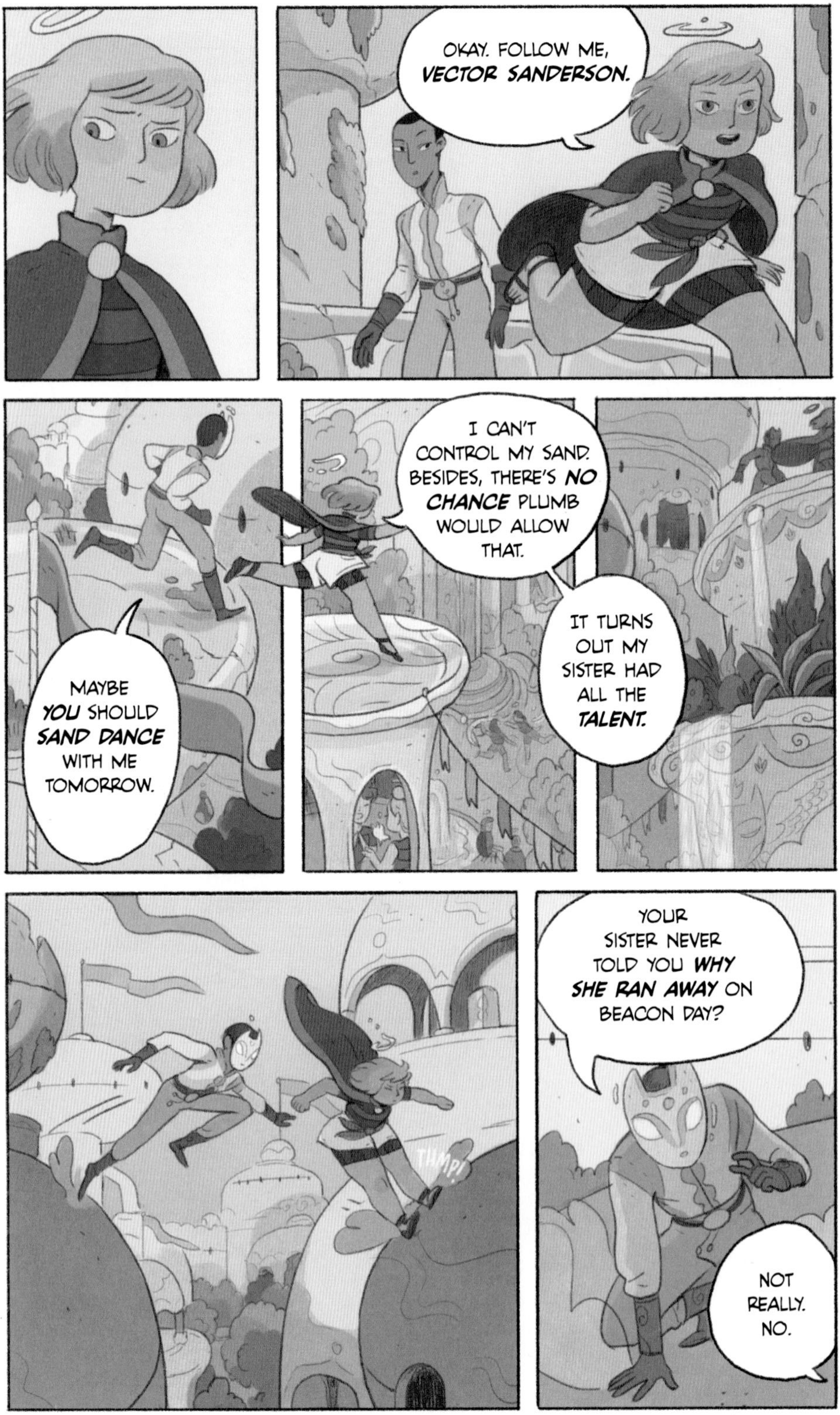
OKAY. FOLLOW ME, **VECTOR SANDERSON.**
MAYBE ***YOU*** SHOULD ***SAND DANCE*** WITH ME TOMORROW.
I CAN'T CONTROL MY SAND. BESIDES, THERE'S ***NO CHANCE*** PLUMB WOULD ALLOW THAT.
IT TURNS OUT MY SISTER HAD ALL THE ***TALENT.***
THMP!
YOUR SISTER NEVER TOLD YOU ***WHY SHE RAN AWAY*** ON BEACON DAY?
NOT REALLY. NO.

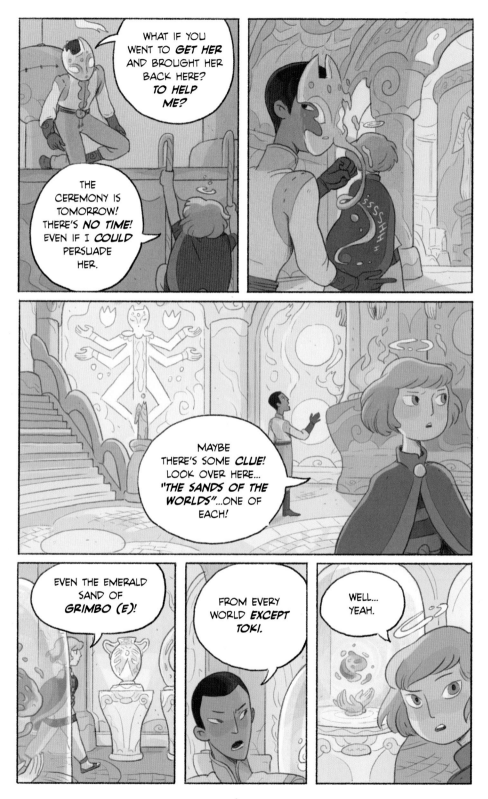

WHAT IF YOU WENT TO *GET HER* AND BROUGHT HER BACK HERE? *TO HELP ME?*

THE CEREMONY IS TOMORROW! THERE'S *NO TIME!* EVEN IF I *COULD* PERSUADE HER.

MAYBE THERE'S SOME *CLUE!* LOOK OVER HERE... *"THE SANDS OF THE WORLDS"*...ONE OF EACH!

EVEN THE EMERALD SAND OF *GRIMBO (E)!*

FROM EVERY WORLD *EXCEPT TOKI.*

WELL... YEAH.

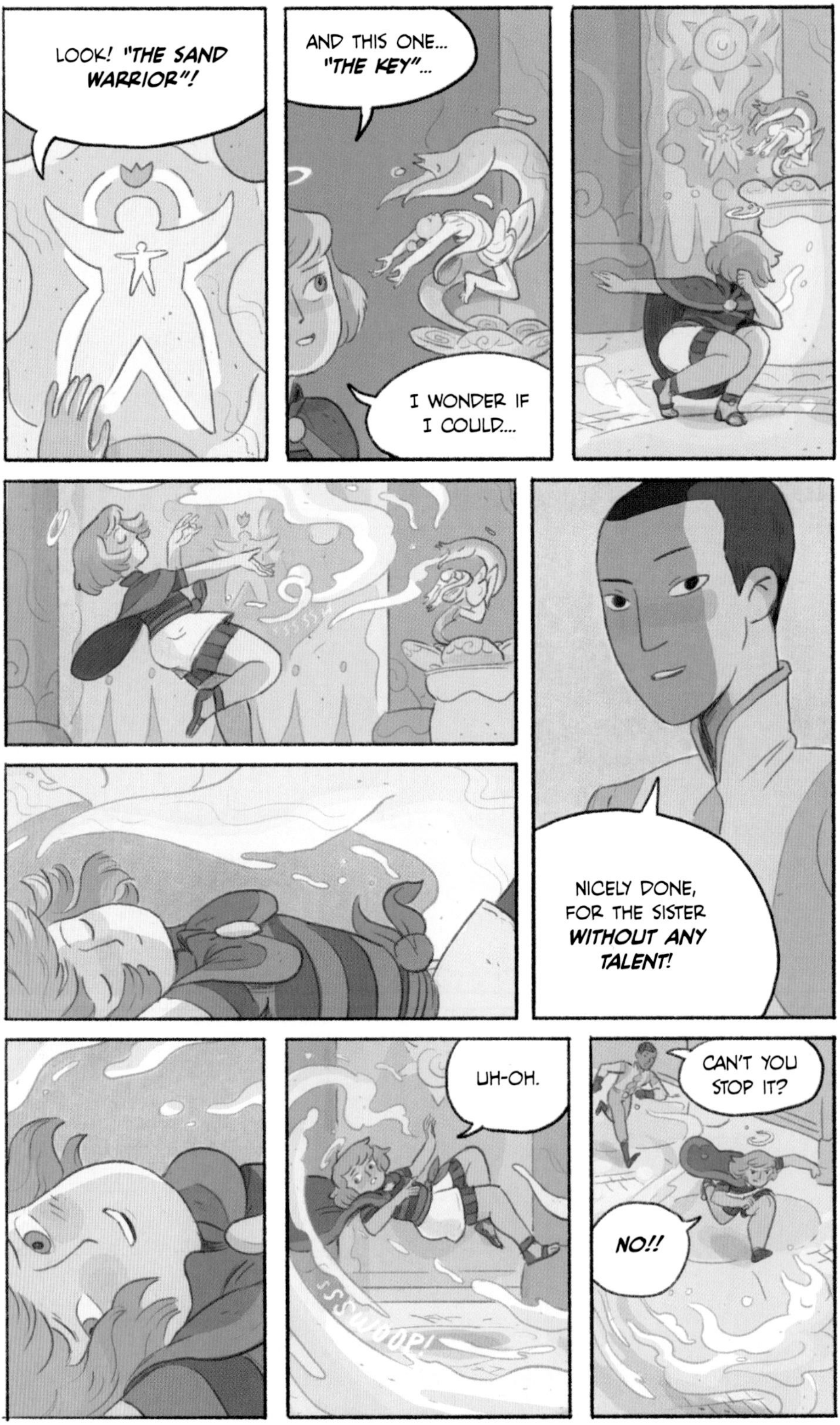
LOOK! "THE SAND WARRIOR"!
AND THIS ONE... "THE KEY"...
I WONDER IF I COULD....
NICELY DONE, FOR THE SISTER WITHOUT ANY TALENT!
UH-OH.
SSSWOOP!
CAN'T YOU STOP IT?
NO!!

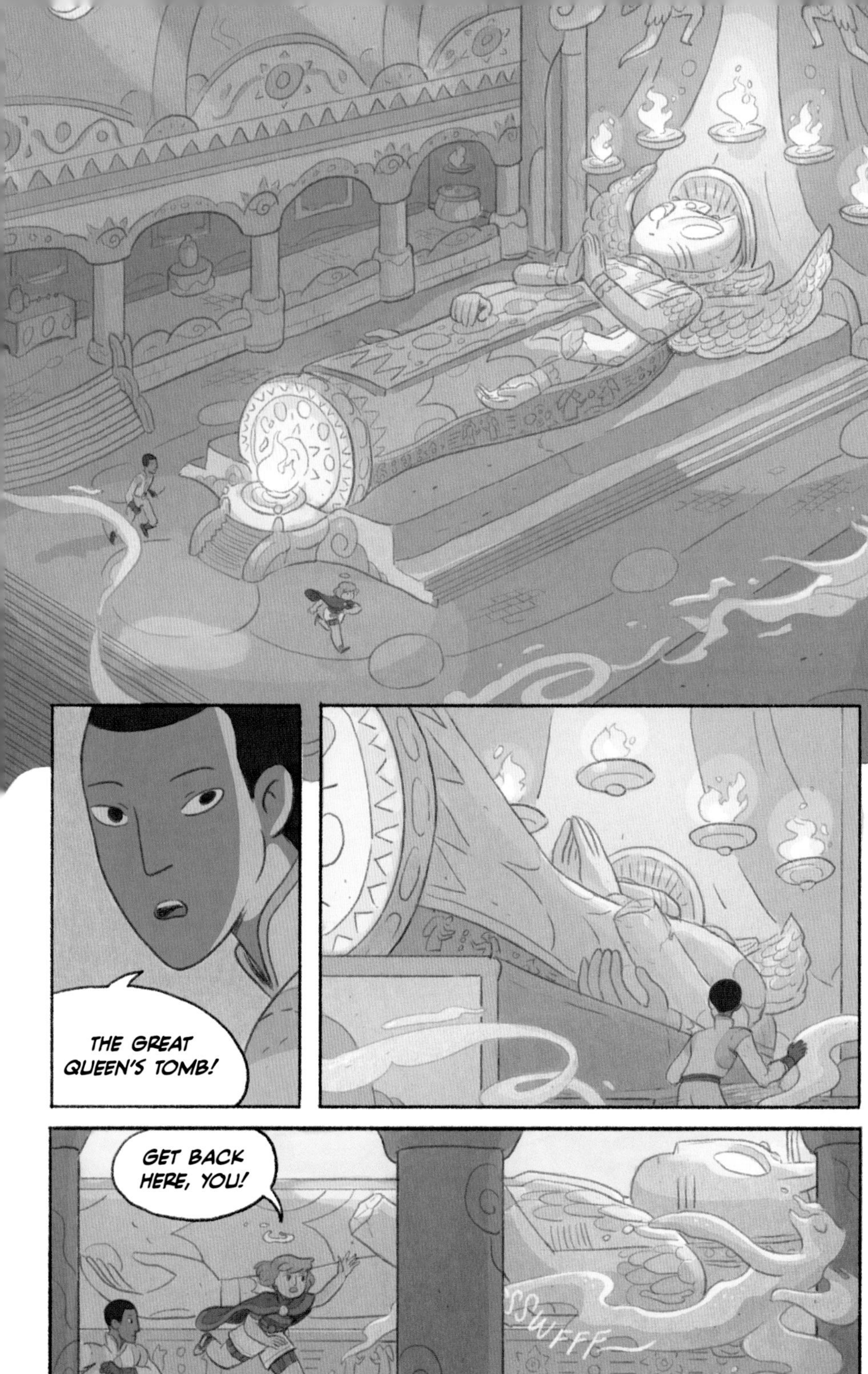
THE GREAT QUEEN'S TOMB!
GET BACK HERE, YOU!
SSWUFFF—

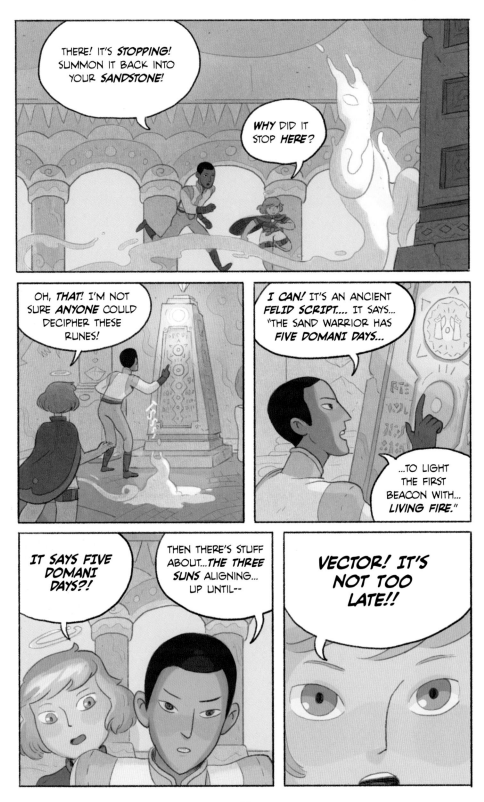

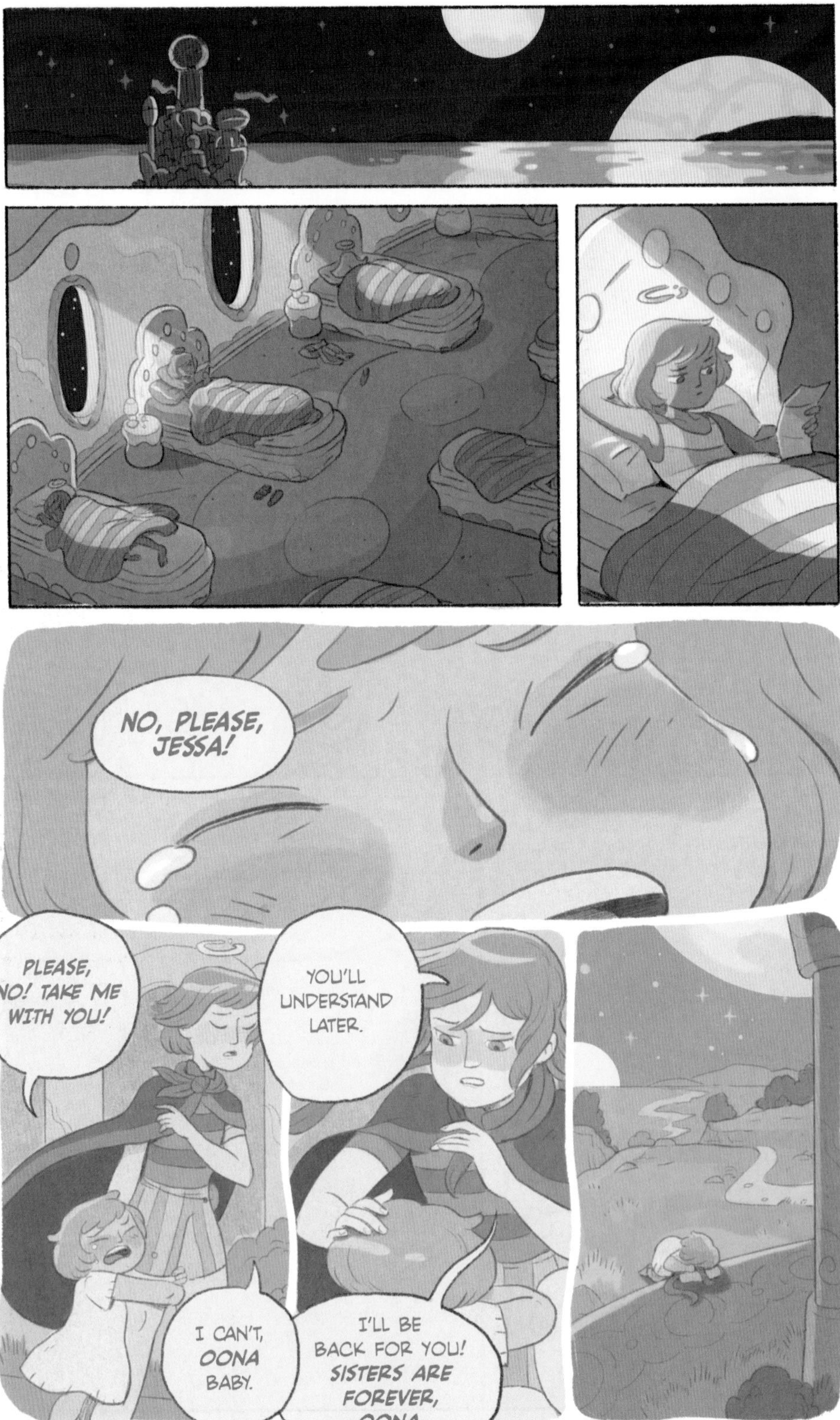
NO, PLEASE, JESSA!
PLEASE, NO! TAKE ME WITH YOU!
YOU'LL UNDERSTAND LATER.
I CAN'T, OONA BABY.
I'LL BE BACK FOR YOU! SISTERS ARE FOREVER, OONA.

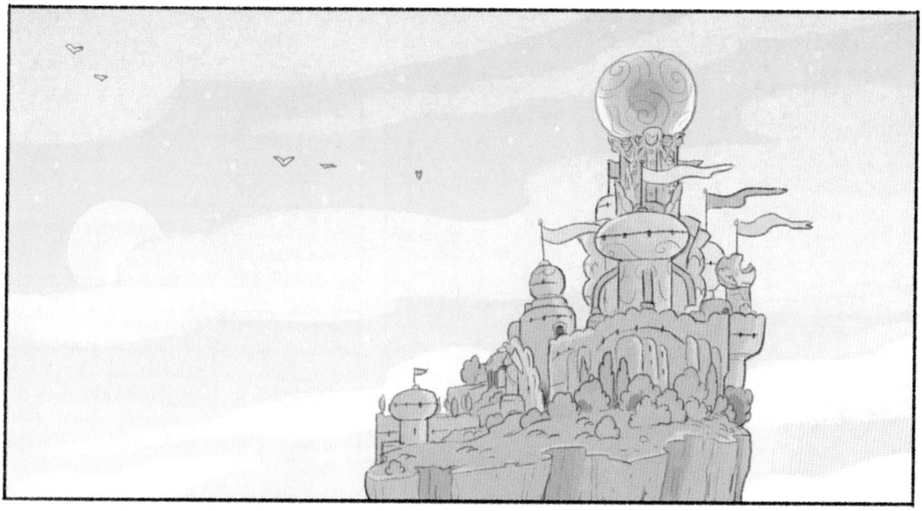

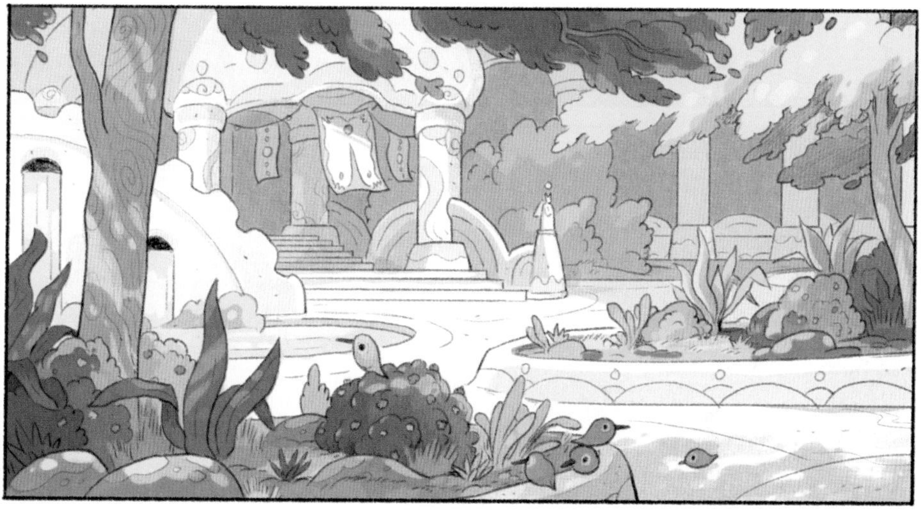

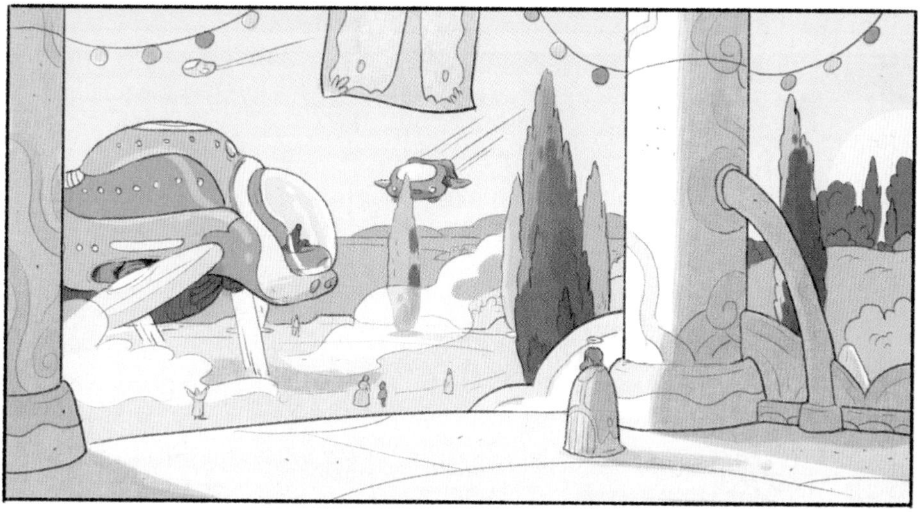

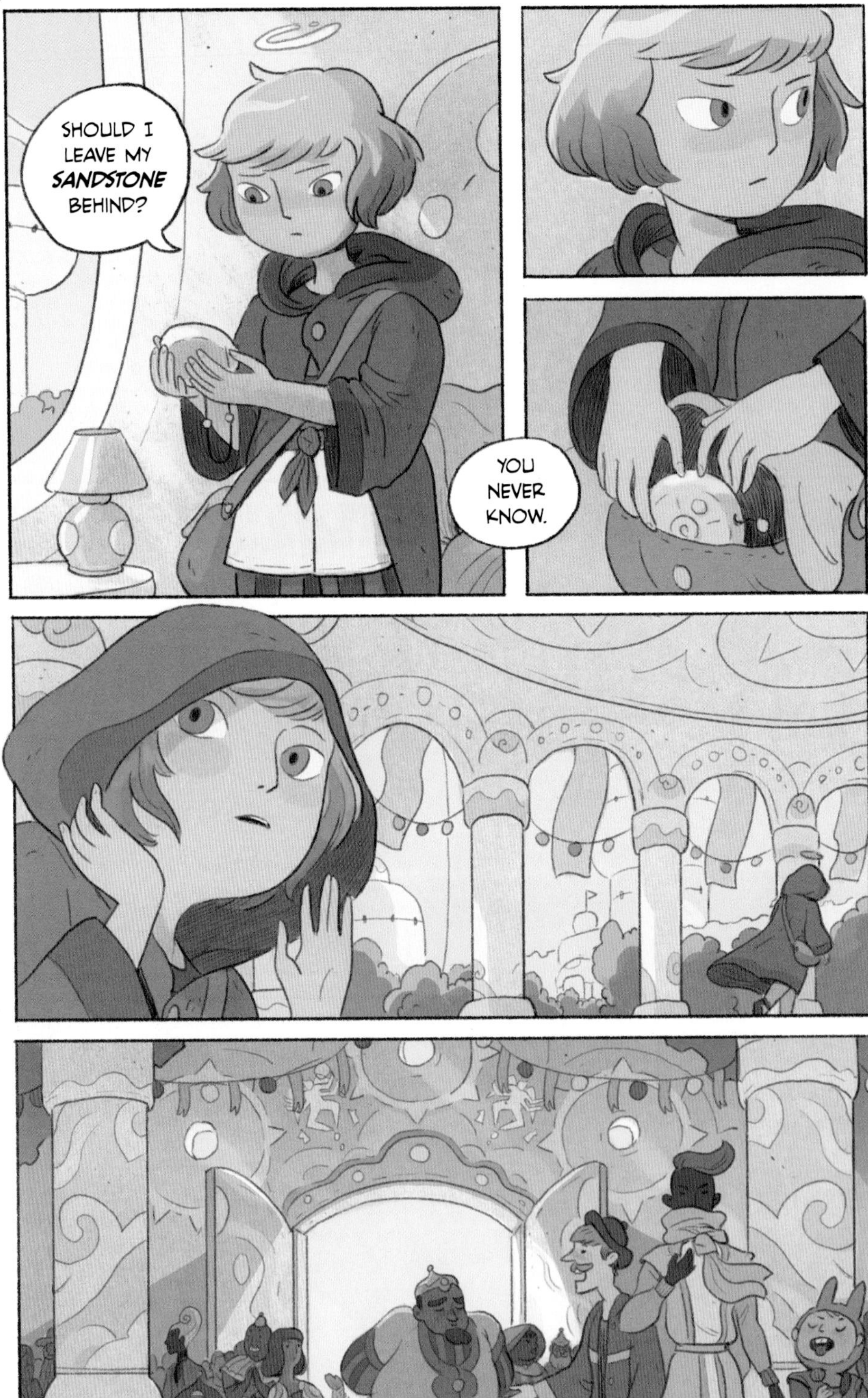
SHOULD I LEAVE MY SANDSTONE BEHIND?
YOU NEVER KNOW.

WELCOME TO THE **177TH BEACON DAY** CEREMONY, HELD ON THE ALIGNMENT OF **THE THREE SUNS**, EVERY SEVEN YEARS--

...AND ON YOUR RIGHT, THESE **FELID** CARVINGS SHOW THE CREATION OF THE FIVE ANCIENT BEACONS...**THE QUEEN** AND HER ARCHITECT... THE QUEEN'S **SACRIFICE**...

COMBINING **MASTERY** OF THE SAND DANCING ARTS WITH THE **INNOCENCE** OF YOUTH, THE CHOSEN ONE INVITES **THE LIVING FIRE**...

...**WATCH** YOUR STEP HERE! THIS WAY TO **THE SAND MUSEUM**, WHERE THE GREAT QUEEN'S **BONES** ARE LAID TO REST. THANKS TO THEM, THE SAND CASTLE HAS **HELD ITS FORM** FOR GENERATIONS!

AW, MOM, IT'S TIME! ALL MY FRIENDS ARE AT THE **STARBALL** GAME!

CHAWLEY, ANY MORE WHINING AND **I SWEAR**...

47

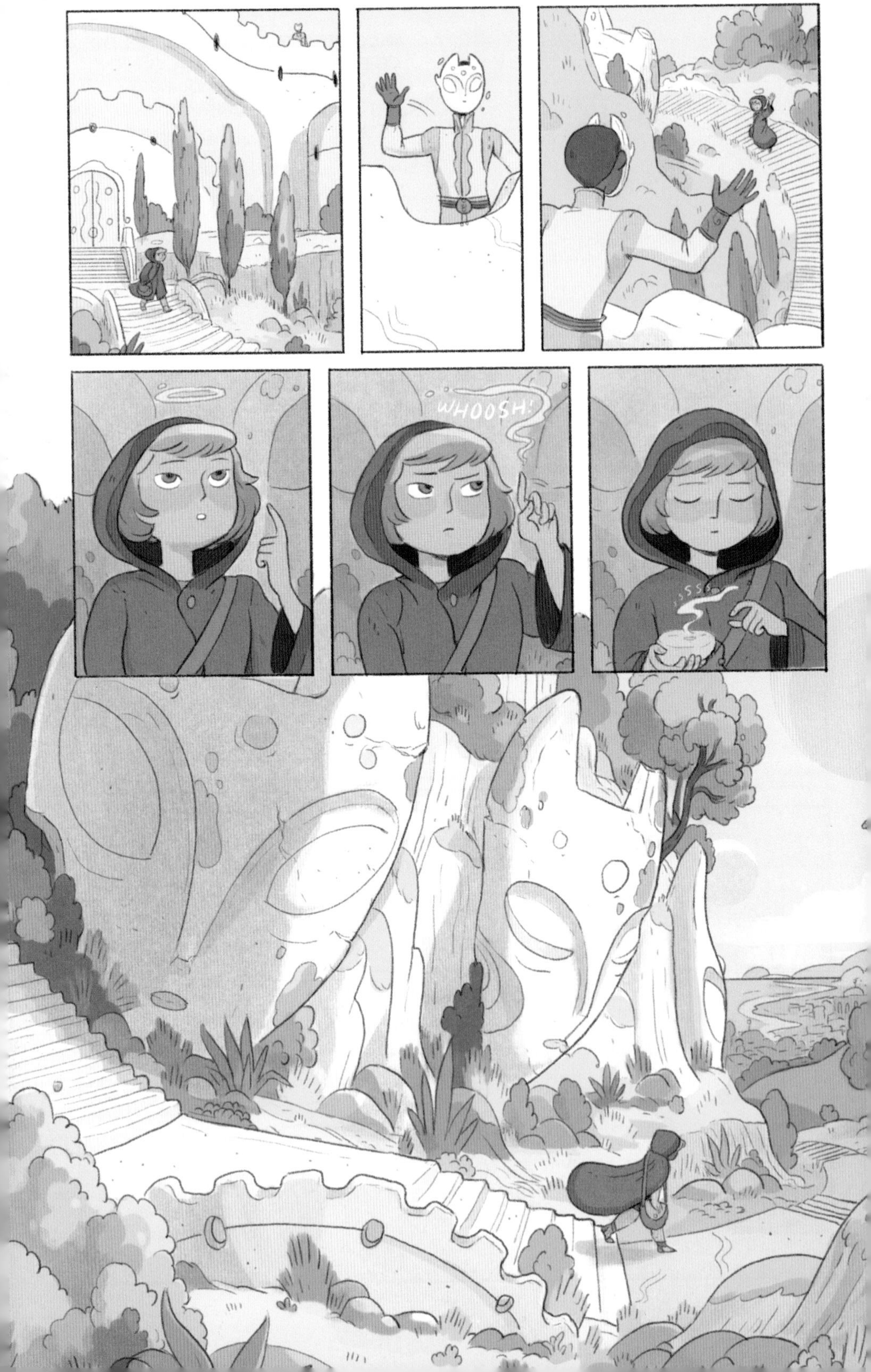
WHOOSH!
SSSSS

Chapter 3

COLLISION AT STARBALL STADIUM

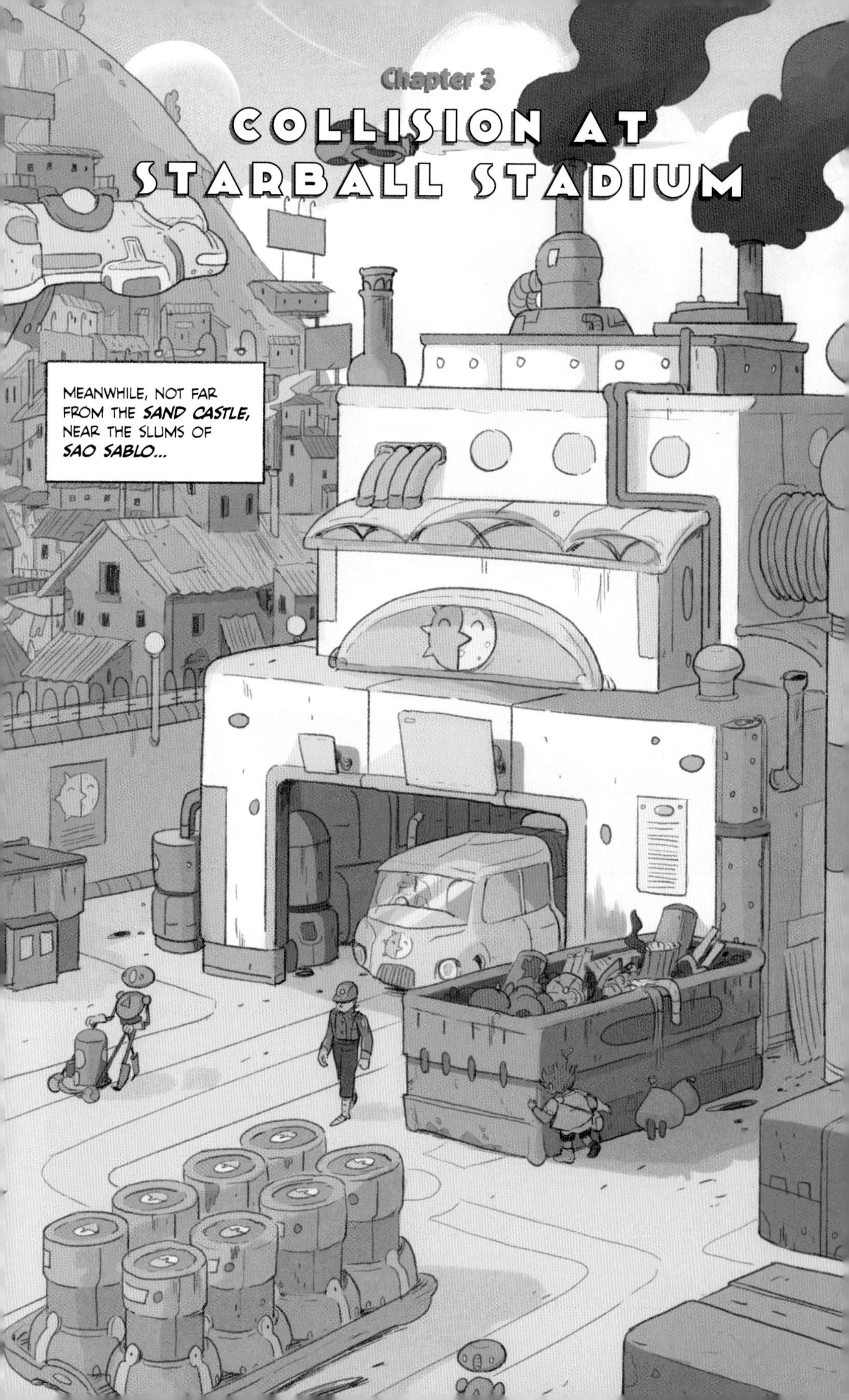
MEANWHILE, NOT FAR FROM THE SAND CASTLE, NEAR THE SLUMS OF SAO SABLO...

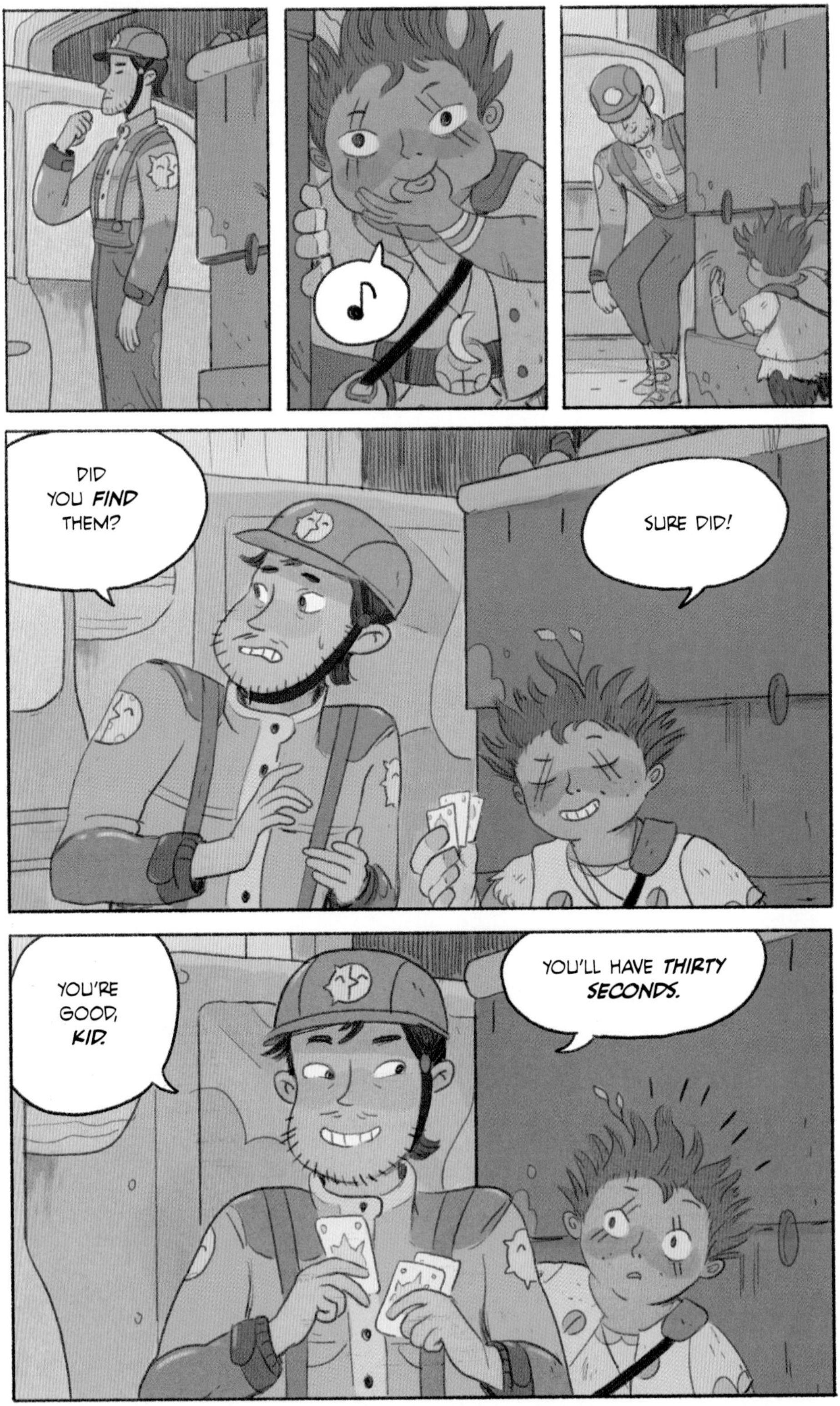
♪
DID YOU FIND THEM?
SURE DID!
YOU'RE GOOD, KID.
YOU'LL HAVE THIRTY SECONDS.

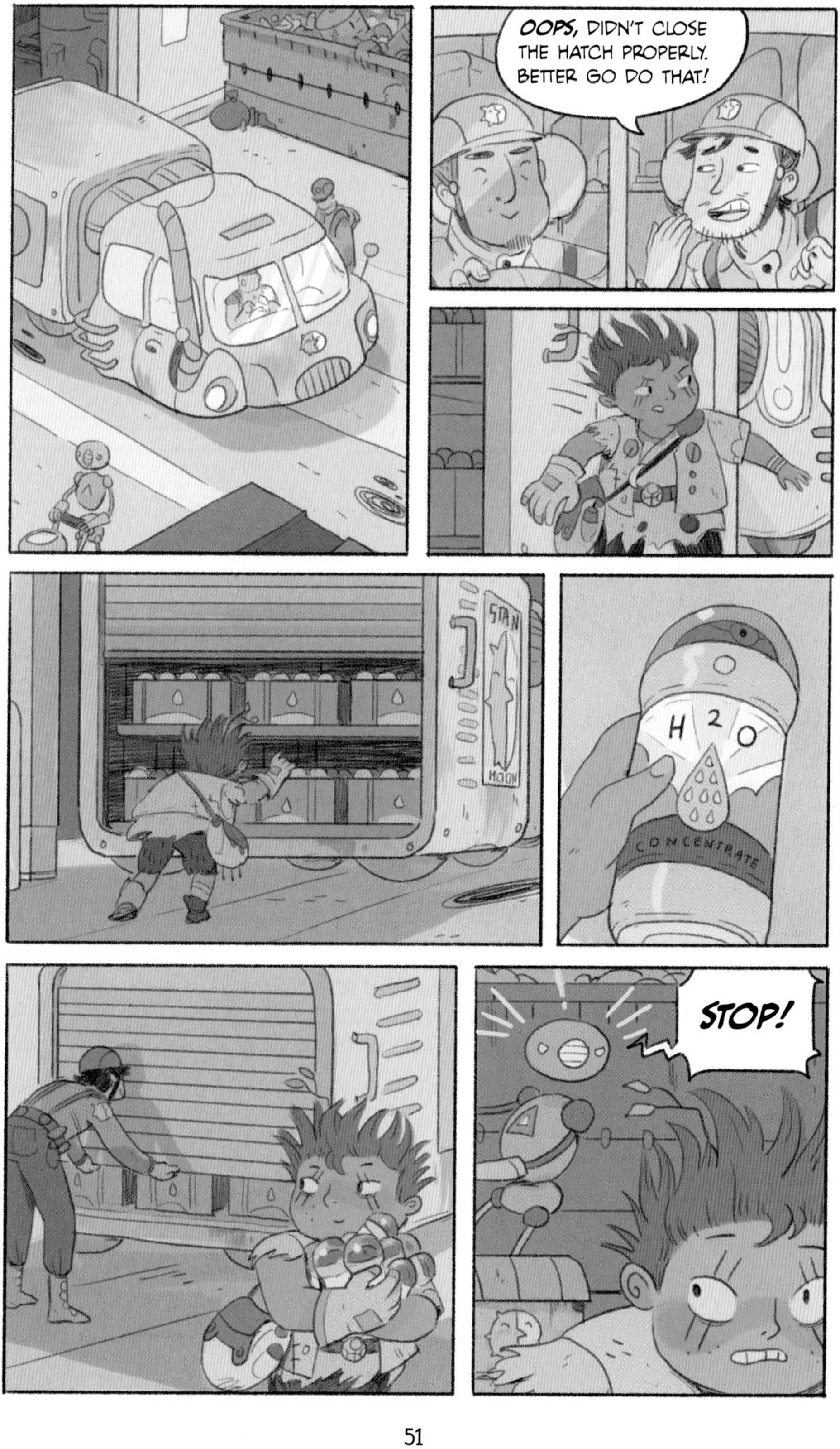
OOPS, DIDN'T CLOSE THE HATCH PROPERLY. BETTER GO DO THAT!
STAN
MOON
H 2 O
CONCENTRATE
STOP!

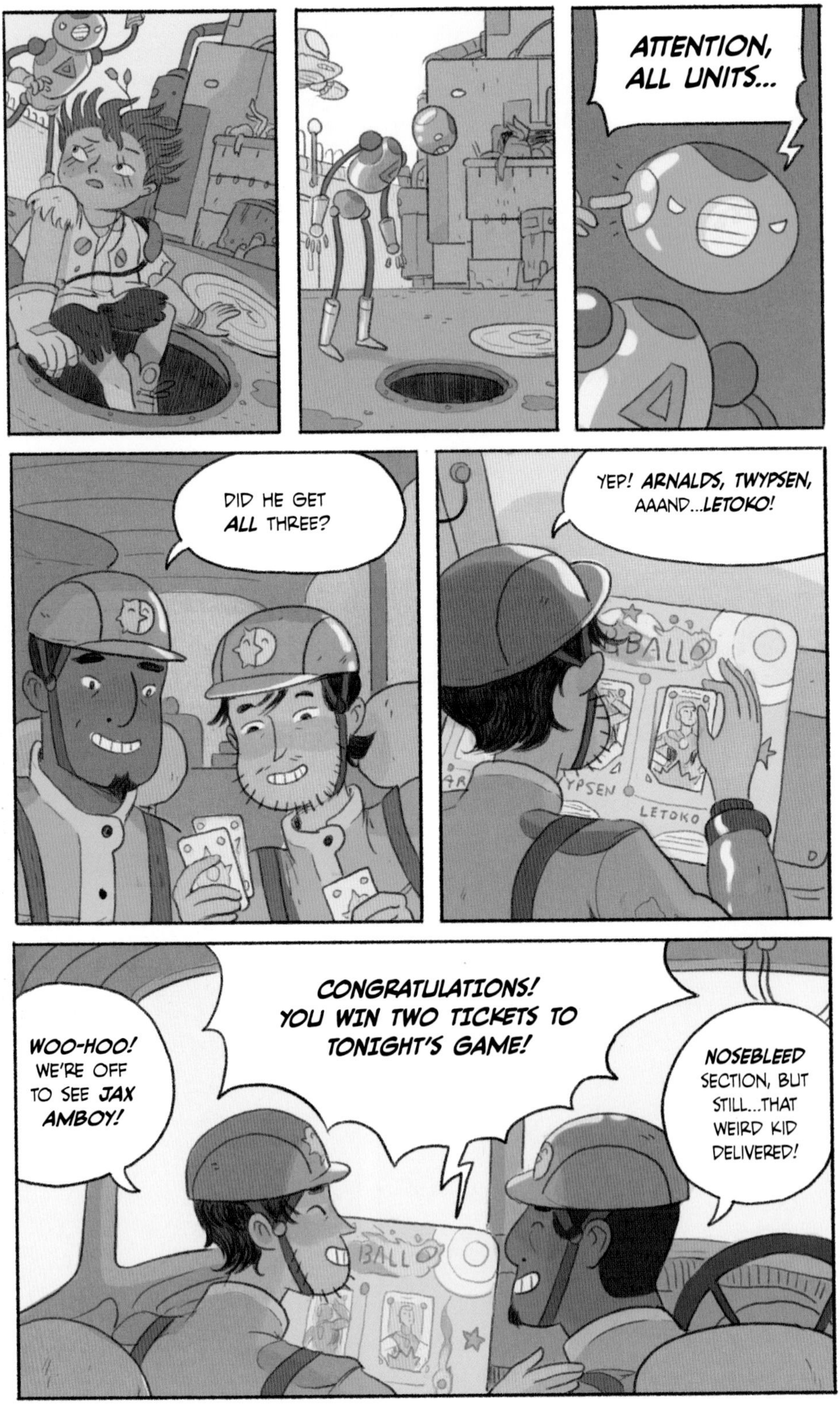
ATTENTION, ALL UNITS...
DID HE GET ALL THREE?
YEP! ARNALDS, TWYPSEN, AAAND...LETOKO!
BALL
YPSEN
LETOKO
CONGRATULATIONS! YOU WIN TWO TICKETS TO TONIGHT'S GAME!
WOO-HOO! WE'RE OFF TO SEE JAX AMBOY!
NOSEBLEED SECTION, BUT STILL...THAT WEIRD KID DELIVERED!
BALL

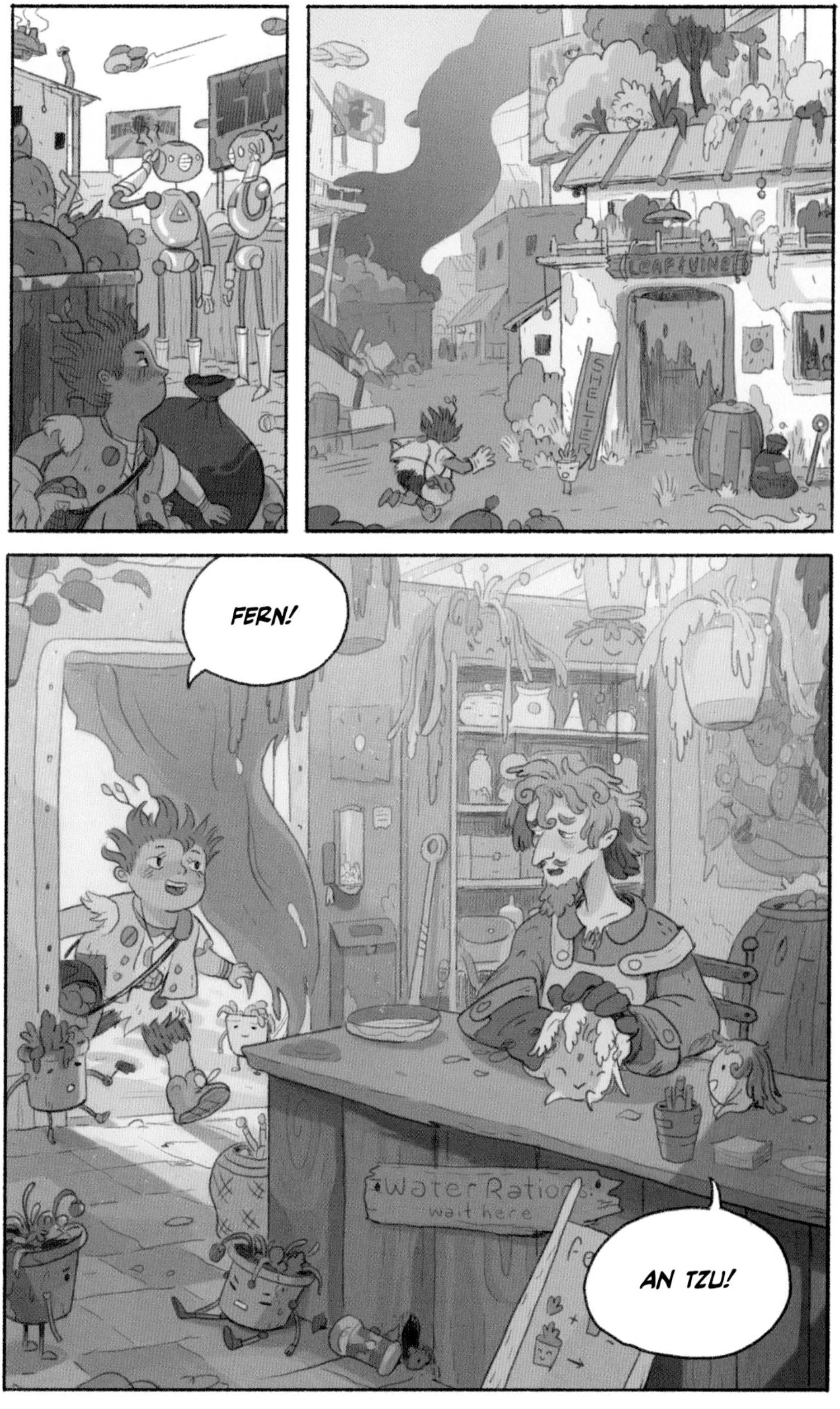
SHELTER
FERN!
wait here
AN TZU!

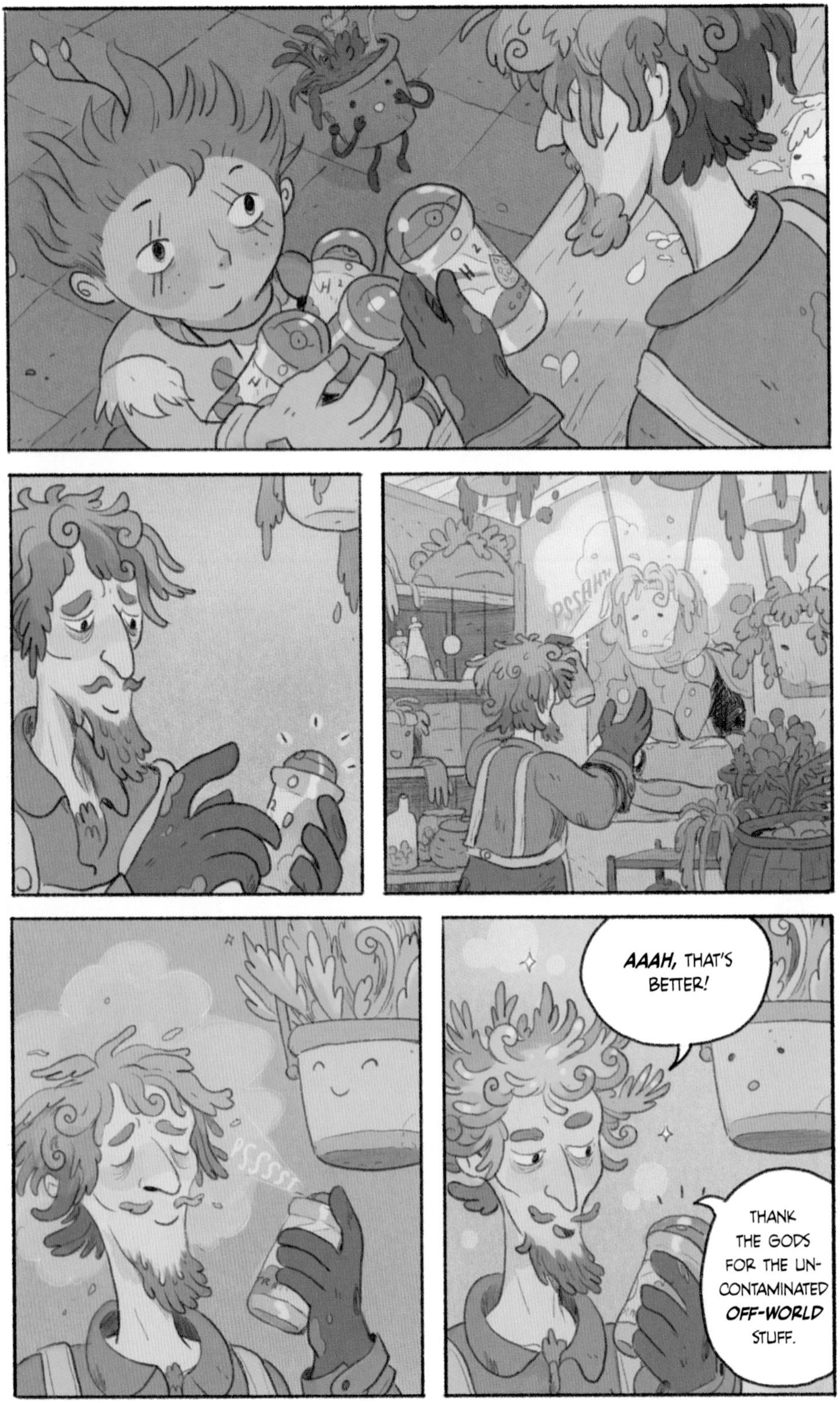
PSSAHH
PSSSSST
AAAH, THAT'S BETTER!
THANK THE GODS FOR THE UN-CONTAMINATED **OFF-WORLD** STUFF.

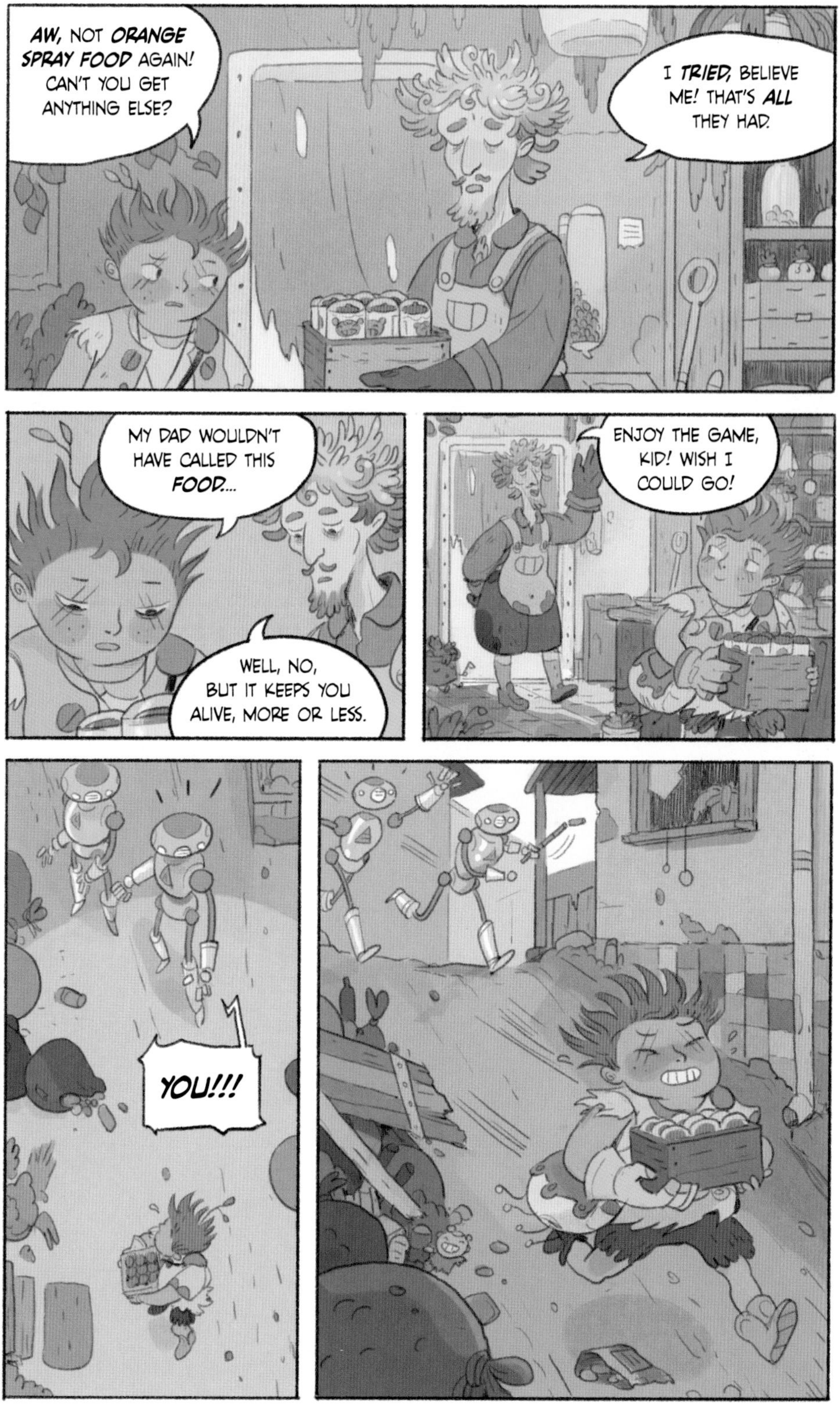
AW, NOT ORANGE SPRAY FOOD AGAIN! CAN'T YOU GET ANYTHING ELSE?
I TRIED, BELIEVE ME! THAT'S ALL THEY HAD.
MY DAD WOULDN'T HAVE CALLED THIS FOOD...
WELL, NO, BUT IT KEEPS YOU ALIVE, MORE OR LESS.
ENJOY THE GAME, KID! WISH I COULD GO!
YOU!!!

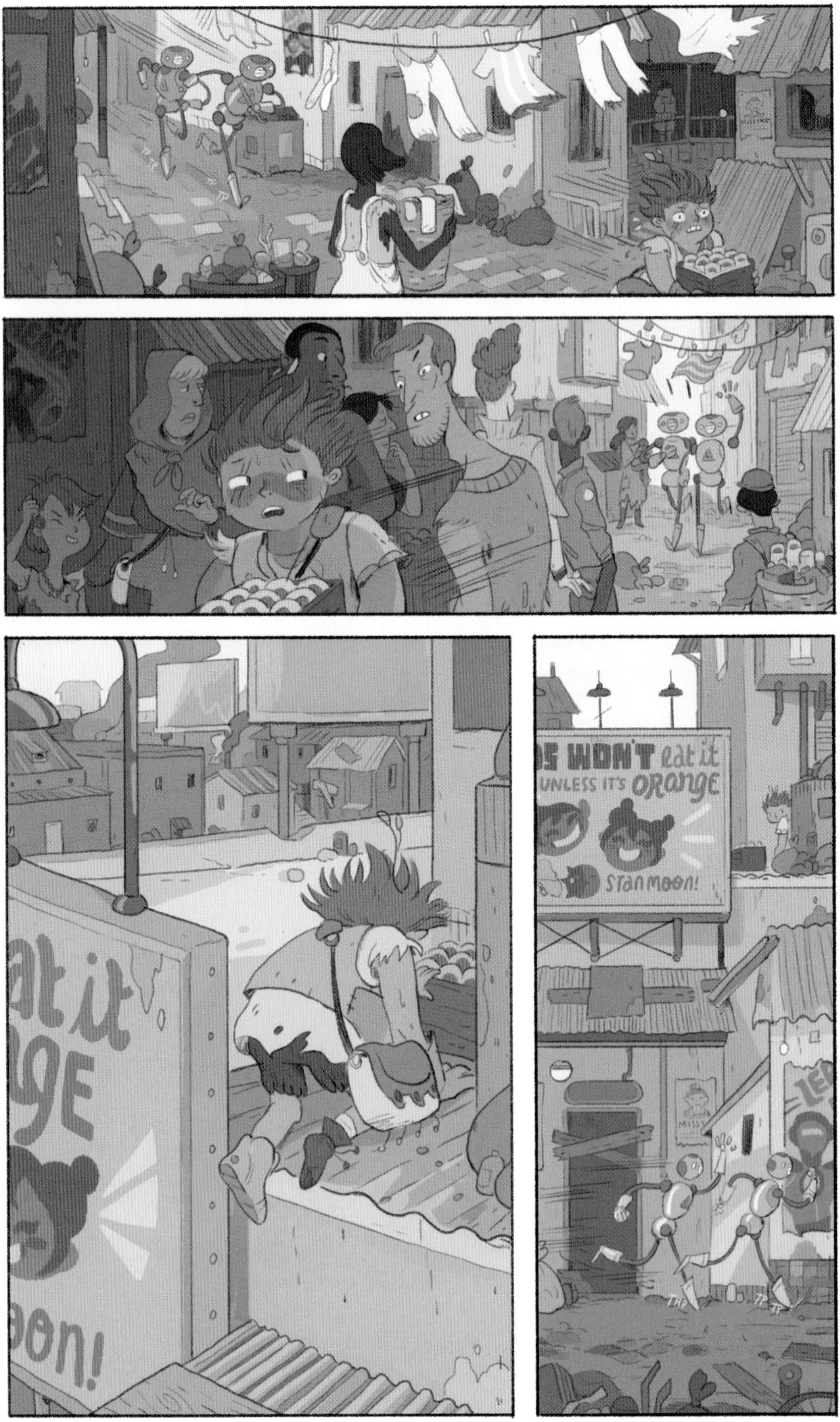
MISSING
WON'T eat it
UNLESS IT'S ORANGE
STAN MOON!

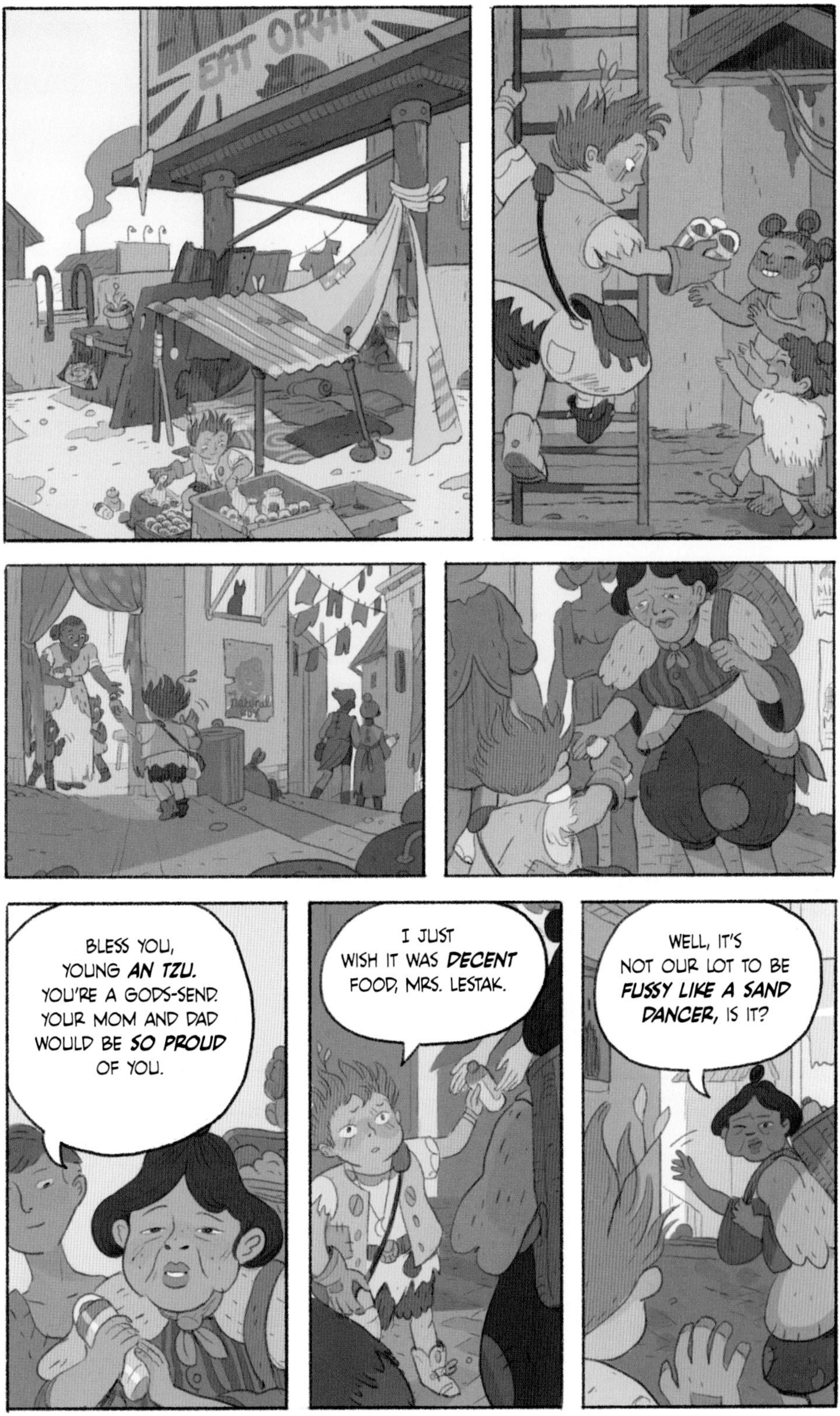
BLESS YOU, YOUNG **AN TZU.** YOU'RE A GODS-SEND. YOUR MOM AND DAD WOULD BE **SO PROUD** OF YOU.
I JUST WISH IT WAS **DECENT** FOOD, MRS. LESTAK.
WELL, IT'S NOT OUR LOT TO BE **FUSSY LIKE A SAND DANCER,** IS IT?

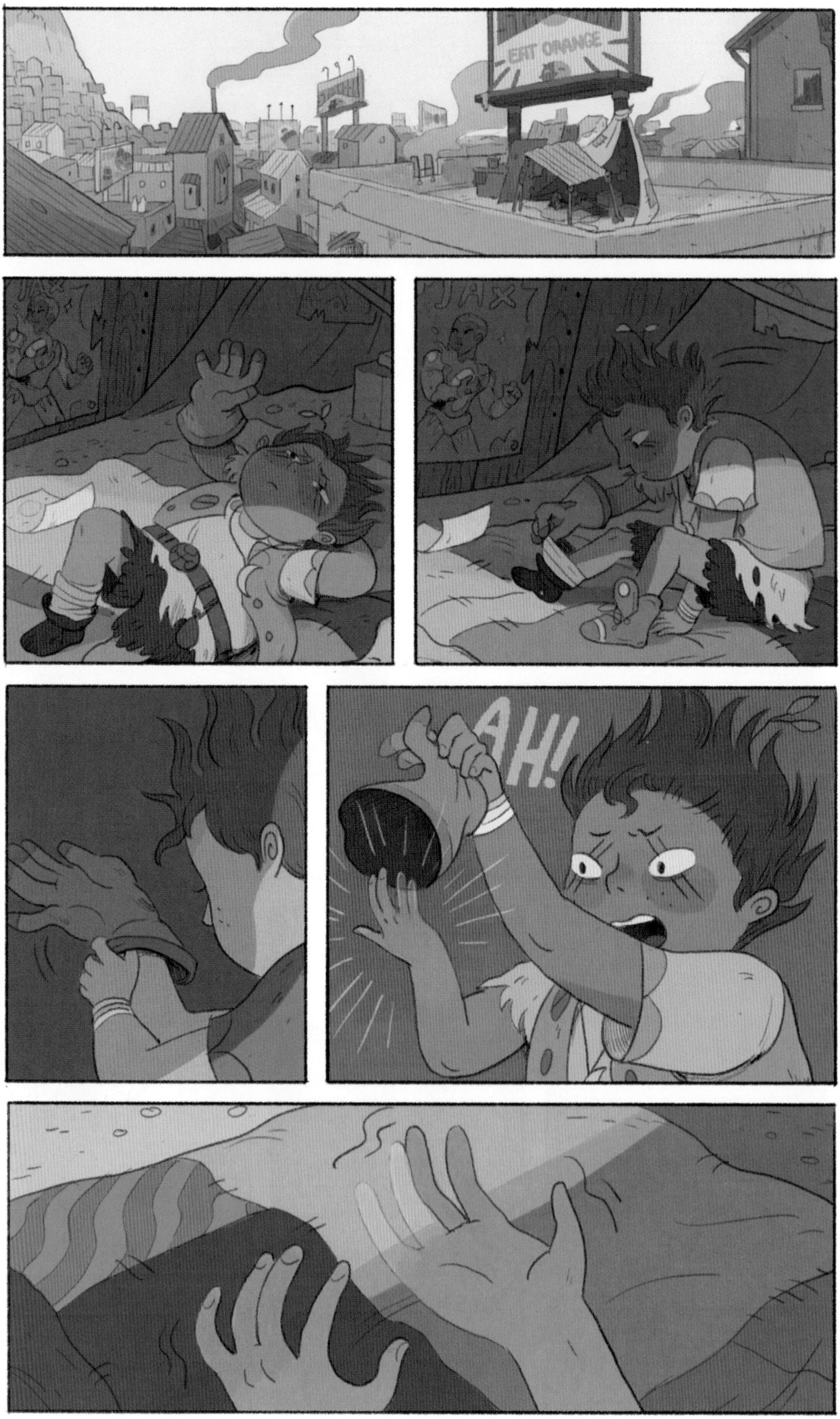
EAT ORANGE
AH!

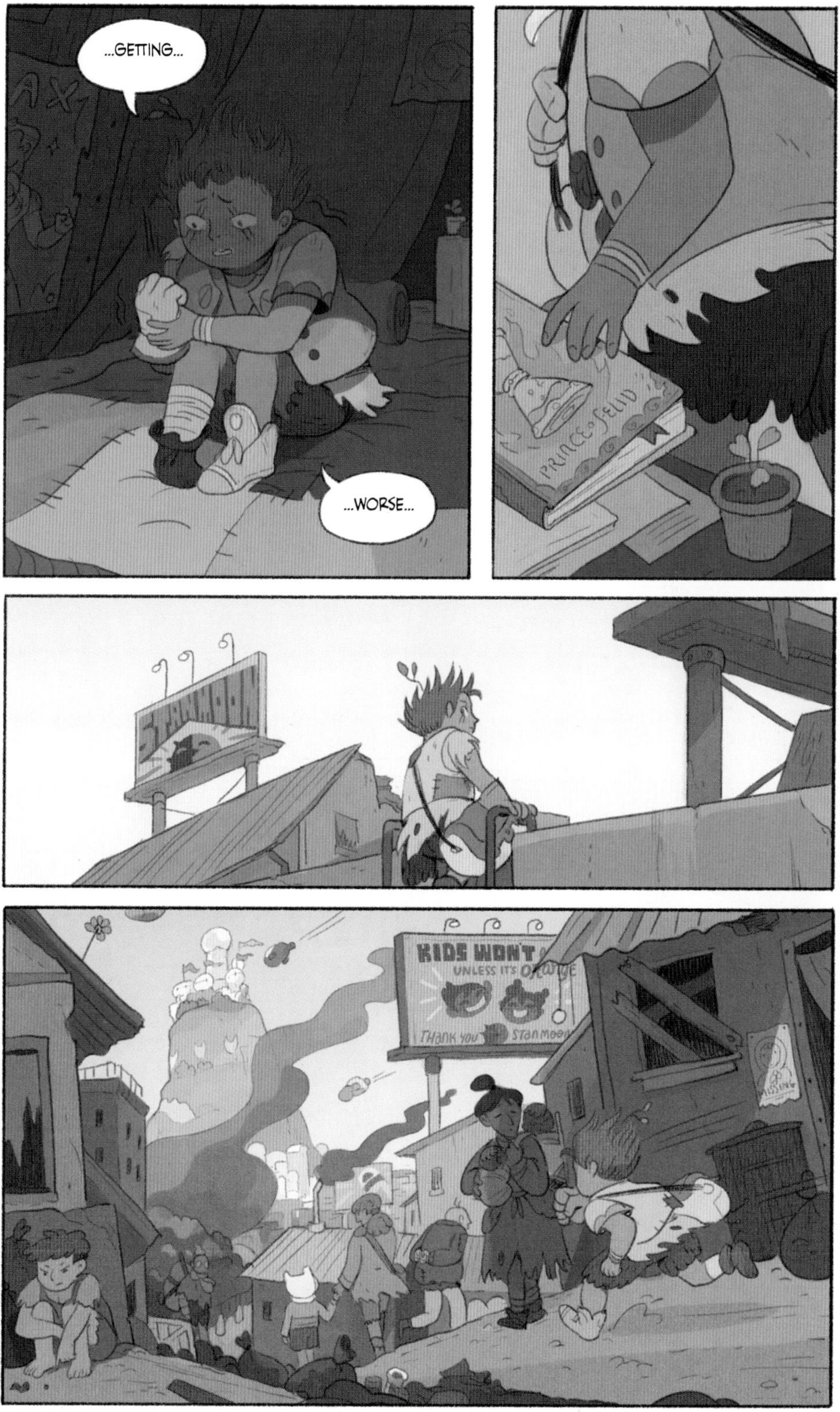
...GETTING...
...WORSE...
PRINCE o FELID
KIDS WON'T
UNLESS IT'S
THANK YOU
STANMOON

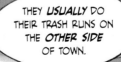

VICTORY PLAZA,
DOWNTOWN **CHRYSALIS**

SHG SHG SHG

SHG SHG

OH MAN! THOSE OLD **TOKI**
GARBAGE BARGES ARE
BLOCKING OUR LIGHT!

THEY **USUALLY** DO
THEIR TRASH RUNS ON
THE **OTHER SIDE**
OF TOWN.

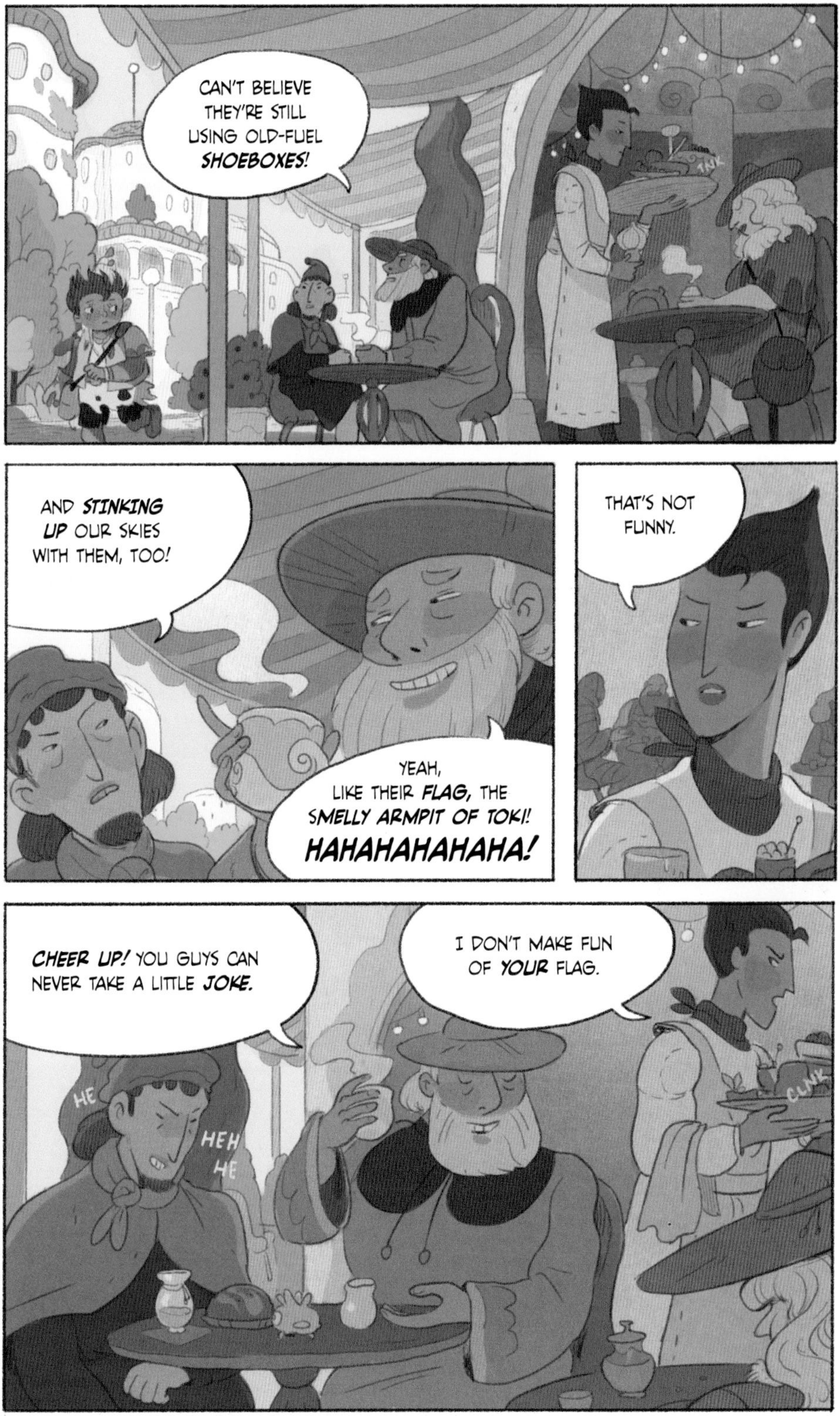
CAN'T BELIEVE THEY'RE STILL USING OLD-FUEL SHOEBOXES!
AND STINKING UP OUR SKIES WITH THEM, TOO!
YEAH, LIKE THEIR FLAG, THE SMELLY ARMPIT OF TOKI! HAHAHAHAHAHA!
THAT'S NOT FUNNY.
CHEER UP! YOU GUYS CAN NEVER TAKE A LITTLE JOKE.
I DON'T MAKE FUN OF YOUR FLAG.
HE
HEH
HE
CLINK

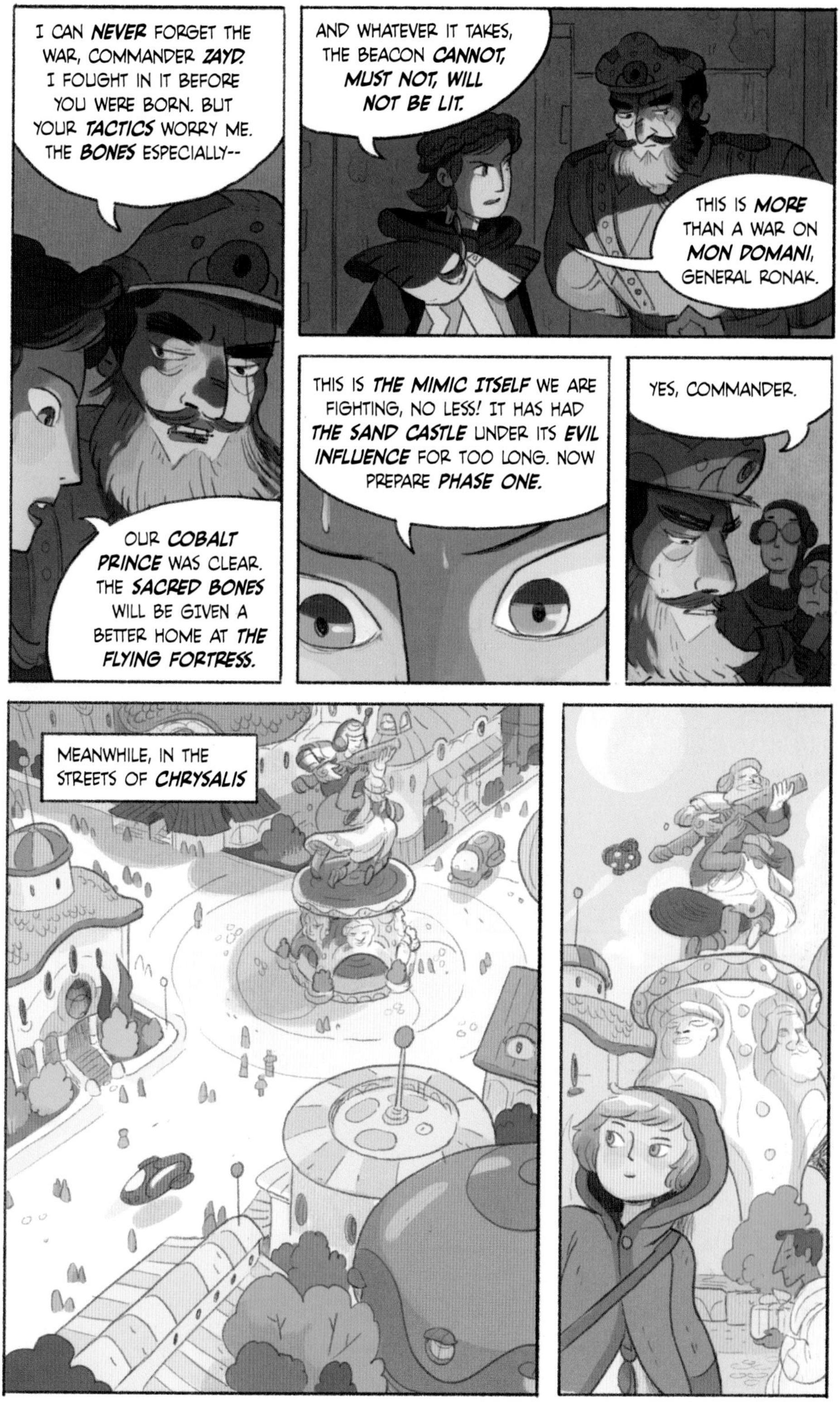
I CAN NEVER FORGET THE WAR, COMMANDER ZAYD. I FOUGHT IN IT BEFORE YOU WERE BORN. BUT YOUR TACTICS WORRY ME. THE BONES ESPECIALLY--
OUR COBALT PRINCE WAS CLEAR. THE SACRED BONES WILL BE GIVEN A BETTER HOME AT THE FLYING FORTRESS.
AND WHATEVER IT TAKES, THE BEACON CANNOT, MUST NOT, WILL NOT BE LIT.
THIS IS MORE THAN A WAR ON MON DOMANI, GENERAL RONAK.
THIS IS THE MIMIC ITSELF WE ARE FIGHTING, NO LESS! IT HAS HAD THE SAND CASTLE UNDER ITS EVIL INFLUENCE FOR TOO LONG. NOW PREPARE PHASE ONE.
YES, COMMANDER.
MEANWHILE, IN THE STREETS OF CHRYSALIS

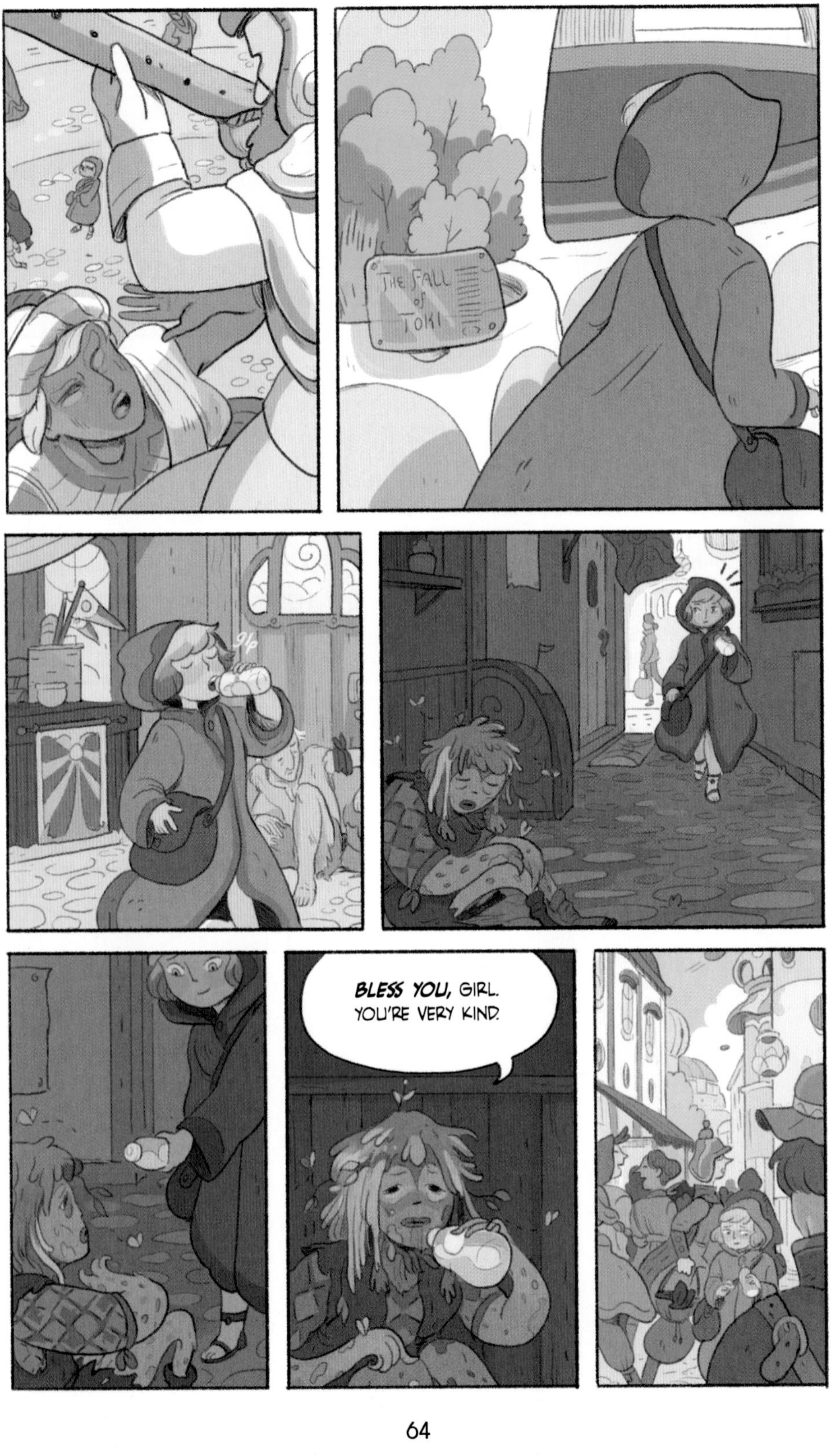
THE FALL of TOKI
glp
BLESS YOU, GIRL.
YOU'RE VERY KIND.

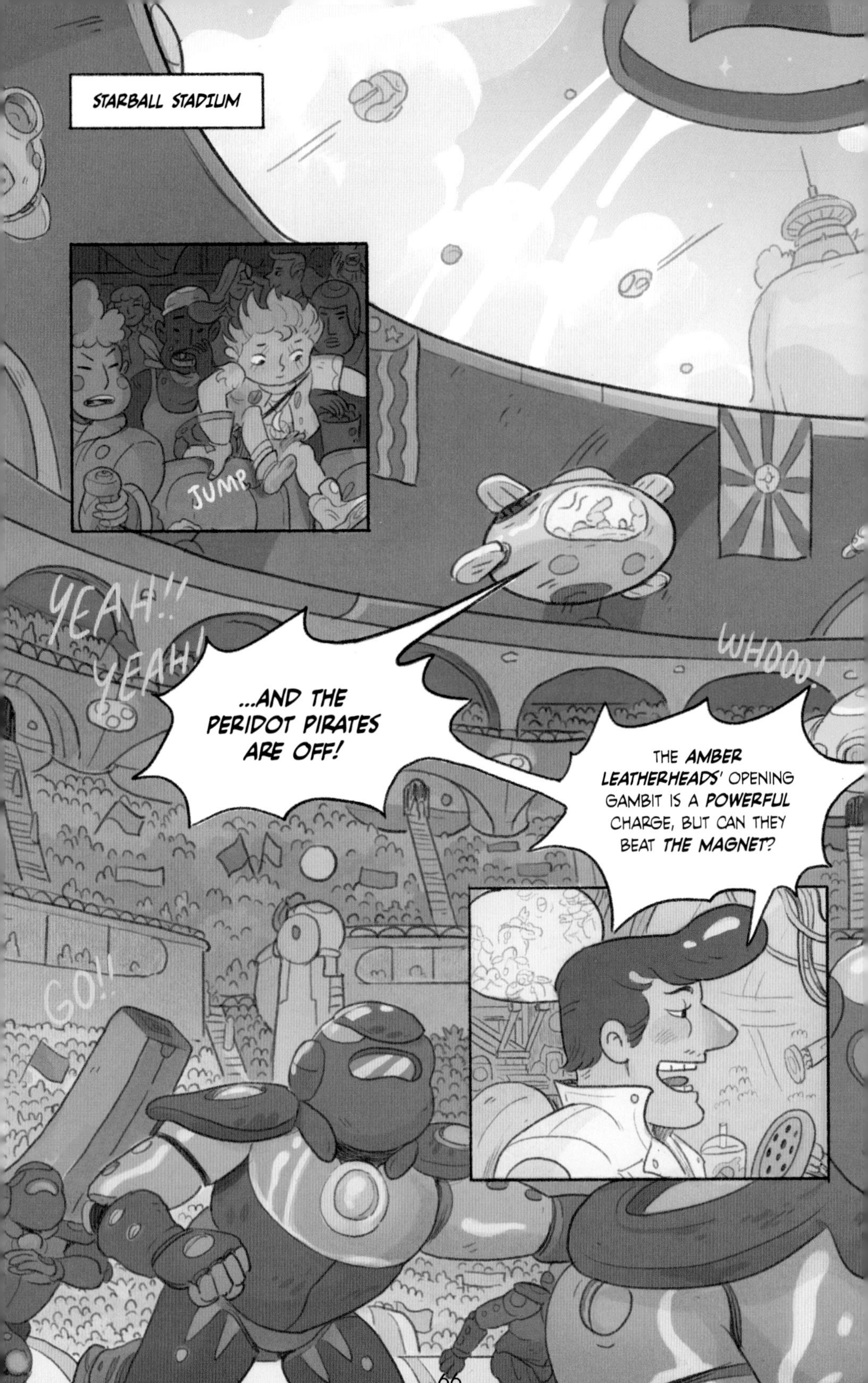
STARBALL STADIUM
JUMP
YEAH!!
YEAH!
...AND THE PERIDOT PIRATES ARE OFF!
WHOOO!
THE AMBER LEATHERHEADS' OPENING GAMBIT IS A POWERFUL CHARGE, BUT CAN THEY BEAT THE MAGNET?
GO!!

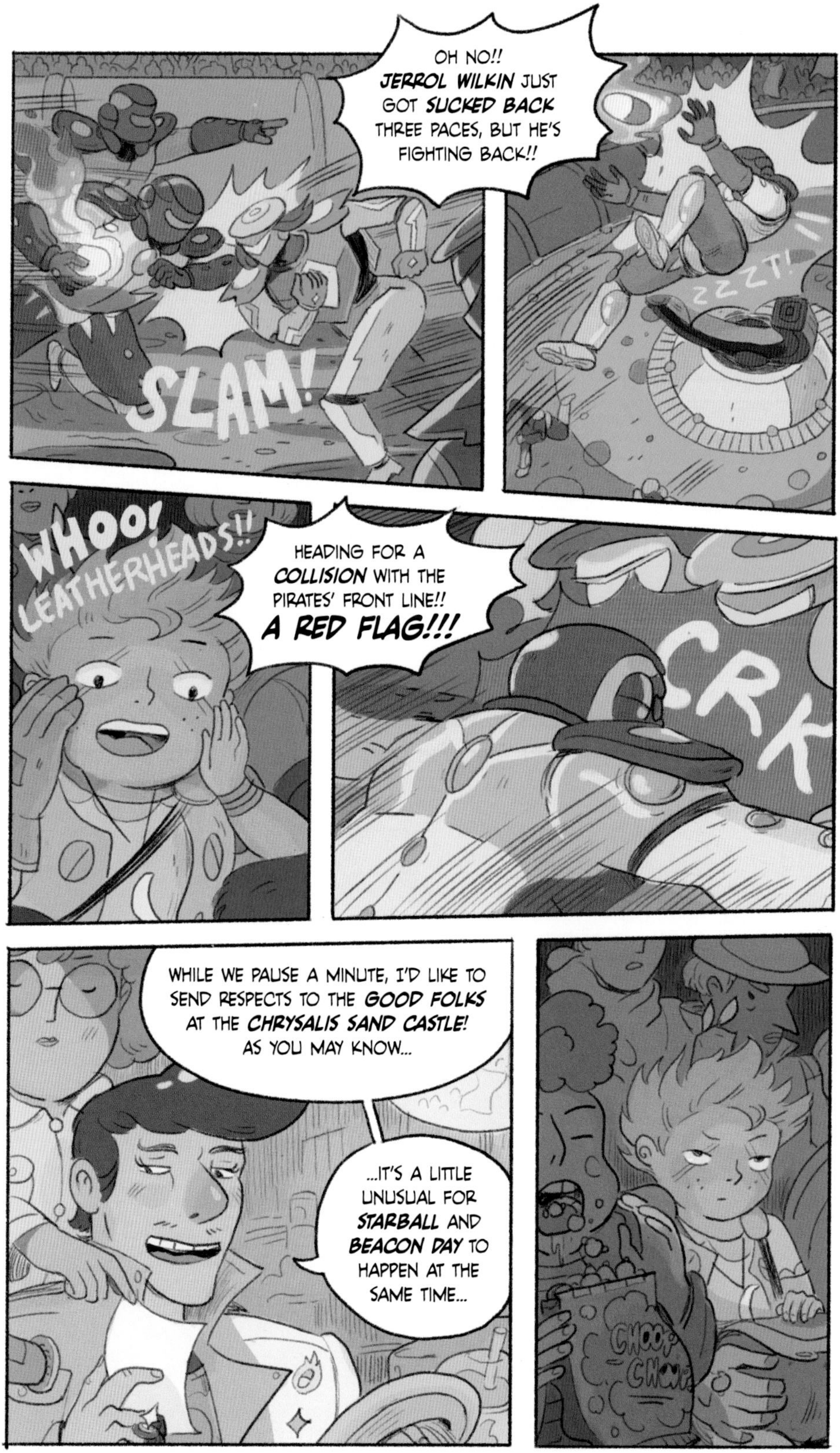
OH NO!! JERROL WILKIN JUST GOT SUCKED BACK THREE PACES, BUT HE'S FIGHTING BACK!!
SLAM!
ZZZT!
WHOO! LEATHERHEADS!!
HEADING FOR A COLLISION WITH THE PIRATES' FRONT LINE!! A RED FLAG!!!
CRK
WHILE WE PAUSE A MINUTE, I'D LIKE TO SEND RESPECTS TO THE GOOD FOLKS AT THE CHRYSALIS SAND CASTLE! AS YOU MAY KNOW...
...IT'S A LITTLE UNUSUAL FOR STARBALL AND BEACON DAY TO HAPPEN AT THE SAME TIME...
CHOOP CHOW

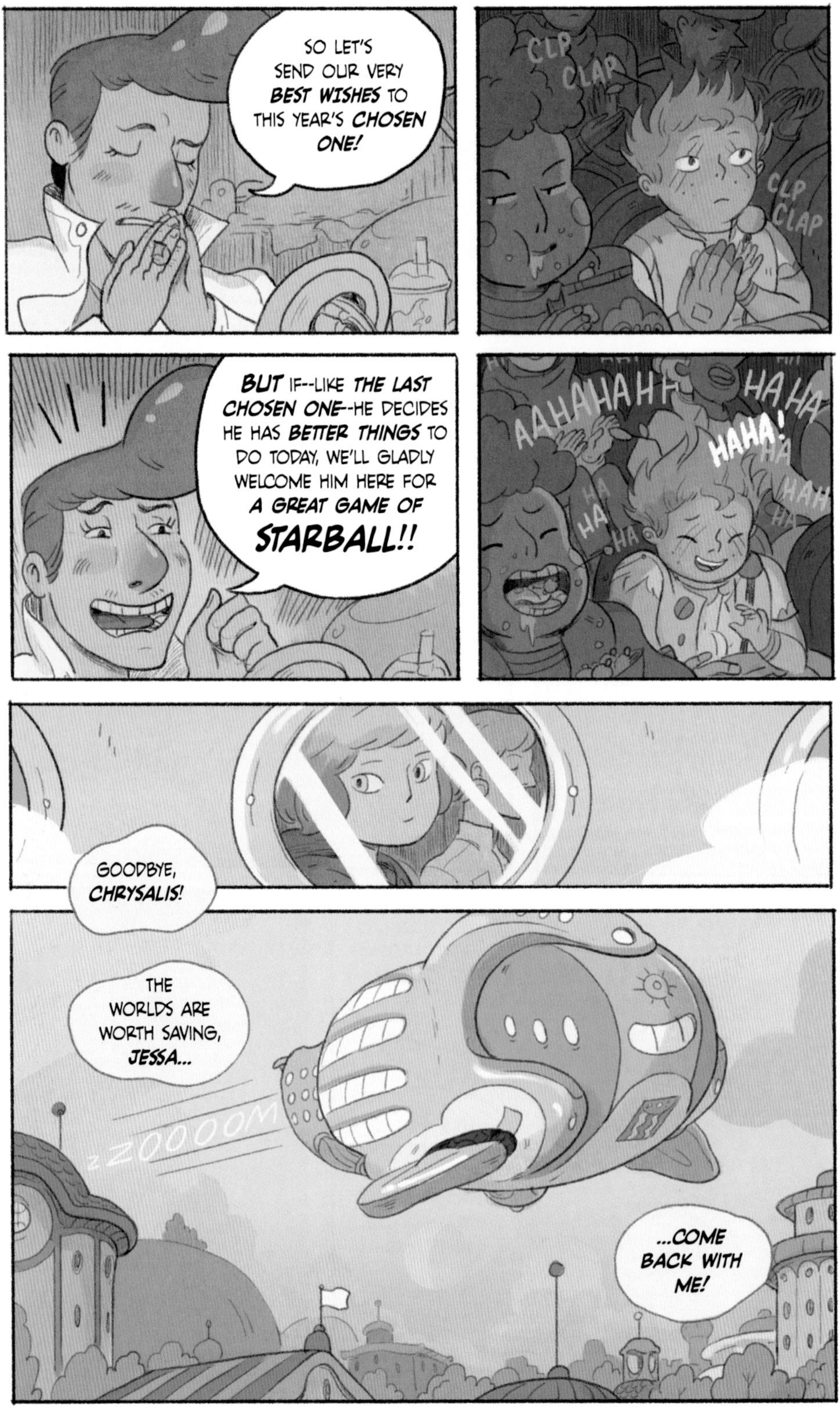
SO LET'S SEND OUR VERY BEST WISHES TO THIS YEAR'S CHOSEN ONE!
CLP CLAP
CLP CLAP
BUT IF--LIKE THE LAST CHOSEN ONE--HE DECIDES HE HAS BETTER THINGS TO DO TODAY, WE'LL GLADLY WELCOME HIM HERE FOR A GREAT GAME OF STARBALL!!
AAHAHAHH
HAHA
HAHA!
HA HA
HA
HAH
GOODBYE, CHRYSALIS!
THE WORLDS ARE WORTH SAVING, JESSA...
zZOOOOM
...COME BACK WITH ME!

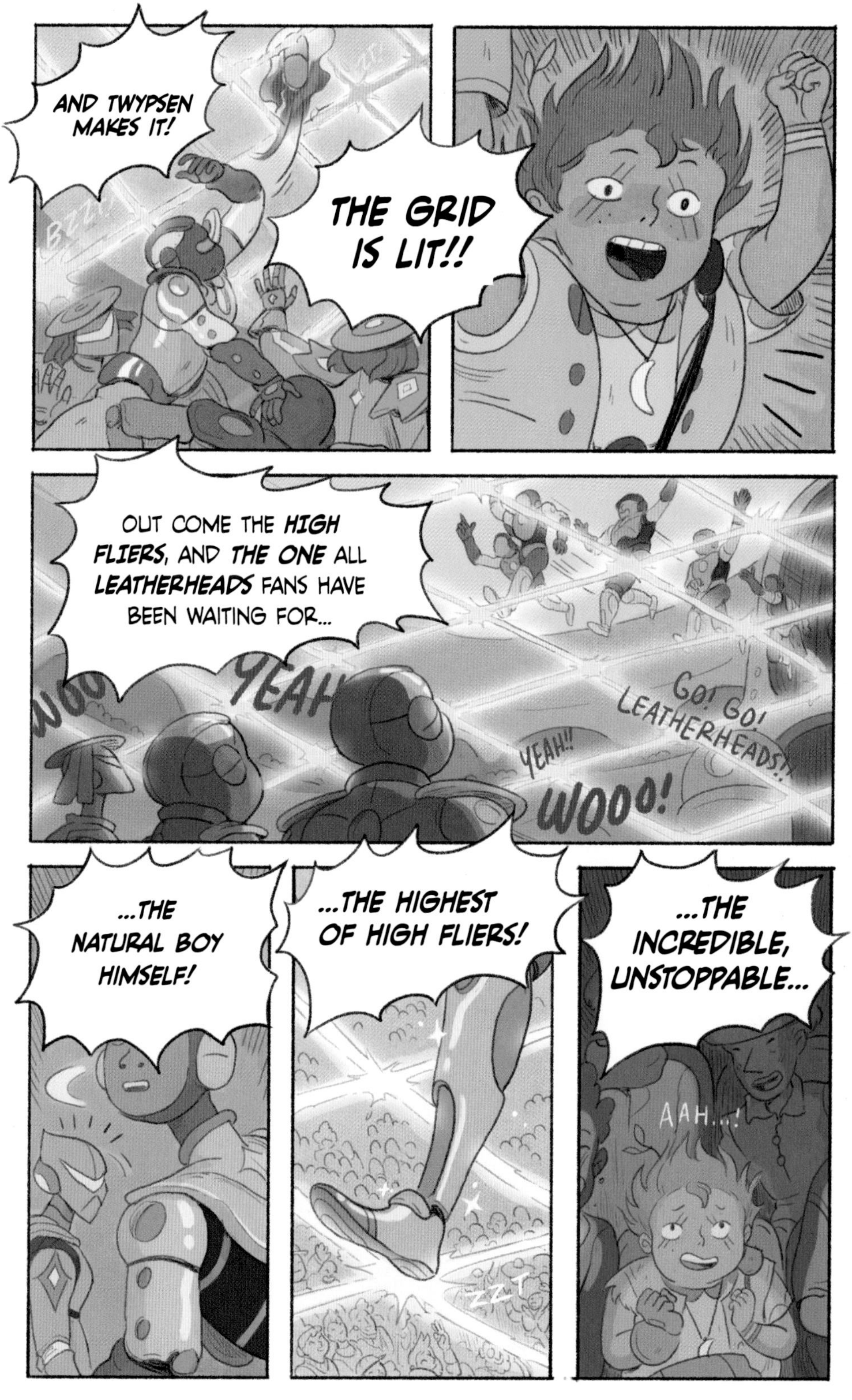
AND TWYPSEN MAKES IT!
BZZZT
THE GRID IS LIT!!
OUT COME THE HIGH FLIERS, AND THE ONE ALL LEATHERHEADS FANS HAVE BEEN WAITING FOR...
WOO
YEAH
GO! GO! LEATHERHEADS!!
YEAH!!
WOOO!
...THE NATURAL BOY HIMSELF!
...THE HIGHEST OF HIGH FLIERS!
ZZT
...THE INCREDIBLE, UNSTOPPABLE...
AAH...!

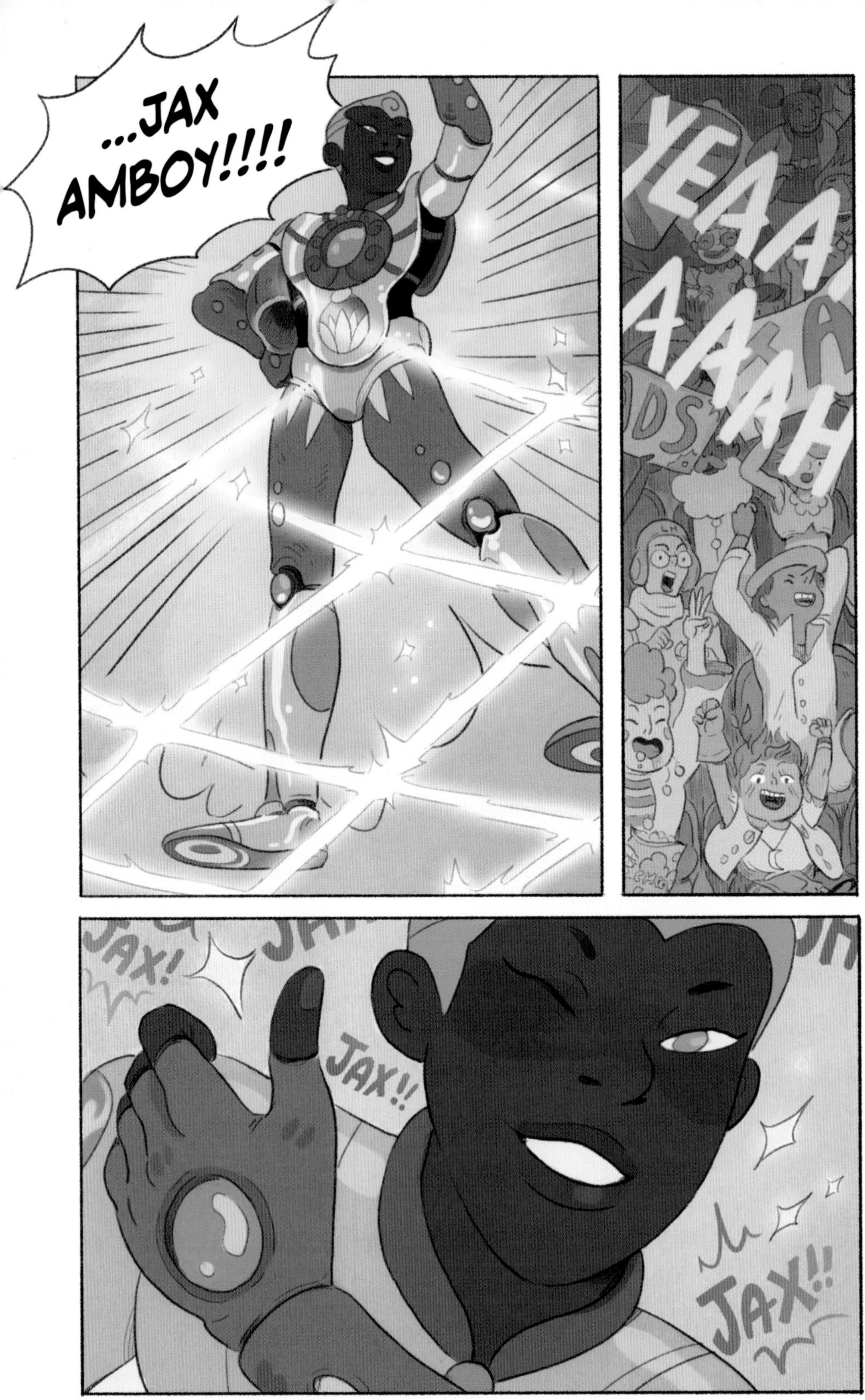
...JAX AMBOY!!!!
YEAA AAAAH
JAX!
JAX!!
JAX!!

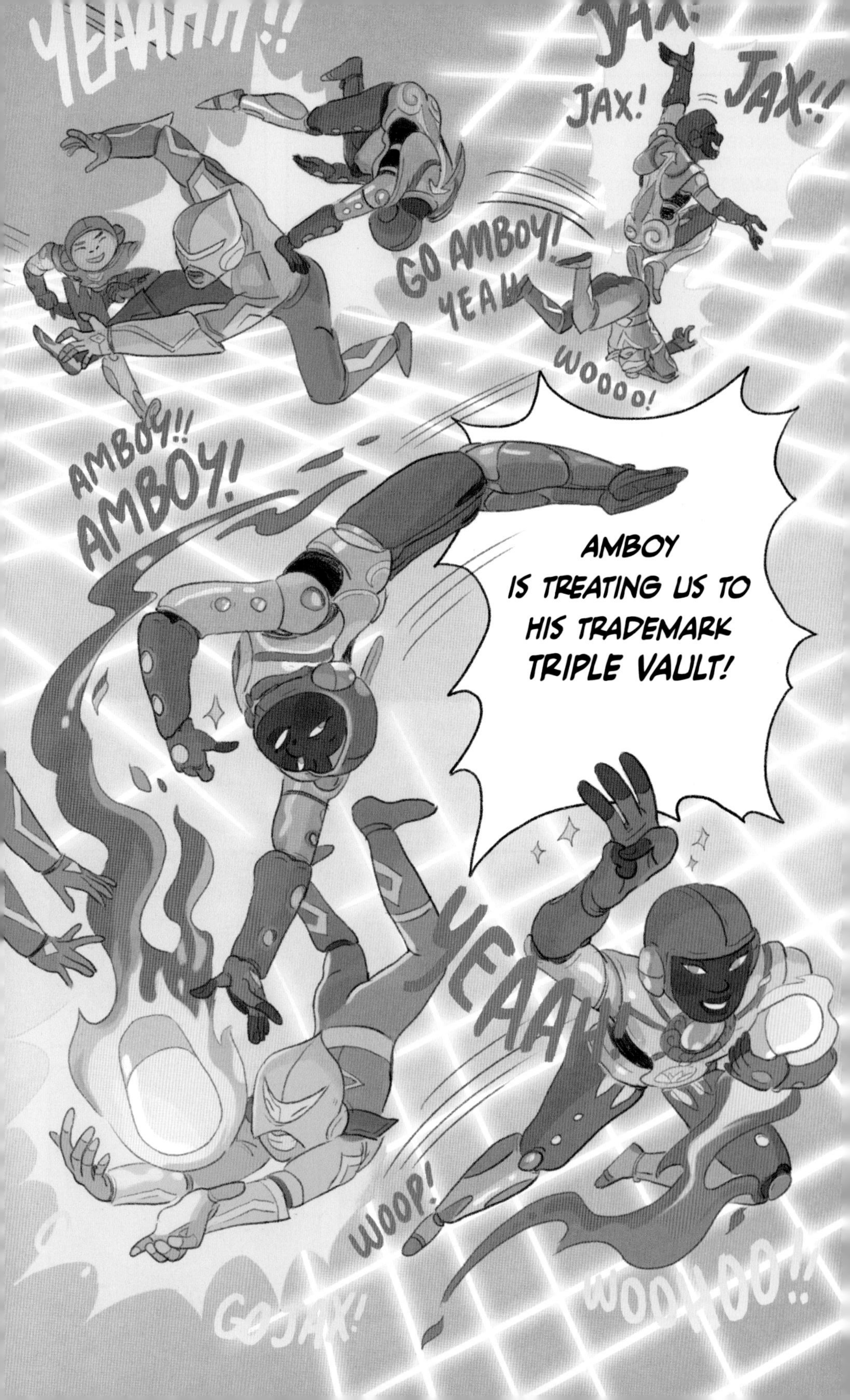
YEAAHH!!
JAX!
JAX!
JAX!!
GO AMBOY!
YEAH
WOOOOO!
AMBOY!!
AMBOY!
AMBOY IS TREATING US TO HIS TRADEMARK TRIPLE VAULT!
YEAAH
WOOP!
GO JAX!
WOOHOO!!

72

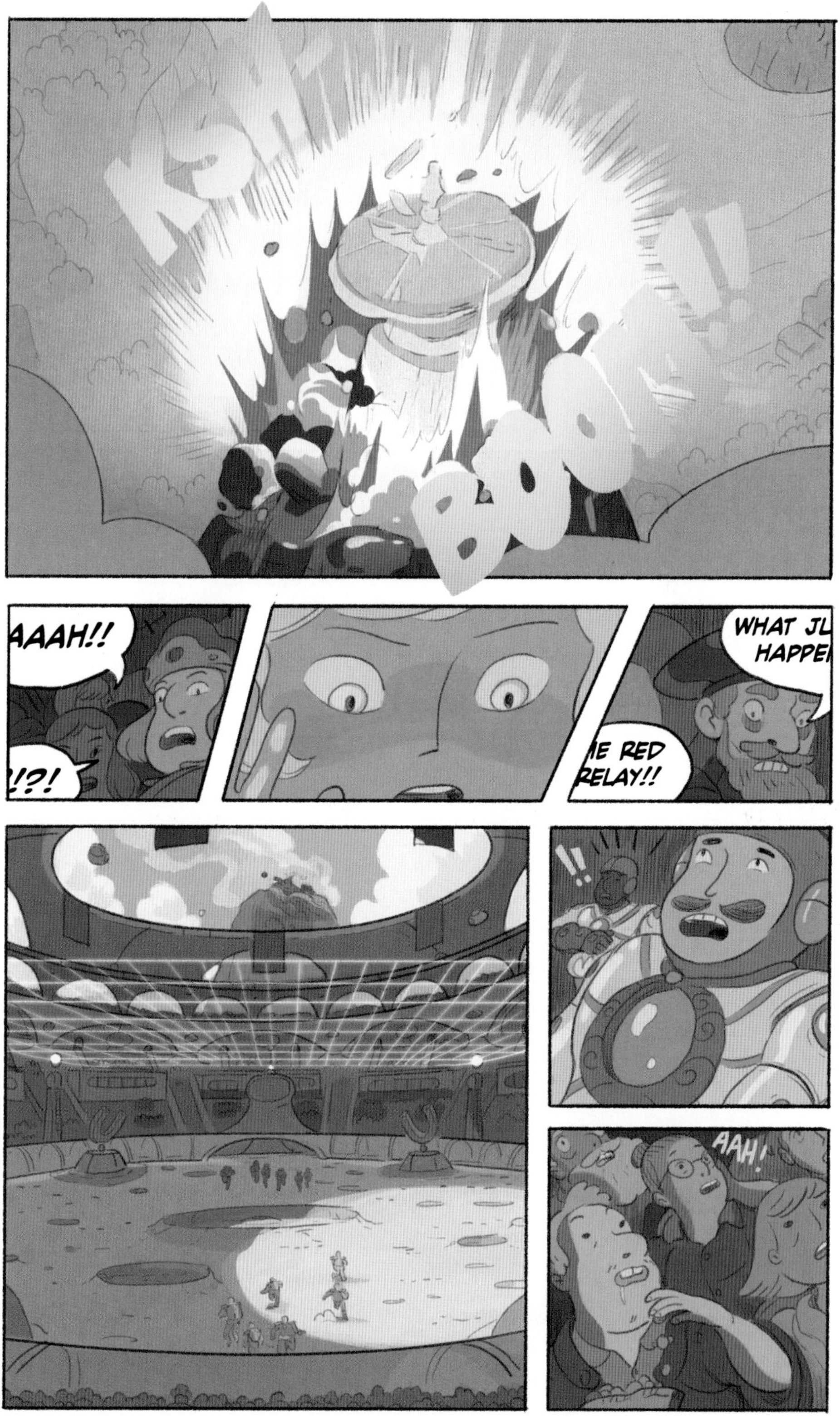
KSH
BOOM!
AAAH!!
!?!
WHAT JU
HAPPE
E RED
RELAY!!
!!
AAH!

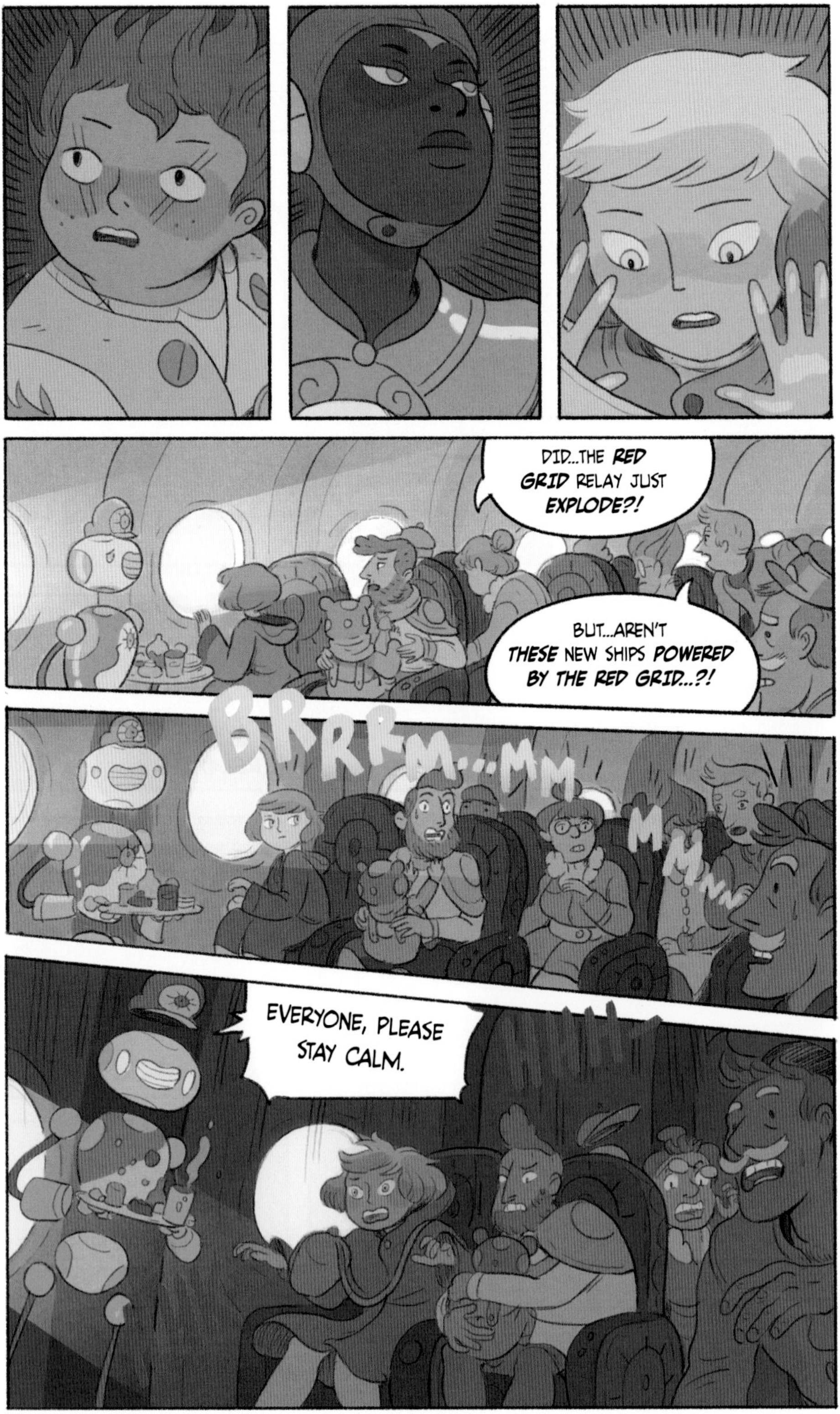
DID...THE RED GRID RELAY JUST EXPLODE?!
BUT...AREN'T THESE NEW SHIPS POWERED BY THE RED GRID...?!
BRRRM...MM
MMNN
EVERYONE, PLEASE STAY CALM.

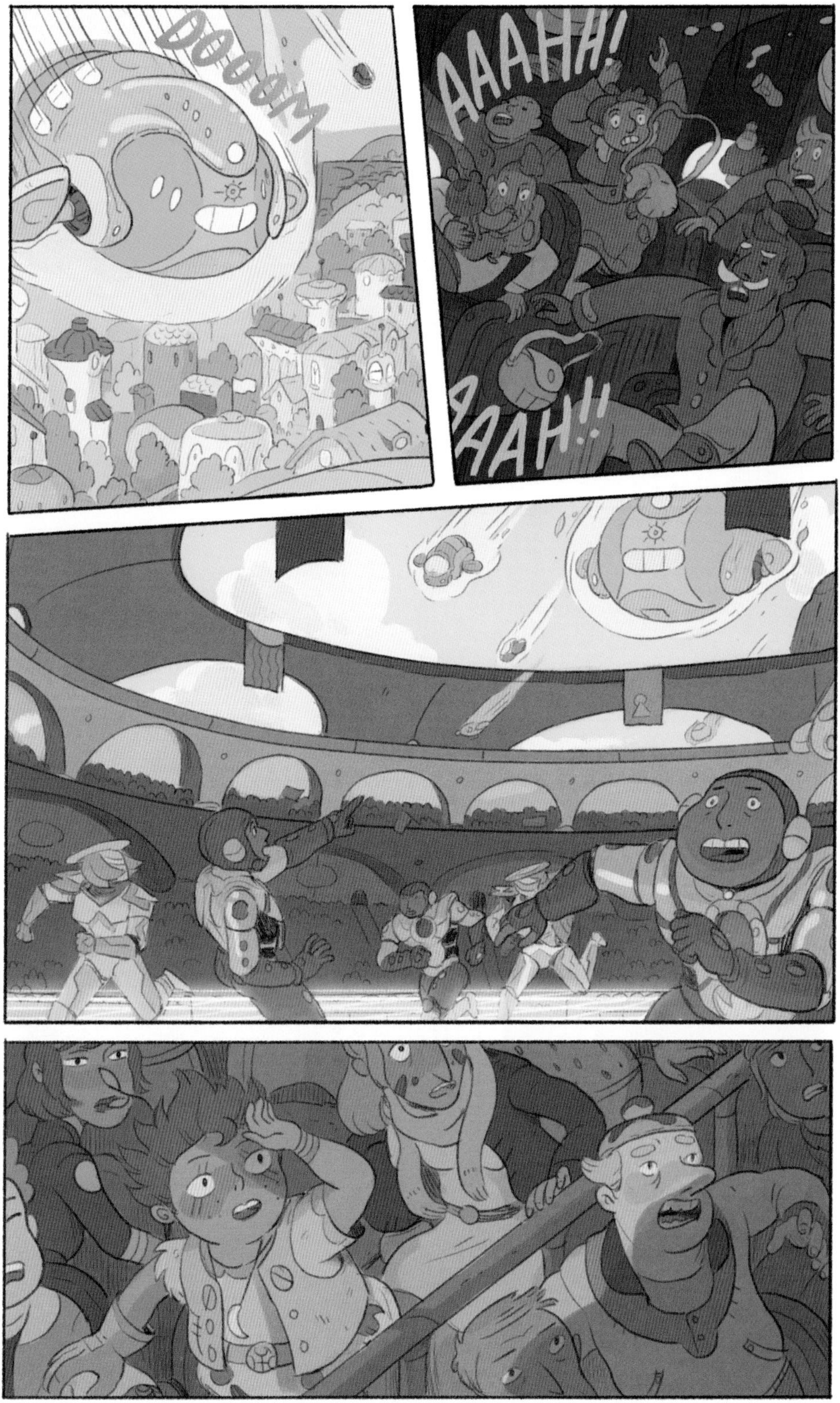
DOOOOM
AAAHH!
AAAH!!

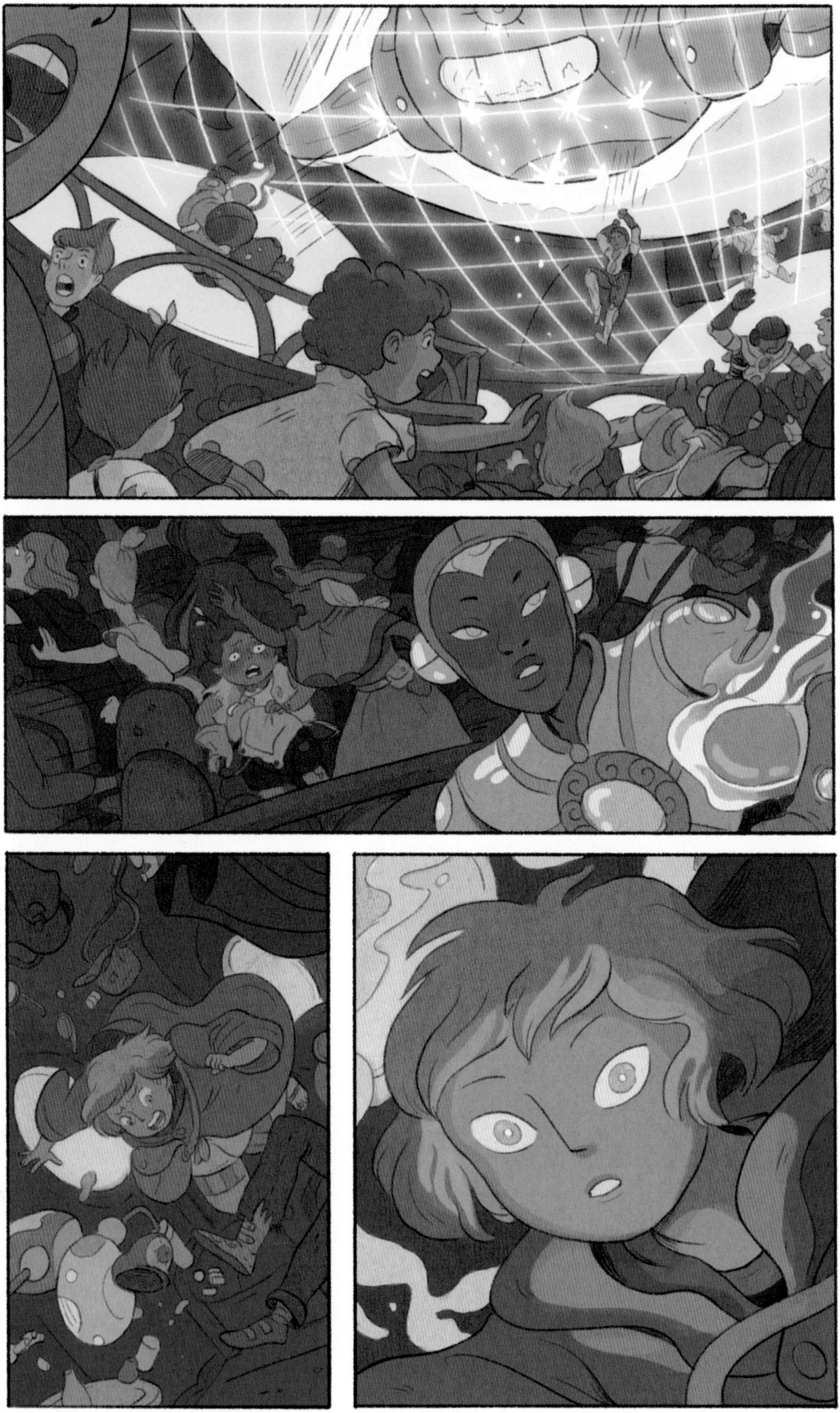

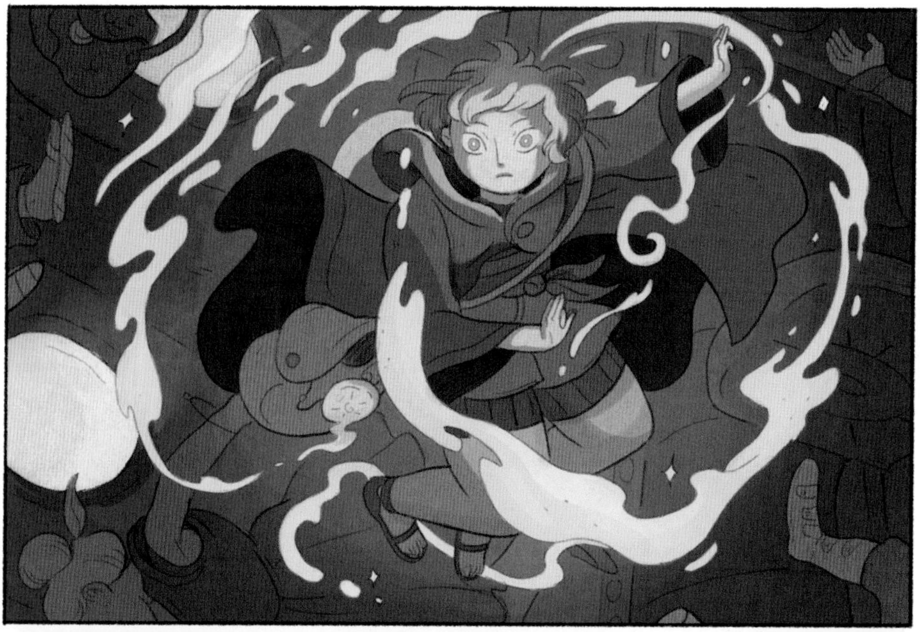

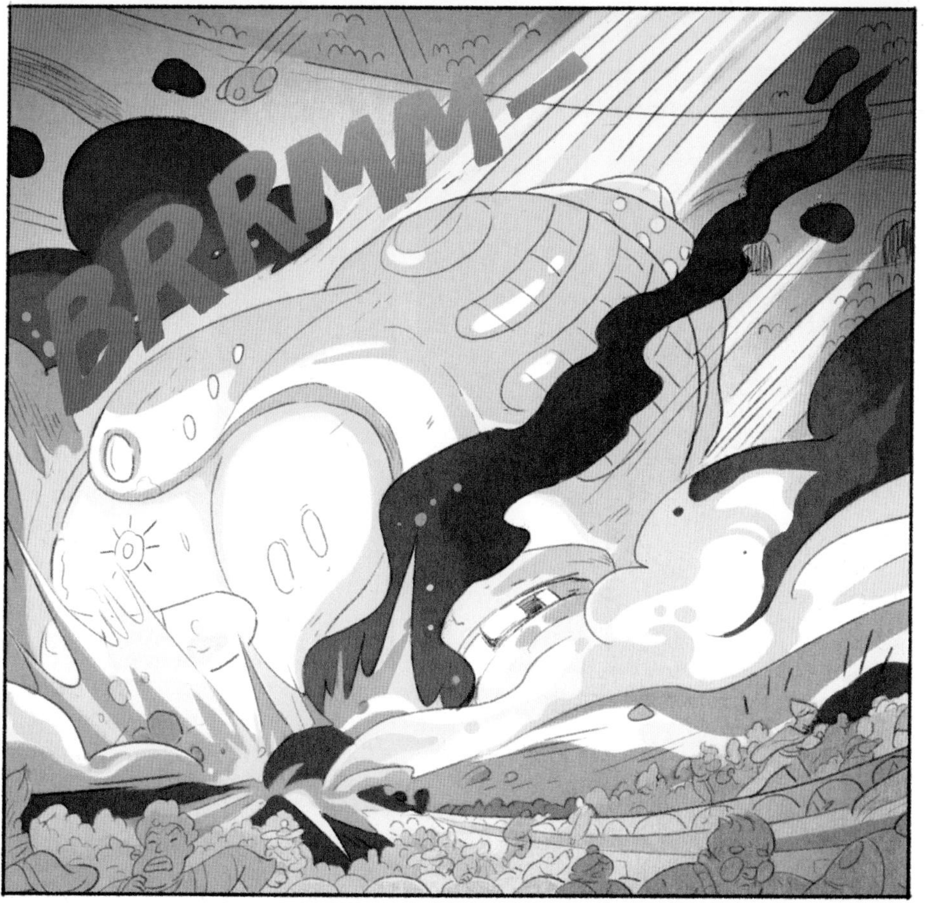

BRRMM—

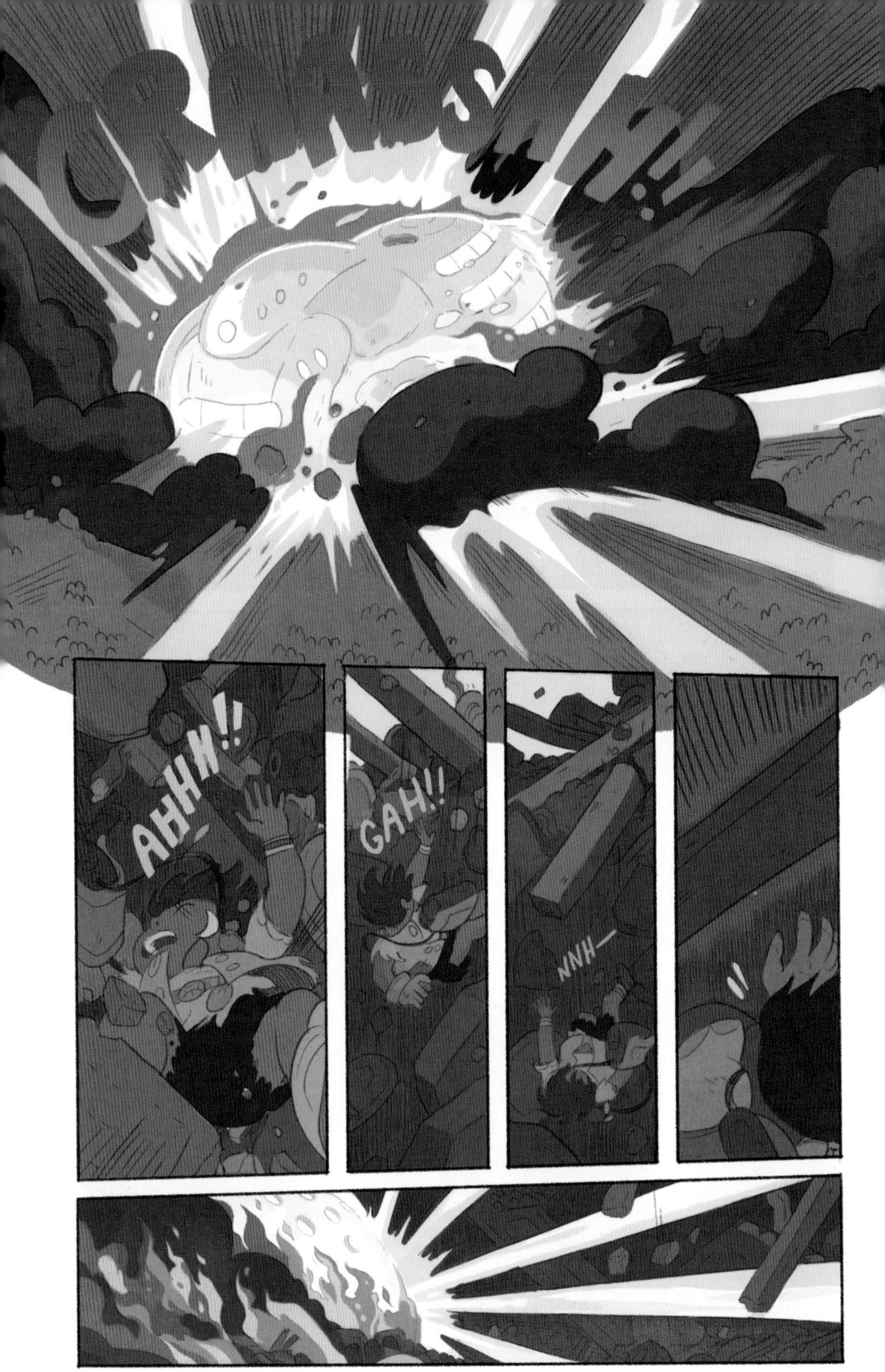
CRASH!
AHHH!!
GAH!!
NNH—
!!

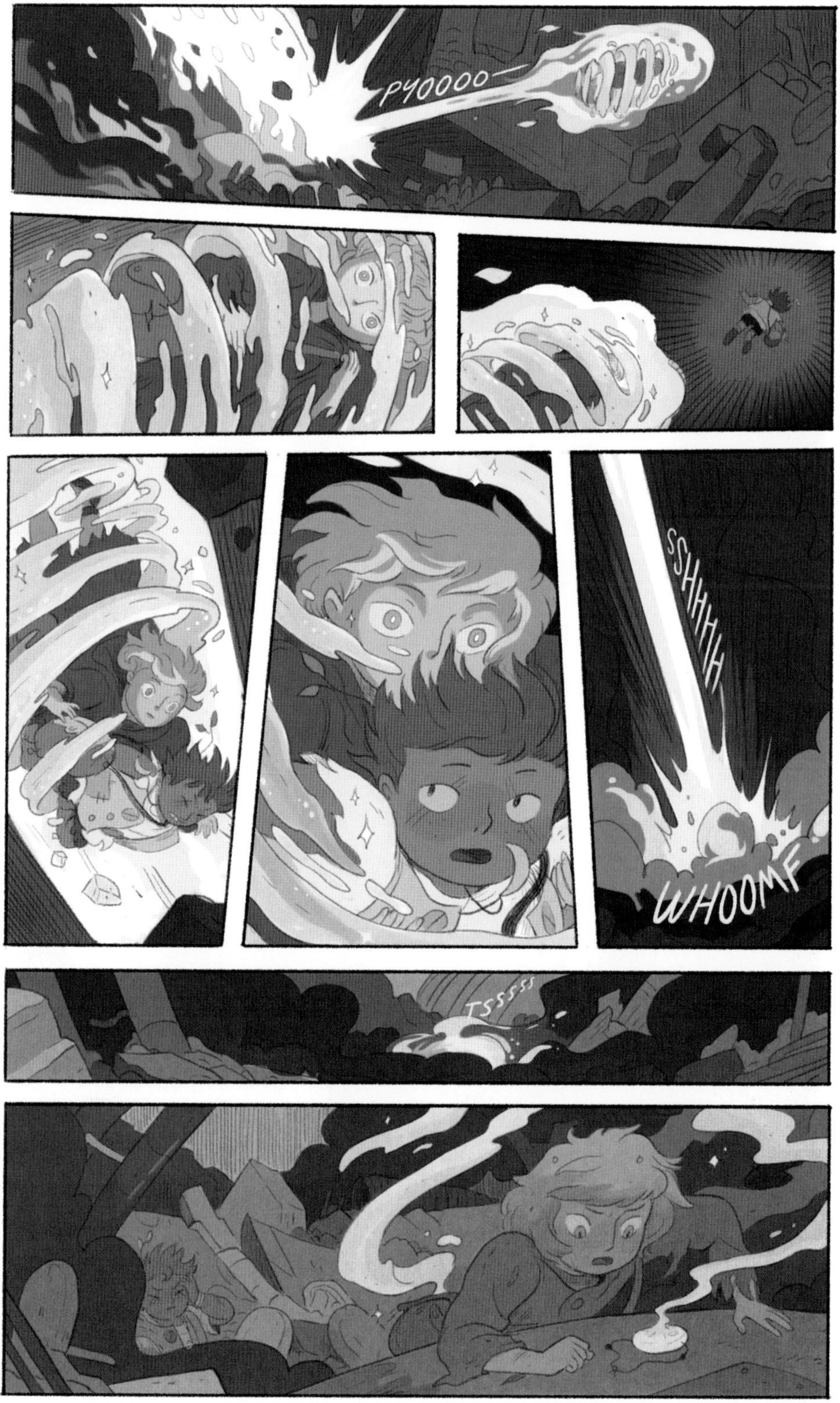
PYOOOO—
SSHHHHH
WHOOMF
TSSSSS

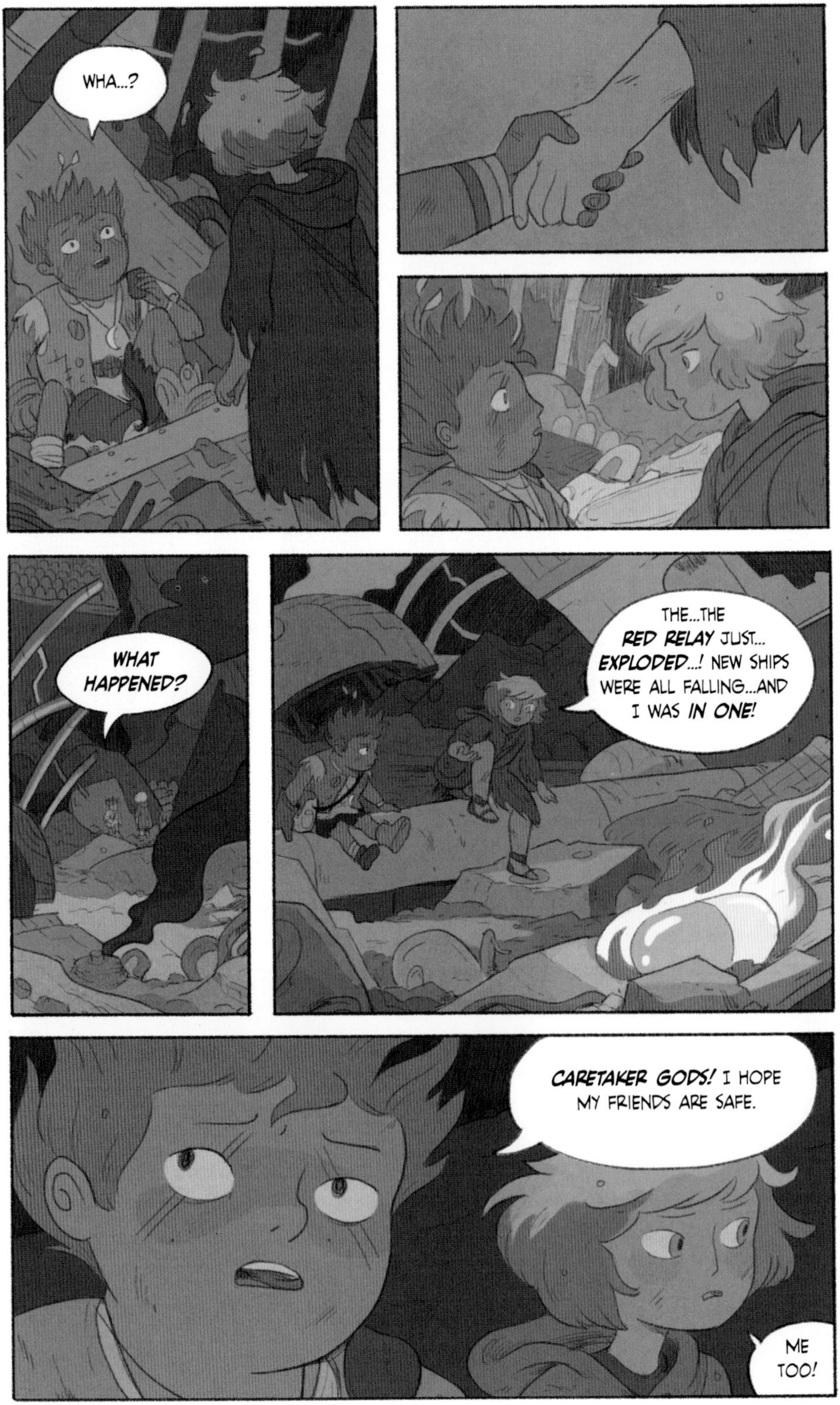
WHA...?
WHAT HAPPENED?
THE...THE RED RELAY JUST... EXPLODED...! NEW SHIPS WERE ALL FALLING...AND I WAS IN ONE!
CARETAKER GODS! I HOPE MY FRIENDS ARE SAFE.
ME TOO!

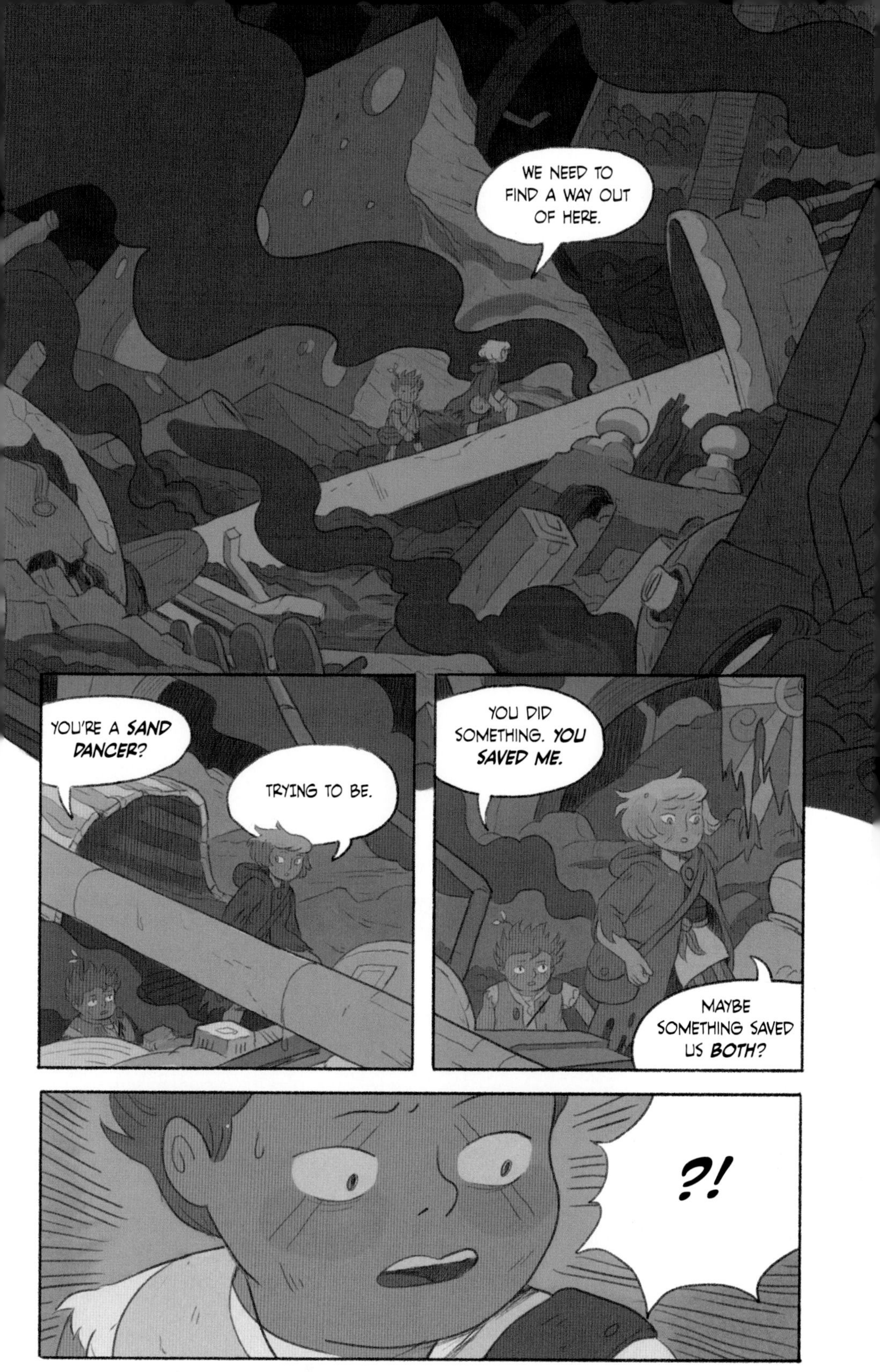
WE NEED TO FIND A WAY OUT OF HERE.
YOU'RE A **SAND DANCER?**
TRYING TO BE.
YOU DID SOMETHING. ***YOU SAVED ME.***
MAYBE SOMETHING SAVED US ***BOTH?***
?!

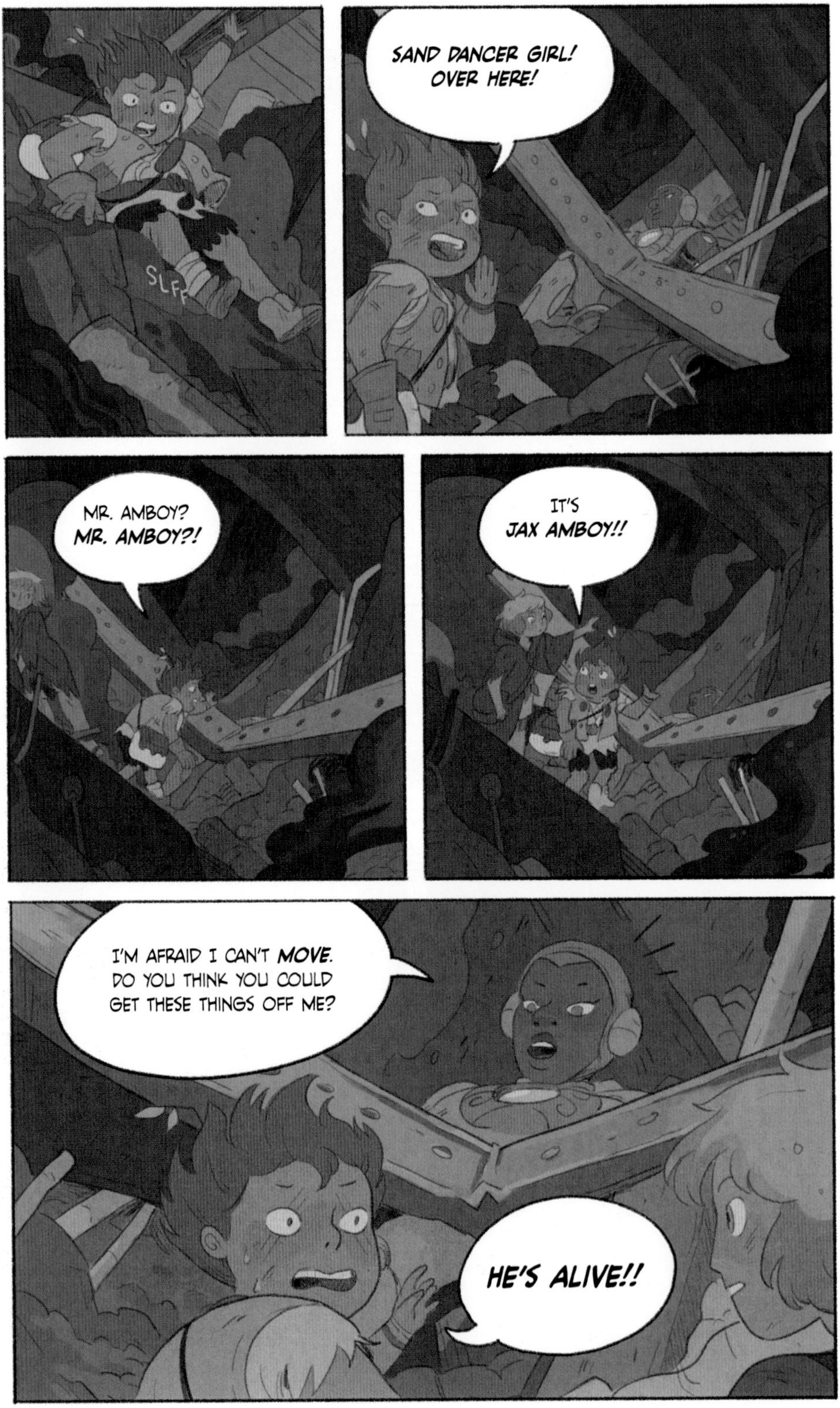
SLFF
SAND DANCER GIRL! OVER HERE!
MR. AMBOY? MR. AMBOY?!
IT'S JAX AMBOY!!
I'M AFRAID I CAN'T MOVE. DO YOU THINK YOU COULD GET THESE THINGS OFF ME?
HE'S ALIVE!!

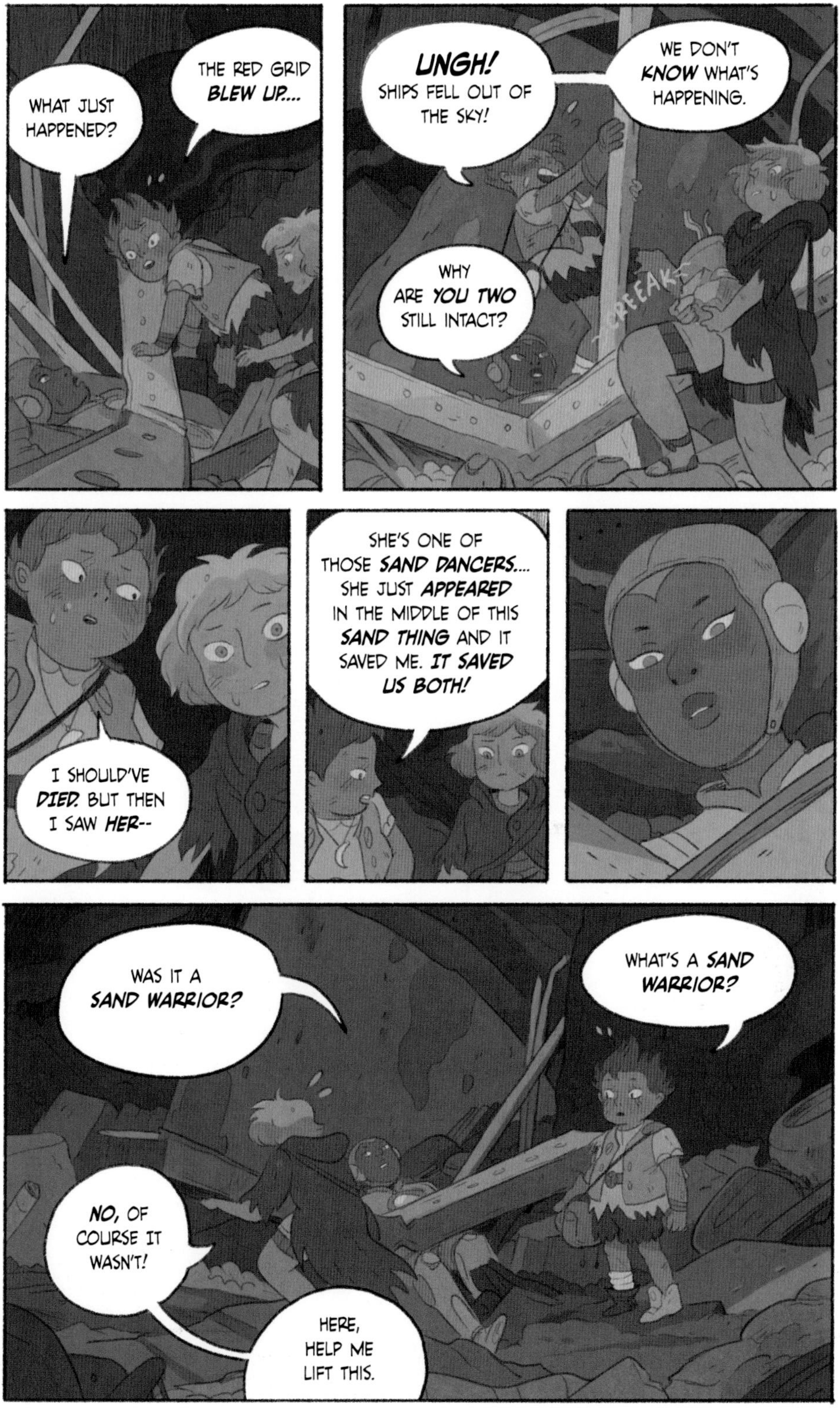
WHAT JUST HAPPENED?
THE RED GRID BLEW UP....
UNGH! SHIPS FELL OUT OF THE SKY!
WE DON'T KNOW WHAT'S HAPPENING.
WHY ARE YOU TWO STILL INTACT?
CREEAK
I SHOULD'VE DIED. BUT THEN I SAW HER--
SHE'S ONE OF THOSE SAND DANCERS.... SHE JUST APPEARED IN THE MIDDLE OF THIS SAND THING AND IT SAVED ME. IT SAVED US BOTH!
WAS IT A SAND WARRIOR?
WHAT'S A SAND WARRIOR?
NO, OF COURSE IT WASN'T!
HERE, HELP ME LIFT THIS.

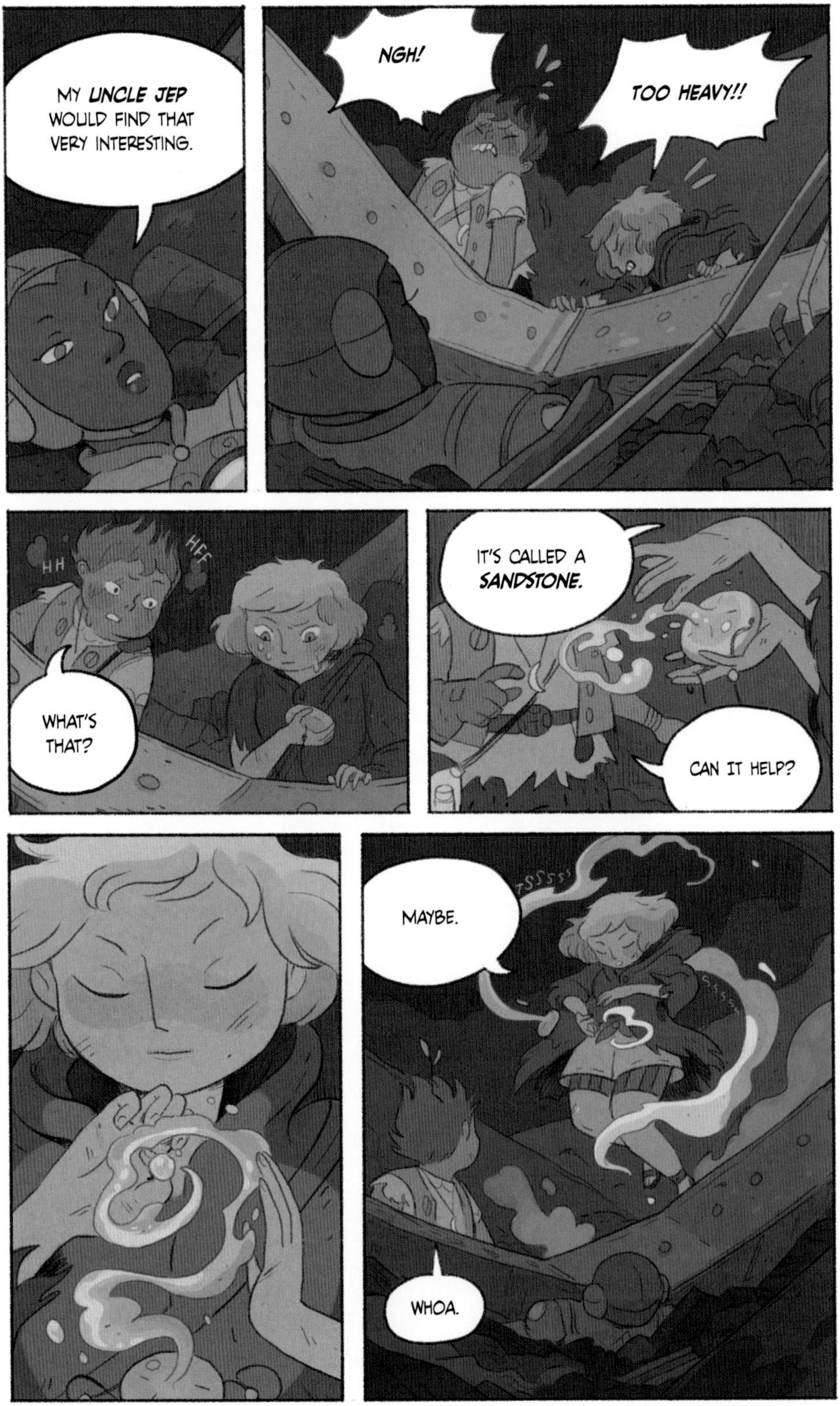
MY UNCLE JEP WOULD FIND THAT VERY INTERESTING.
NGH!
TOO HEAVY!!
HH
HFF
WHAT'S THAT?
IT'S CALLED A SANDSTONE.
CAN IT HELP?
MAYBE.
WHOA.

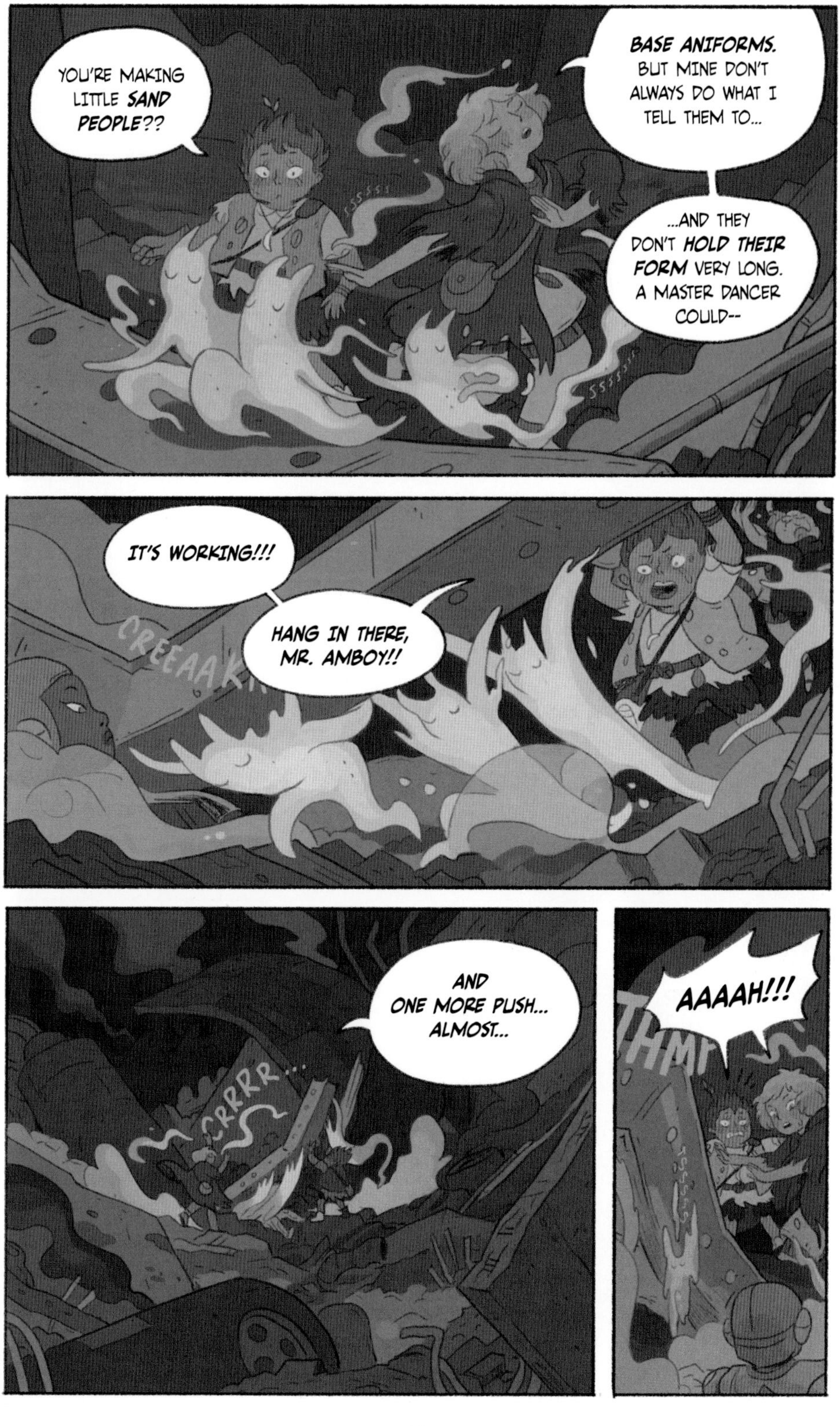
YOU'RE MAKING LITTLE SAND PEOPLE??
BASE ANIFORMS. BUT MINE DON'T ALWAYS DO WHAT I TELL THEM TO...
...AND THEY DON'T HOLD THEIR FORM VERY LONG. A MASTER DANCER COULD--
IT'S WORKING!!!
HANG IN THERE, MR. AMBOY!!
CREEAAK
AND ONE MORE PUSH... ALMOST...
CRRRR...
AAAAH!!!
THM

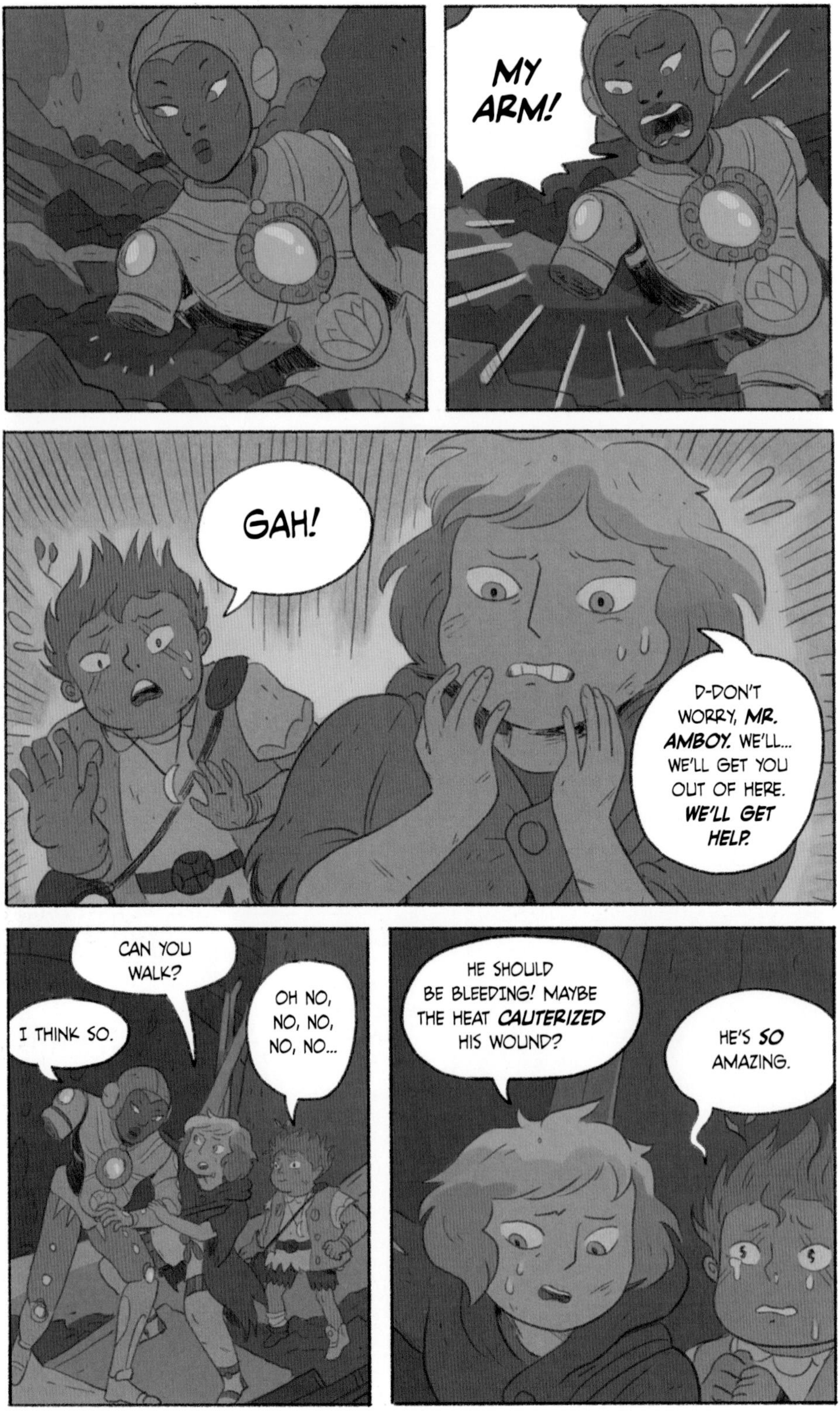
MY ARM!
GAH!
D-DON'T WORRY, MR. AMBOY. WE'LL... WE'LL GET YOU OUT OF HERE. WE'LL GET HELP.
CAN YOU WALK?
I THINK SO.
OH NO, NO, NO, NO, NO...
HE SHOULD BE BLEEDING! MAYBE THE HEAT CAUTERIZED HIS WOUND?
HE'S SO AMAZING.

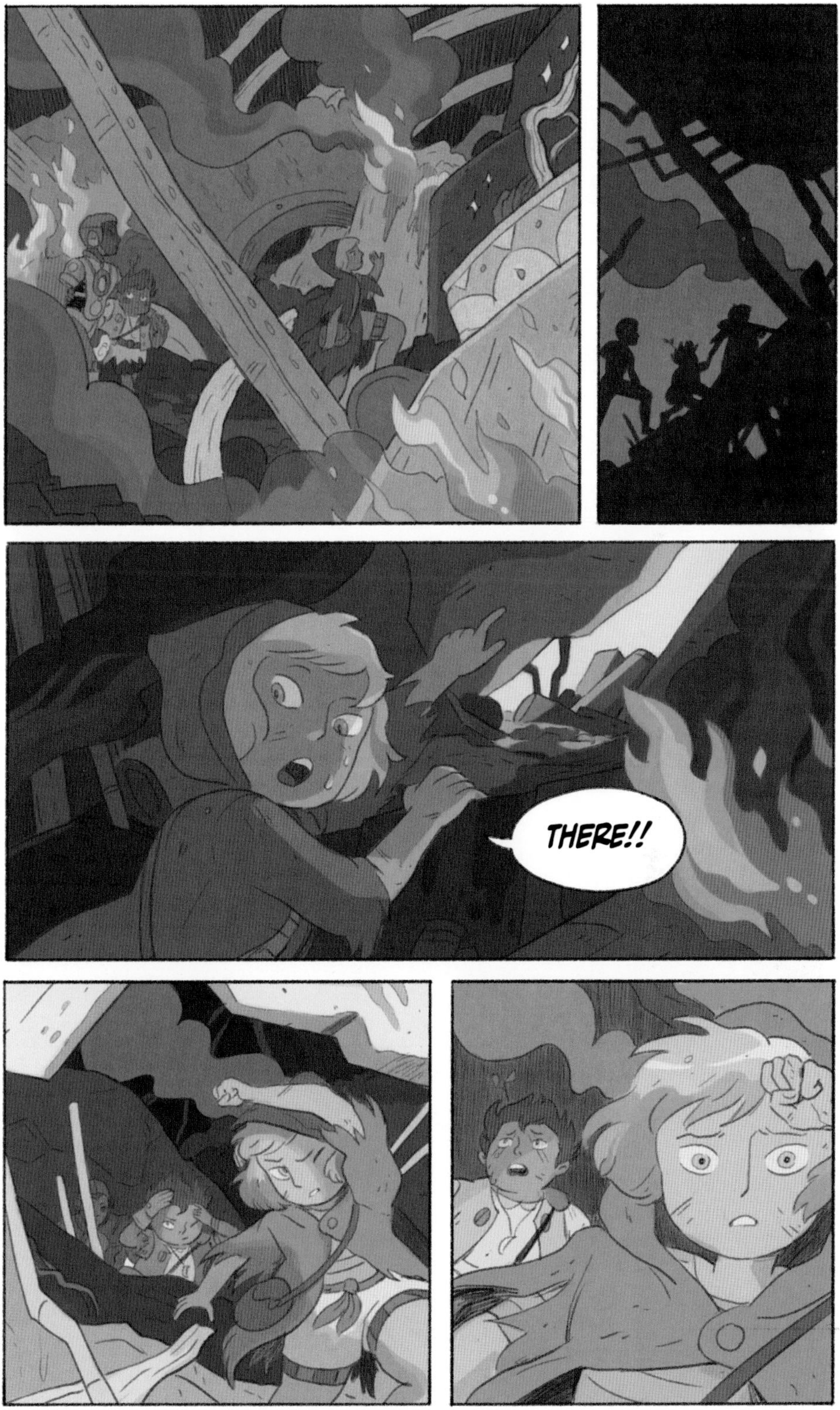
THERE!!

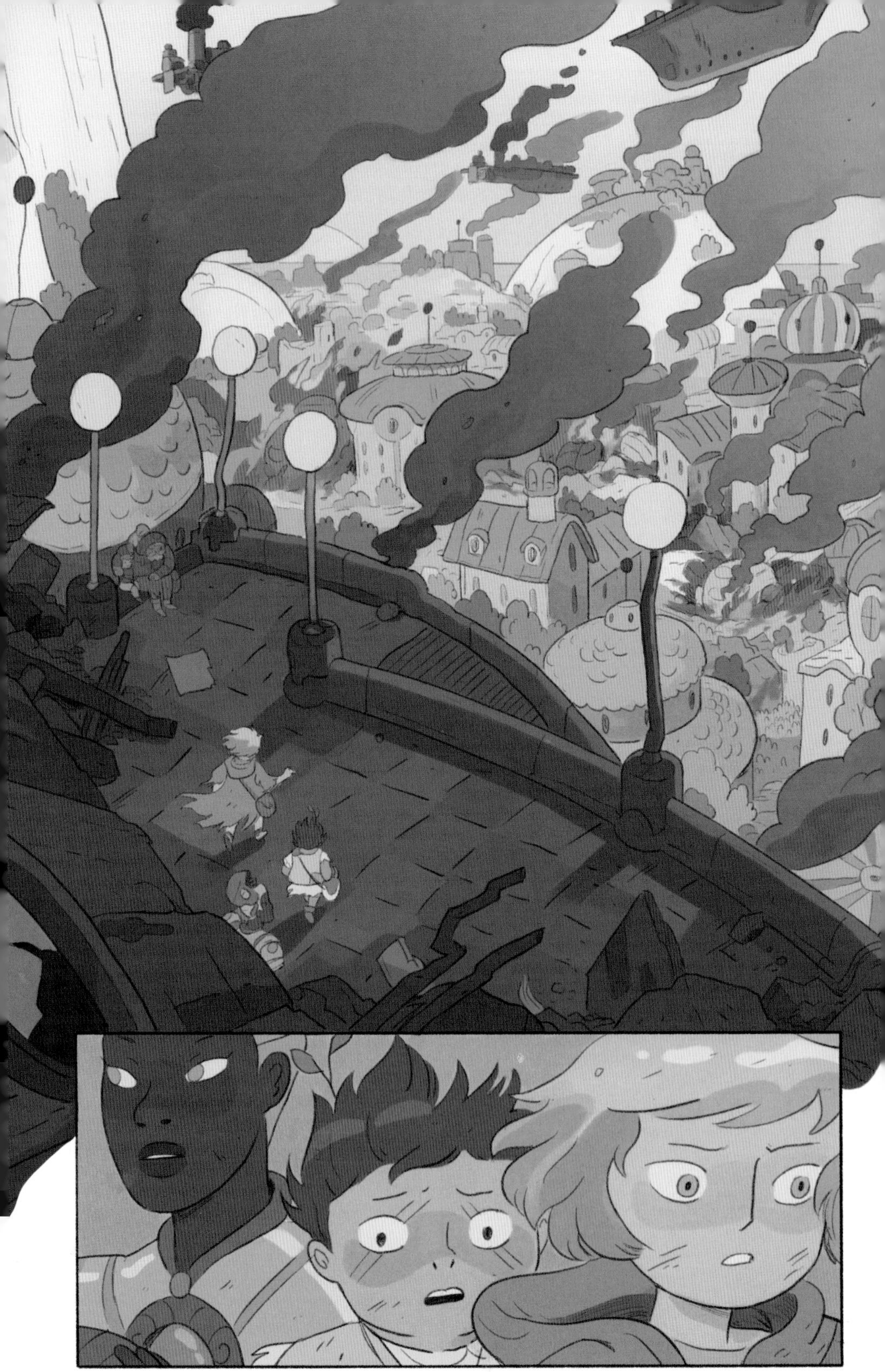

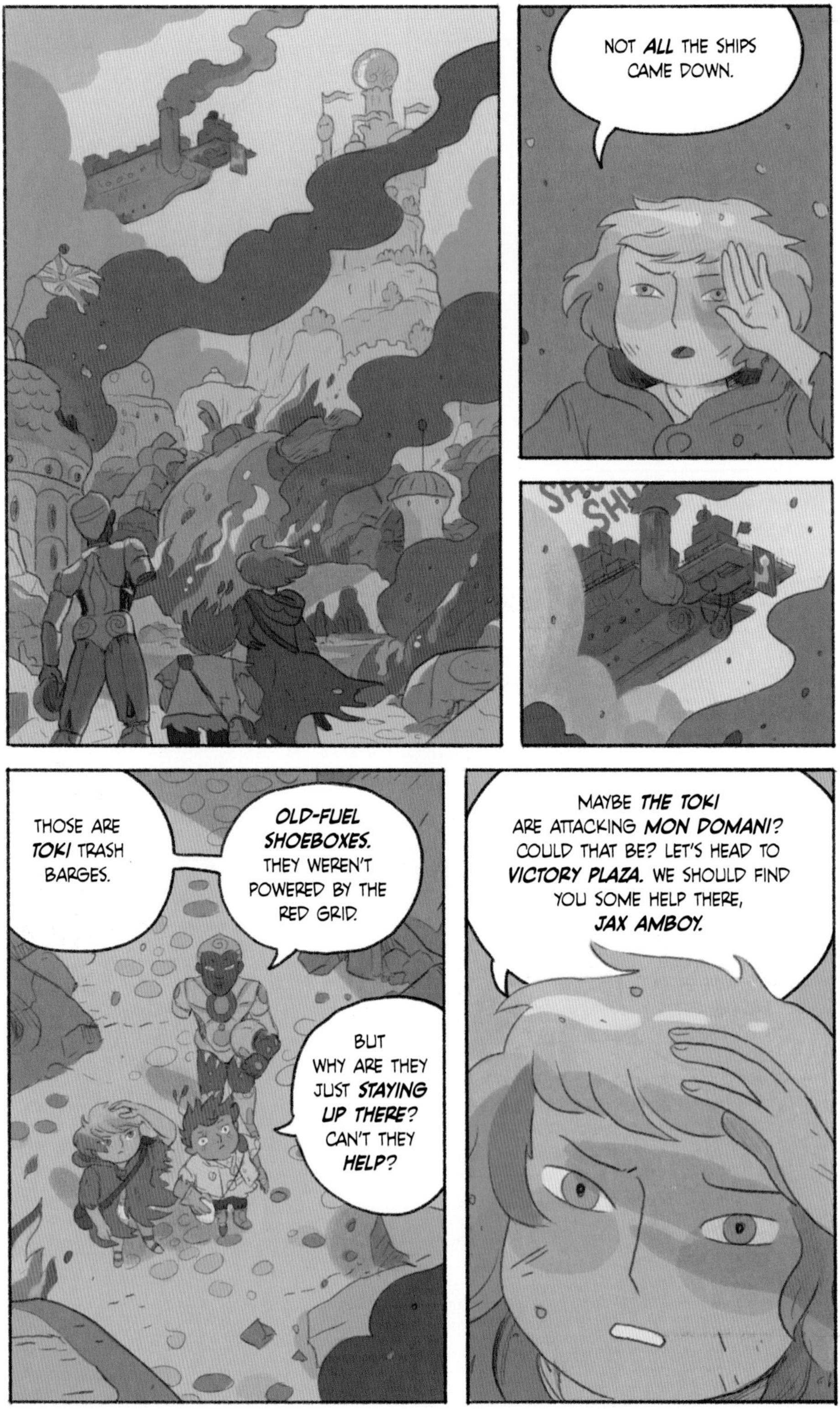
NOT ALL THE SHIPS CAME DOWN.
THOSE ARE TOKI TRASH BARGES.
OLD-FUEL SHOEBOXES. THEY WEREN'T POWERED BY THE RED GRID.
BUT WHY ARE THEY JUST STAYING UP THERE? CAN'T THEY HELP?
MAYBE THE TOKI ARE ATTACKING MON DOMANI? COULD THAT BE? LET'S HEAD TO VICTORY PLAZA. WE SHOULD FIND YOU SOME HELP THERE, JAX AMBOY.

Chapter 4
THE FALL OF THE SAND CASTLE

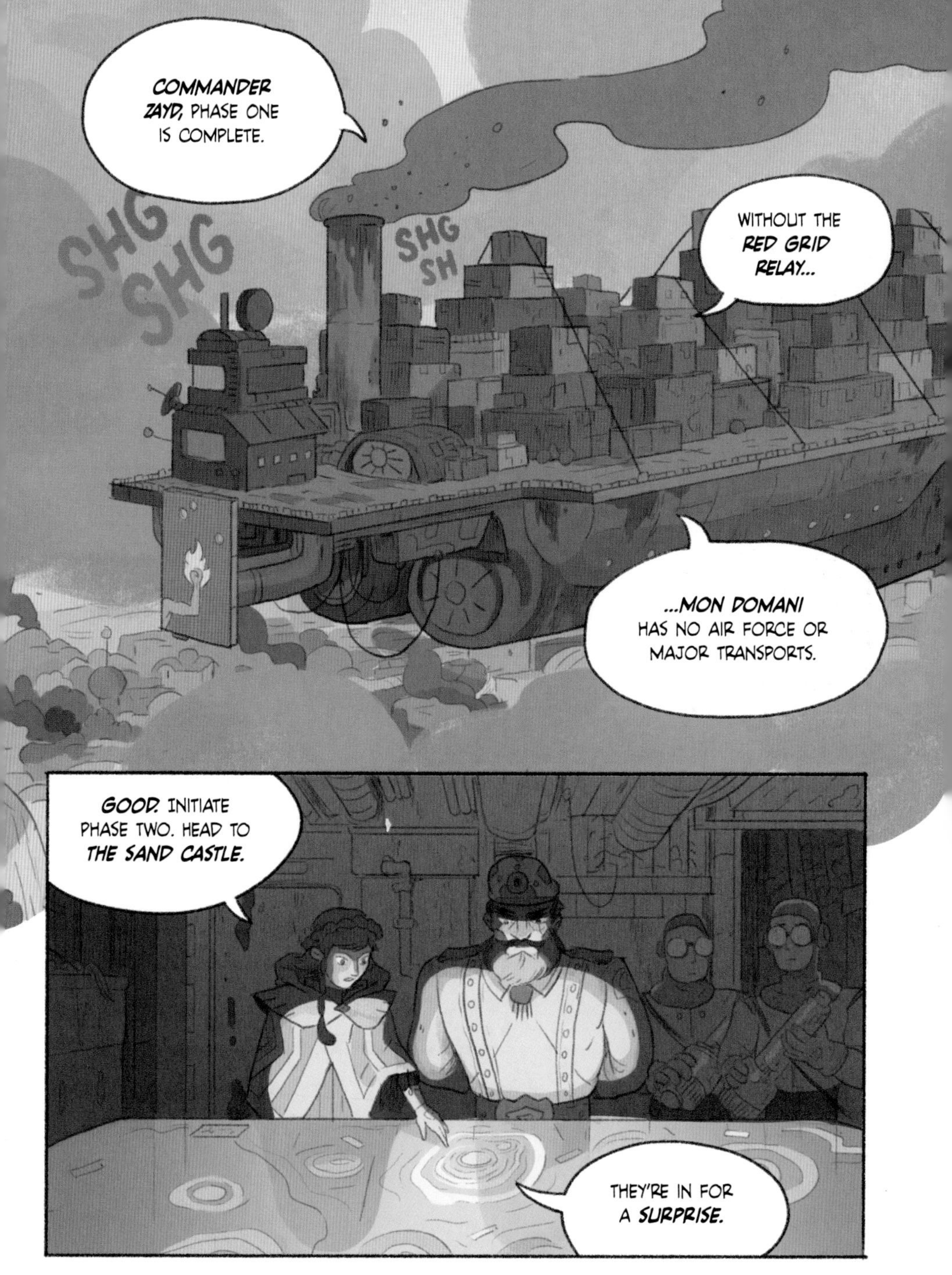
COMMANDER ZAYD, PHASE ONE IS COMPLETE.
SHG SHG
SHG SH
WITHOUT THE RED GRID RELAY...
...MON DOMANI HAS NO AIR FORCE OR MAJOR TRANSPORTS.
GOOD. INITIATE PHASE TWO. HEAD TO THE SAND CASTLE.
THEY'RE IN FOR A SURPRISE.

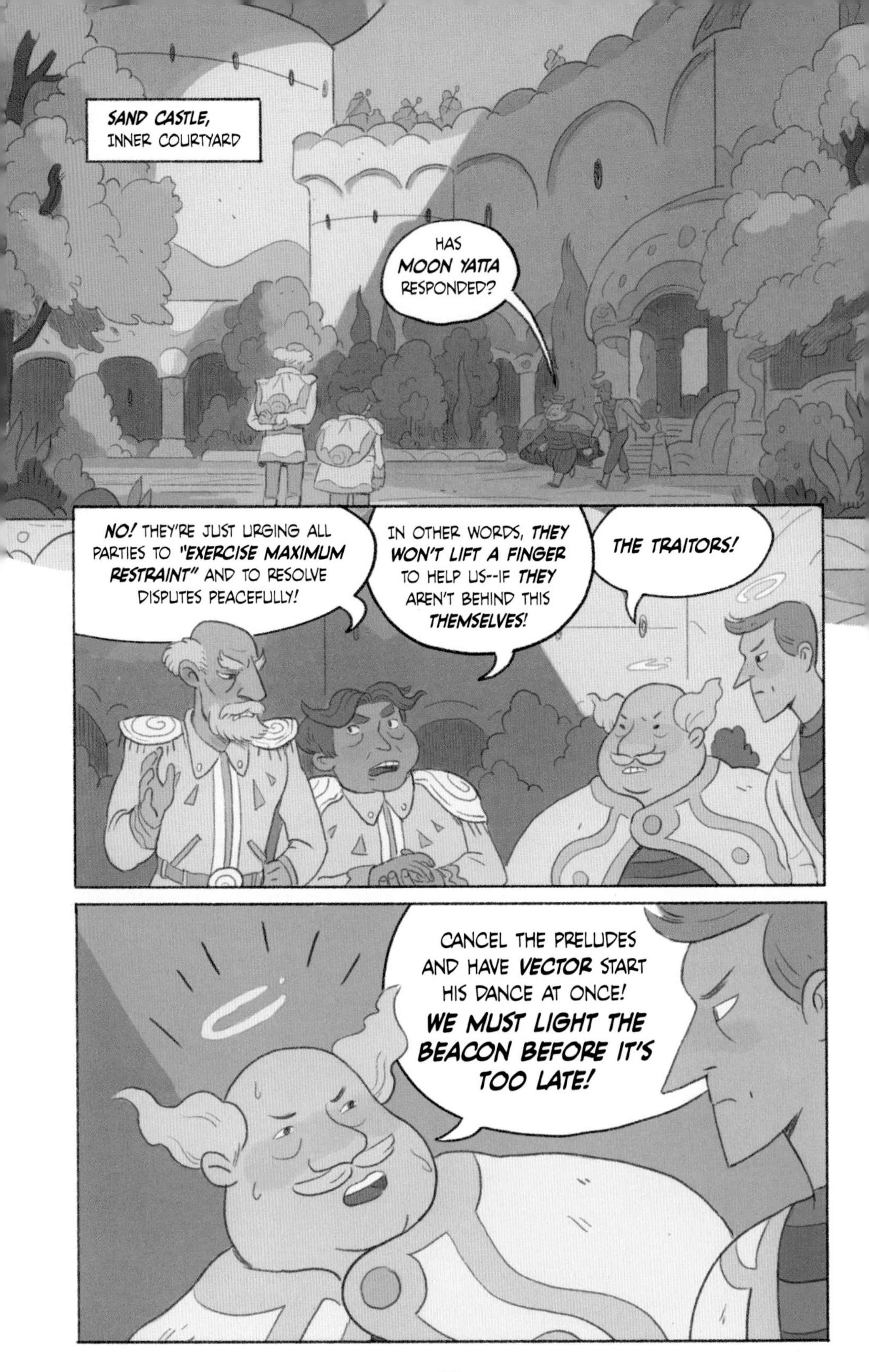
SAND CASTLE,
INNER COURTYARD
HAS MOON YATTA RESPONDED?
NO! THEY'RE JUST URGING ALL PARTIES TO "EXERCISE MAXIMUM RESTRAINT" AND TO RESOLVE DISPUTES PEACEFULLY!
IN OTHER WORDS, THEY WON'T LIFT A FINGER TO HELP US--IF THEY AREN'T BEHIND THIS THEMSELVES!
THE TRAITORS!
CANCEL THE PRELUDES AND HAVE VECTOR START HIS DANCE AT ONCE! WE MUST LIGHT THE BEACON BEFORE IT'S TOO LATE!

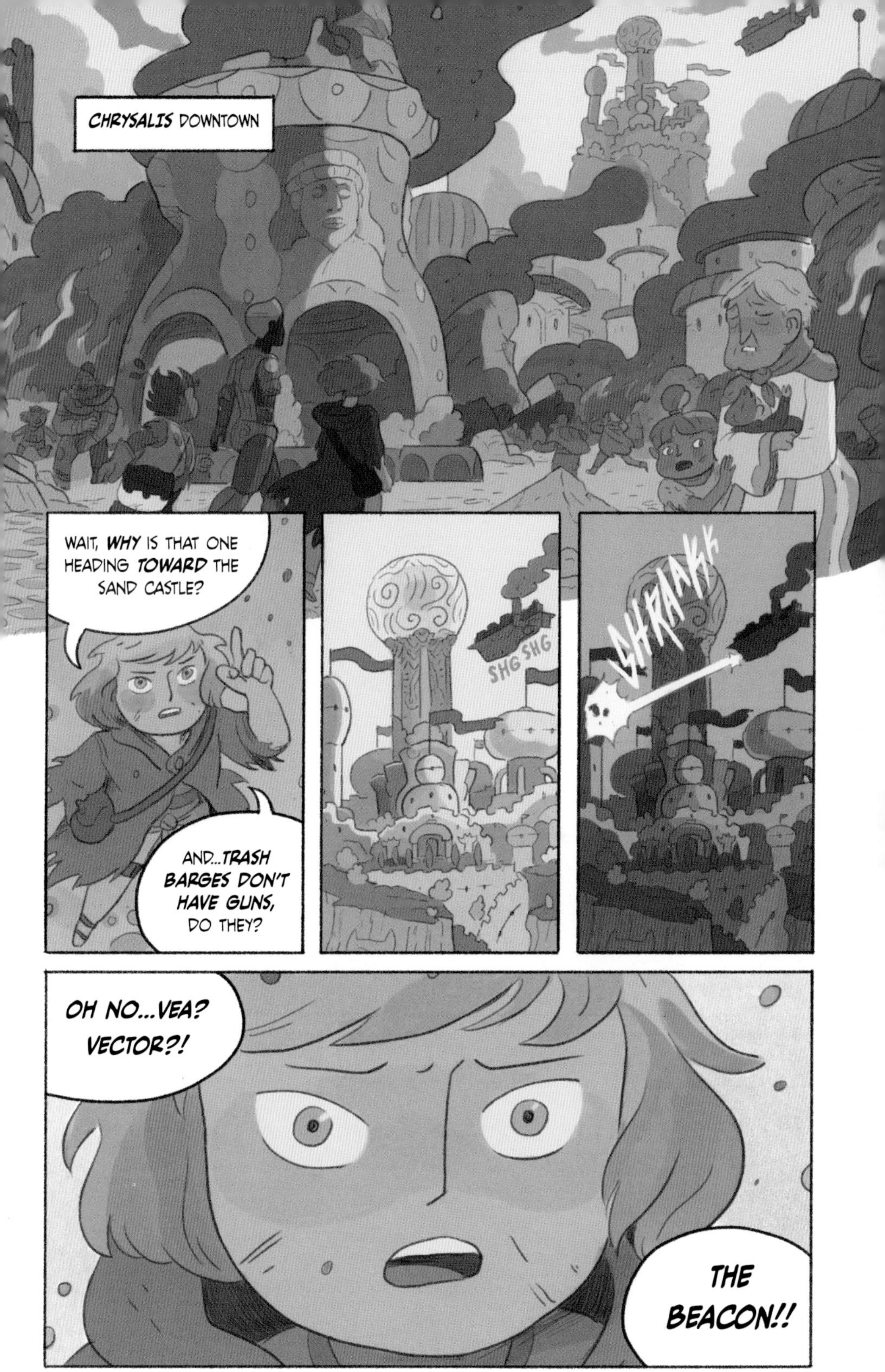
CHRYSALIS DOWNTOWN
WAIT, WHY IS THAT ONE HEADING TOWARD THE SAND CASTLE?
AND...TRASH BARGES DON'T HAVE GUNS, DO THEY?
SHG SHG
SHRAAK!
OH NO...VEA? VECTOR?!
THE BEACON!!

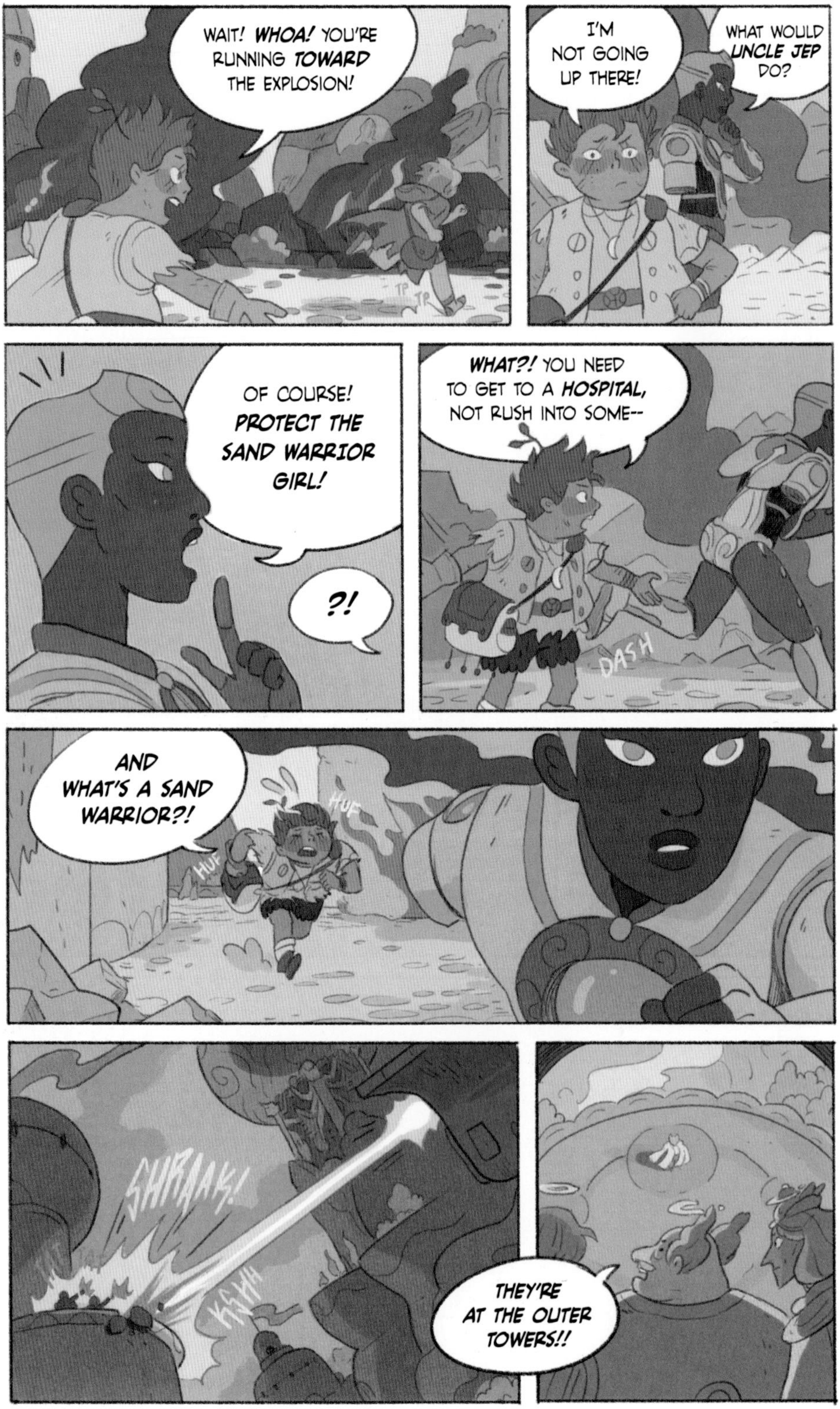

WAIT! WHOA! YOU'RE RUNNING TOWARD THE EXPLOSION!
I'M NOT GOING UP THERE!
WHAT WOULD UNCLE JEP DO?
OF COURSE! PROTECT THE SAND WARRIOR GIRL!
?!
WHAT?! YOU NEED TO GET TO A HOSPITAL, NOT RUSH INTO SOME--
DASH
AND WHAT'S A SAND WARRIOR?!
HUF
HUF
SHRAAK!
THEY'RE AT THE OUTER TOWERS!!

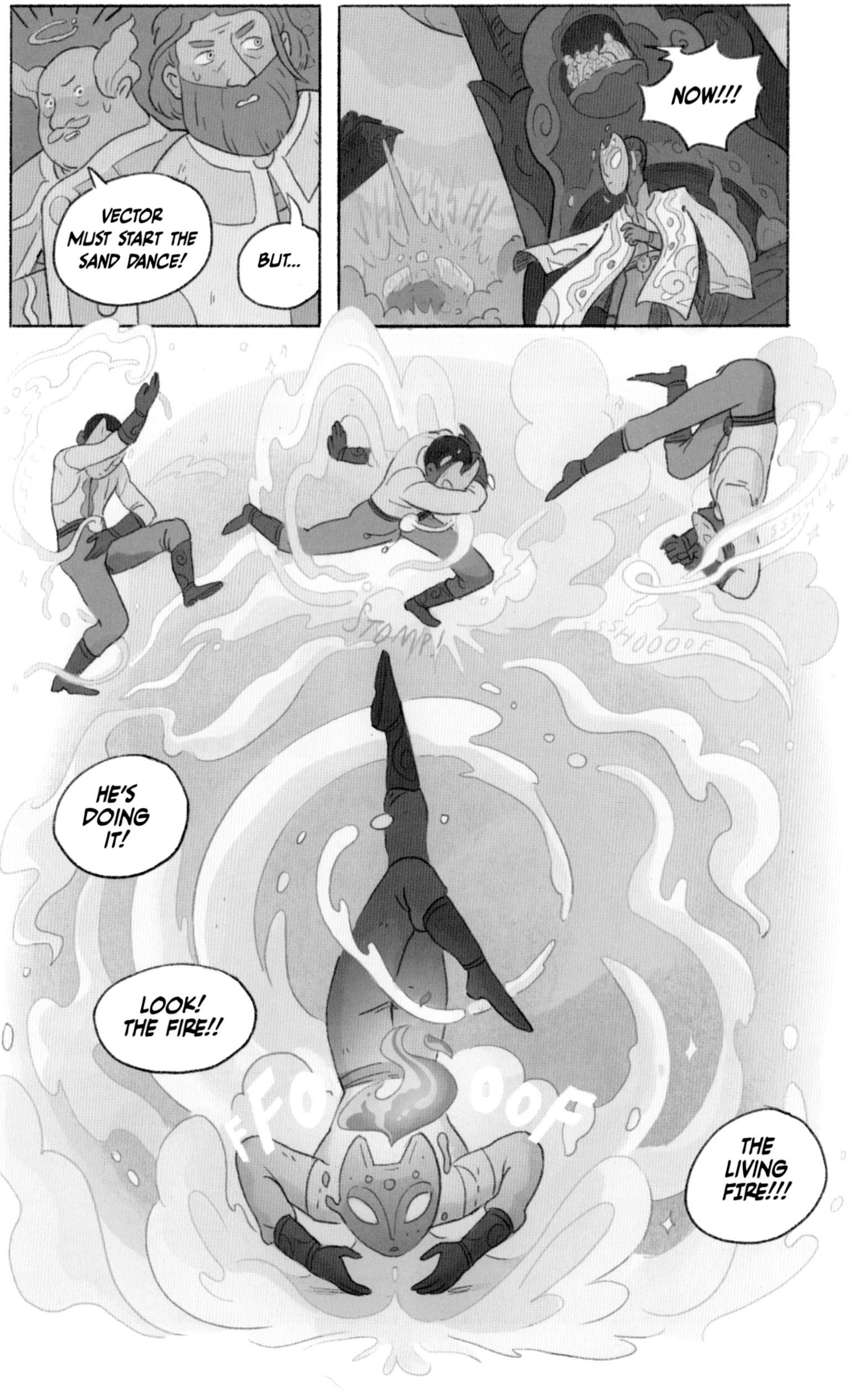
VECTOR MUST START THE SAND DANCE!
BUT...
NOW!!!
STOMP!
SSHOOOOF
HE'S DOING IT!
LOOK! THE FIRE!!
THE LIVING FIRE!!!

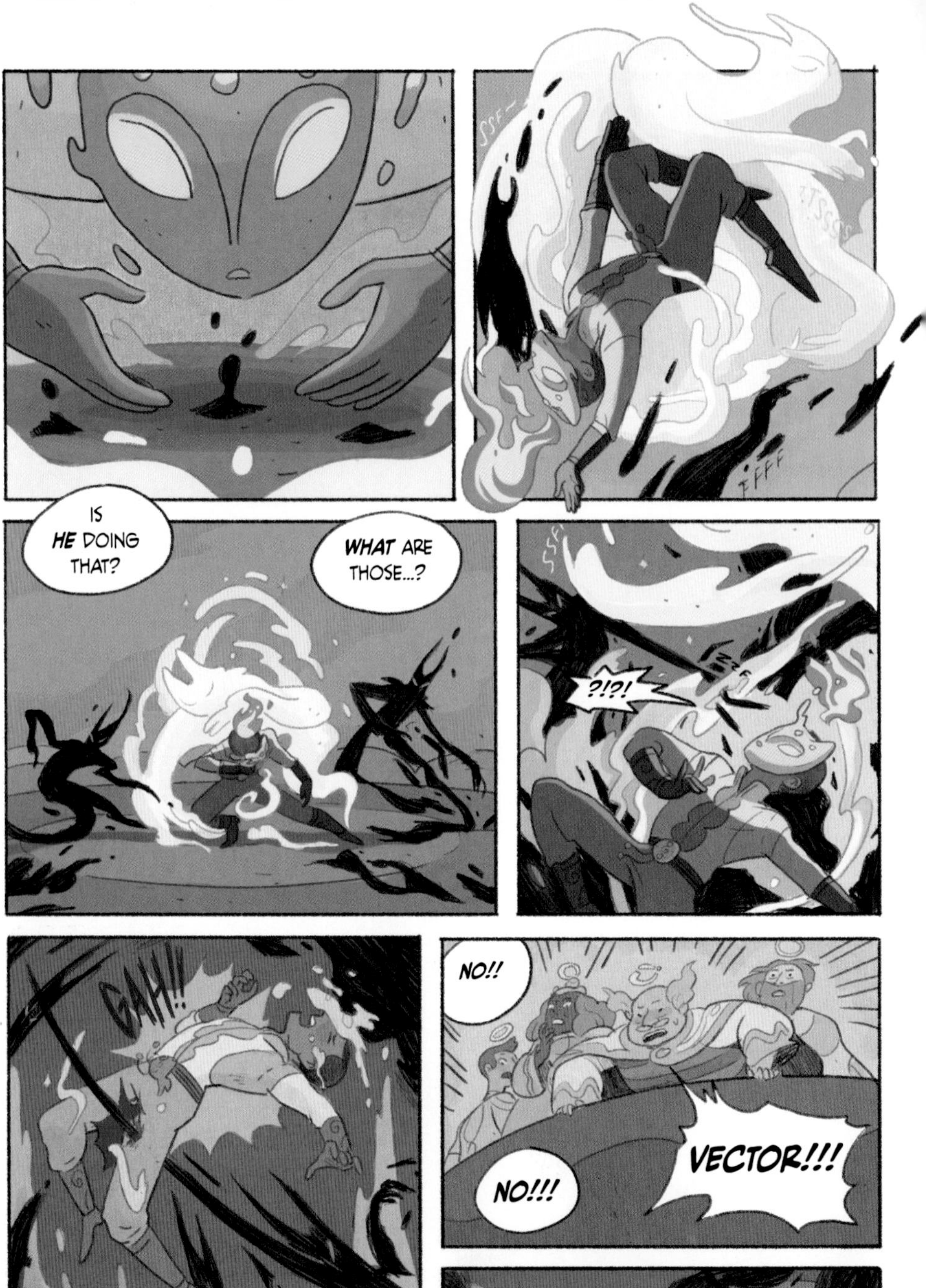
SSF~
TSSSS
FFFF
IS HE DOING THAT?
WHAT ARE THOSE...?
SSF
?!?!
GAH!!
NO!!
VECTOR!!!
NO!!!

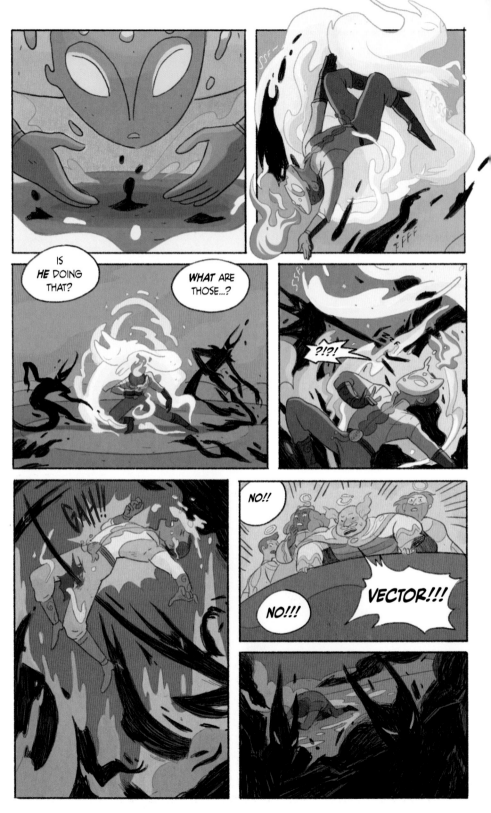

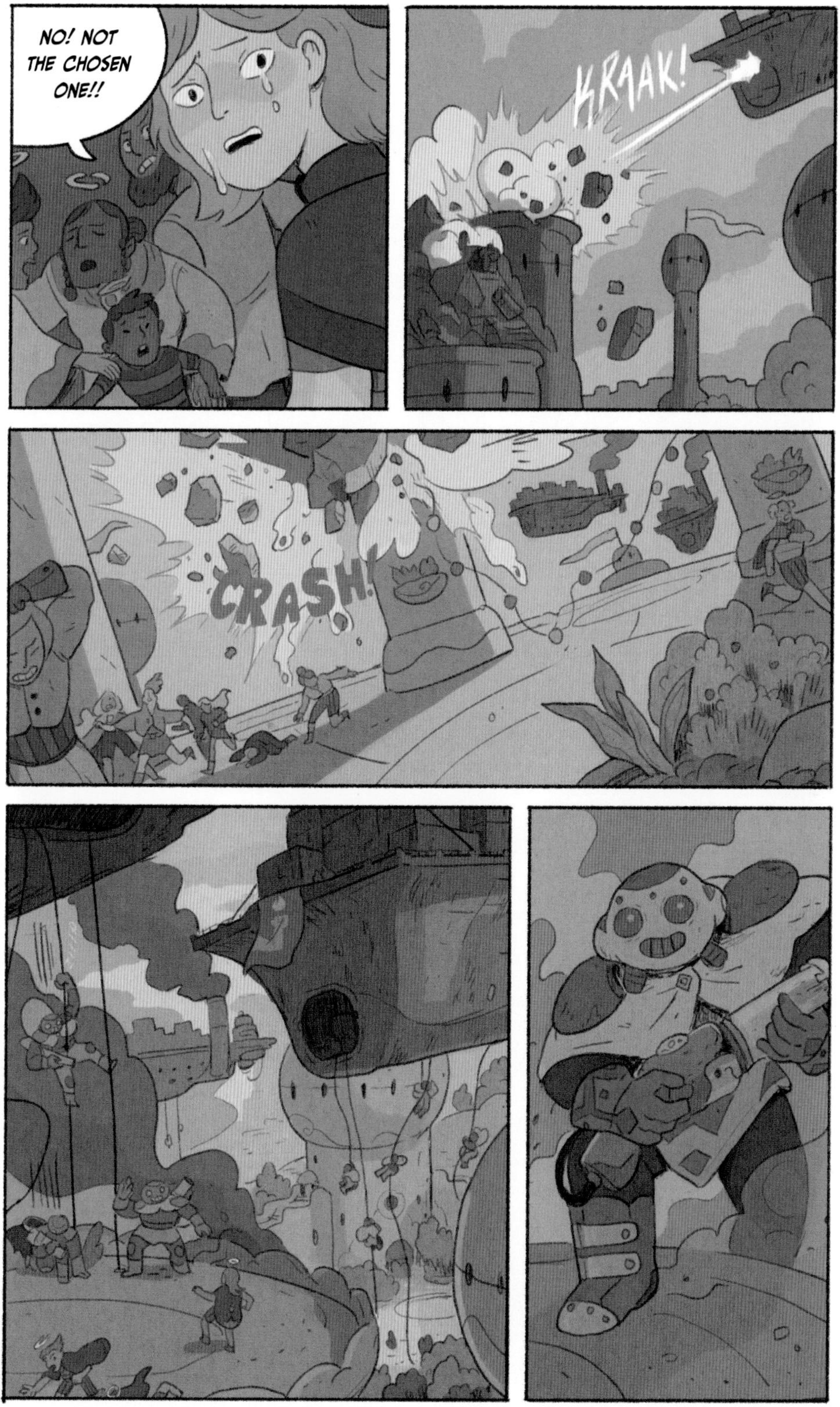
NO! NOT THE CHOSEN ONE!!
KRAAK!
CRASH!

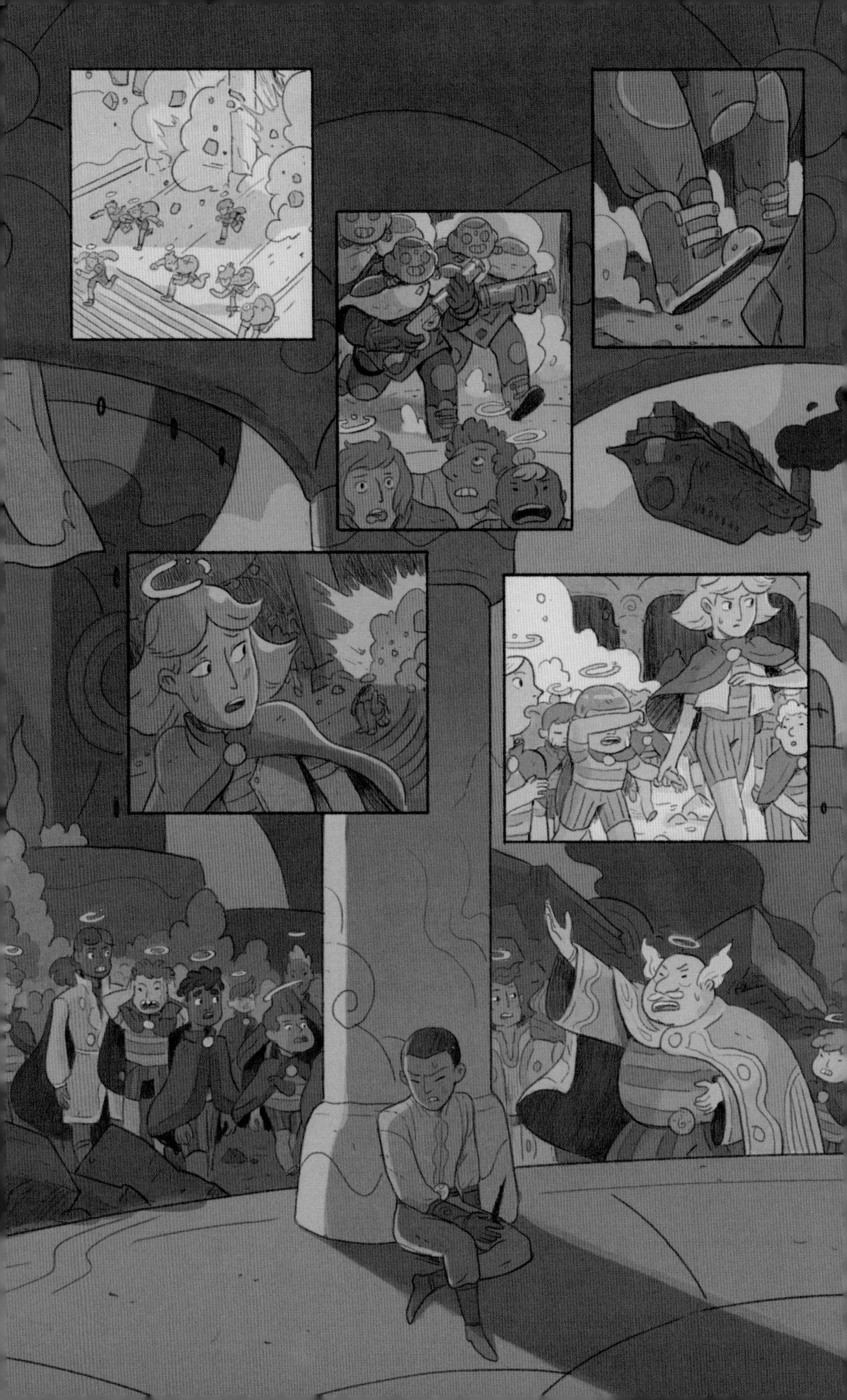

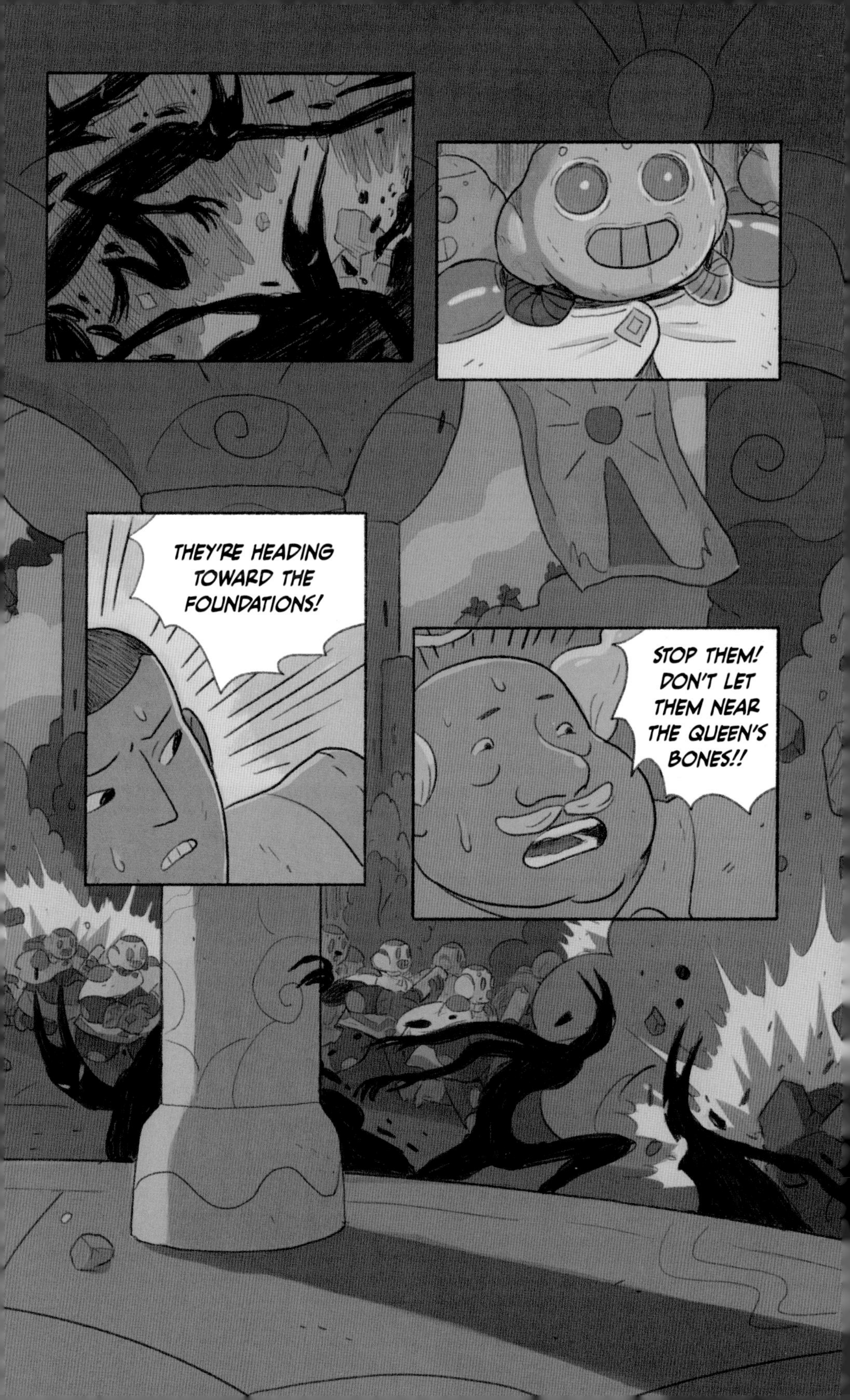
THEY'RE HEADING TOWARD THE FOUNDATIONS!
STOP THEM! DON'T LET THEM NEAR THE QUEEN'S BONES!!

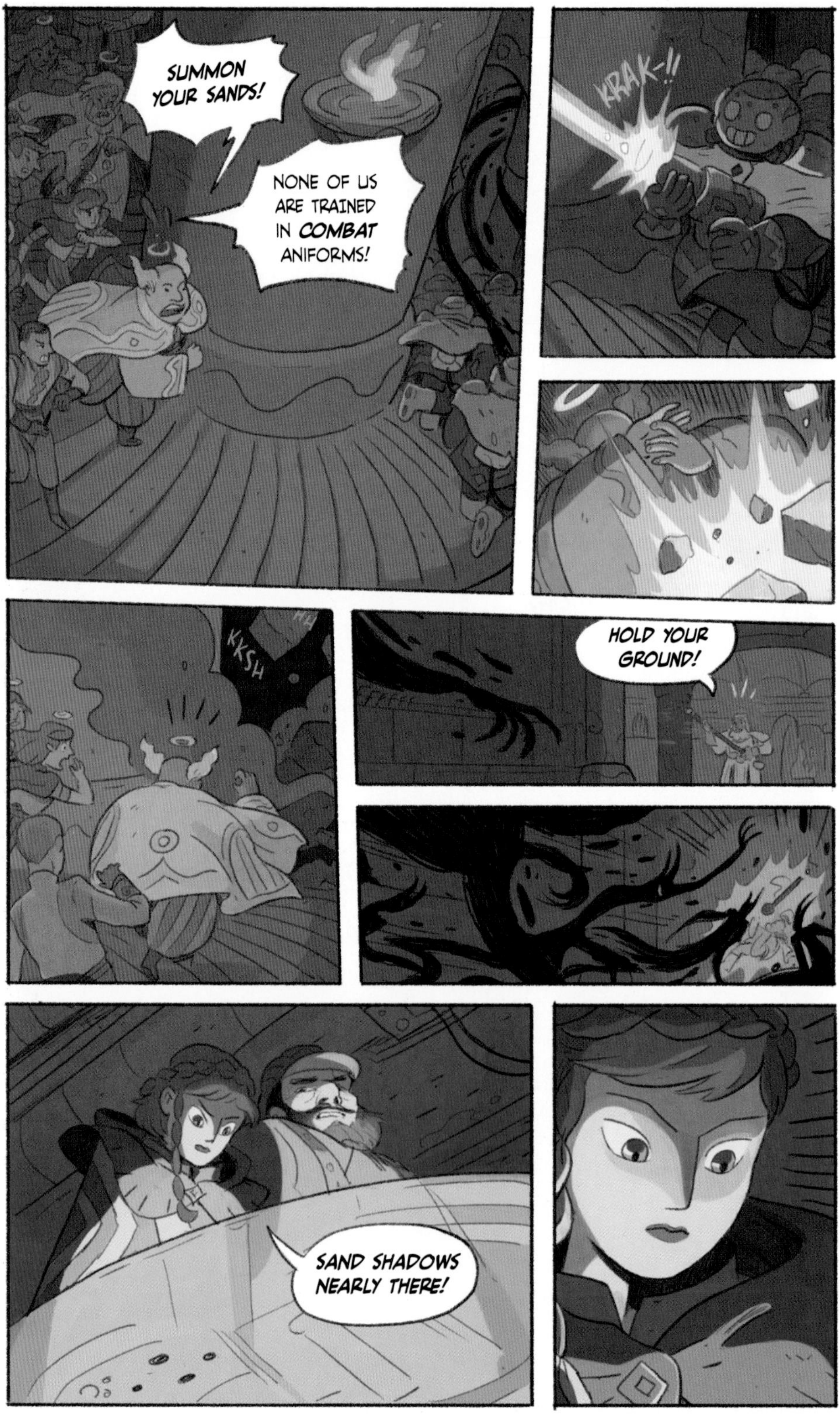

SUMMON YOUR SANDS!
NONE OF US ARE TRAINED IN COMBAT ANIFORMS!
KRAK-!!
KKSH
HOLD YOUR GROUND!
SAND SHADOWS NEARLY THERE!

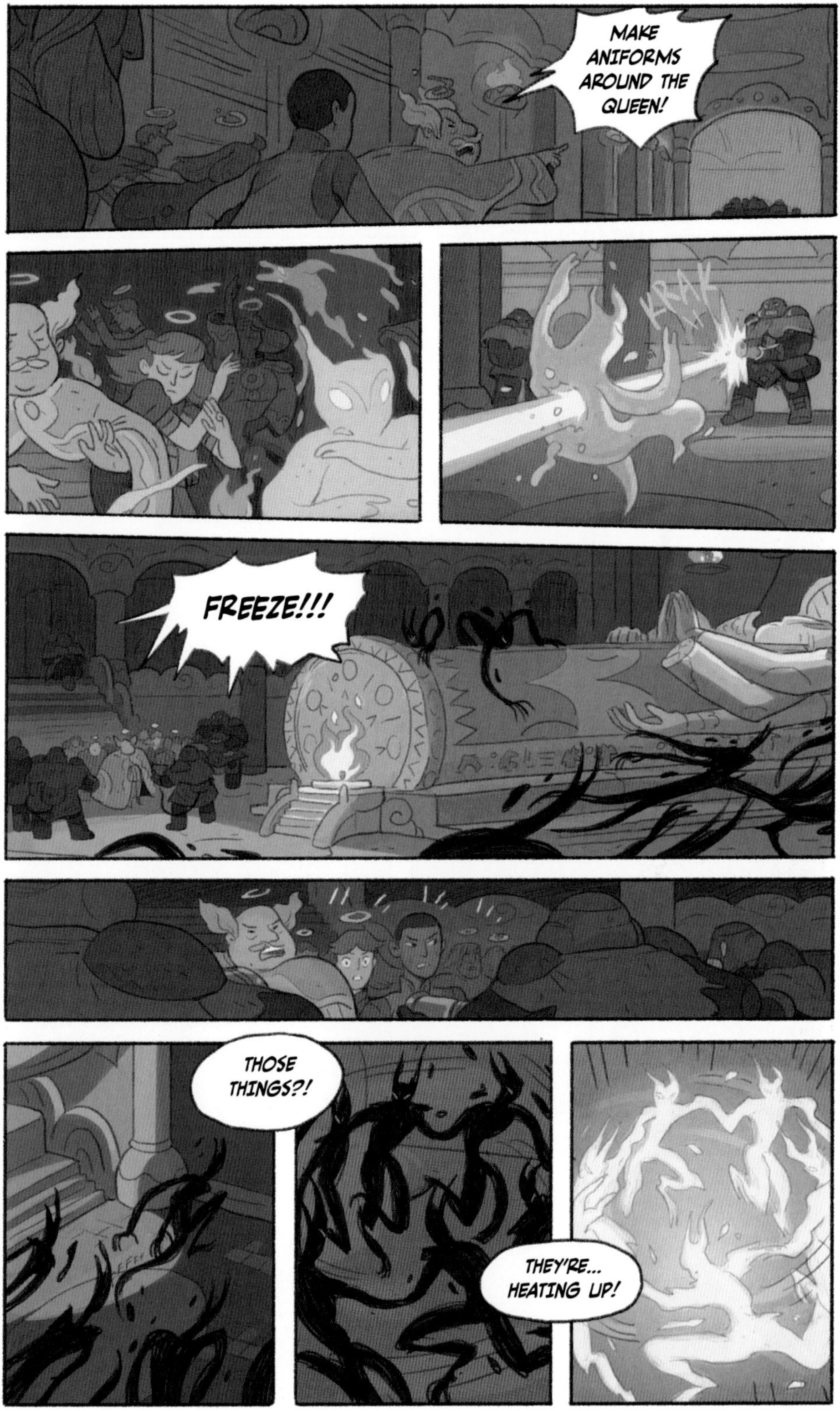
MAKE ANIFORMS AROUND THE QUEEN!
KRAK
FREEZE!!!
THOSE THINGS?!
THEY'RE... HEATING UP!

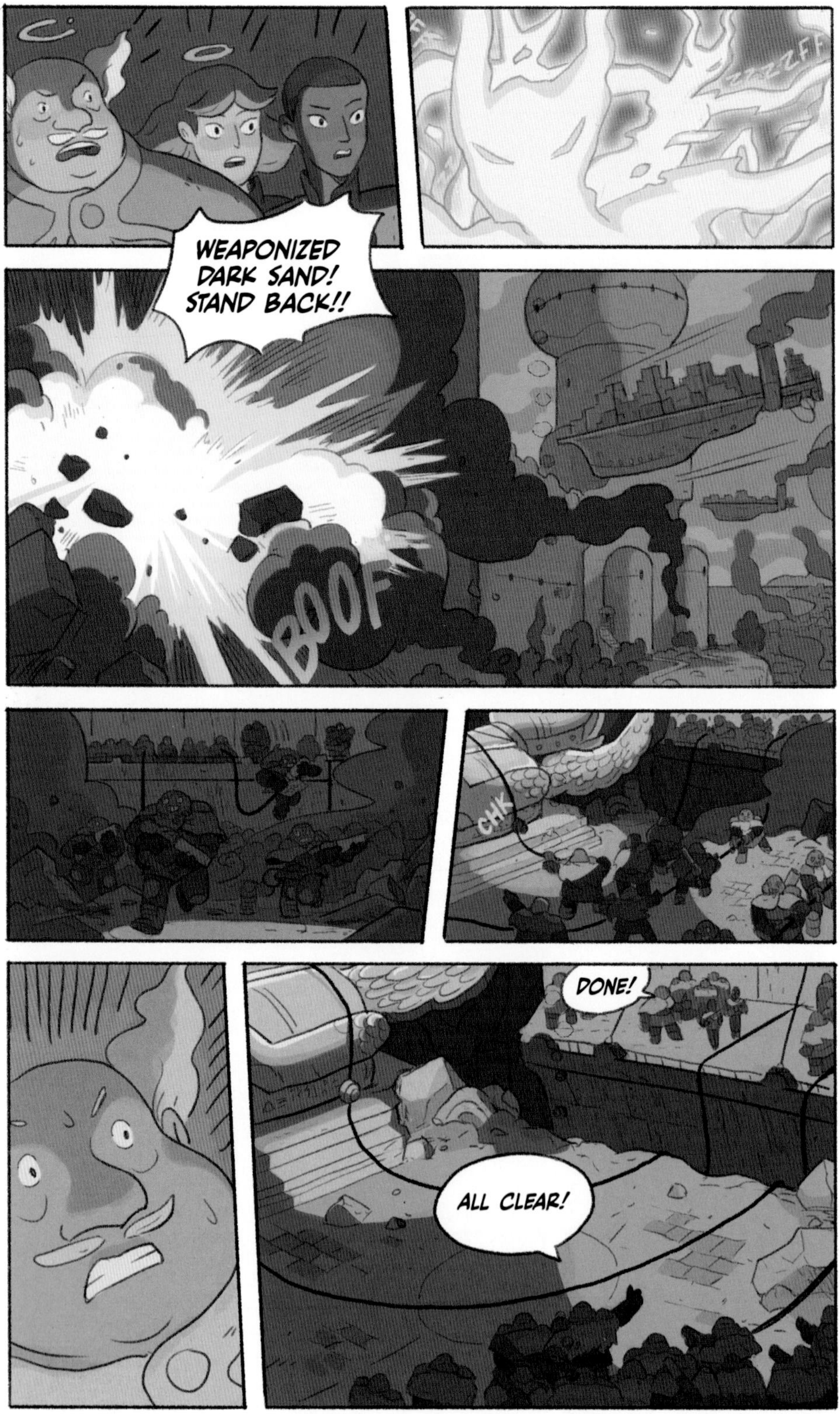
ZZZZFF
WEAPONIZED DARK SAND! STAND BACK!!
BOOF
CHK
DONE!
ALL CLEAR!

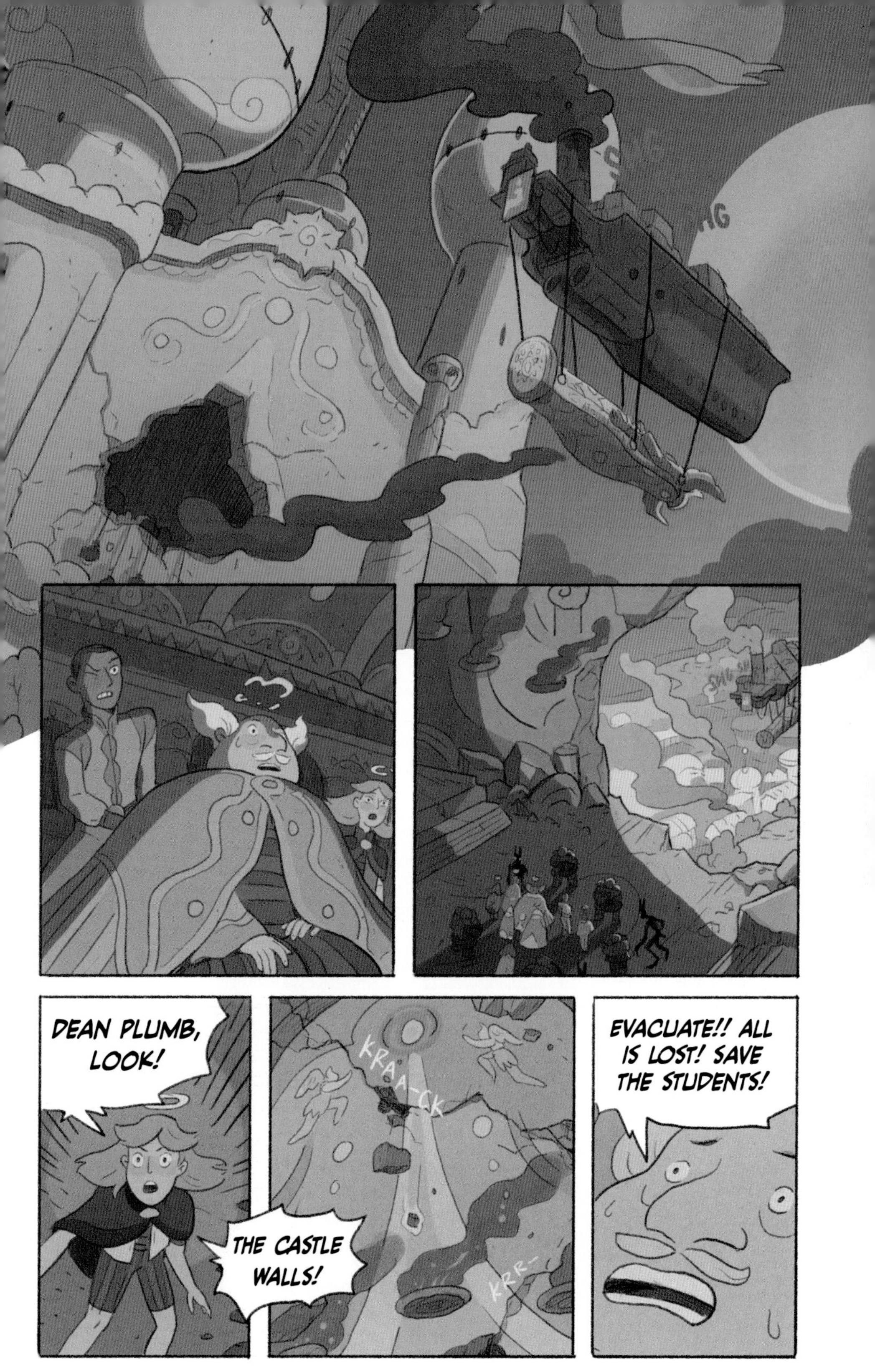
DEAN PLUMB, LOOK!
THE CASTLE WALLS!
KRAA-CK
KRR-
EVACUATE!! ALL IS LOST! SAVE THE STUDENTS!

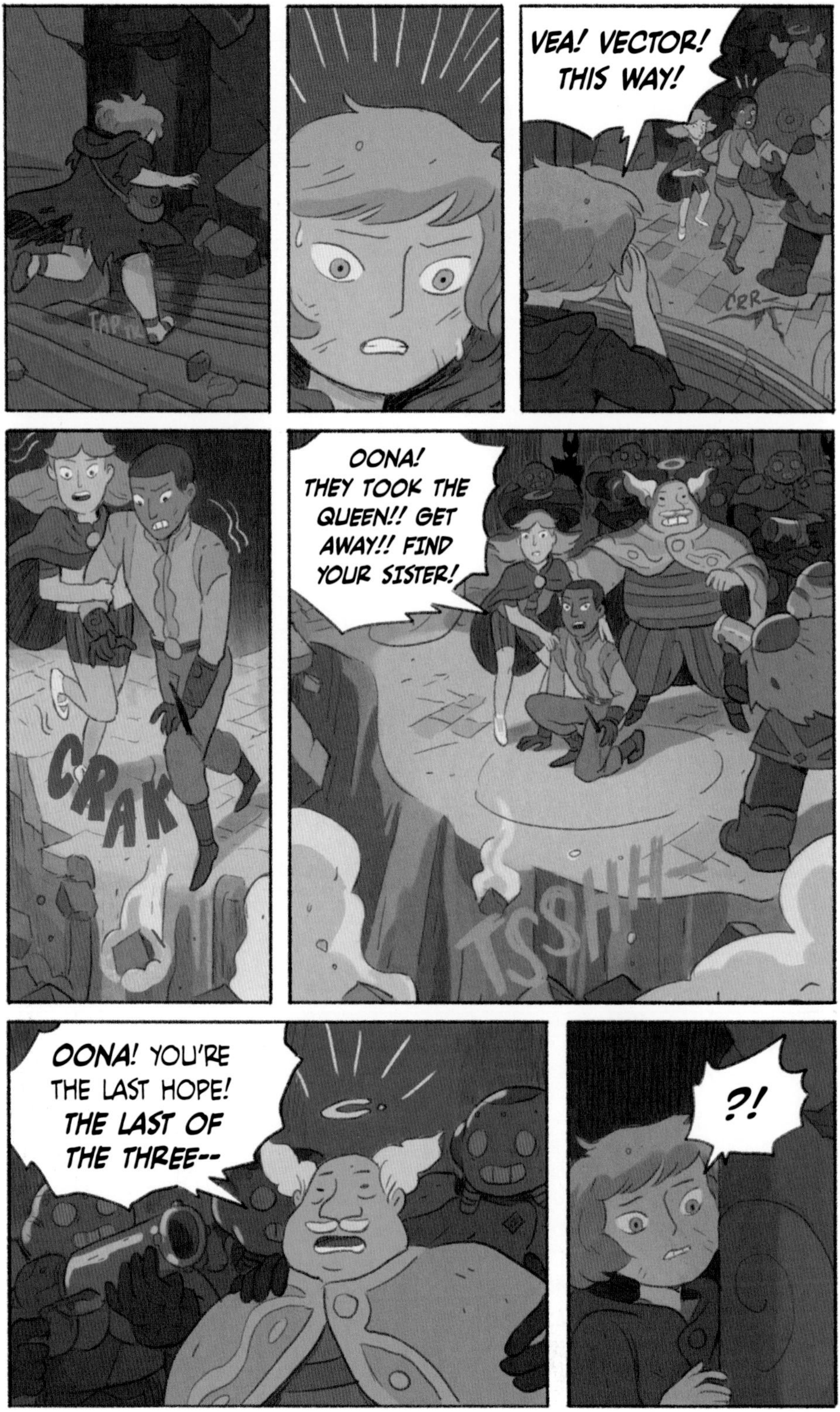
VEA! VECTOR! THIS WAY!
CRR—
CRAK
OONA! THEY TOOK THE QUEEN!! GET AWAY!! FIND YOUR SISTER!
TSSHH
OONA! YOU'RE THE LAST HOPE! THE LAST OF THE THREE--
?!

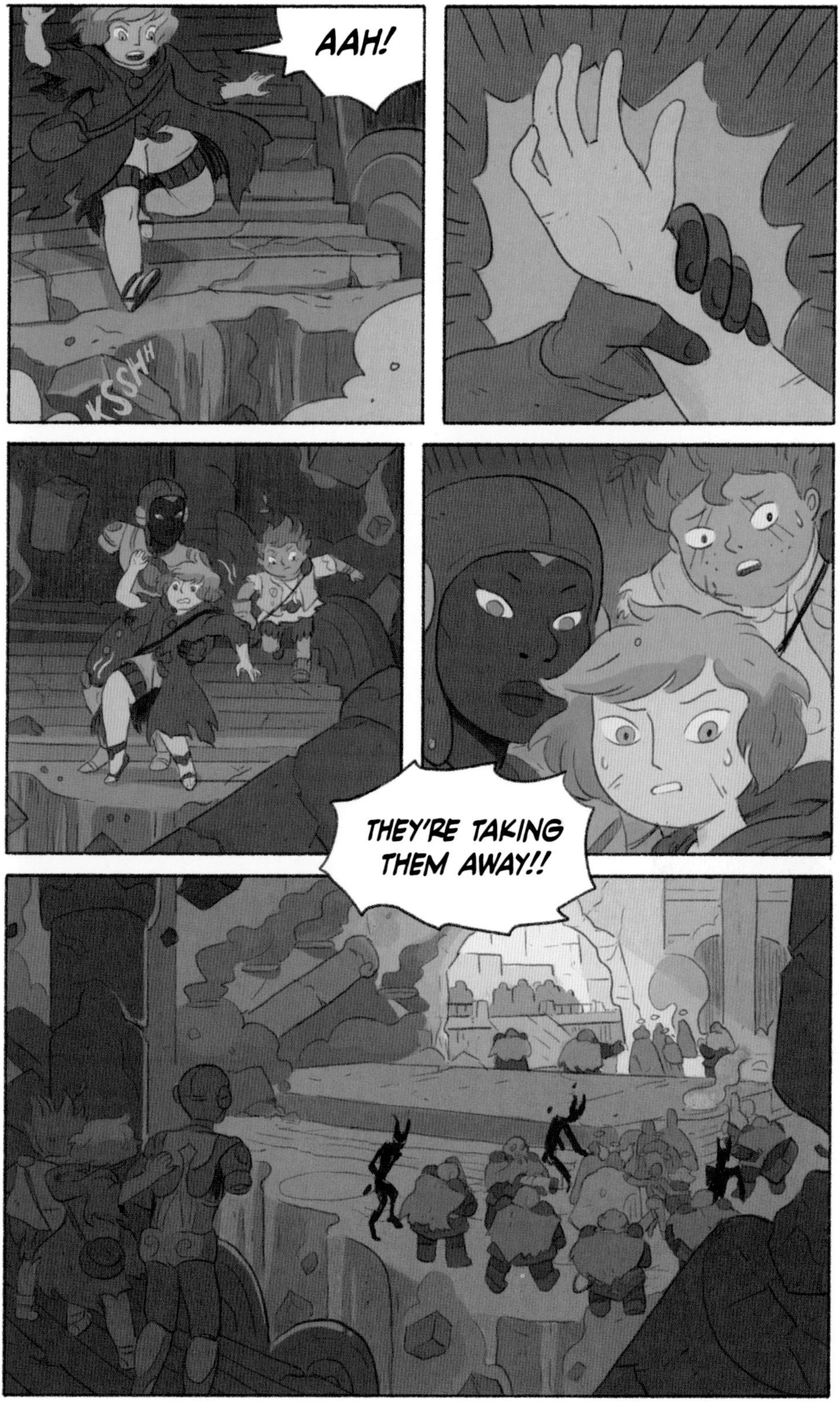
AAH!
KSSHH
THEY'RE TAKING THEM AWAY!!

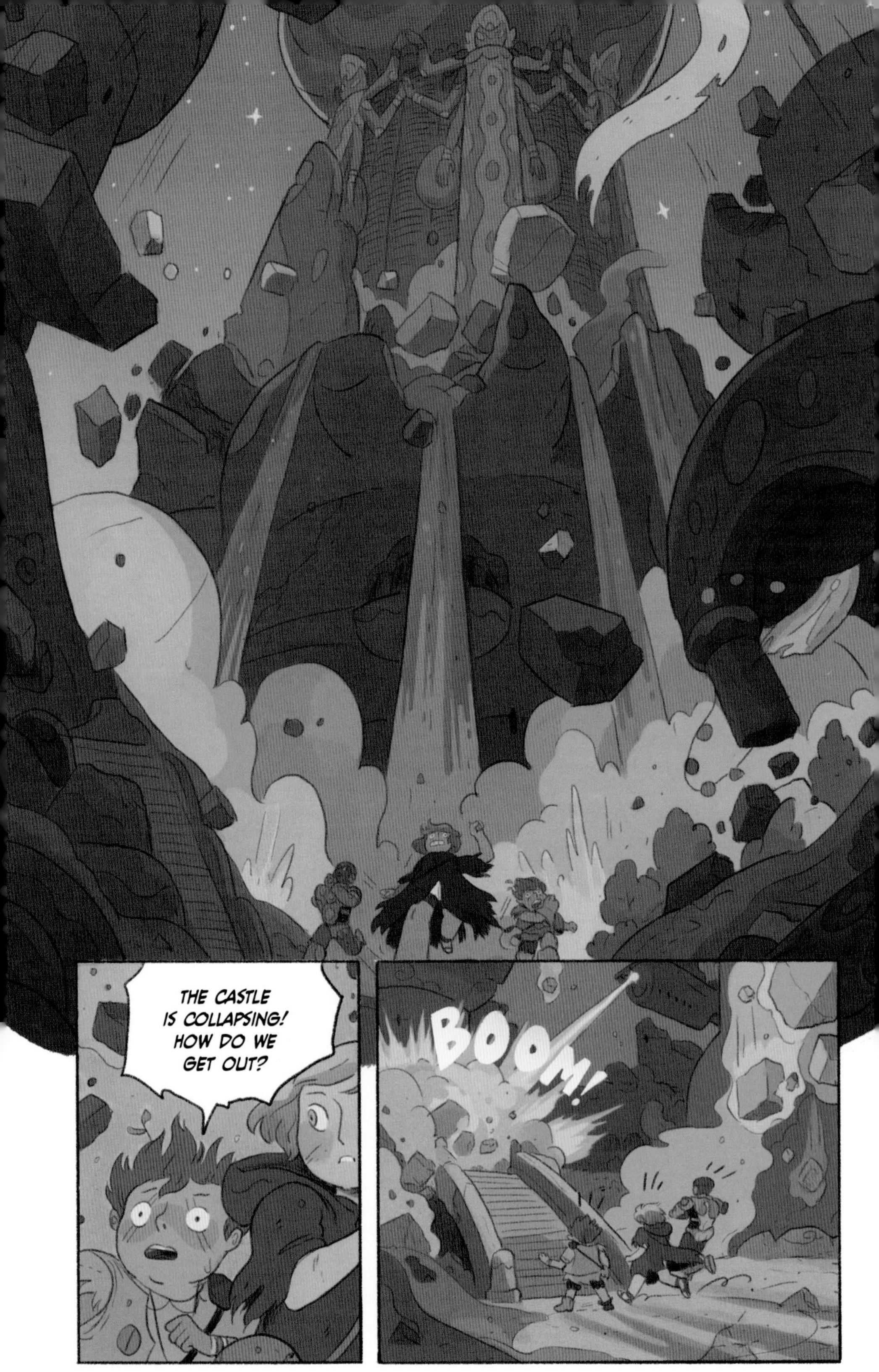
THE CASTLE IS COLLAPSING! HOW DO WE GET OUT?
BOOOM!

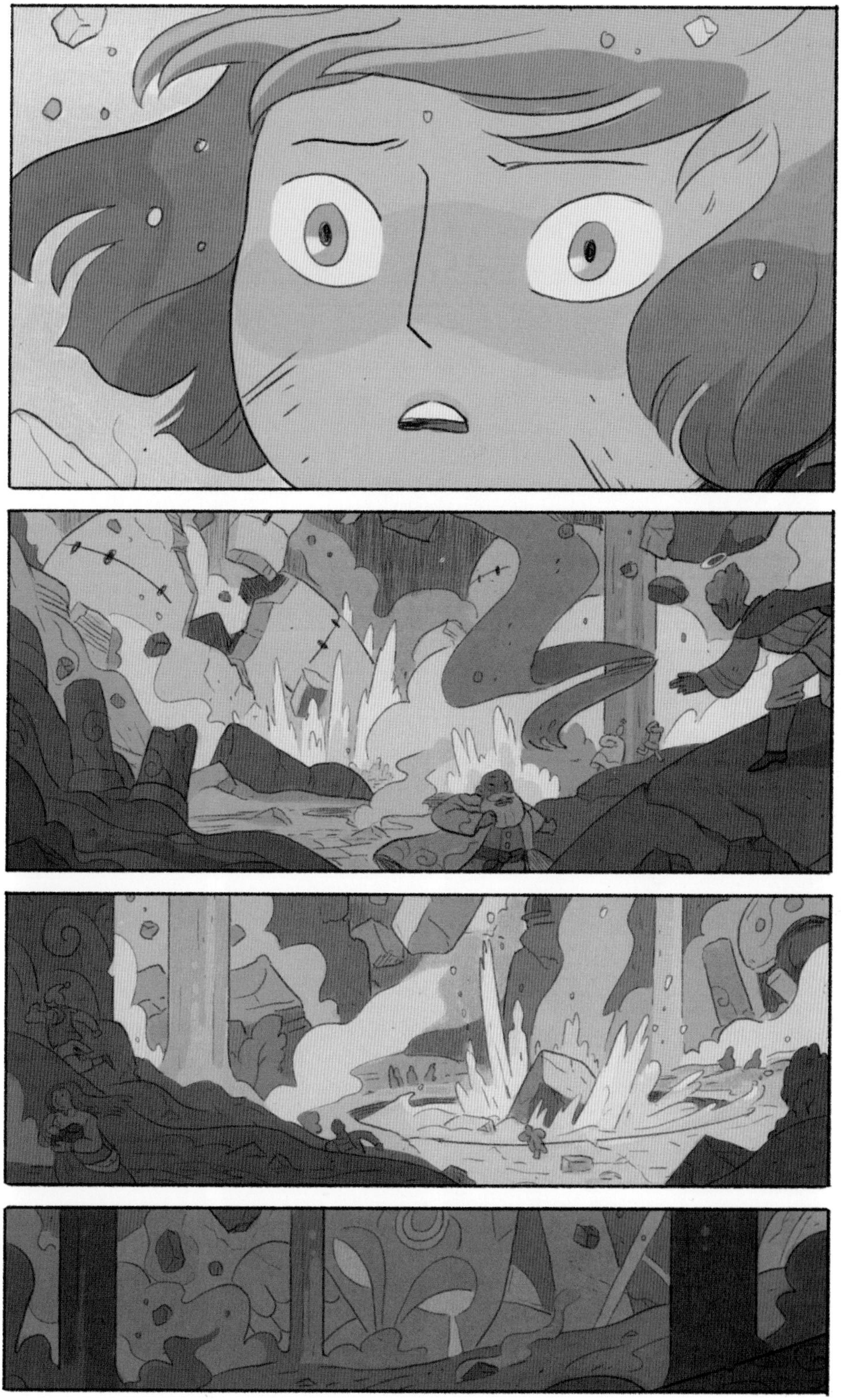

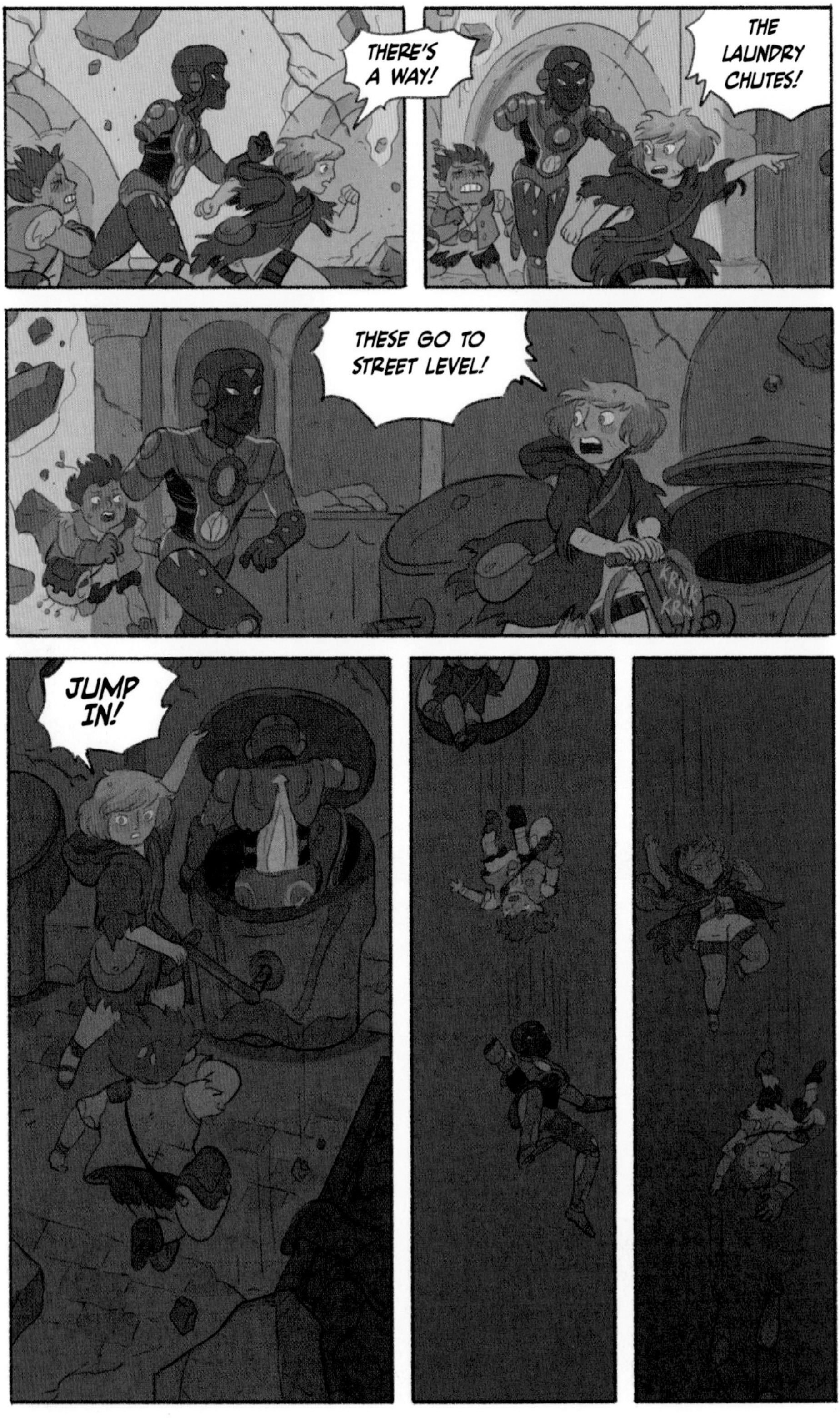
THERE'S A WAY!
THE LAUNDRY CHUTES!
THESE GO TO STREET LEVEL!
KRNK KRN
JUMP IN!

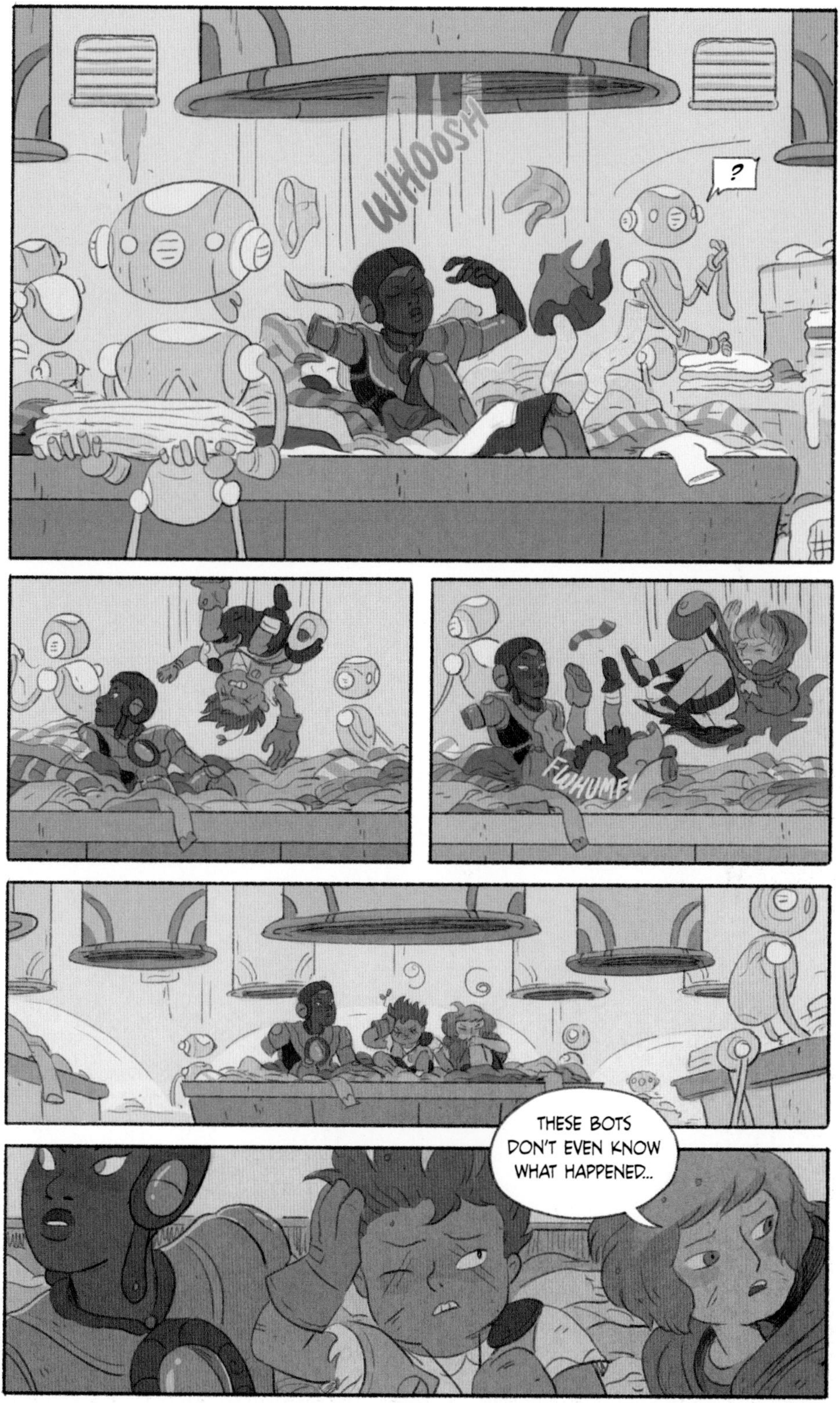
WHOOSH
?
FWHUMF!
THESE BOTS DON'T EVEN KNOW WHAT HAPPENED...

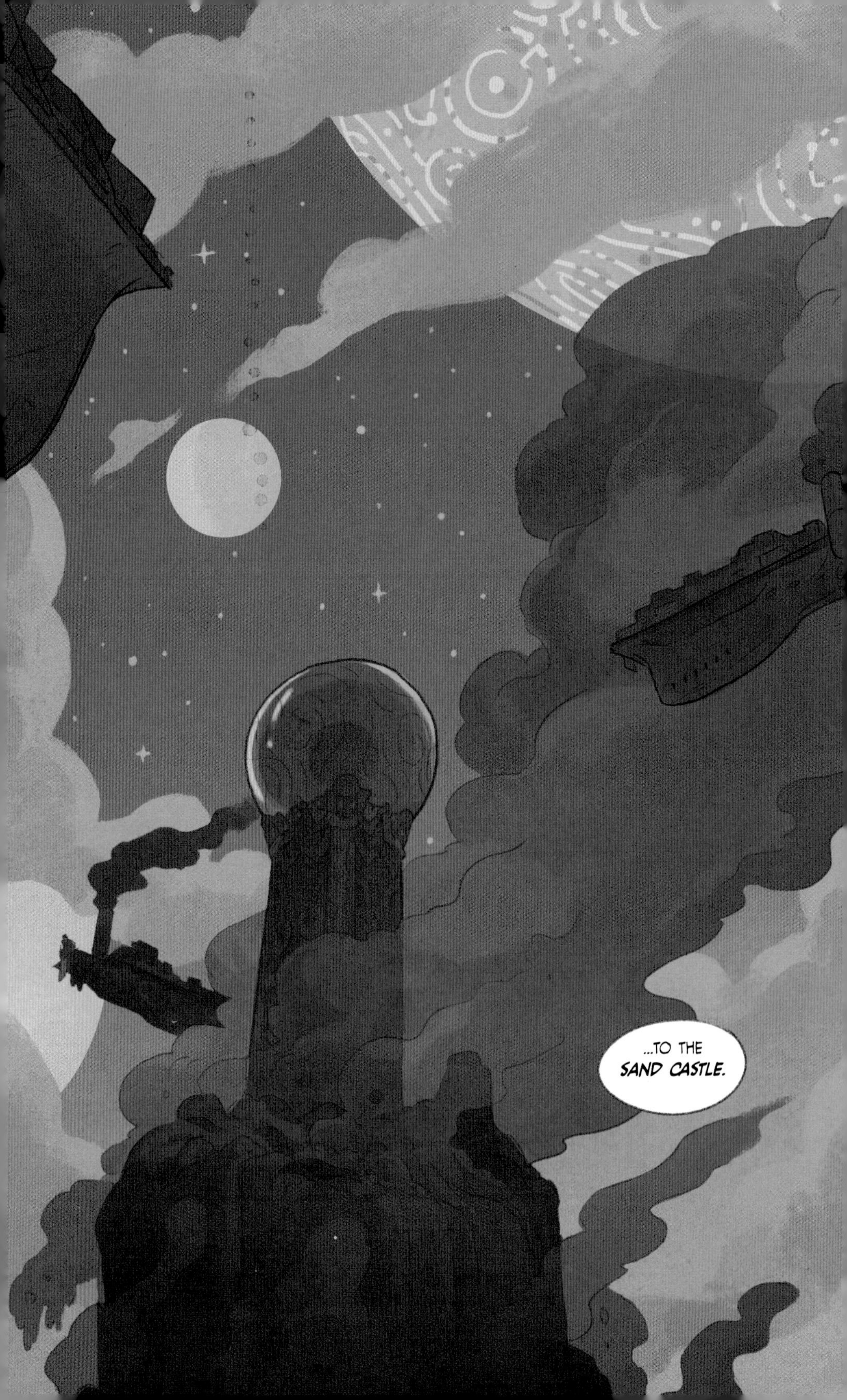
...TO THE
SAND CASTLE.

Chapter 5

PASSAGE TO MAYAPOLIS

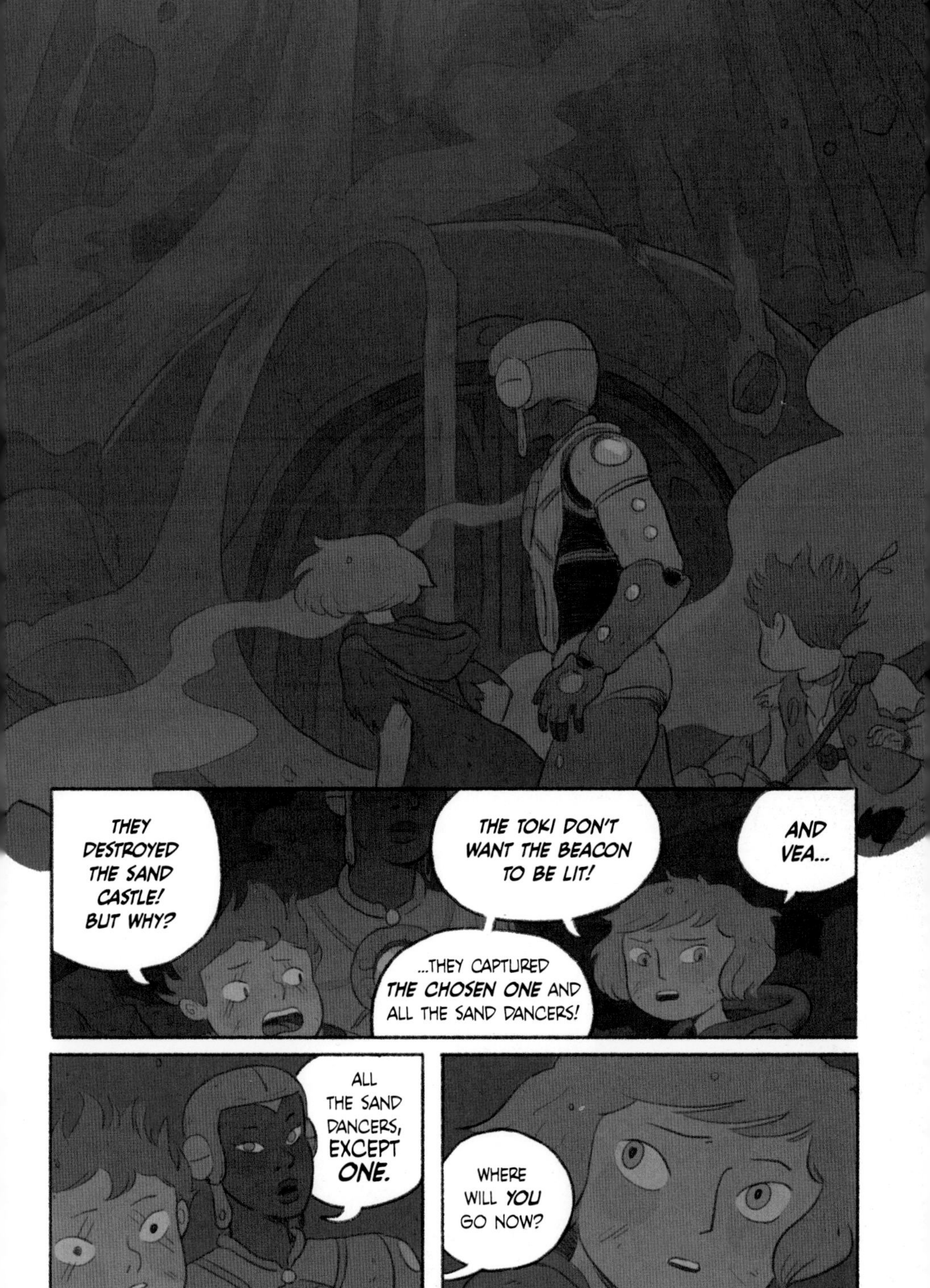
THEY DESTROYED THE SAND CASTLE! BUT WHY?
THE TOKI DON'T WANT THE BEACON TO BE LIT!
AND VEA...
...THEY CAPTURED *THE CHOSEN ONE* AND ALL THE SAND DANCERS!
ALL THE SAND DANCERS, **EXCEPT *ONE.***
WHERE WILL *YOU* GO NOW?

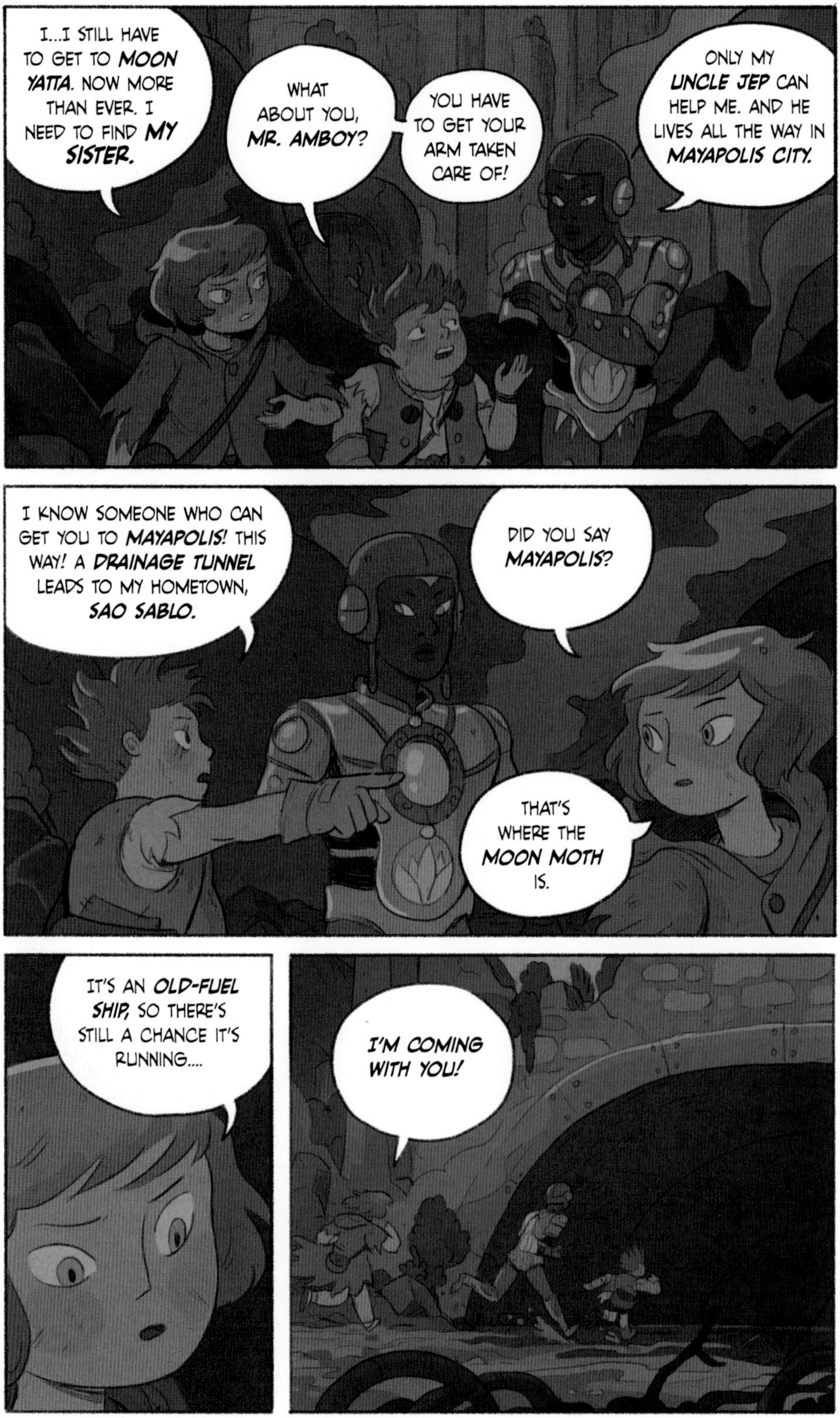
I...I STILL HAVE TO GET TO MOON YATTA. NOW MORE THAN EVER. I NEED TO FIND MY SISTER.
WHAT ABOUT YOU, MR. AMBOY?
YOU HAVE TO GET YOUR ARM TAKEN CARE OF!
ONLY MY UNCLE JEP CAN HELP ME. AND HE LIVES ALL THE WAY IN MAYAPOLIS CITY.
I KNOW SOMEONE WHO CAN GET YOU TO MAYAPOLIS! THIS WAY! A DRAINAGE TUNNEL LEADS TO MY HOMETOWN, SAO SABLO.
DID YOU SAY MAYAPOLIS?
THAT'S WHERE THE MOON MOTH IS.
IT'S AN OLD-FUEL SHIP, SO THERE'S STILL A CHANCE IT'S RUNNING....
I'M COMING WITH YOU!

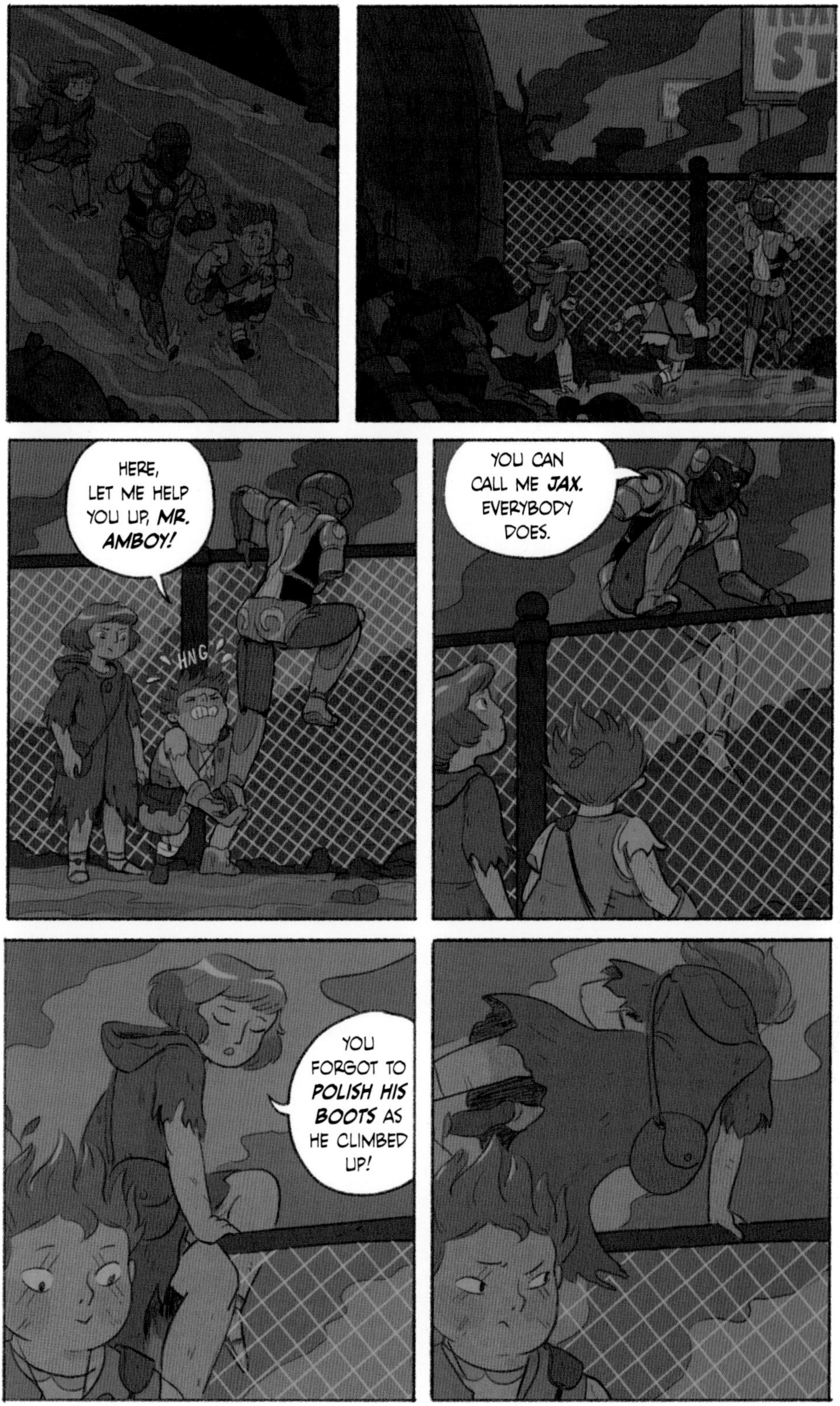
HERE, LET ME HELP YOU UP, MR. AMBOY!
HNG
YOU CAN CALL ME JAX. EVERYBODY DOES.
YOU FORGOT TO POLISH HIS BOOTS AS HE CLIMBED UP!

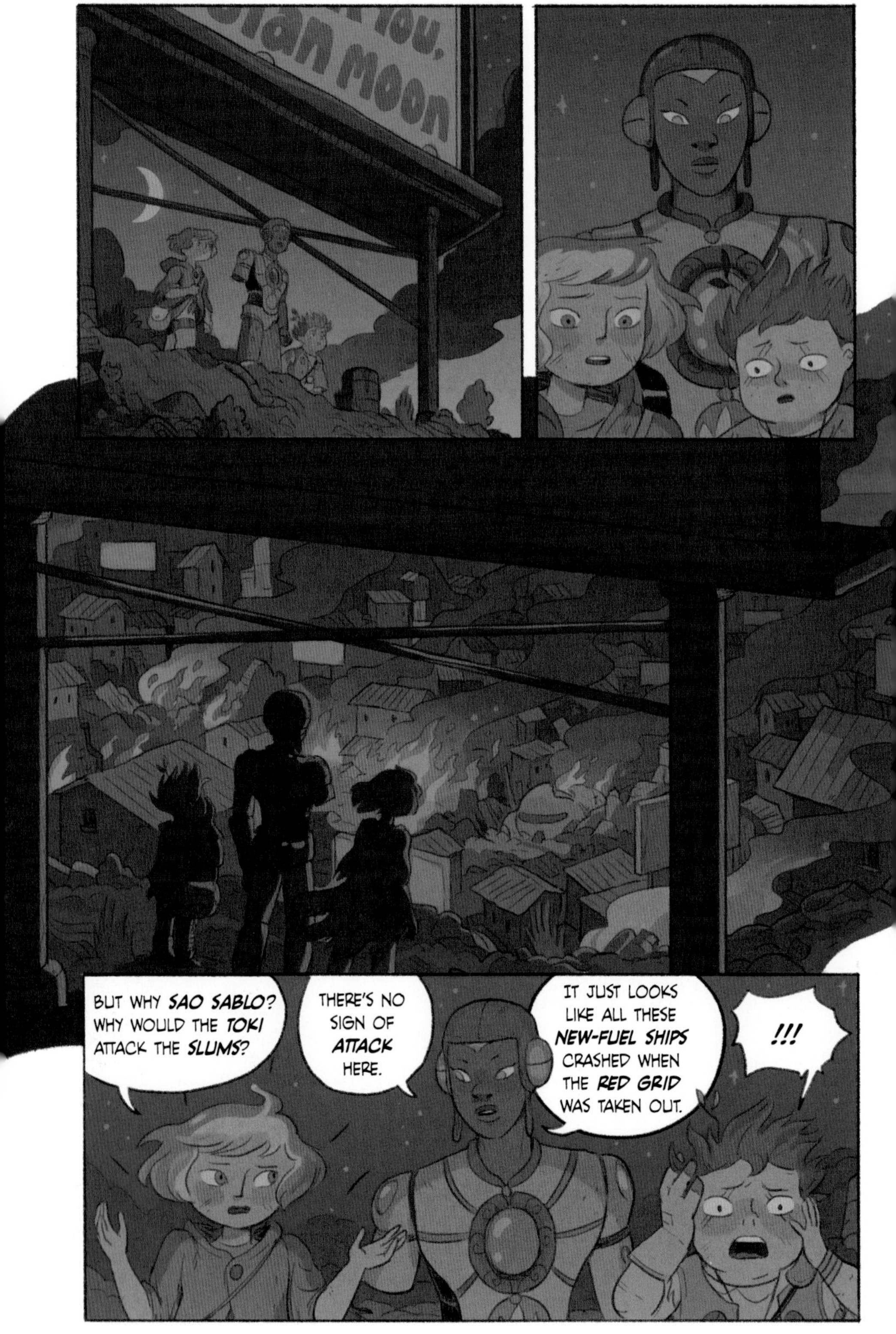
BUT WHY SAO SABLO? WHY WOULD THE TOKI ATTACK THE SLUMS?
THERE'S NO SIGN OF ATTACK HERE.
IT JUST LOOKS LIKE ALL THESE NEW-FUEL SHIPS CRASHED WHEN THE RED GRID WAS TAKEN OUT.
!!!

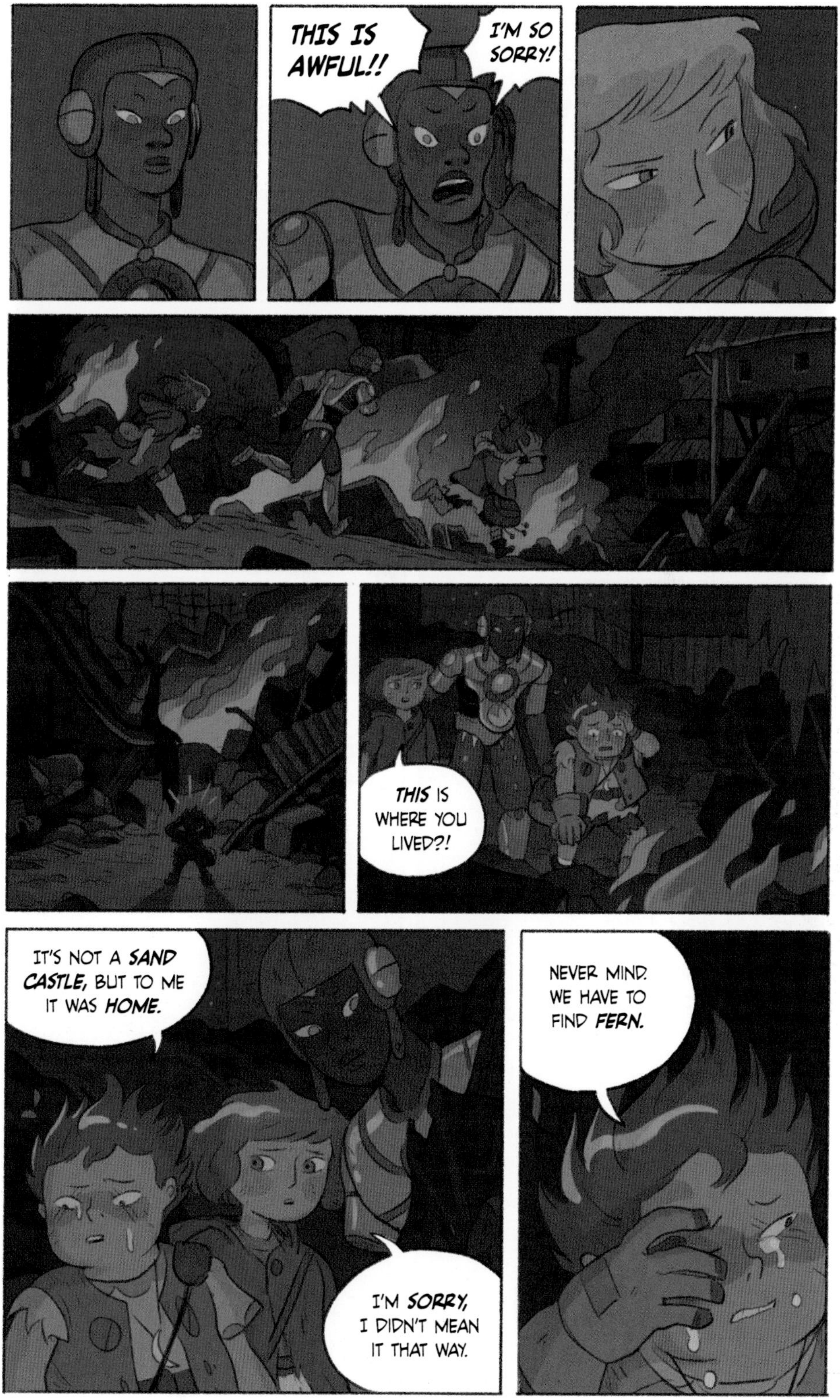
THIS IS AWFUL!!
I'M SO SORRY!
THIS IS WHERE YOU LIVED?!
IT'S NOT A SAND CASTLE, BUT TO ME IT WAS HOME.
I'M SORRY, I DIDN'T MEAN IT THAT WAY.
NEVER MIND. WE HAVE TO FIND FERN.

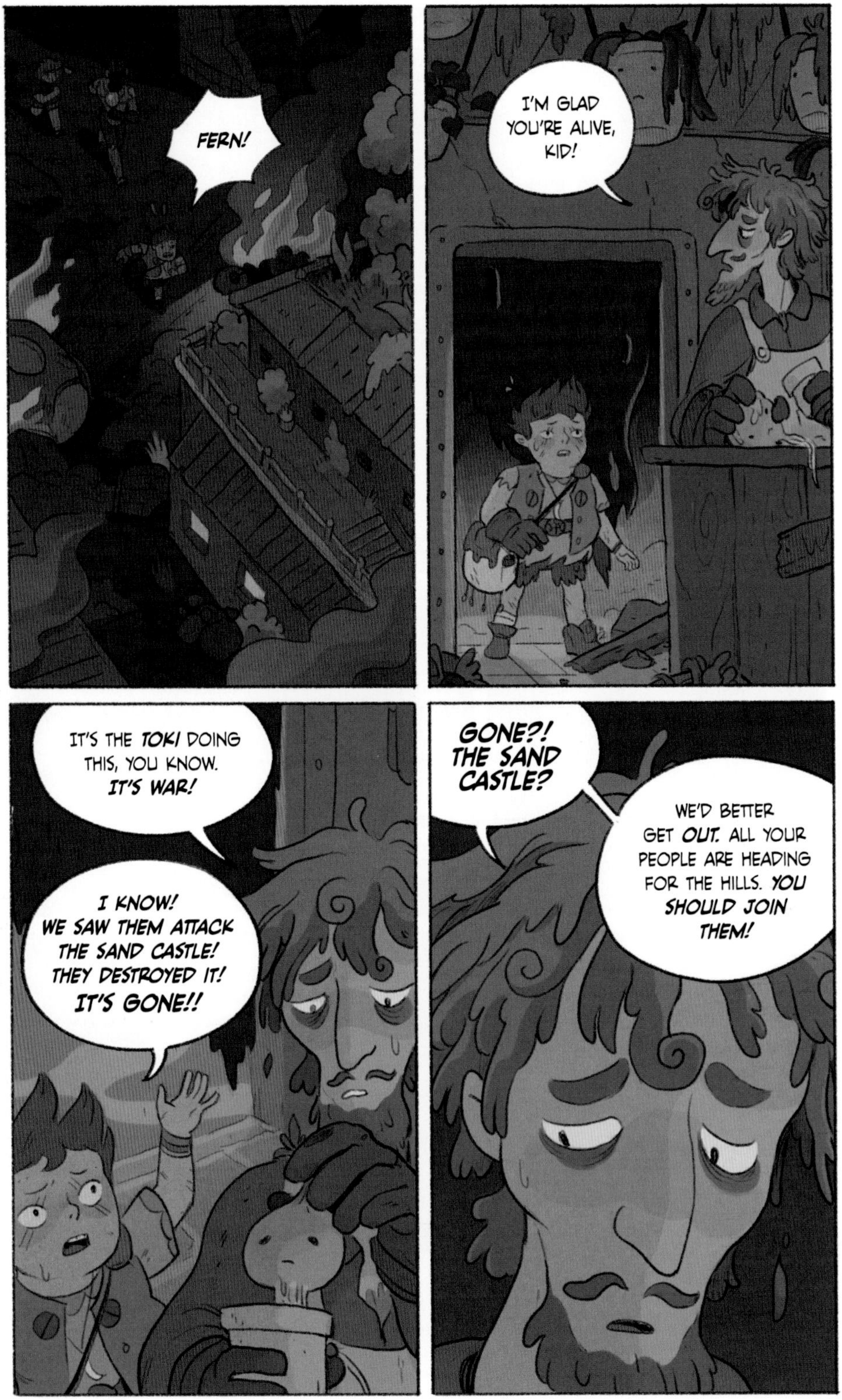
FERN!
I'M GLAD YOU'RE ALIVE, KID!
IT'S THE TOKI DOING THIS, YOU KNOW. IT'S WAR!
I KNOW! WE SAW THEM ATTACK THE SAND CASTLE! THEY DESTROYED IT! IT'S GONE!!
GONE?! THE SAND CASTLE?
WE'D BETTER GET OUT. ALL YOUR PEOPLE ARE HEADING FOR THE HILLS. YOU SHOULD JOIN THEM!

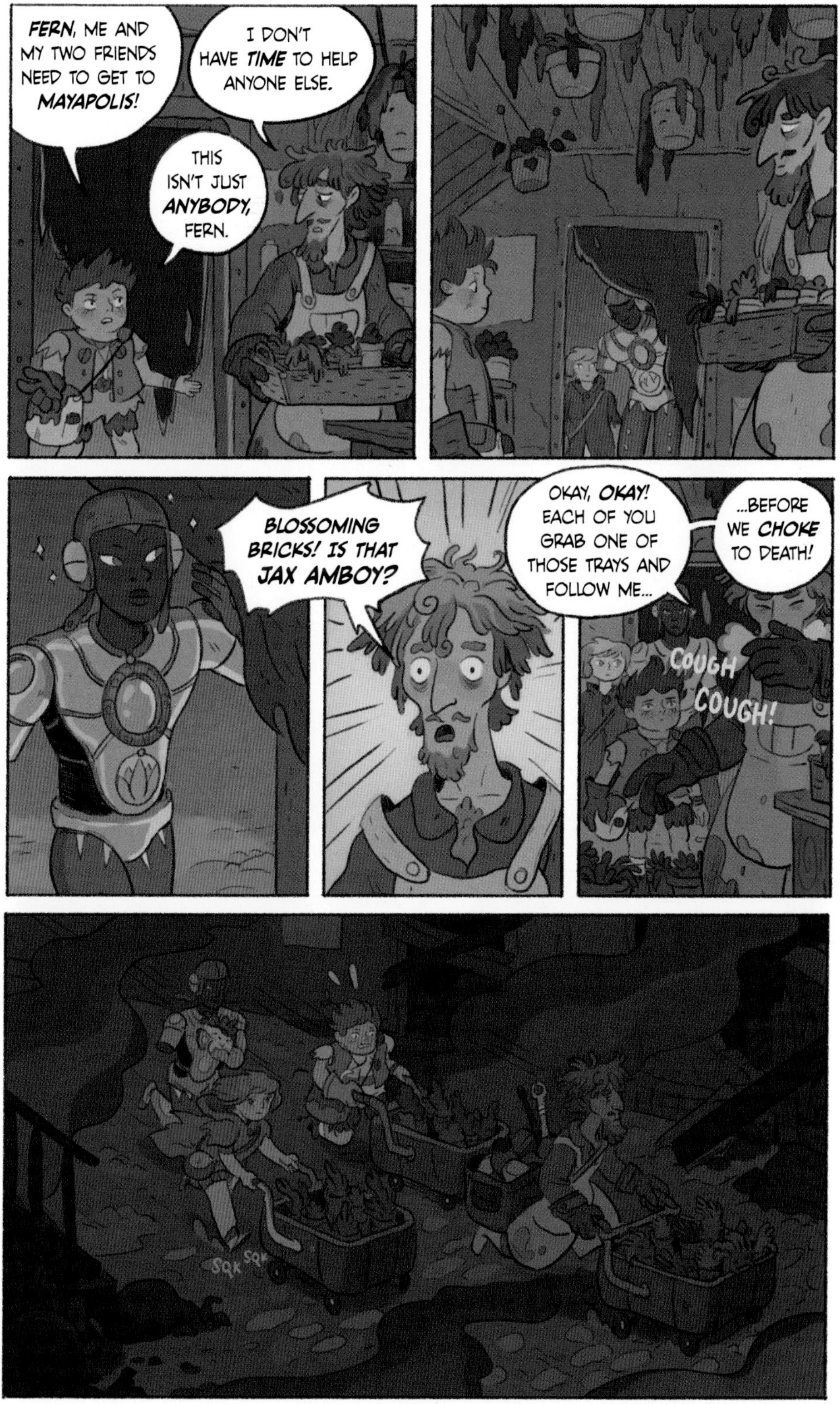
FERN, ME AND MY TWO FRIENDS NEED TO GET TO MAYAPOLIS!
I DON'T HAVE TIME TO HELP ANYONE ELSE.
THIS ISN'T JUST ANYBODY, FERN.
BLOSSOMING BRICKS! IS THAT JAX AMBOY?
OKAY, OKAY! EACH OF YOU GRAB ONE OF THOSE TRAYS AND FOLLOW ME...
...BEFORE WE CHOKE TO DEATH!
COUGH
COUGH!
SQK SQK

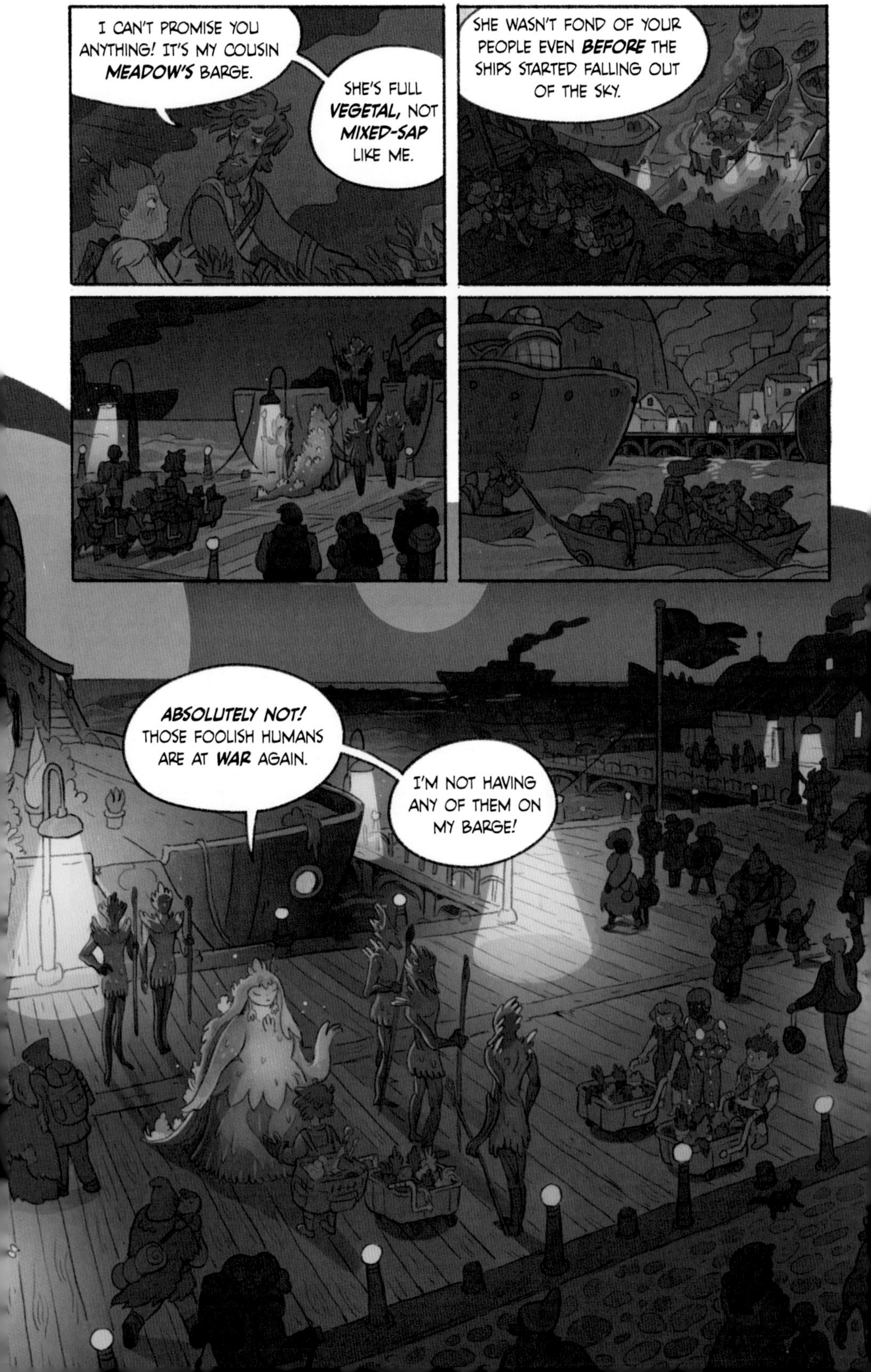
I CAN'T PROMISE YOU ANYTHING! IT'S MY COUSIN MEADOW'S BARGE.
SHE'S FULL VEGETAL, NOT MIXED-SAP LIKE ME.
SHE WASN'T FOND OF YOUR PEOPLE EVEN BEFORE THE SHIPS STARTED FALLING OUT OF THE SKY.
ABSOLUTELY NOT! THOSE FOOLISH HUMANS ARE AT WAR AGAIN.
I'M NOT HAVING ANY OF THEM ON MY BARGE!

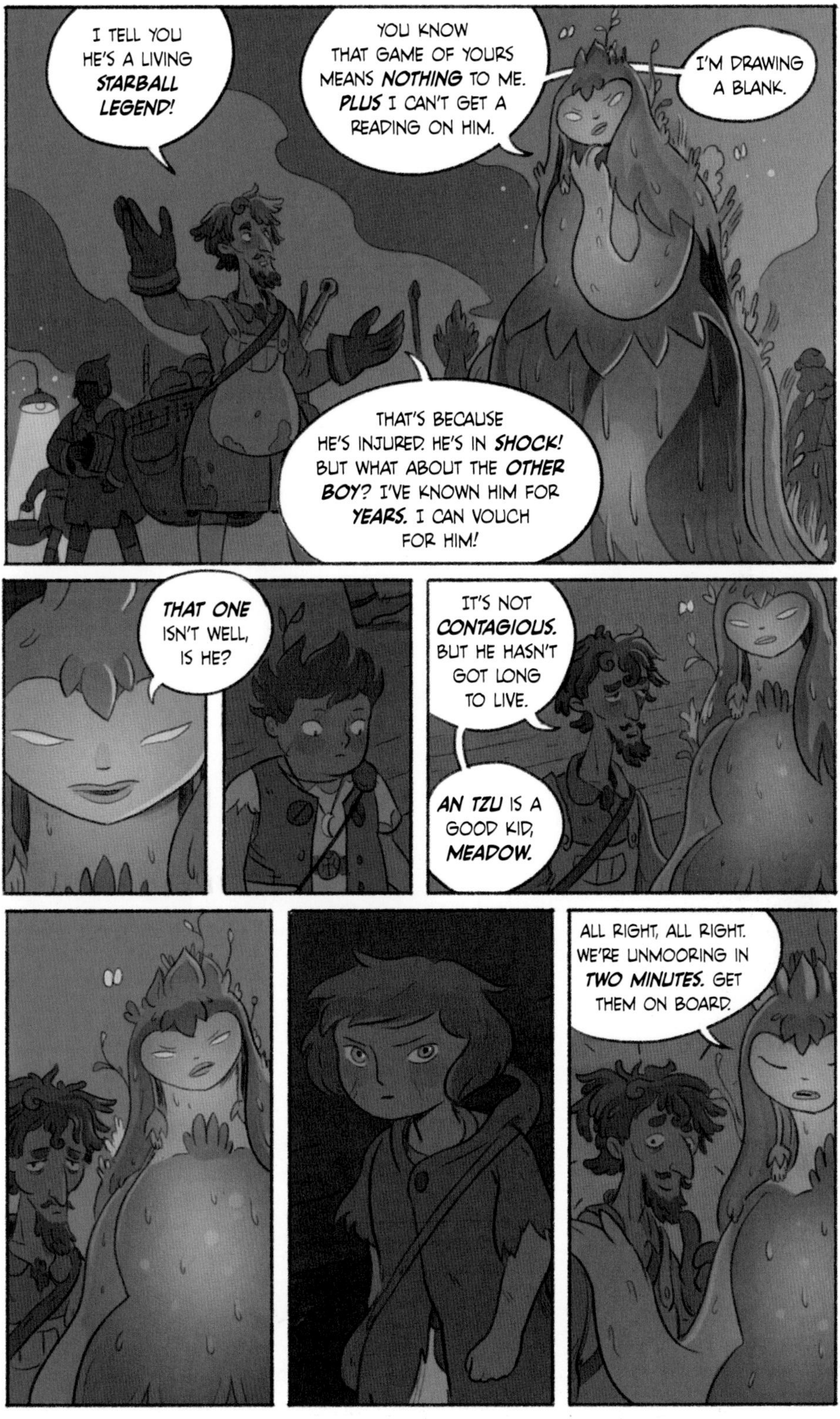
I TELL YOU HE'S A LIVING **STARBALL LEGEND!**
YOU KNOW THAT GAME OF YOURS MEANS **NOTHING** TO ME. **PLUS** I CAN'T GET A READING ON HIM.
I'M DRAWING A BLANK.
THAT'S BECAUSE HE'S INJURED. HE'S IN **SHOCK!** BUT WHAT ABOUT THE **OTHER BOY?** I'VE KNOWN HIM FOR **YEARS.** I CAN VOUCH FOR HIM!
THAT ONE ISN'T WELL, IS HE?
IT'S NOT **CONTAGIOUS.** BUT HE HASN'T GOT LONG TO LIVE.
AN TZU IS A GOOD KID, **MEADOW.**
ALL RIGHT, ALL RIGHT. WE'RE UNMOORING IN **TWO MINUTES.** GET THEM ON BOARD.

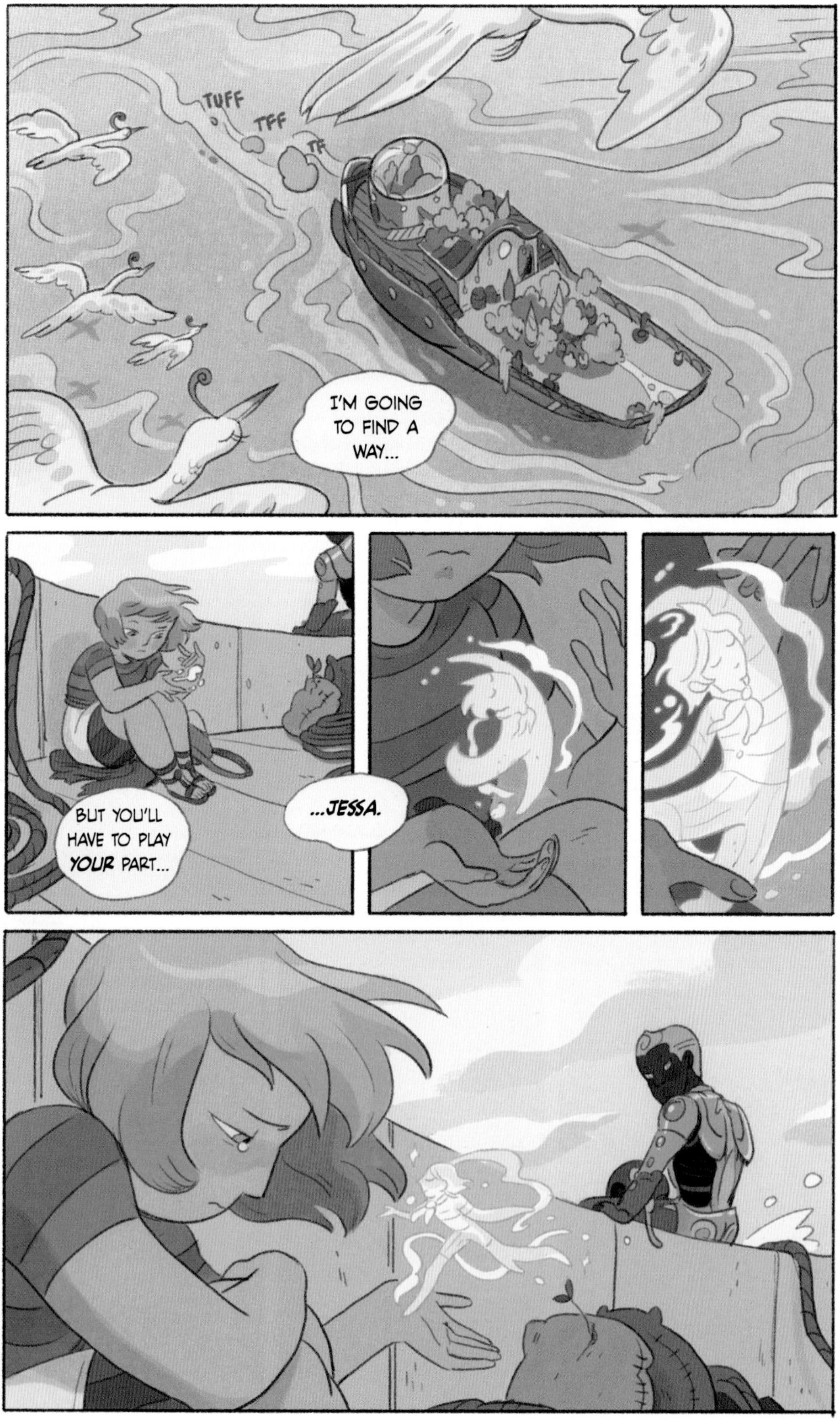
TUFF
TFF
TF
I'M GOING TO FIND A WAY...
BUT YOU'LL HAVE TO PLAY YOUR PART...
...JESSA.

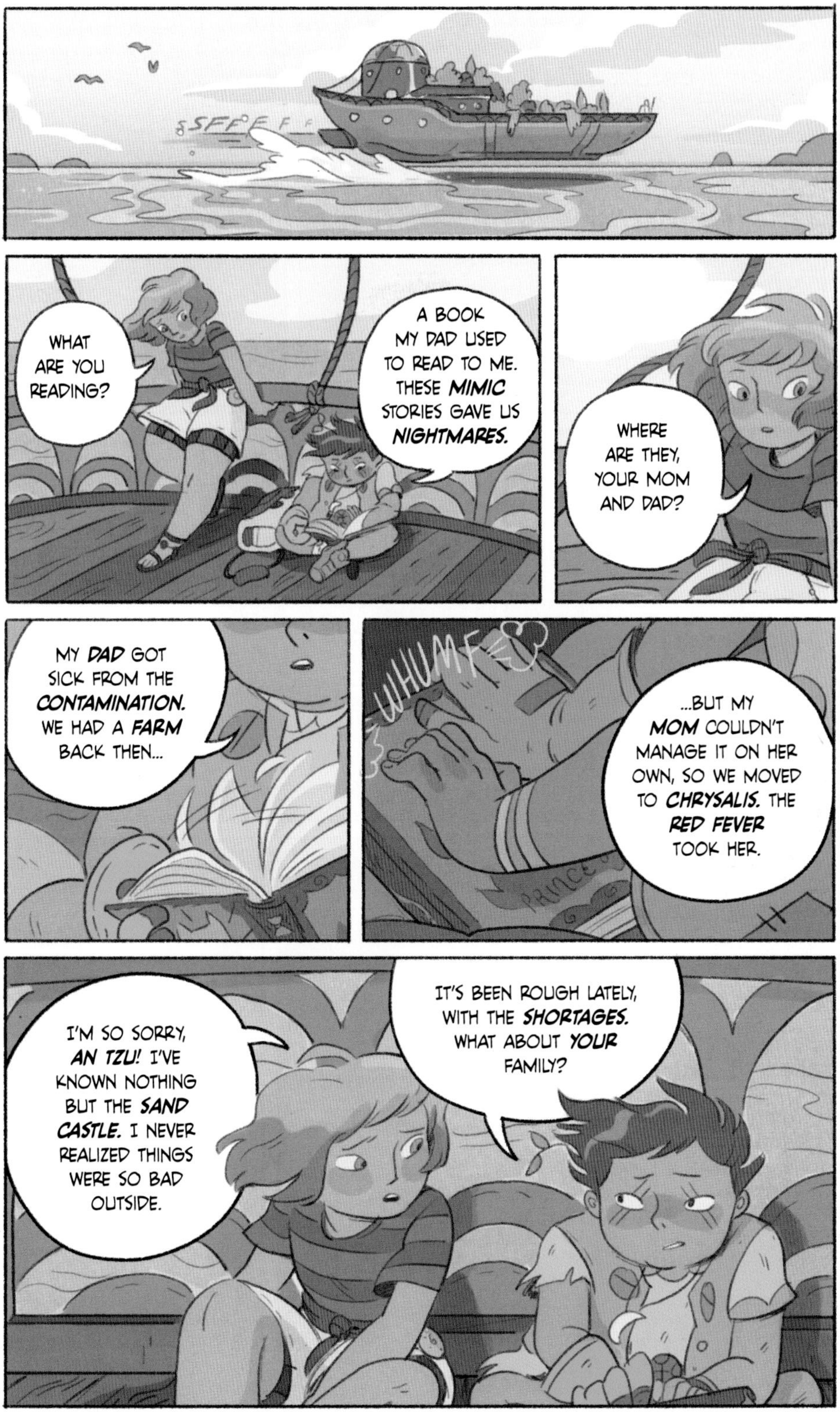
SFFFFF
WHAT ARE YOU READING?
A BOOK MY DAD USED TO READ TO ME. THESE MIMIC STORIES GAVE US NIGHTMARES.
WHERE ARE THEY, YOUR MOM AND DAD?
MY DAD GOT SICK FROM THE CONTAMINATION. WE HAD A FARM BACK THEN...
WHUMF
...BUT MY MOM COULDN'T MANAGE IT ON HER OWN, SO WE MOVED TO CHRYSALIS. THE RED FEVER TOOK HER.
IT'S BEEN ROUGH LATELY, WITH THE SHORTAGES. WHAT ABOUT YOUR FAMILY?
I'M SO SORRY, AN TZU! I'VE KNOWN NOTHING BUT THE SAND CASTLE. I NEVER REALIZED THINGS WERE SO BAD OUTSIDE.

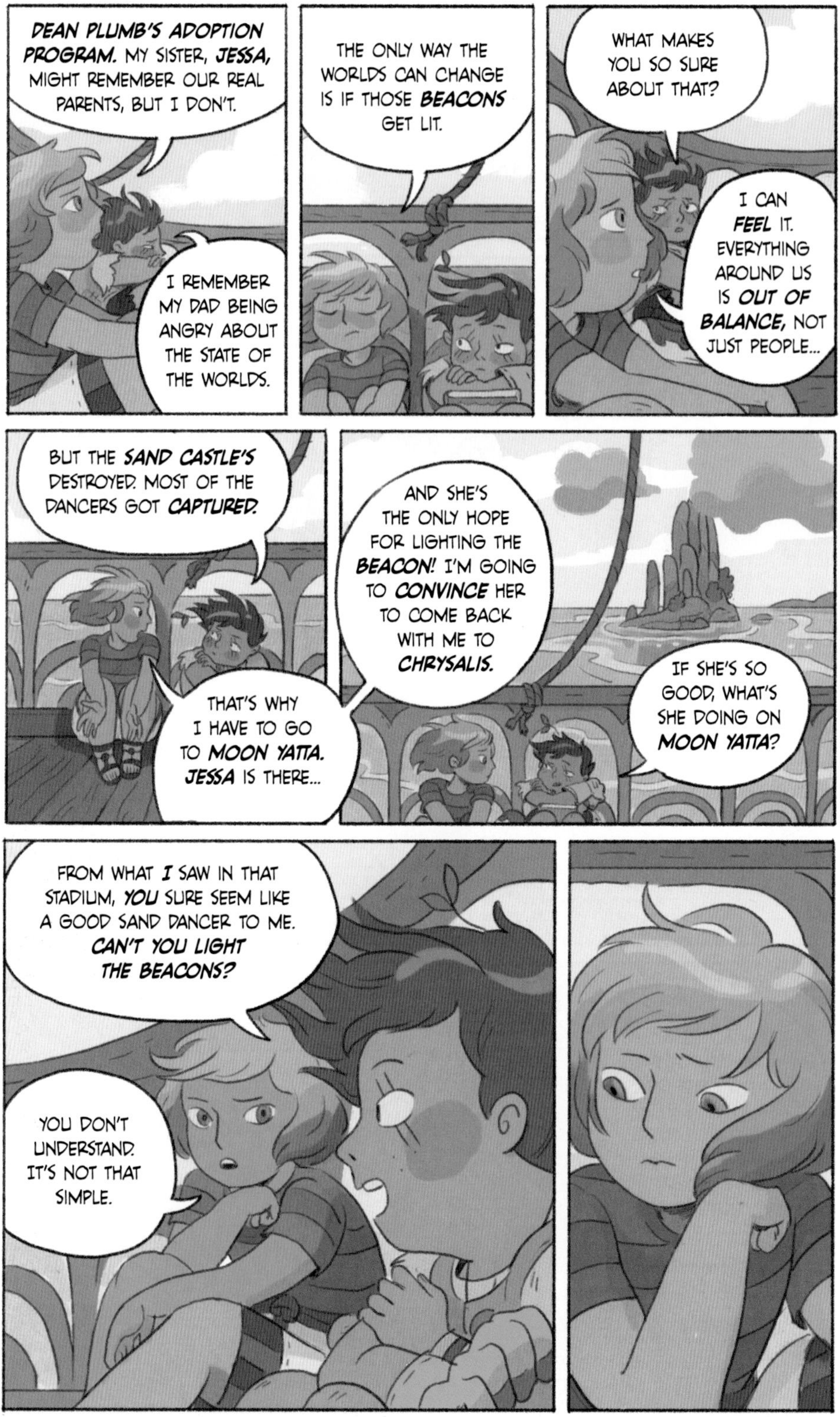
DEAN PLUMB'S ADOPTION PROGRAM. MY SISTER, JESSA, MIGHT REMEMBER OUR REAL PARENTS, BUT I DON'T.
I REMEMBER MY DAD BEING ANGRY ABOUT THE STATE OF THE WORLDS.
THE ONLY WAY THE WORLDS CAN CHANGE IS IF THOSE BEACONS GET LIT.
WHAT MAKES YOU SO SURE ABOUT THAT?
I CAN FEEL IT. EVERYTHING AROUND US IS OUT OF BALANCE, NOT JUST PEOPLE...
BUT THE SAND CASTLE'S DESTROYED. MOST OF THE DANCERS GOT CAPTURED.
THAT'S WHY I HAVE TO GO TO MOON YATTA. JESSA IS THERE...
AND SHE'S THE ONLY HOPE FOR LIGHTING THE BEACON! I'M GOING TO CONVINCE HER TO COME BACK WITH ME TO CHRYSALIS.
IF SHE'S SO GOOD, WHAT'S SHE DOING ON MOON YATTA?
FROM WHAT I SAW IN THAT STADIUM, YOU SURE SEEM LIKE A GOOD SAND DANCER TO ME. CAN'T YOU LIGHT THE BEACONS?
YOU DON'T UNDERSTAND. IT'S NOT THAT SIMPLE.

Chapter 6

CAT ISLAND

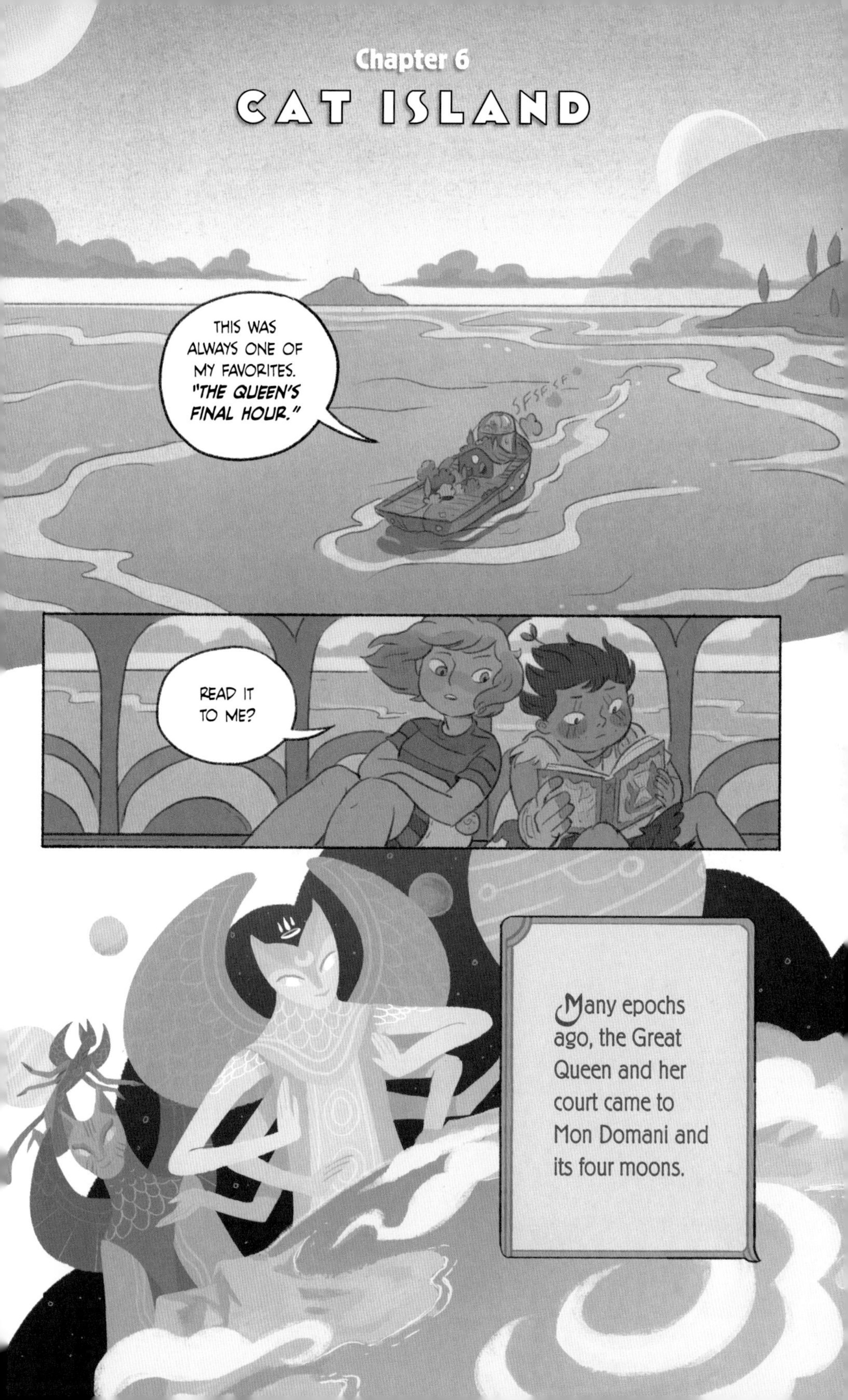
THIS WAS ALWAYS ONE OF MY FAVORITES. "THE QUEEN'S FINAL HOUR."
READ IT TO ME?
Many epochs ago, the Great Queen and her court came to Mon Domani and its four moons.

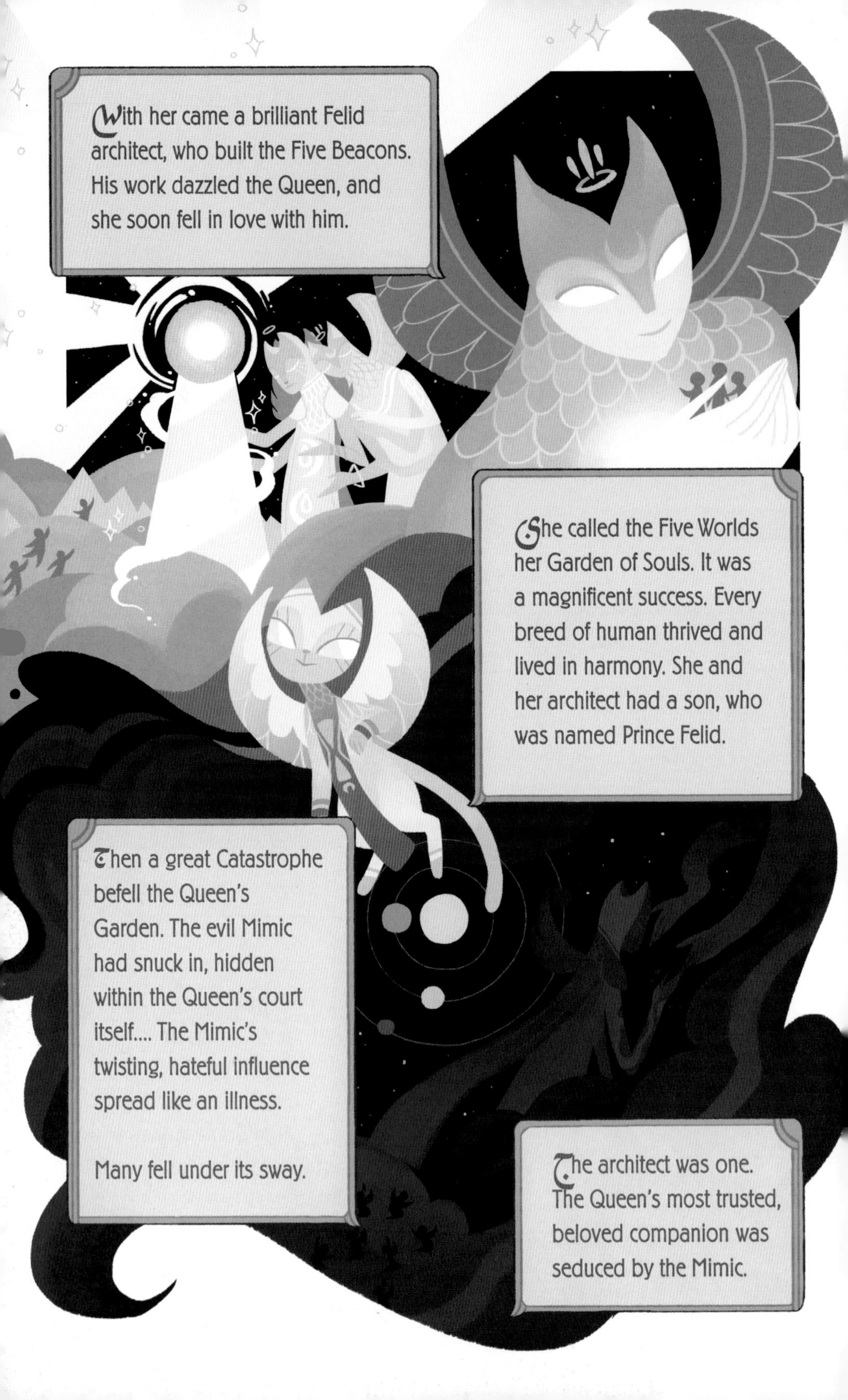
With her came a brilliant Felid architect, who built the Five Beacons. His work dazzled the Queen, and she soon fell in love with him.
She called the Five Worlds her Garden of Souls. It was a magnificent success. Every breed of human thrived and lived in harmony. She and her architect had a son, who was named Prince Felid.
Then a great Catastrophe befell the Queen's Garden. The evil Mimic had snuck in, hidden within the Queen's court itself.... The Mimic's twisting, hateful influence spread like an illness.
Many fell under its sway.
The architect was one. The Queen's most trusted, beloved companion was seduced by the Mimic.

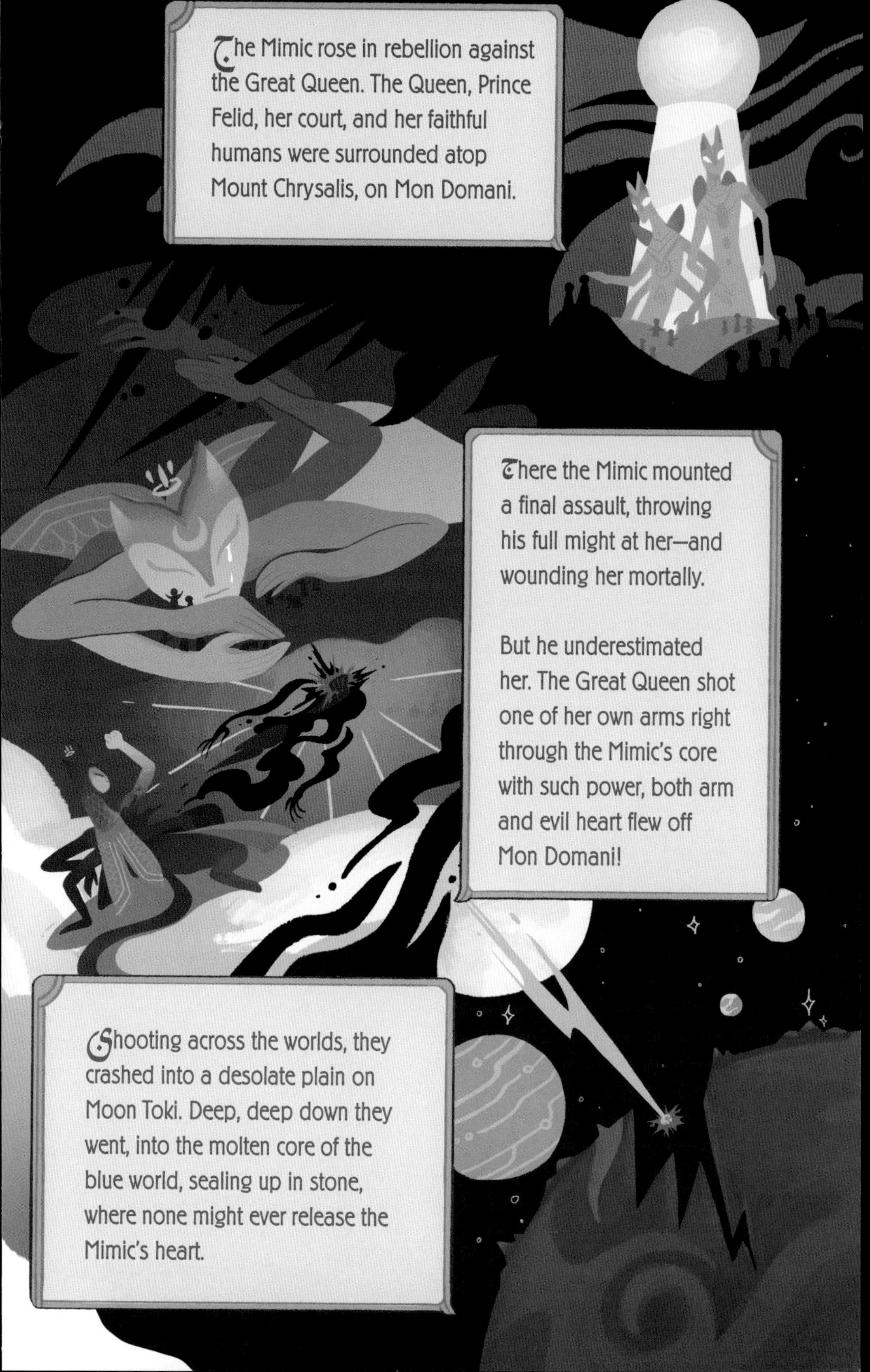
The Mimic rose in rebellion against the Great Queen. The Queen, Prince Felid, her court, and her faithful humans were surrounded atop Mount Chrysalis, on Mon Domani.
There the Mimic mounted a final assault, throwing his full might at her—and wounding her mortally.
But he underestimated her. The Great Queen shot one of her own arms right through the Mimic's core with such power, both arm and evil heart flew off Mon Domani!
Shooting across the worlds, they crashed into a desolate plain on Moon Toki. Deep, deep down they went, into the molten core of the blue world, sealing up in stone, where none might ever release the Mimic's heart.

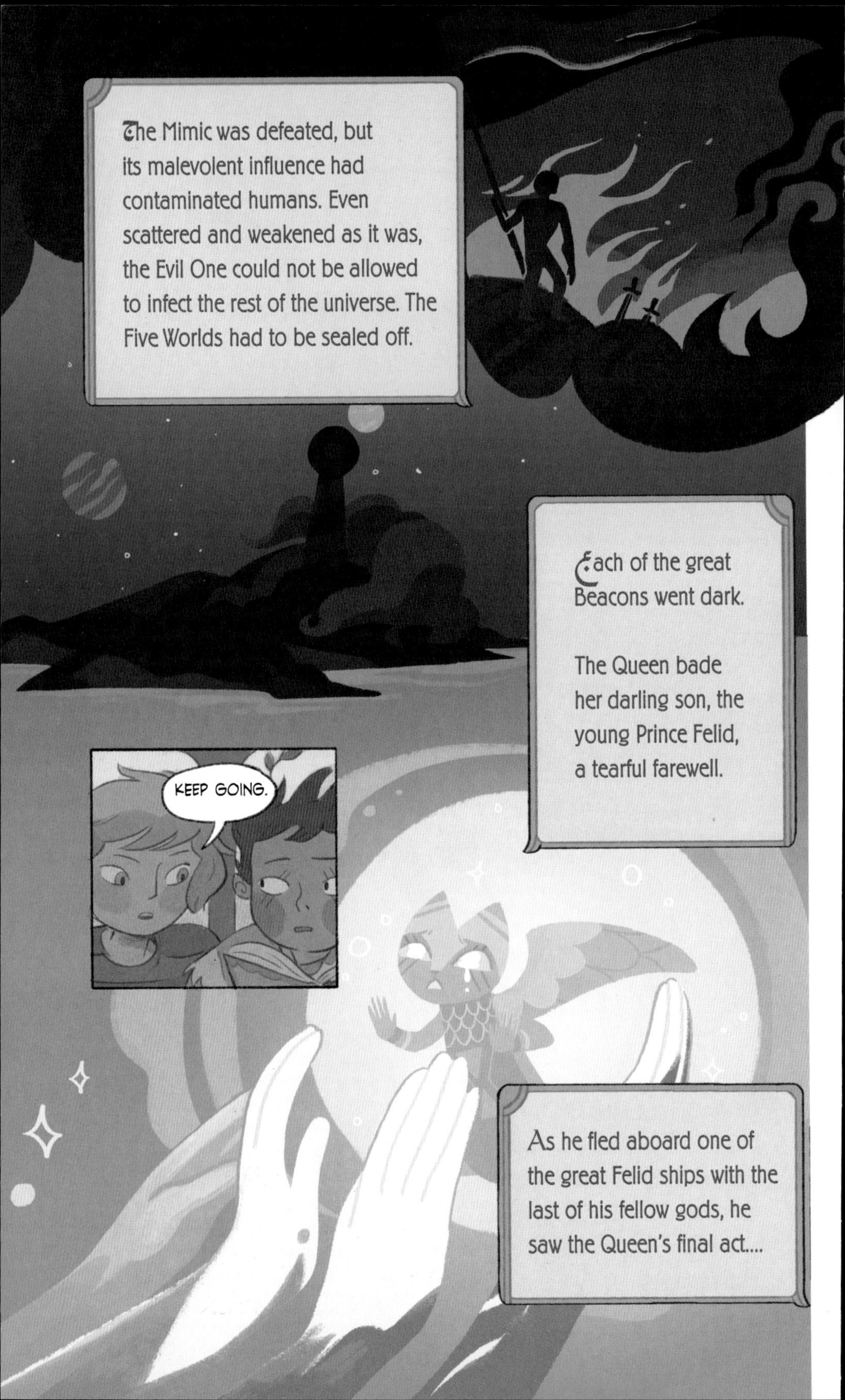
The Mimic was defeated, but its malevolent influence had contaminated humans. Even scattered and weakened as it was, the Evil One could not be allowed to infect the rest of the universe. The Five Worlds had to be sealed off.
Each of the great Beacons went dark.
The Queen bade her darling son, the young Prince Felid, a tearful farewell.
KEEP GOING.
As he fled aboard one of the great Felid ships with the last of his fellow gods, he saw the Queen's final act....

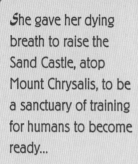

She gave her dying breath to raise the Sand Castle, atop Mount Chrysalis, to be a sanctuary of training for humans to become ready...

...to one day defeat the Mimic, and reignite the great Beacons...

...or risk losing the Five Worlds altogether.

MOST **DEPRESSING** CHILDREN'S BOOK EVER WRITTEN, I KNOW.

THEY TAUGHT THE STORY DIFFERENTLY AT THE **SAND CASTLE.** DO YOU BELIEVE THE **MIMIC** REALLY EXISTS?

I DUNNO. I WAS **TERRIFIED** OF IT AS A KID. BUT NOBODY'S EVER SEEN IT, SO I'M NOT SO SURE.

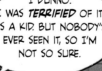

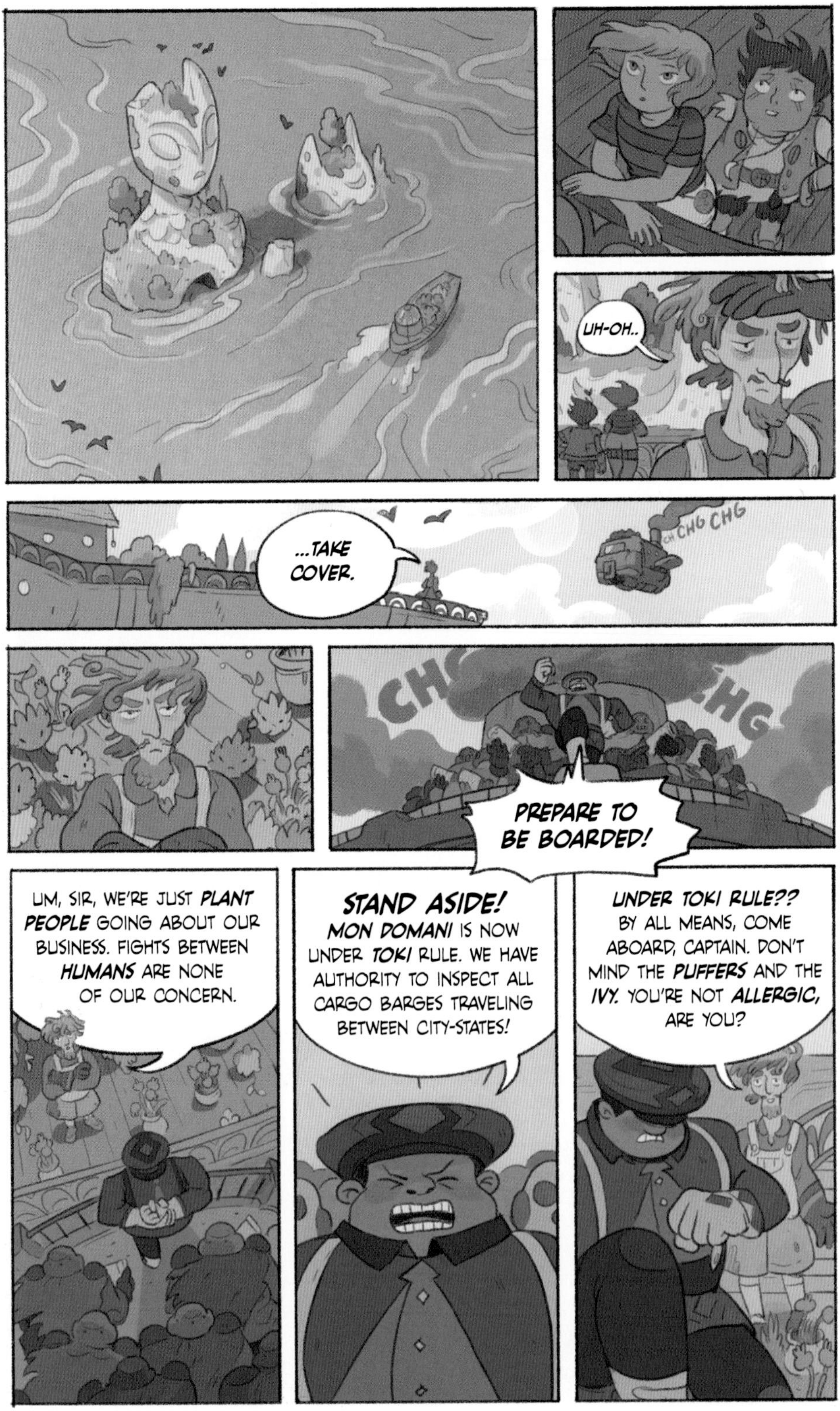

UH-OH..
...TAKE COVER.
CHG CHG CHG
CHG CHG
PREPARE TO BE BOARDED!
UM, SIR, WE'RE JUST PLANT PEOPLE GOING ABOUT OUR BUSINESS. FIGHTS BETWEEN HUMANS ARE NONE OF OUR CONCERN.
STAND ASIDE! MON DOMANI IS NOW UNDER TOKI RULE. WE HAVE AUTHORITY TO INSPECT ALL CARGO BARGES TRAVELING BETWEEN CITY-STATES!
UNDER TOKI RULE?? BY ALL MEANS, COME ABOARD, CAPTAIN. DON'T MIND THE PUFFERS AND THE IVY. YOU'RE NOT ALLERGIC, ARE YOU?

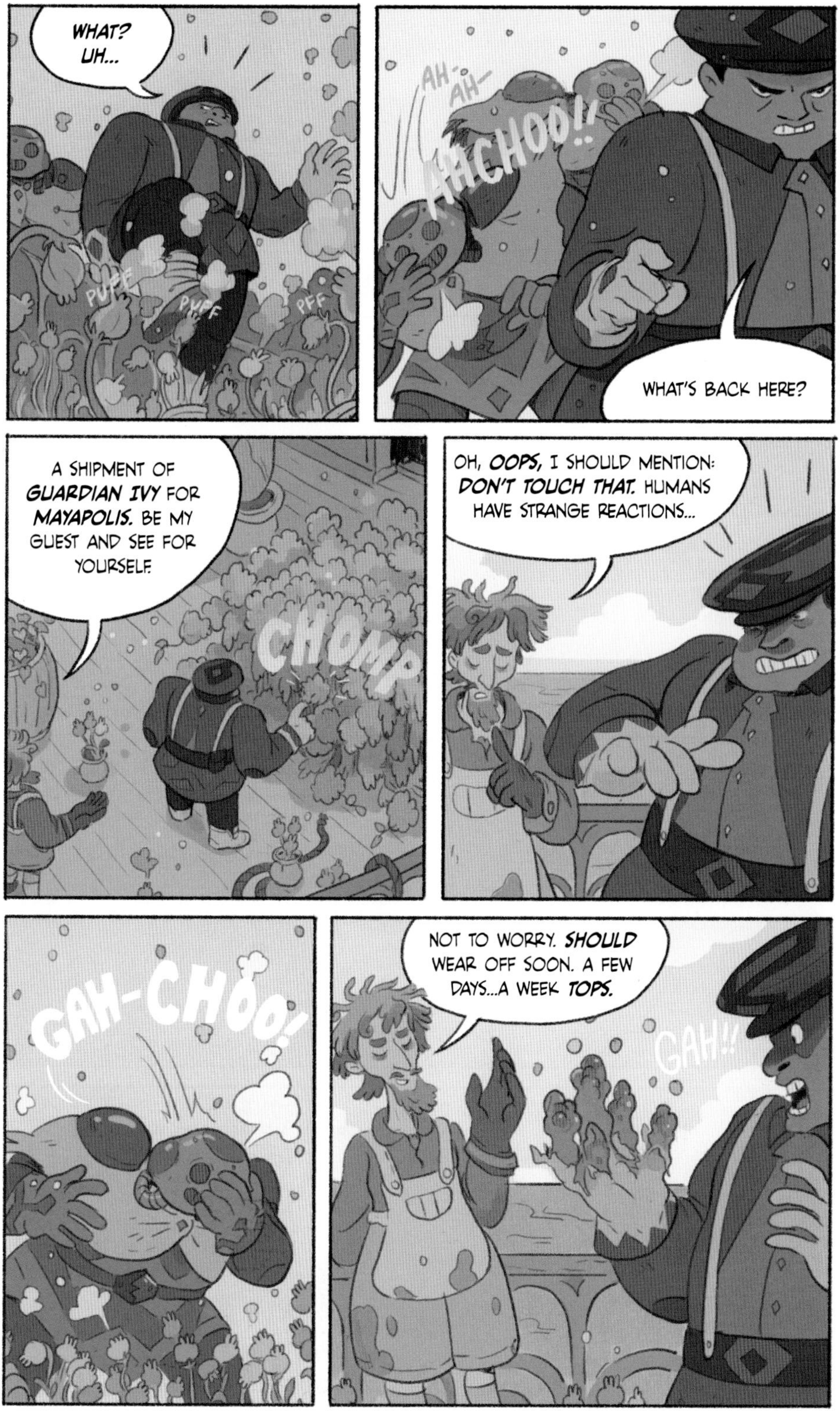
WHAT? UH...
PUFF
PUFF
PFF
AH- AH-
AHCHOO!!
WHAT'S BACK HERE?
A SHIPMENT OF GUARDIAN IVY FOR MAYAPOLIS. BE MY GUEST AND SEE FOR YOURSELF.
CHOMP
OH, OOPS, I SHOULD MENTION: DON'T TOUCH THAT. HUMANS HAVE STRANGE REACTIONS...
GAH-CHOO!
NOT TO WORRY. SHOULD WEAR OFF SOON. A FEW DAYS...A WEEK TOPS.
GAH!!

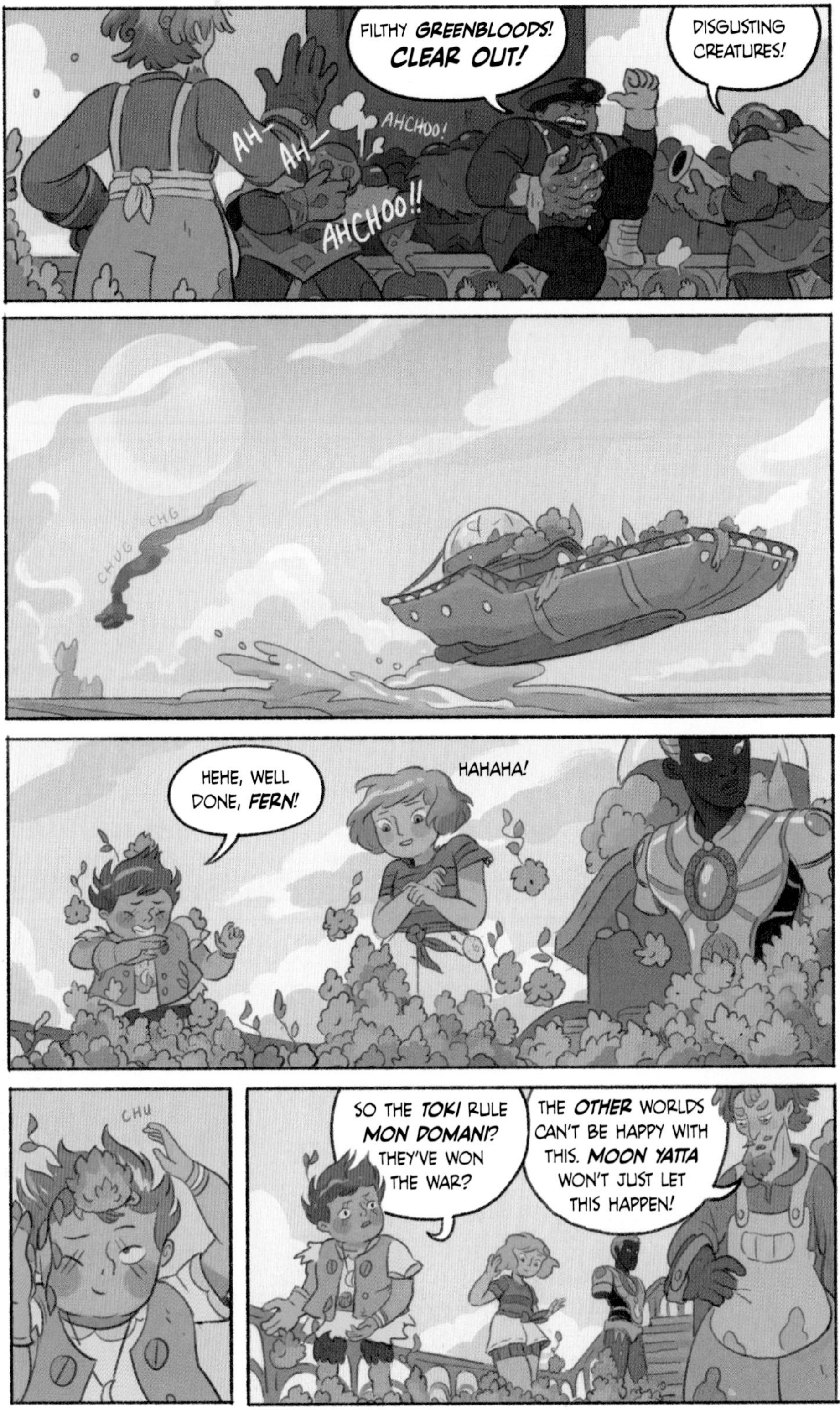
FILTHY GREENBLOODS! CLEAR OUT!
DISGUSTING CREATURES!
AH- AH-
AHCHOO!
AHCHOO!!
CHUG CHG
HEHE, WELL DONE, FERN!
HAHAHA!
CHU
SO THE TOKI RULE MON DOMANI? THEY'VE WON THE WAR?
THE OTHER WORLDS CAN'T BE HAPPY WITH THIS. MOON YATTA WON'T JUST LET THIS HAPPEN!

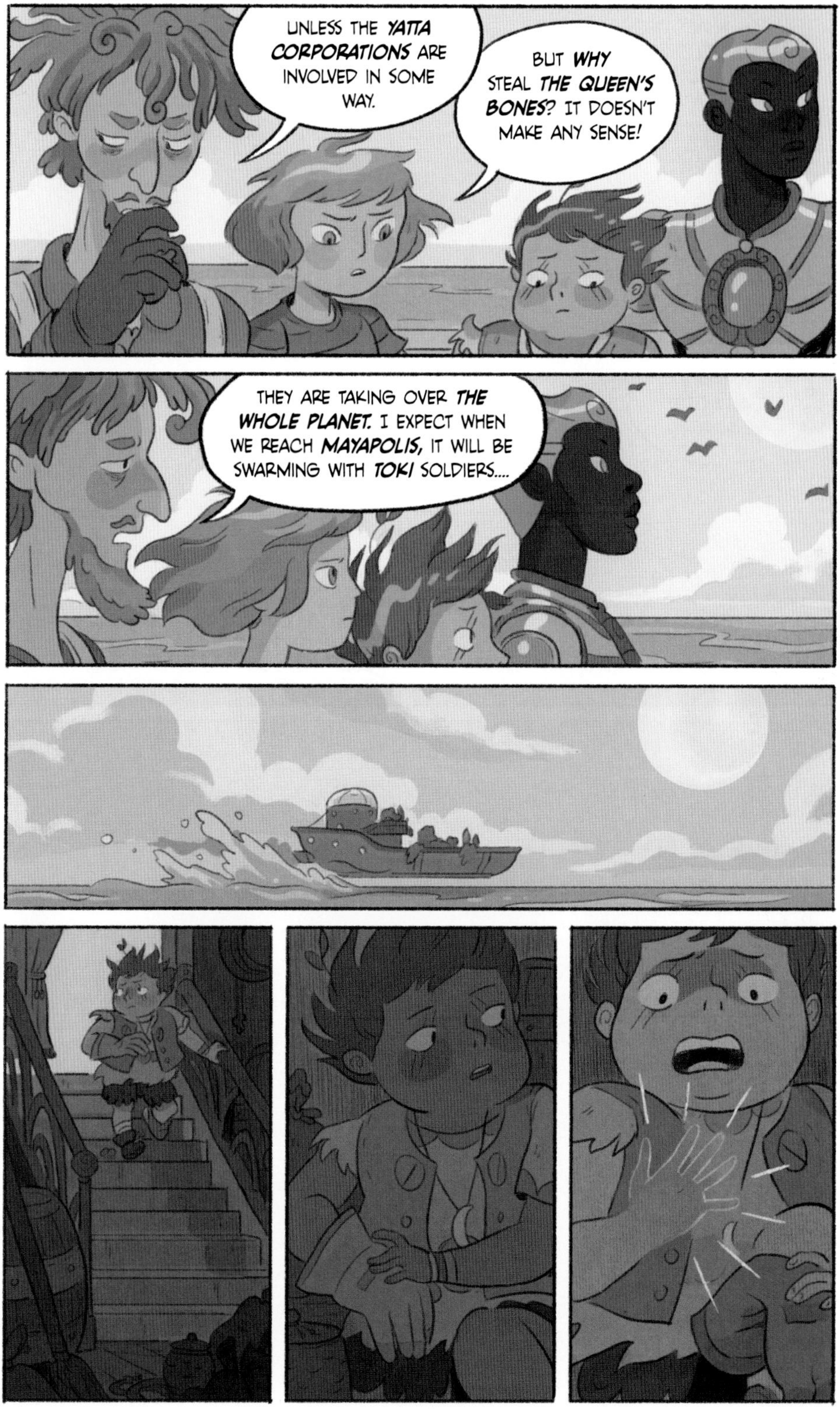
UNLESS THE YATTA CORPORATIONS ARE INVOLVED IN SOME WAY.
BUT WHY STEAL THE QUEEN'S BONES? IT DOESN'T MAKE ANY SENSE!
THEY ARE TAKING OVER THE WHOLE PLANET. I EXPECT WHEN WE REACH MAYAPOLIS, IT WILL BE SWARMING WITH TOKI SOLDIERS....

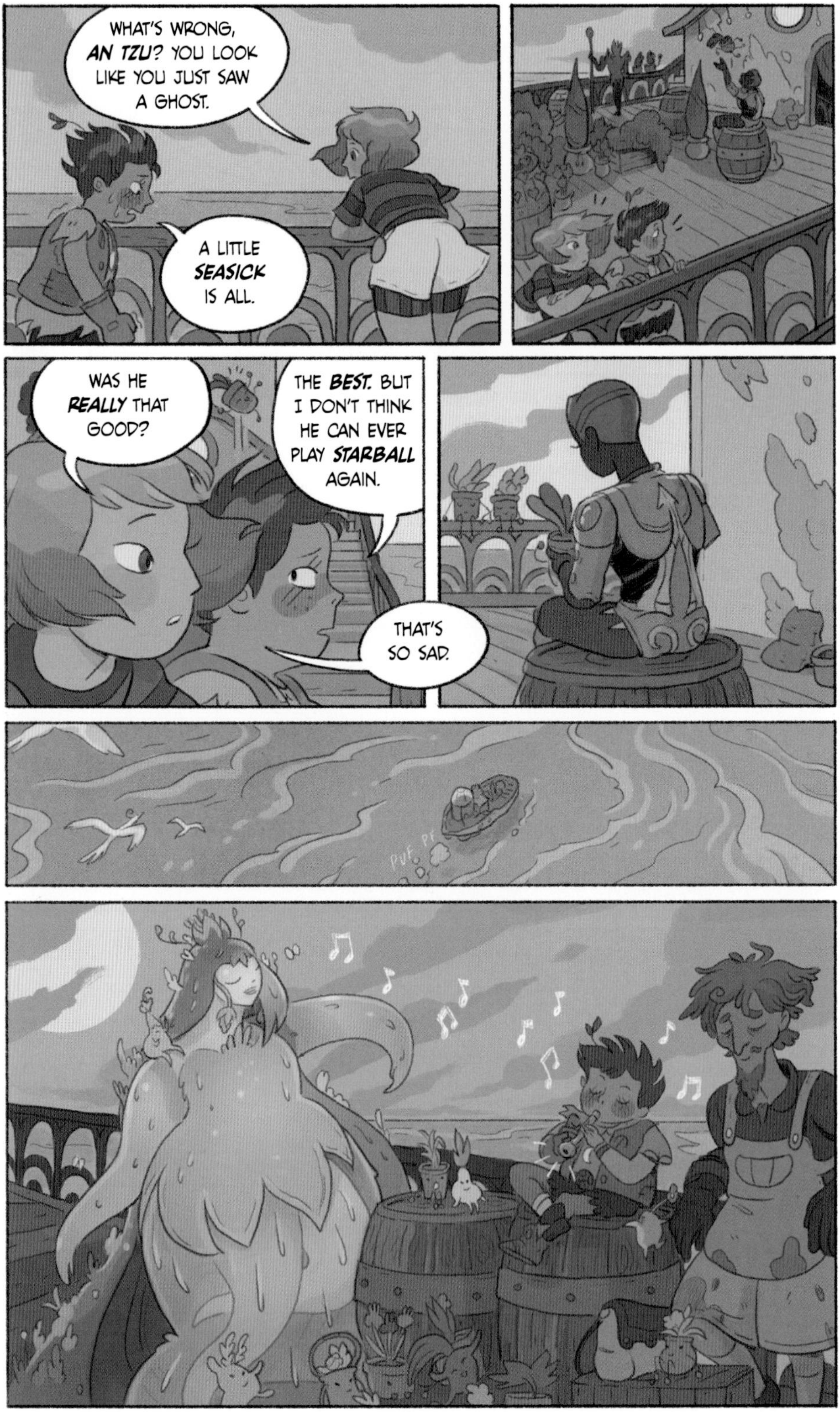
WHAT'S WRONG, AN TZU? YOU LOOK LIKE YOU JUST SAW A GHOST.
A LITTLE SEASICK IS ALL.
WAS HE REALLY THAT GOOD?
THE BEST. BUT I DON'T THINK HE CAN EVER PLAY STARBALL AGAIN.
THAT'S SO SAD.
PUF PF

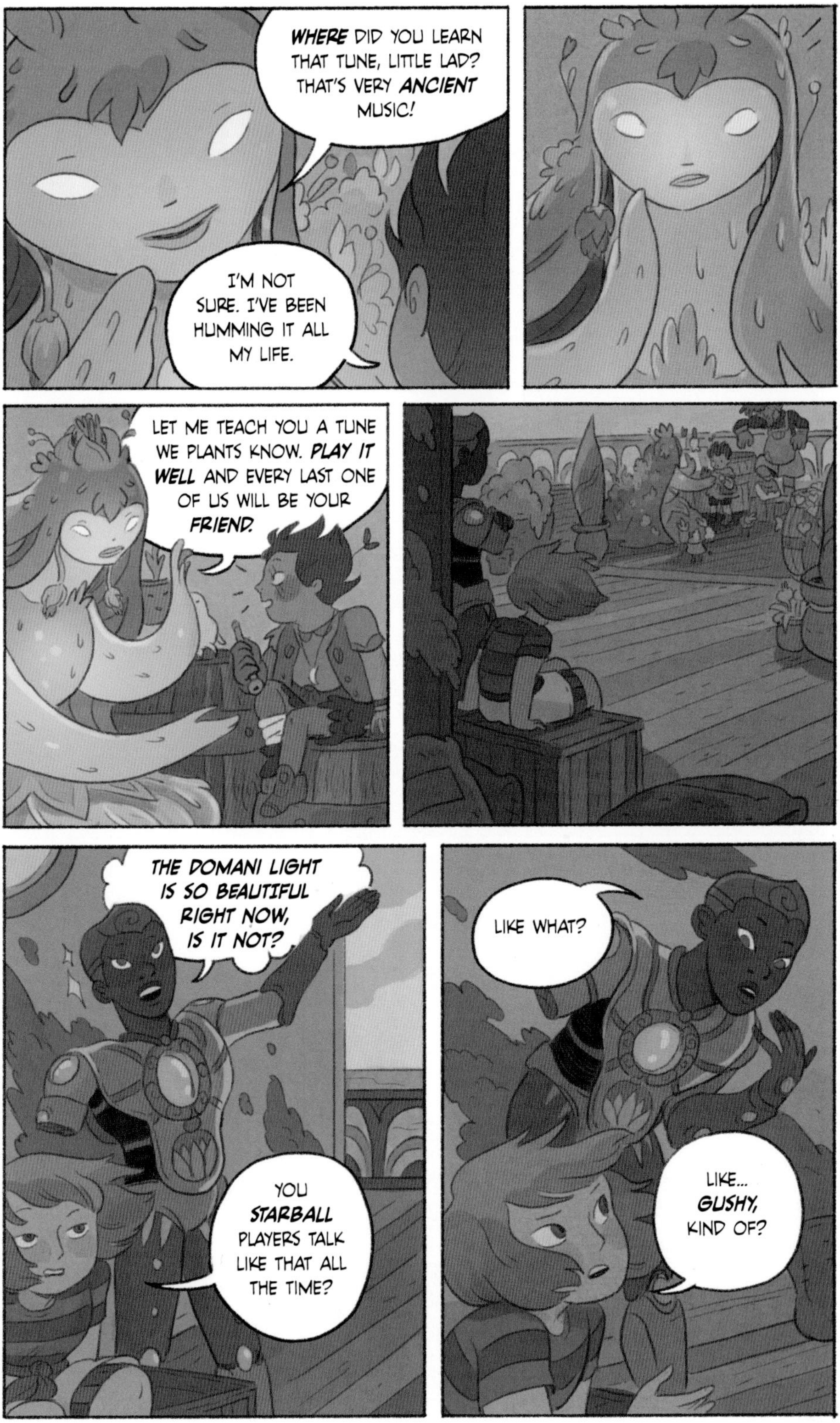
WHERE DID YOU LEARN THAT TUNE, LITTLE LAD? THAT'S VERY ANCIENT MUSIC!
I'M NOT SURE. I'VE BEEN HUMMING IT ALL MY LIFE.
LET ME TEACH YOU A TUNE WE PLANTS KNOW. PLAY IT WELL AND EVERY LAST ONE OF US WILL BE YOUR FRIEND.
THE DOMANI LIGHT IS SO BEAUTIFUL RIGHT NOW, IS IT NOT?
YOU STARBALL PLAYERS TALK LIKE THAT ALL THE TIME?
LIKE WHAT?
LIKE... GUSHY, KIND OF?

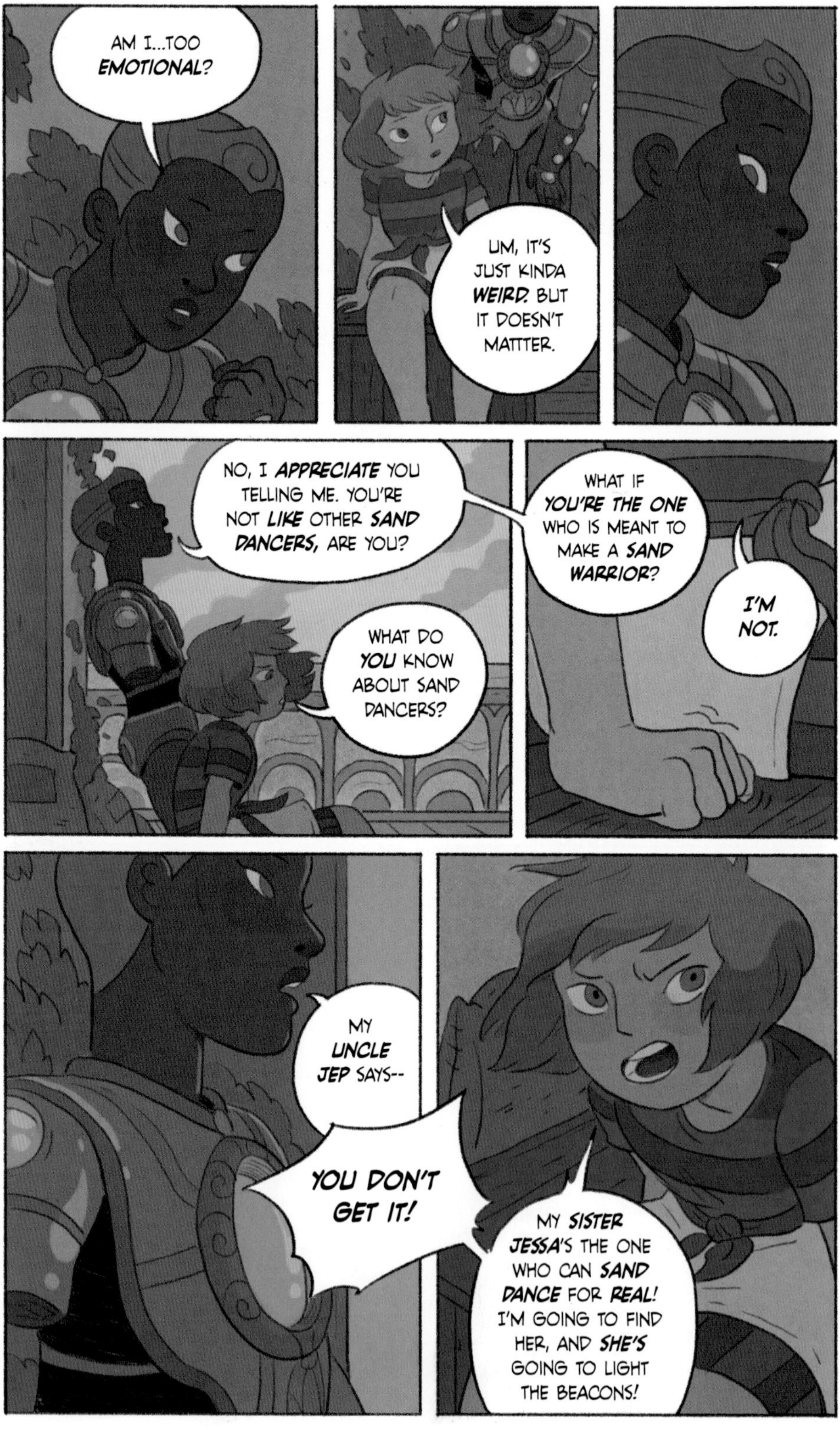
AM I...TOO EMOTIONAL?
UM, IT'S JUST KINDA WEIRD. BUT IT DOESN'T MATTTER.
NO, I APPRECIATE YOU TELLING ME. YOU'RE NOT LIKE OTHER SAND DANCERS, ARE YOU?
WHAT DO YOU KNOW ABOUT SAND DANCERS?
WHAT IF YOU'RE THE ONE WHO IS MEANT TO MAKE A SAND WARRIOR?
I'M NOT.
MY UNCLE JEP SAYS--
YOU DON'T GET IT!
MY SISTER JESSA'S THE ONE WHO CAN SAND DANCE FOR REAL! I'M GOING TO FIND HER, AND SHE'S GOING TO LIGHT THE BEACONS!

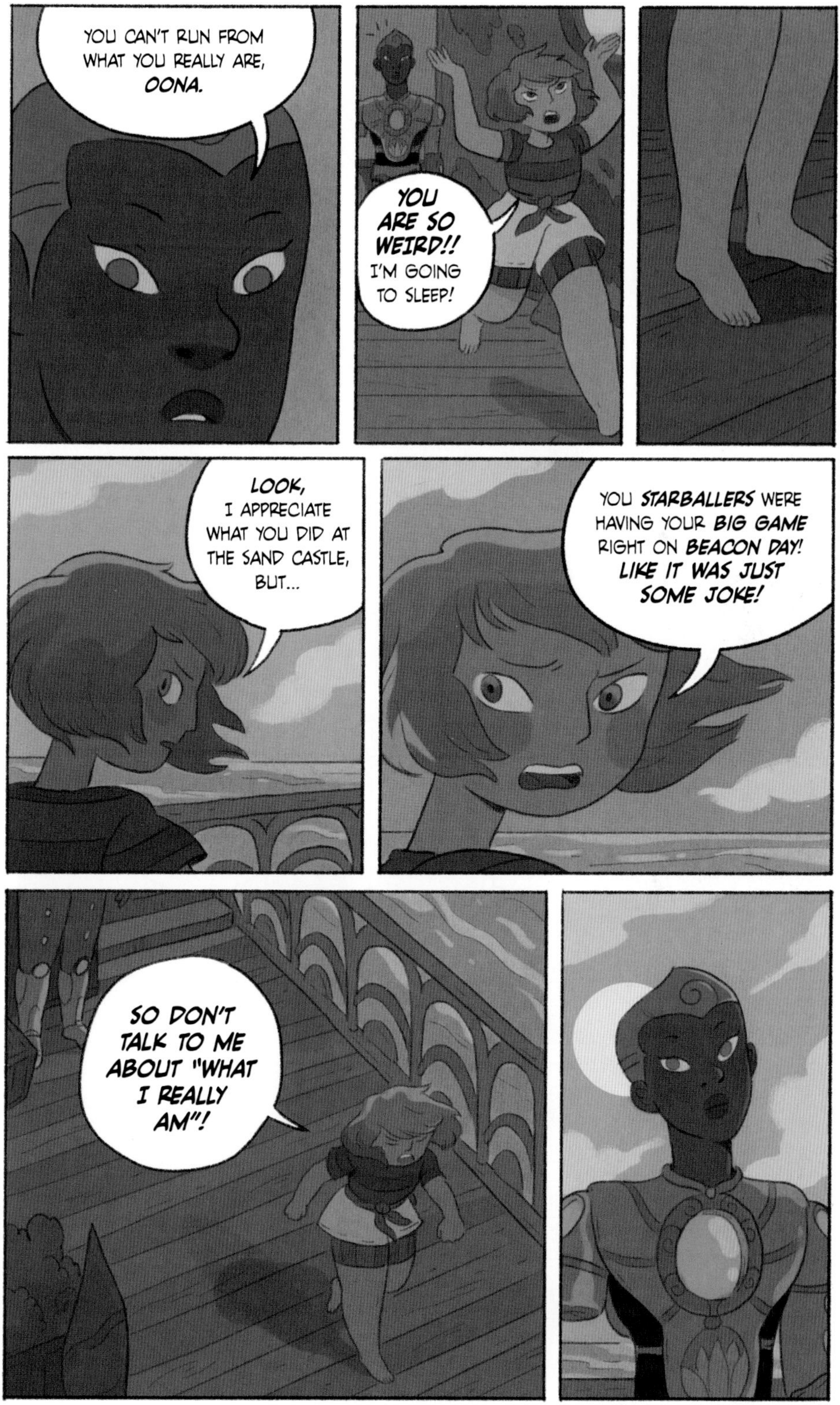
YOU CAN'T RUN FROM WHAT YOU REALLY ARE, OONA.
YOU ARE SO WEIRD!! I'M GOING TO SLEEP!
LOOK, I APPRECIATE WHAT YOU DID AT THE SAND CASTLE, BUT...
YOU STARBALLERS WERE HAVING YOUR BIG GAME RIGHT ON BEACON DAY! LIKE IT WAS JUST SOME JOKE!
SO DON'T TALK TO ME ABOUT "WHAT I REALLY AM"!

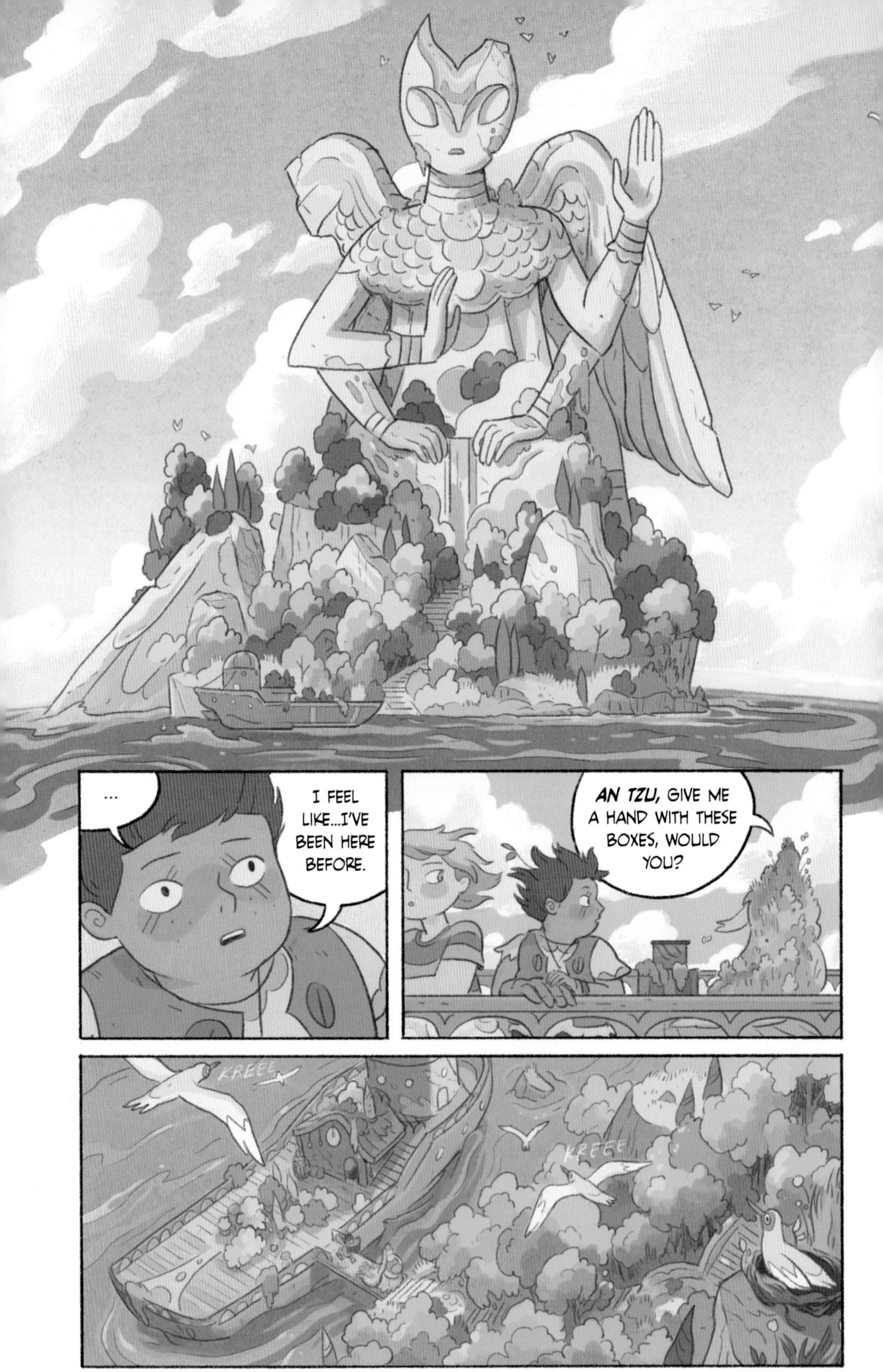
...
I FEEL LIKE...I'VE BEEN HERE BEFORE.
AN TZU, GIVE ME A HAND WITH THESE BOXES, WOULD YOU?
KREEE
KREEE

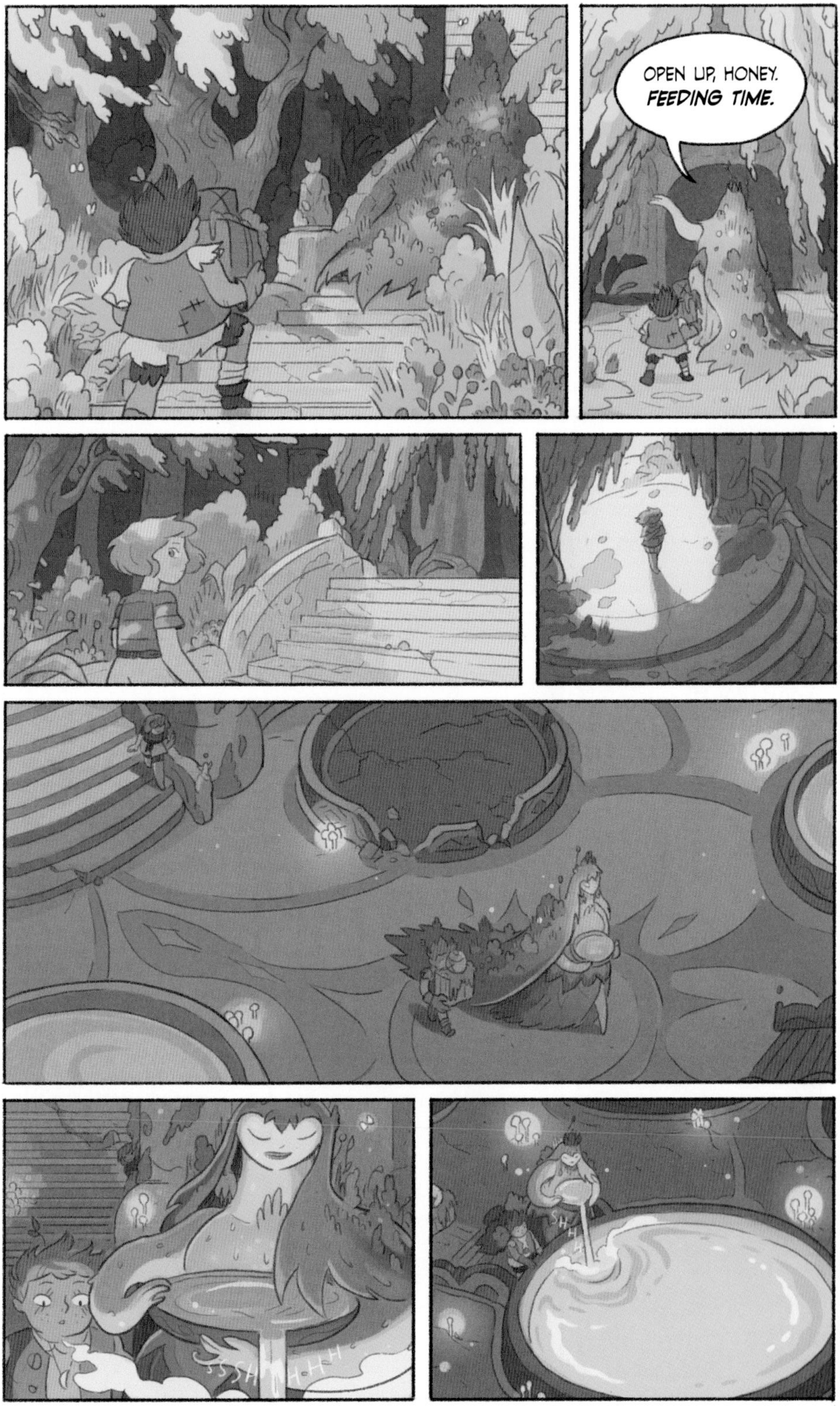
OPEN UP, HONEY.
FEEDING TIME.

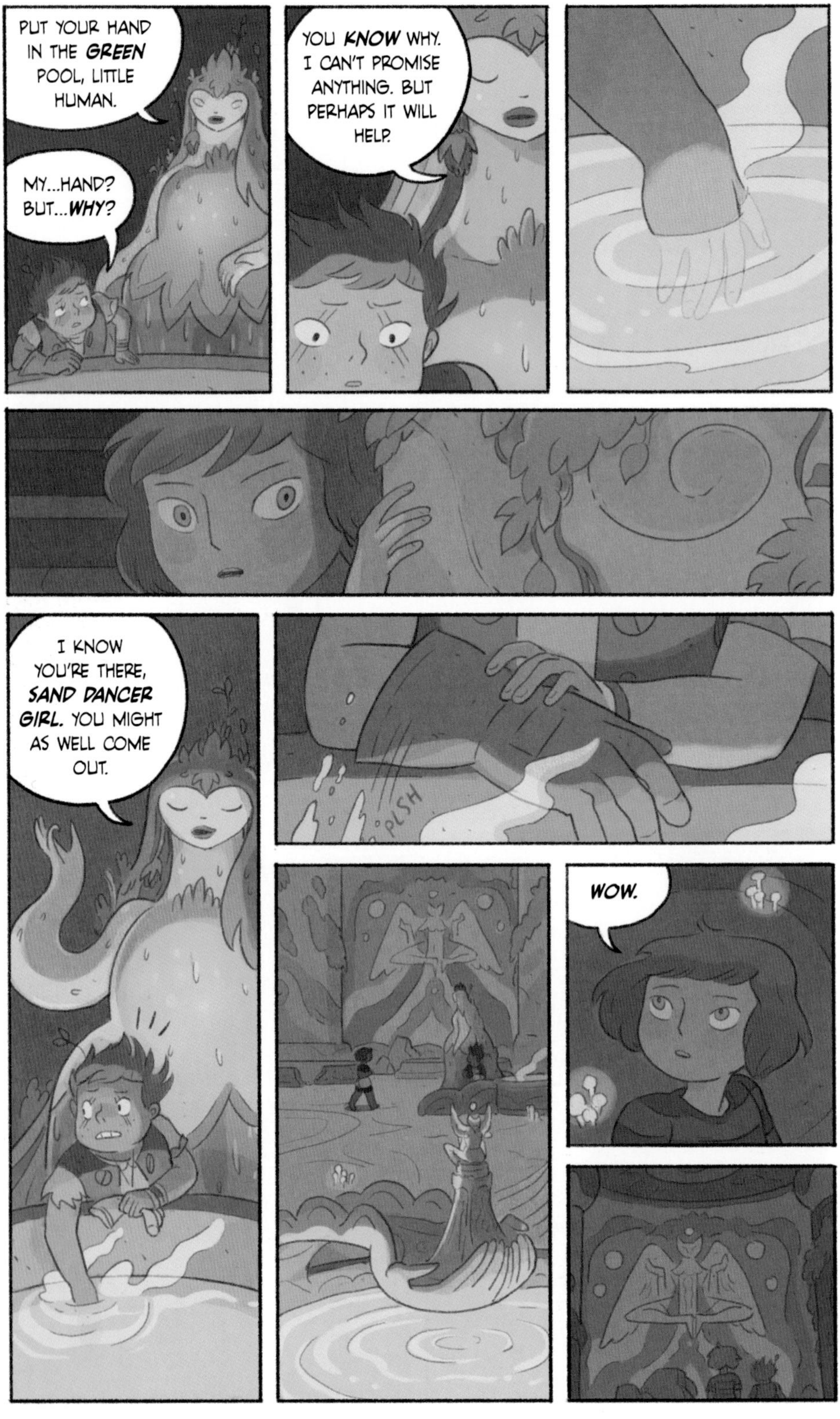
PUT YOUR HAND IN THE GREEN POOL, LITTLE HUMAN.
MY...HAND? BUT...WHY?
YOU KNOW WHY. I CAN'T PROMISE ANYTHING. BUT PERHAPS IT WILL HELP.
I KNOW YOU'RE THERE, SAND DANCER GIRL. YOU MIGHT AS WELL COME OUT.
PLSH
WOW.

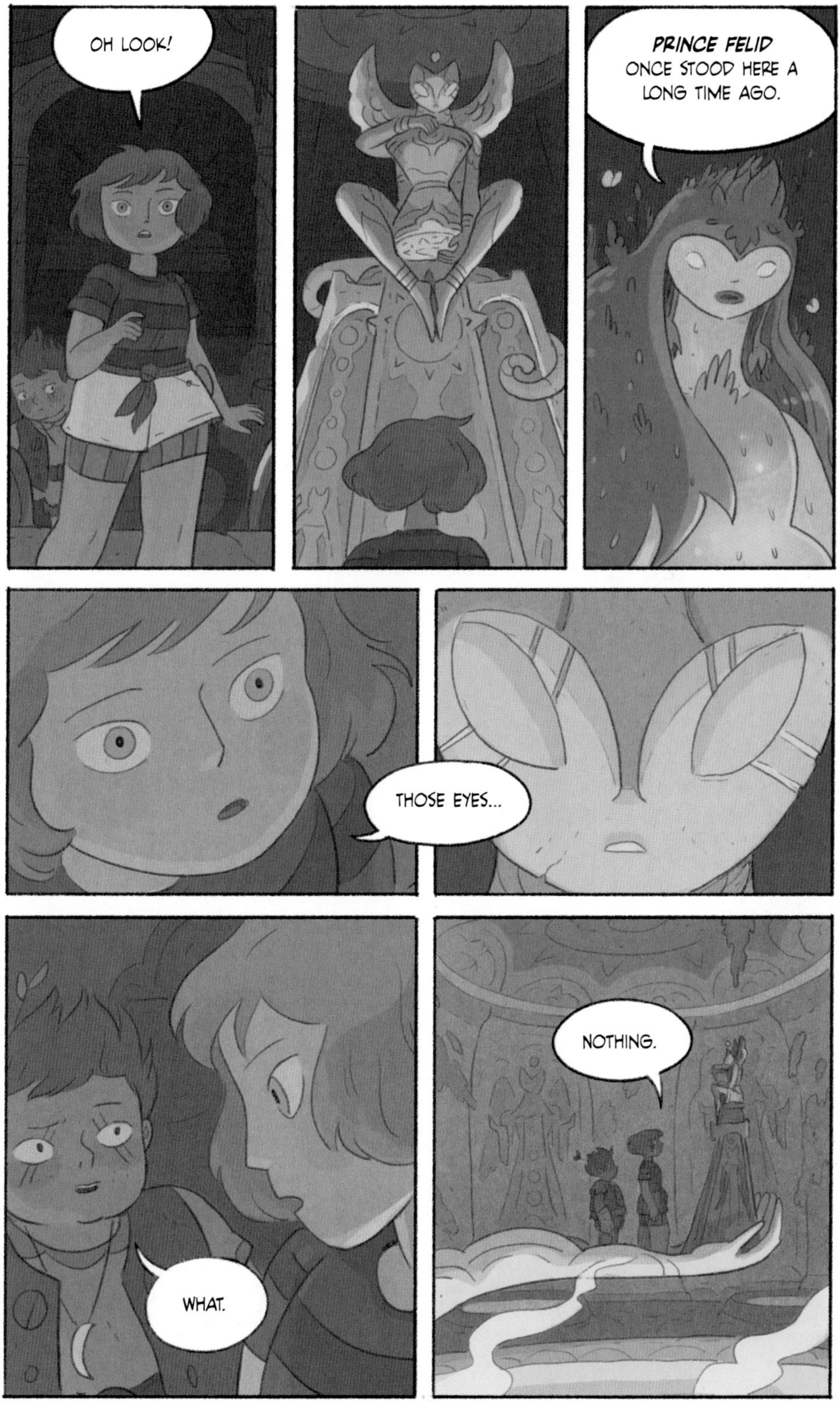
OH LOOK!
PRINCE FELID ONCE STOOD HERE A LONG TIME AGO.
THOSE EYES...
WHAT.
NOTHING.

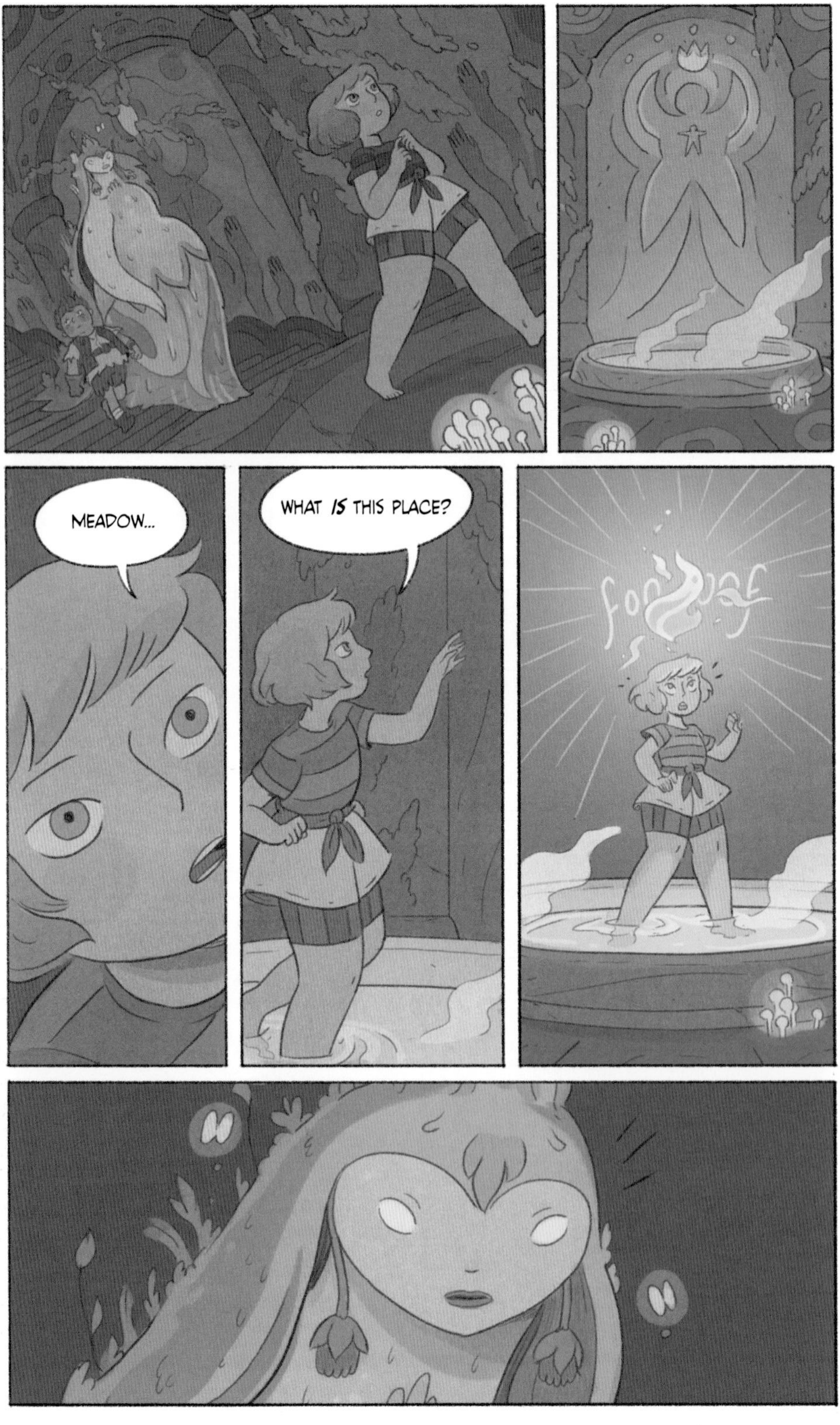
MEADOW...
WHAT *IS* THIS PLACE?

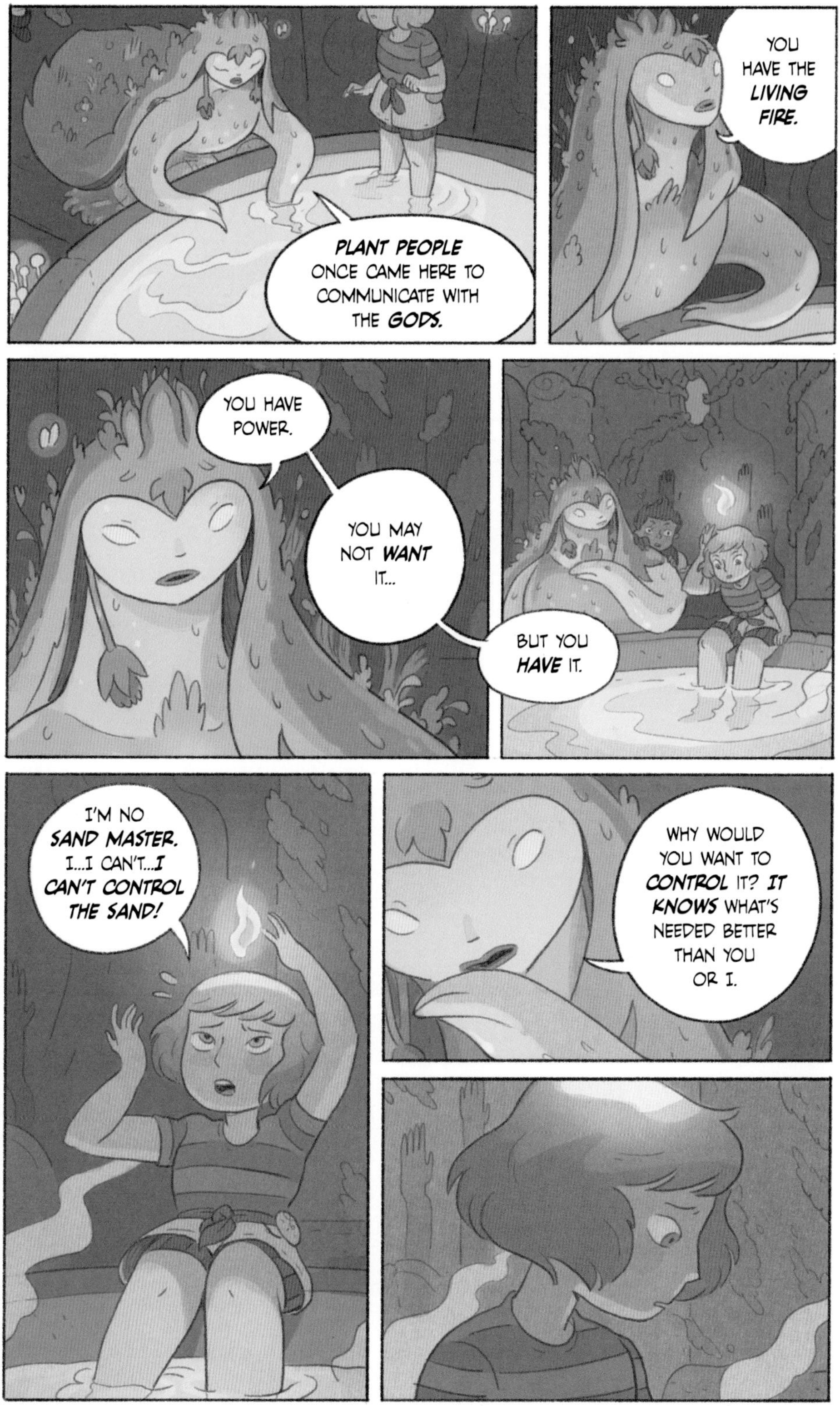
PLANT PEOPLE ONCE CAME HERE TO COMMUNICATE WITH THE GODS.
YOU HAVE THE LIVING FIRE.
YOU HAVE POWER.
YOU MAY NOT WANT IT...
BUT YOU HAVE IT.
I'M NO SAND MASTER. I...I CAN'T...I CAN'T CONTROL THE SAND!
WHY WOULD YOU WANT TO CONTROL IT? IT KNOWS WHAT'S NEEDED BETTER THAN YOU OR I.

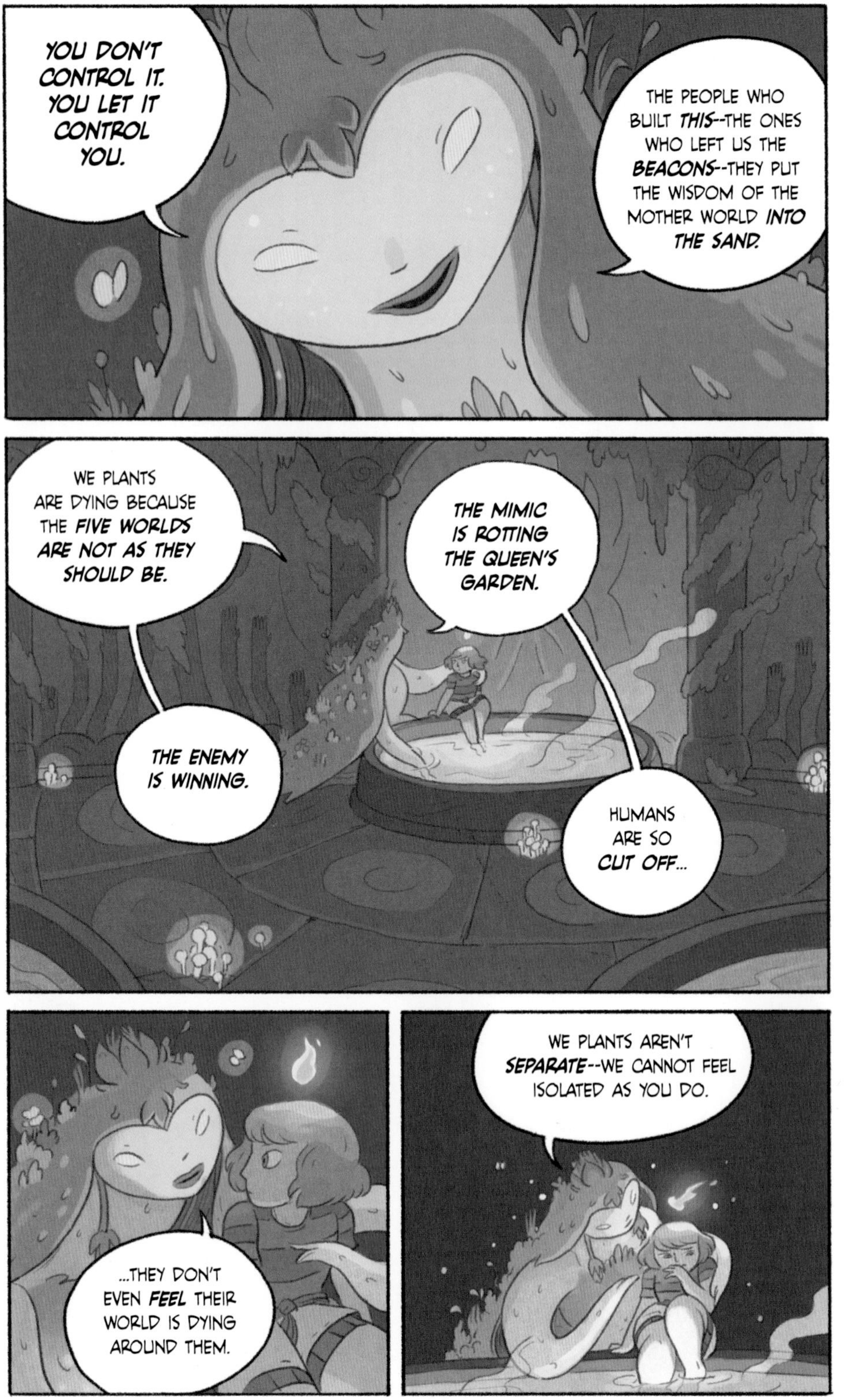
YOU DON'T CONTROL IT. YOU LET IT CONTROL YOU.
THE PEOPLE WHO BUILT THIS--THE ONES WHO LEFT US THE BEACONS--THEY PUT THE WISDOM OF THE MOTHER WORLD INTO THE SAND.
WE PLANTS ARE DYING BECAUSE THE FIVE WORLDS ARE NOT AS THEY SHOULD BE.
THE ENEMY IS WINNING.
THE MIMIC IS ROTTING THE QUEEN'S GARDEN.
HUMANS ARE SO CUT OFF...
...THEY DON'T EVEN FEEL THEIR WORLD IS DYING AROUND THEM.
WE PLANTS AREN'T SEPARATE--WE CANNOT FEEL ISOLATED AS YOU DO.

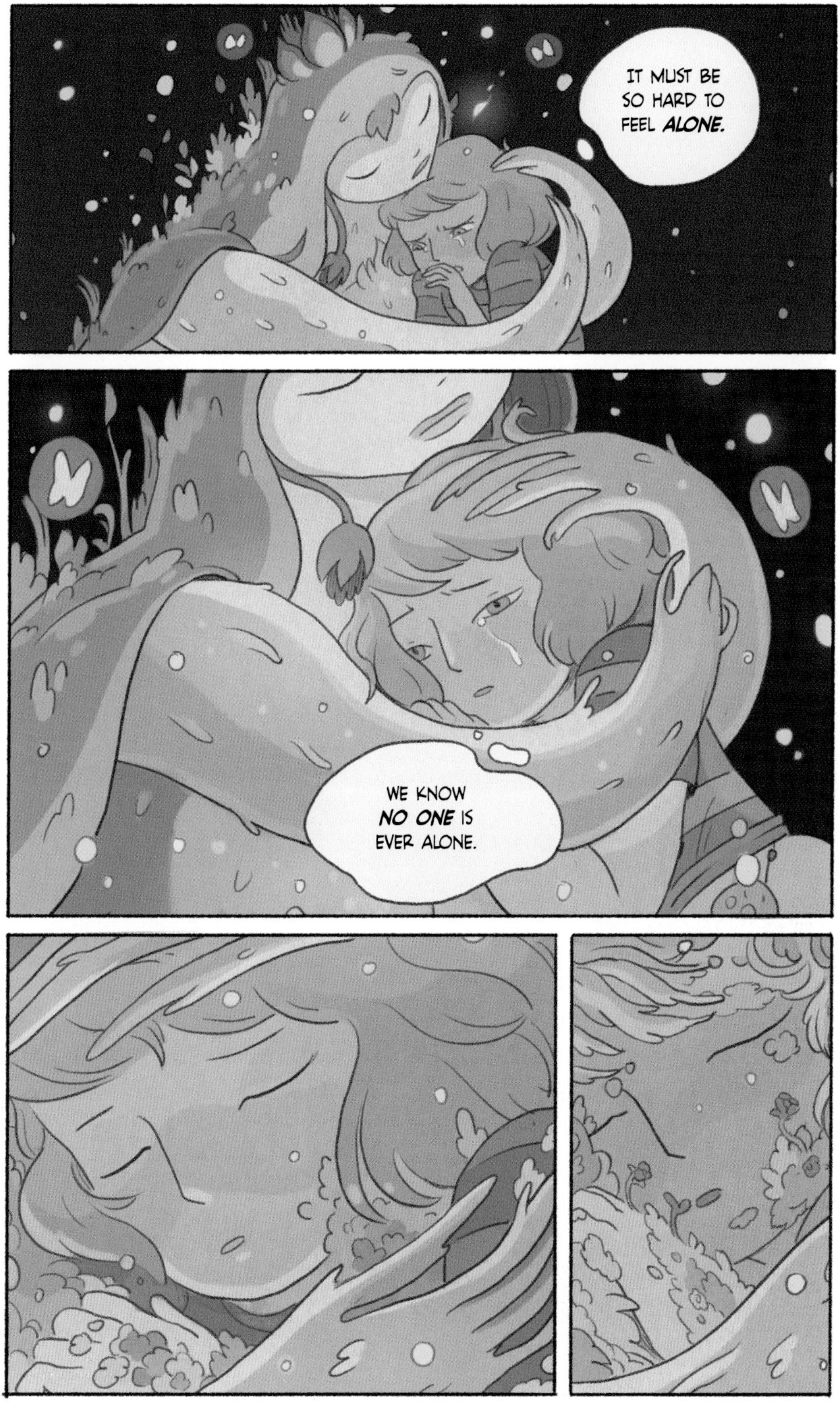
IT MUST BE SO HARD TO FEEL ALONE.
WE KNOW NO ONE IS EVER ALONE.

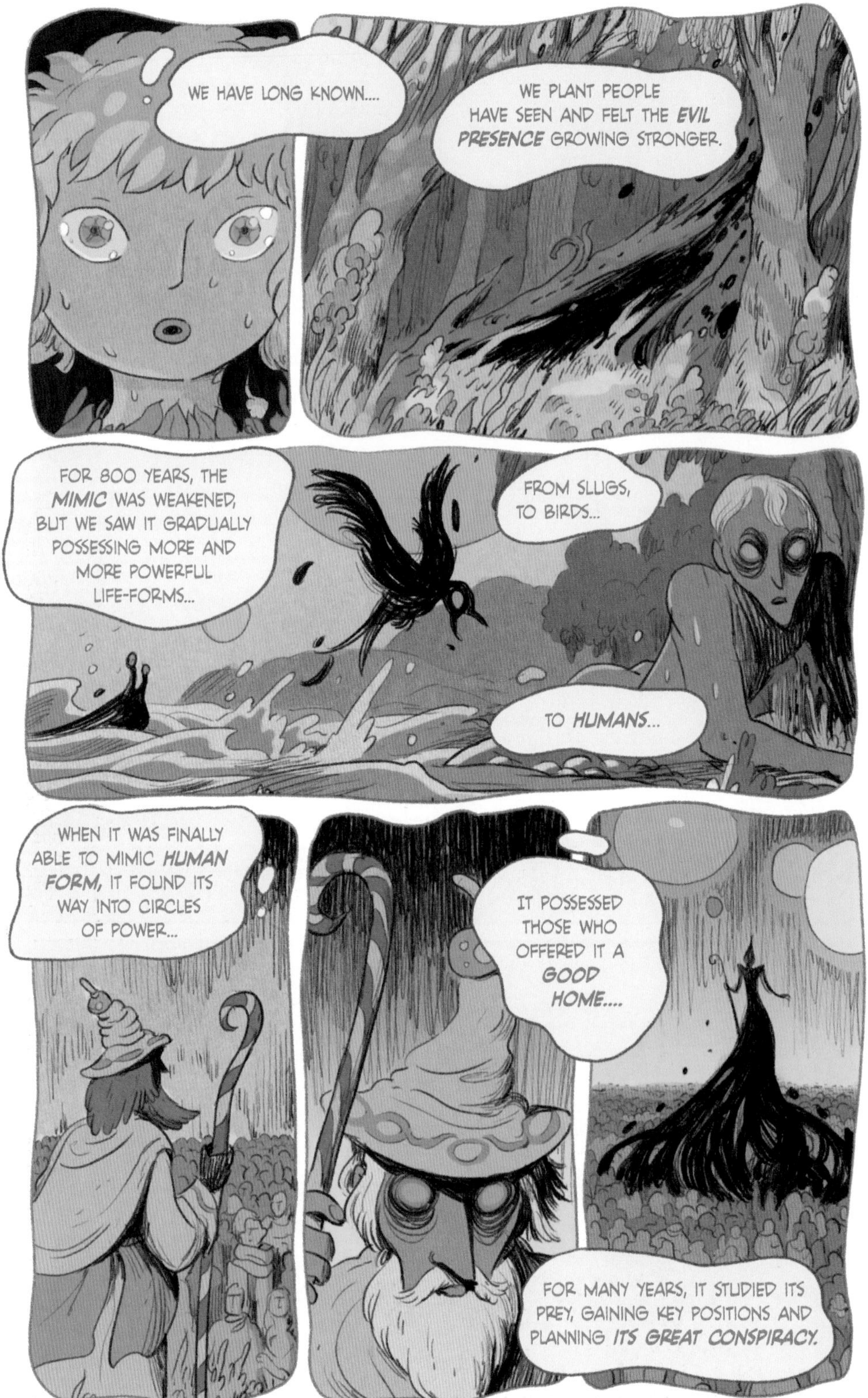
WE HAVE LONG KNOWN....
WE PLANT PEOPLE HAVE SEEN AND FELT THE *EVIL PRESENCE* GROWING STRONGER.
FOR 800 YEARS, THE *MIMIC* WAS WEAKENED, BUT WE SAW IT GRADUALLY POSSESSING MORE AND MORE POWERFUL LIFE-FORMS...
FROM SLUGS, TO BIRDS...
TO *HUMANS*...
WHEN IT WAS FINALLY ABLE TO MIMIC *HUMAN FORM,* IT FOUND ITS WAY INTO CIRCLES OF POWER...
IT POSSESSED THOSE WHO OFFERED IT A *GOOD HOME....*
FOR MANY YEARS, IT STUDIED ITS PREY, GAINING KEY POSITIONS AND PLANNING *ITS GREAT CONSPIRACY.*

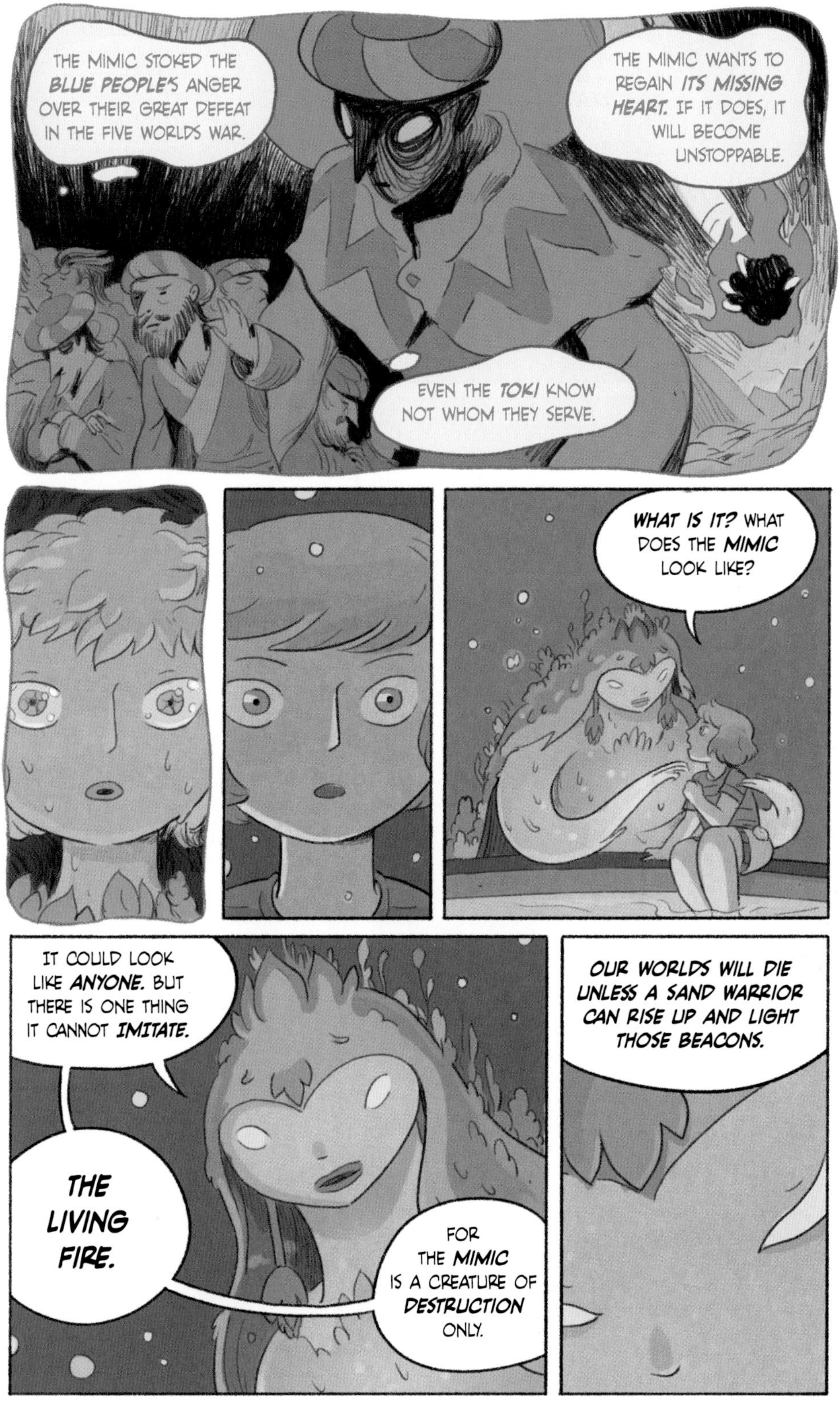

THE MIMIC STOKED THE BLUE PEOPLE'S ANGER OVER THEIR GREAT DEFEAT IN THE FIVE WORLDS WAR.
THE MIMIC WANTS TO REGAIN ITS MISSING HEART. IF IT DOES, IT WILL BECOME UNSTOPPABLE.
EVEN THE TOKI KNOW NOT WHOM THEY SERVE.
WHAT IS IT? WHAT DOES THE MIMIC LOOK LIKE?
IT COULD LOOK LIKE ANYONE. BUT THERE IS ONE THING IT CANNOT IMITATE.
THE LIVING FIRE.
FOR THE MIMIC IS A CREATURE OF DESTRUCTION ONLY.
OUR WORLDS WILL DIE UNLESS A SAND WARRIOR CAN RISE UP AND LIGHT THOSE BEACONS.

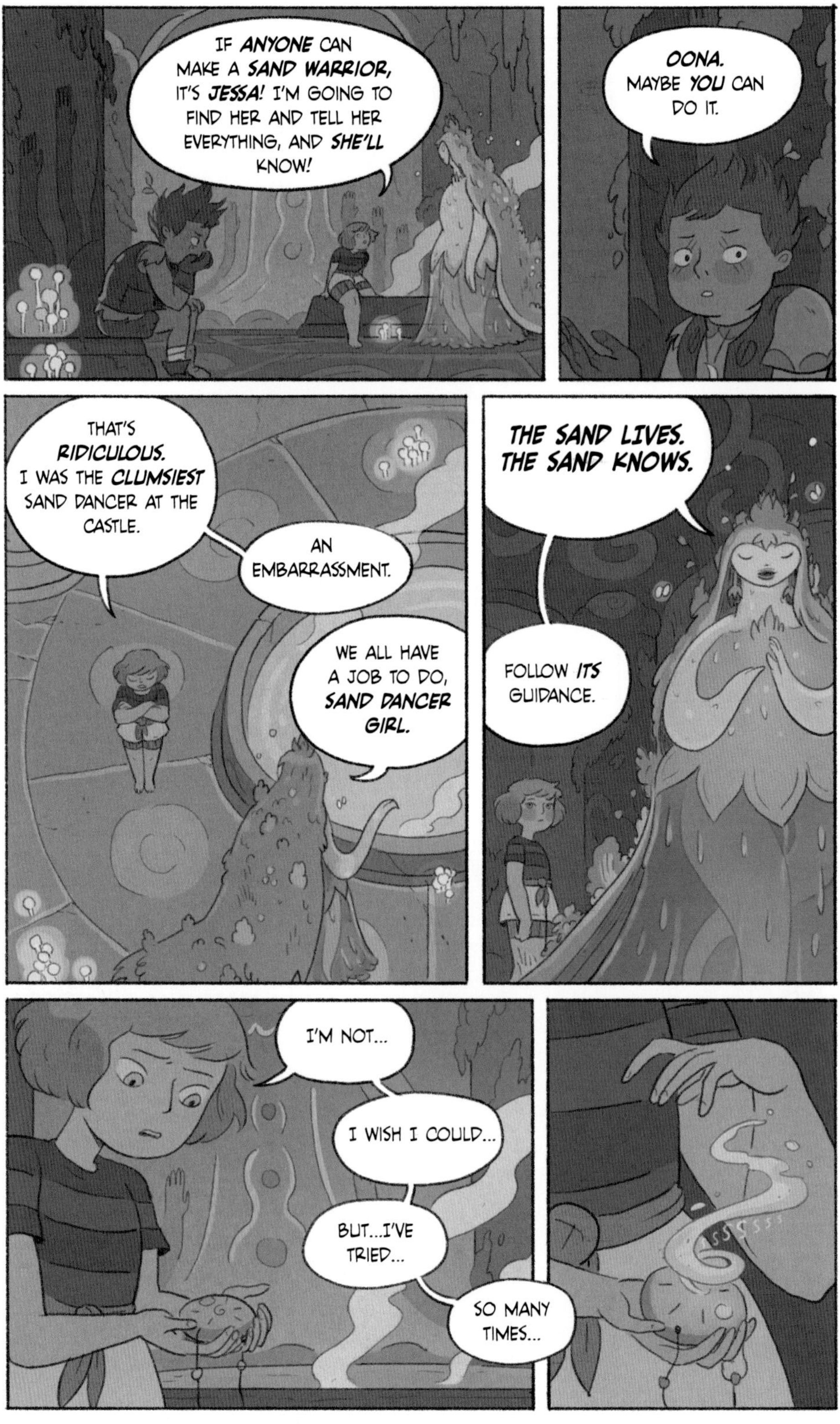
IF ANYONE CAN MAKE A SAND WARRIOR, IT'S JESSA! I'M GOING TO FIND HER AND TELL HER EVERYTHING, AND SHE'LL KNOW!
OONA. MAYBE YOU CAN DO IT.
THAT'S RIDICULOUS. I WAS THE CLUMSIEST SAND DANCER AT THE CASTLE.
AN EMBARRASSMENT.
WE ALL HAVE A JOB TO DO, SAND DANCER GIRL.
THE SAND LIVES. THE SAND KNOWS.
FOLLOW ITS GUIDANCE.
I'M NOT...
I WISH I COULD...
BUT...I'VE TRIED...
SO MANY TIMES...
SSSSSS

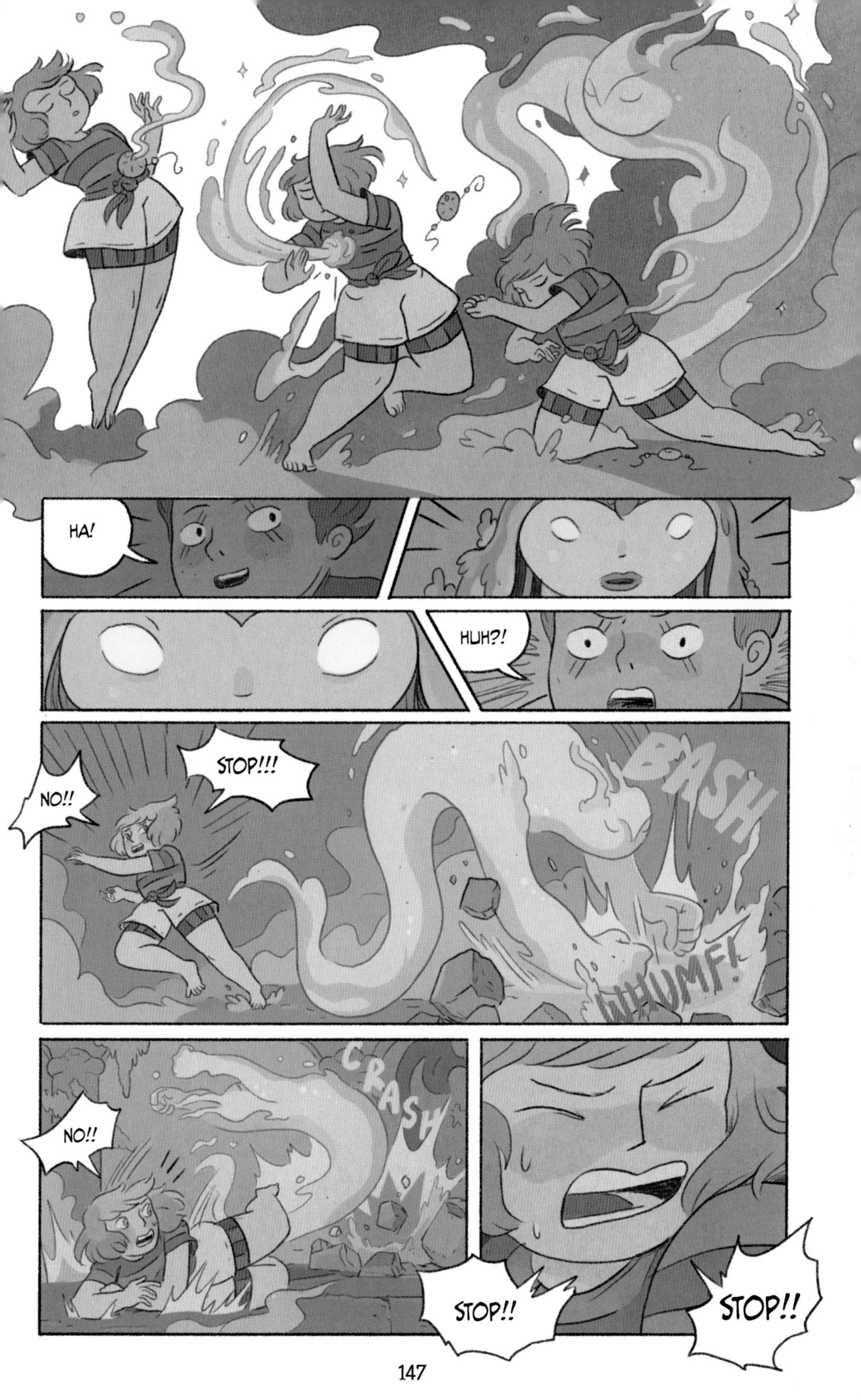
HA!
HUH?!
STOP!!!
NO!!
BASH
WHUMF!
CRASH
NO!!
STOP!!
STOP!!

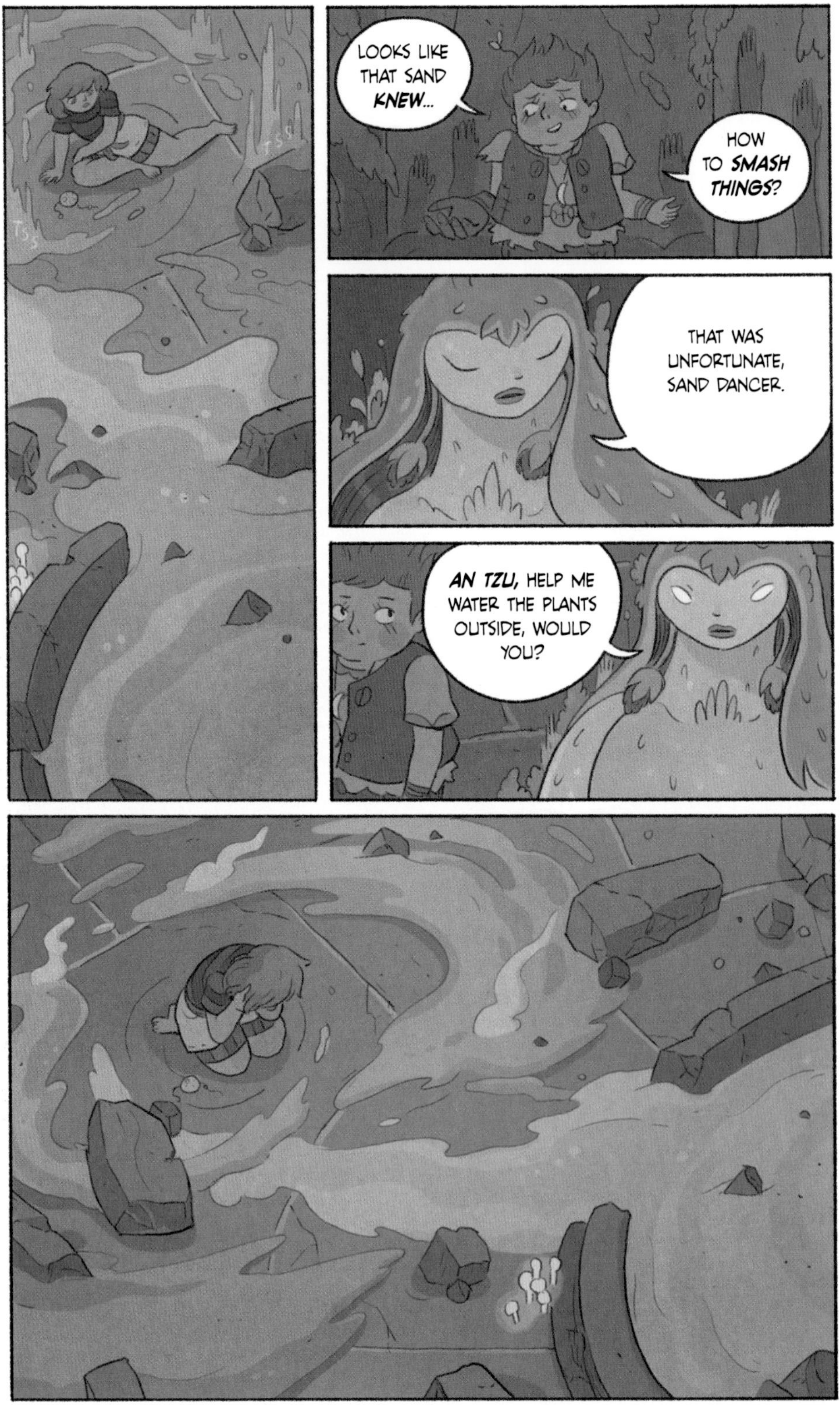
LOOKS LIKE THAT SAND *KNEW*...
HOW TO *SMASH THINGS?*
THAT WAS UNFORTUNATE, SAND DANCER.
AN TZU, HELP ME WATER THE PLANTS OUTSIDE, WOULD YOU?

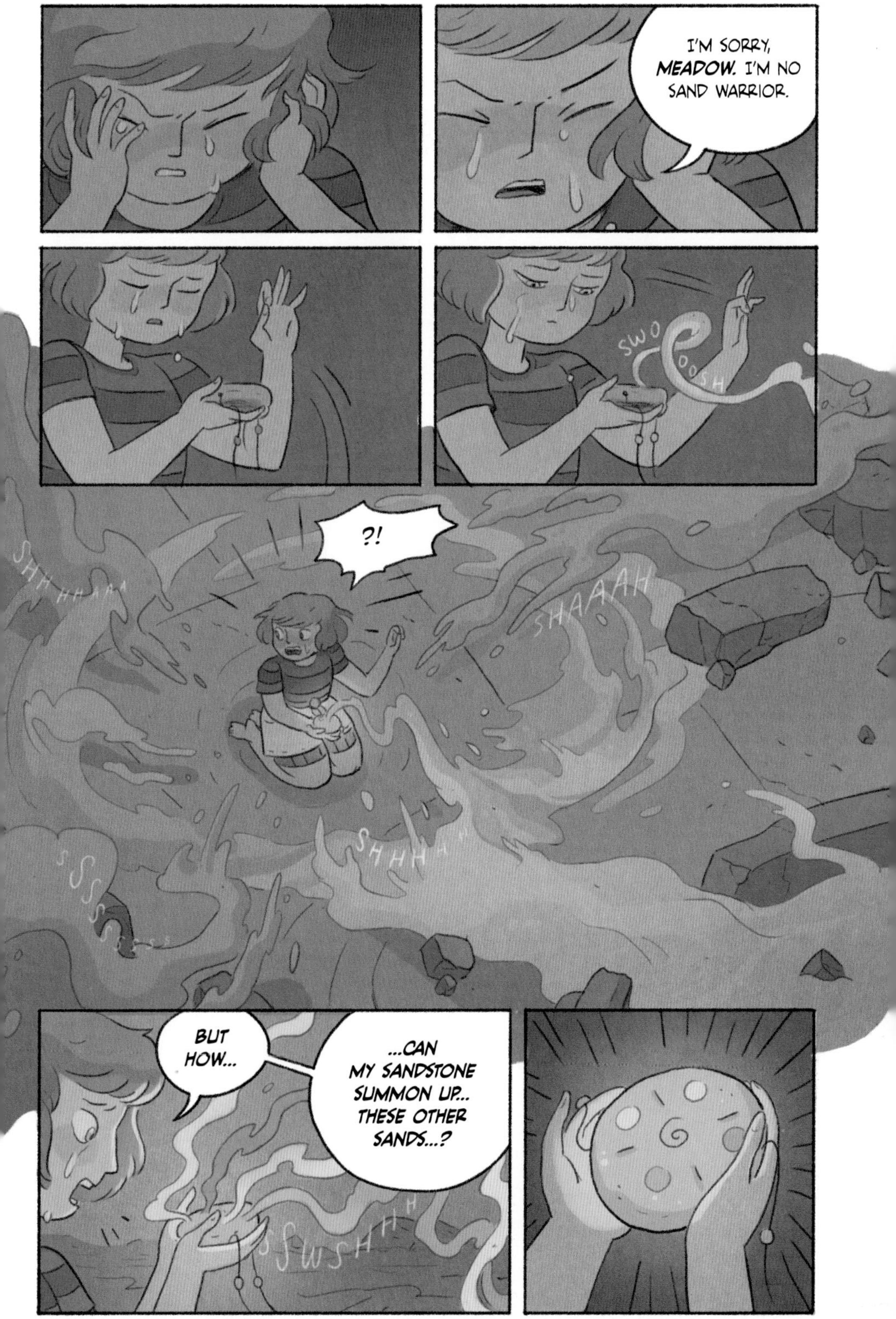
I'M SORRY, MEADOW. I'M NO SAND WARRIOR.
SWOOOSH
?!
SHHHHAAA
SHAAAH
SHHHH
SSSS
BUT HOW...
...CAN MY SANDSTONE SUMMON UP... THESE OTHER SANDS...?
SSWSHHH

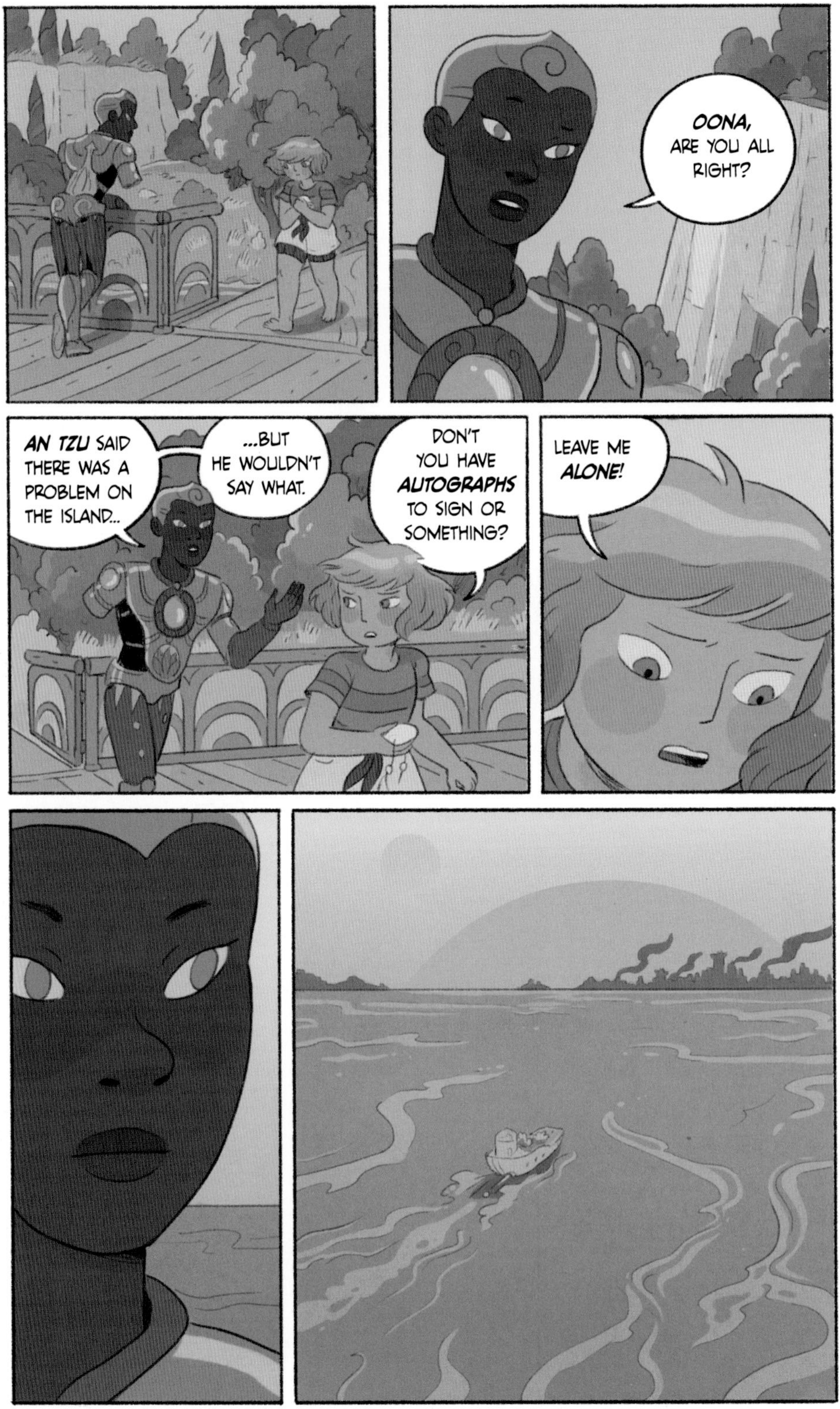
OONA, ARE YOU ALL RIGHT?
AN TZU SAID THERE WAS A PROBLEM ON THE ISLAND...
...BUT HE WOULDN'T SAY WHAT.
DON'T YOU HAVE AUTOGRAPHS TO SIGN OR SOMETHING?
LEAVE ME ALONE!

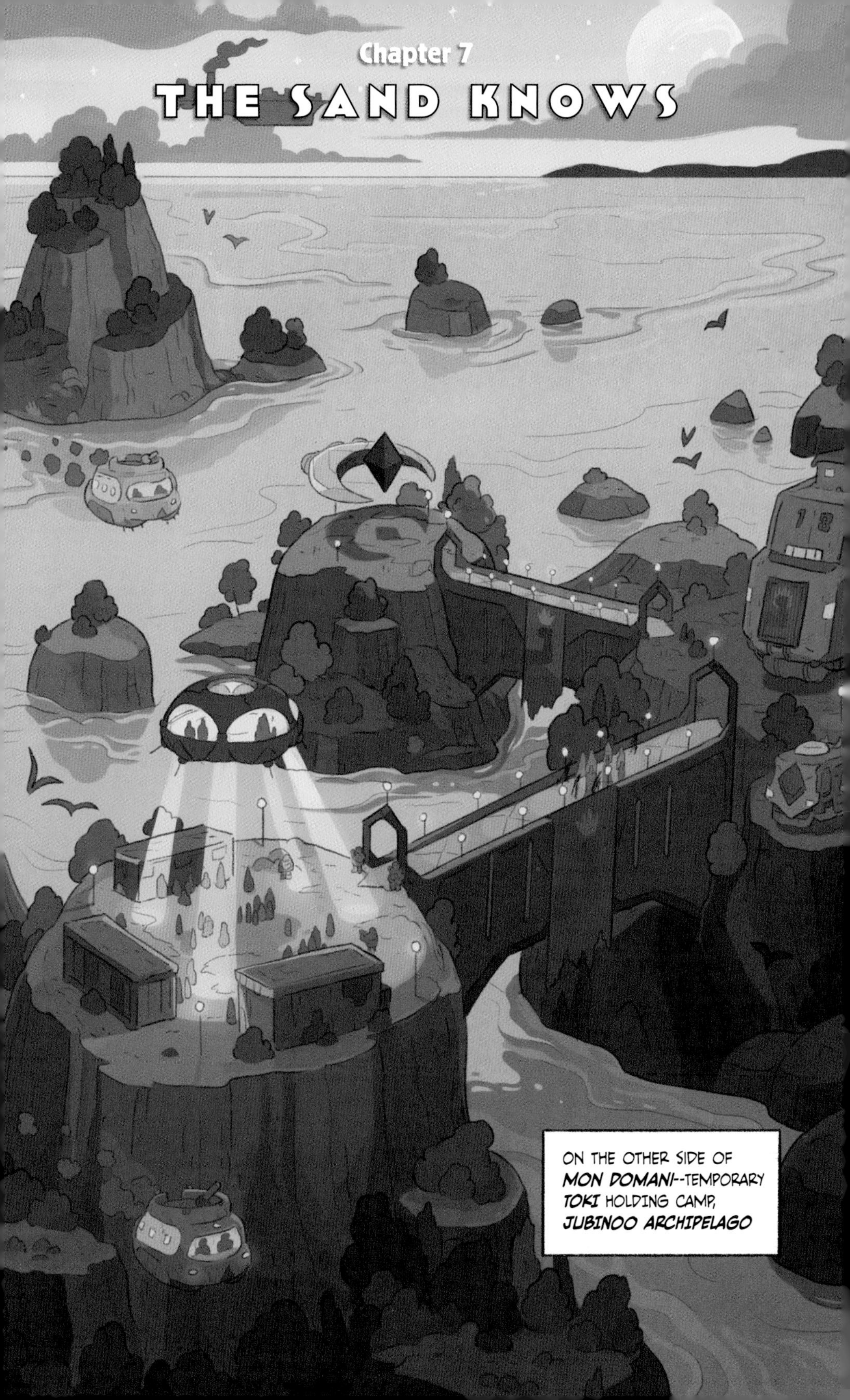

Chapter 7
THE SAND KNOWS
ON THE OTHER SIDE OF MON DOMANI--TEMPORARY TOKI HOLDING CAMP, JUBINOO ARCHIPELAGO

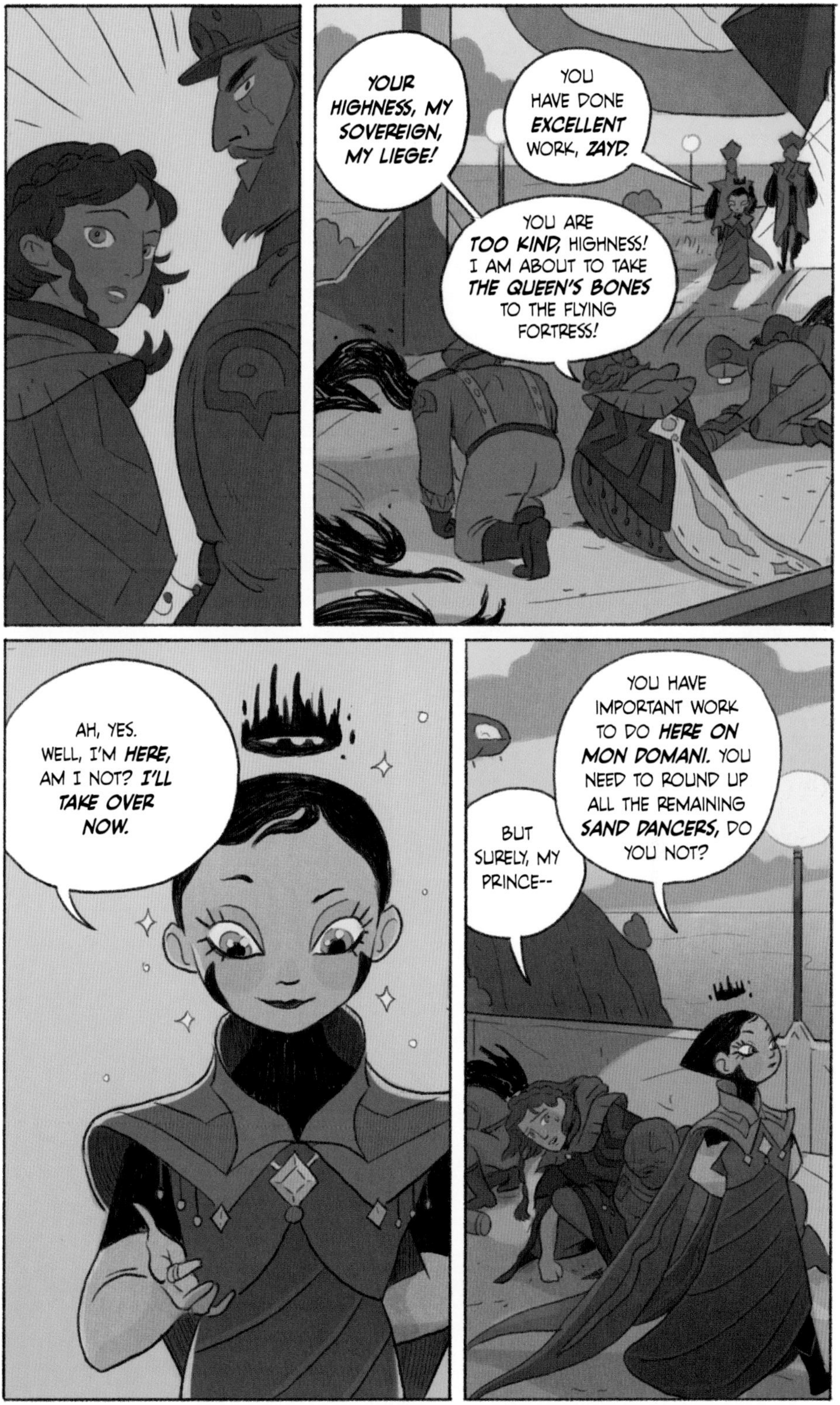
YOUR HIGHNESS, MY SOVEREIGN, MY LIEGE!
YOU HAVE DONE EXCELLENT WORK, ZAYD.
YOU ARE TOO KIND, HIGHNESS! I AM ABOUT TO TAKE THE QUEEN'S BONES TO THE FLYING FORTRESS!
AH, YES. WELL, I'M HERE, AM I NOT? I'LL TAKE OVER NOW.
BUT SURELY, MY PRINCE--
YOU HAVE IMPORTANT WORK TO DO HERE ON MON DOMANI. YOU NEED TO ROUND UP ALL THE REMAINING SAND DANCERS, DO YOU NOT?

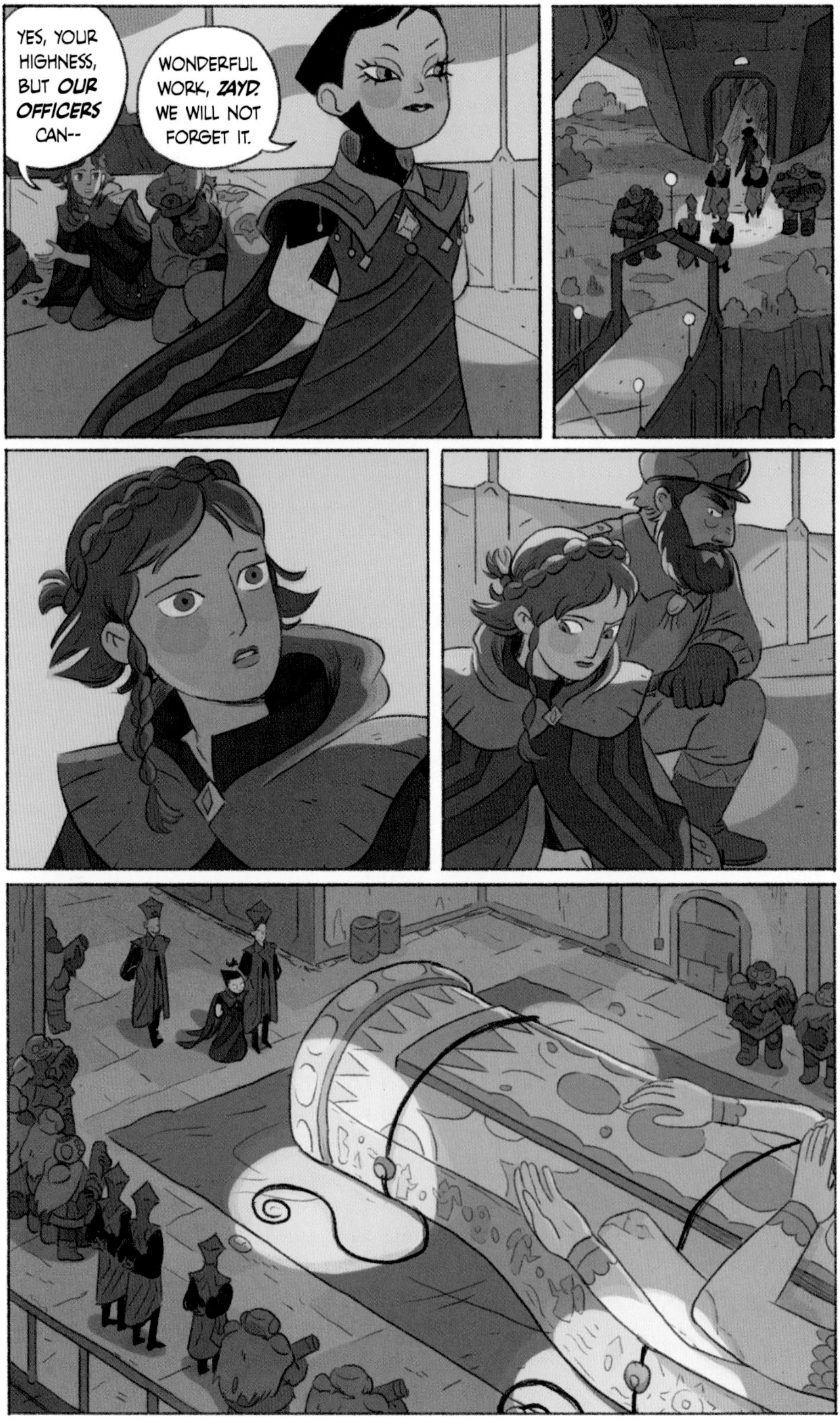
YES, YOUR HIGHNESS, BUT OUR OFFICERS CAN--
WONDERFUL WORK, ZAYD. WE WILL NOT FORGET IT.

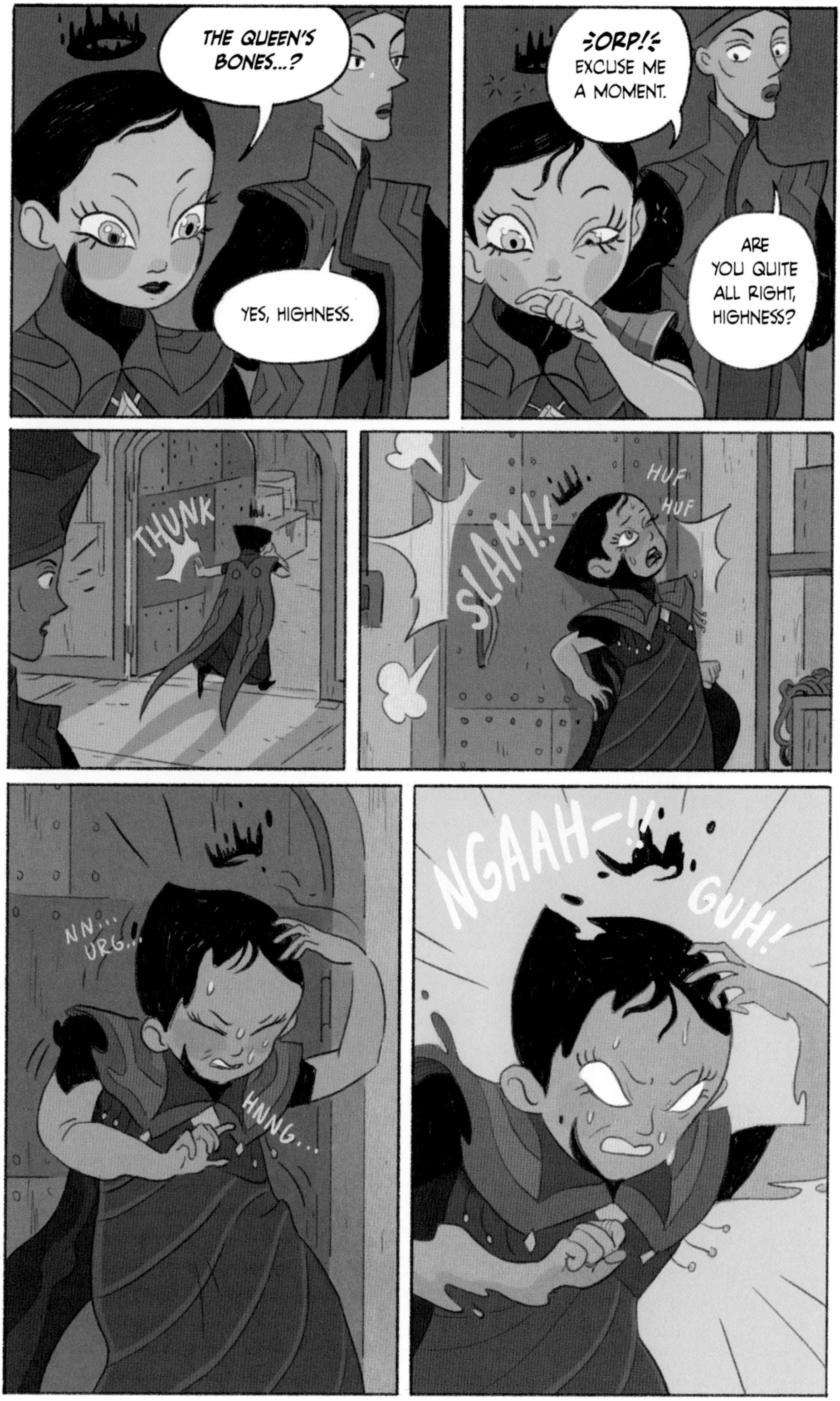
THE QUEEN'S BONES...?
YES, HIGHNESS.
ORP!
EXCUSE ME A MOMENT.
ARE YOU QUITE ALL RIGHT, HIGHNESS?
THUNK
SLAM!!
HUF HUF
NN... URG...
HNNG...
NGAAH-!!
GUH!

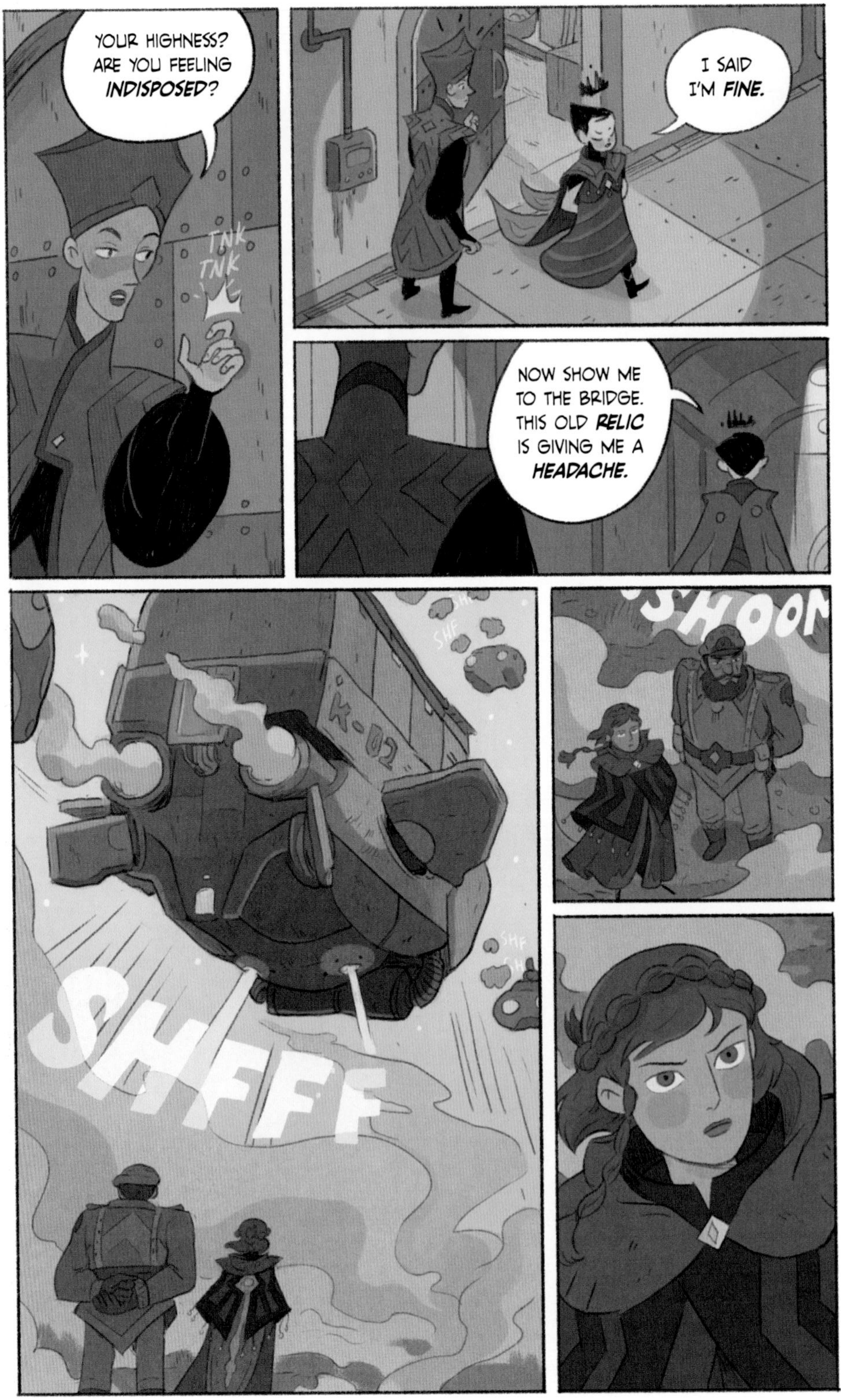
YOUR HIGHNESS? ARE YOU FEELING INDISPOSED?
TNK TNK
I SAID I'M FINE.
NOW SHOW ME TO THE BRIDGE. THIS OLD RELIC IS GIVING ME A HEADACHE.
K-02
SHF
SHFFF
SHOOM

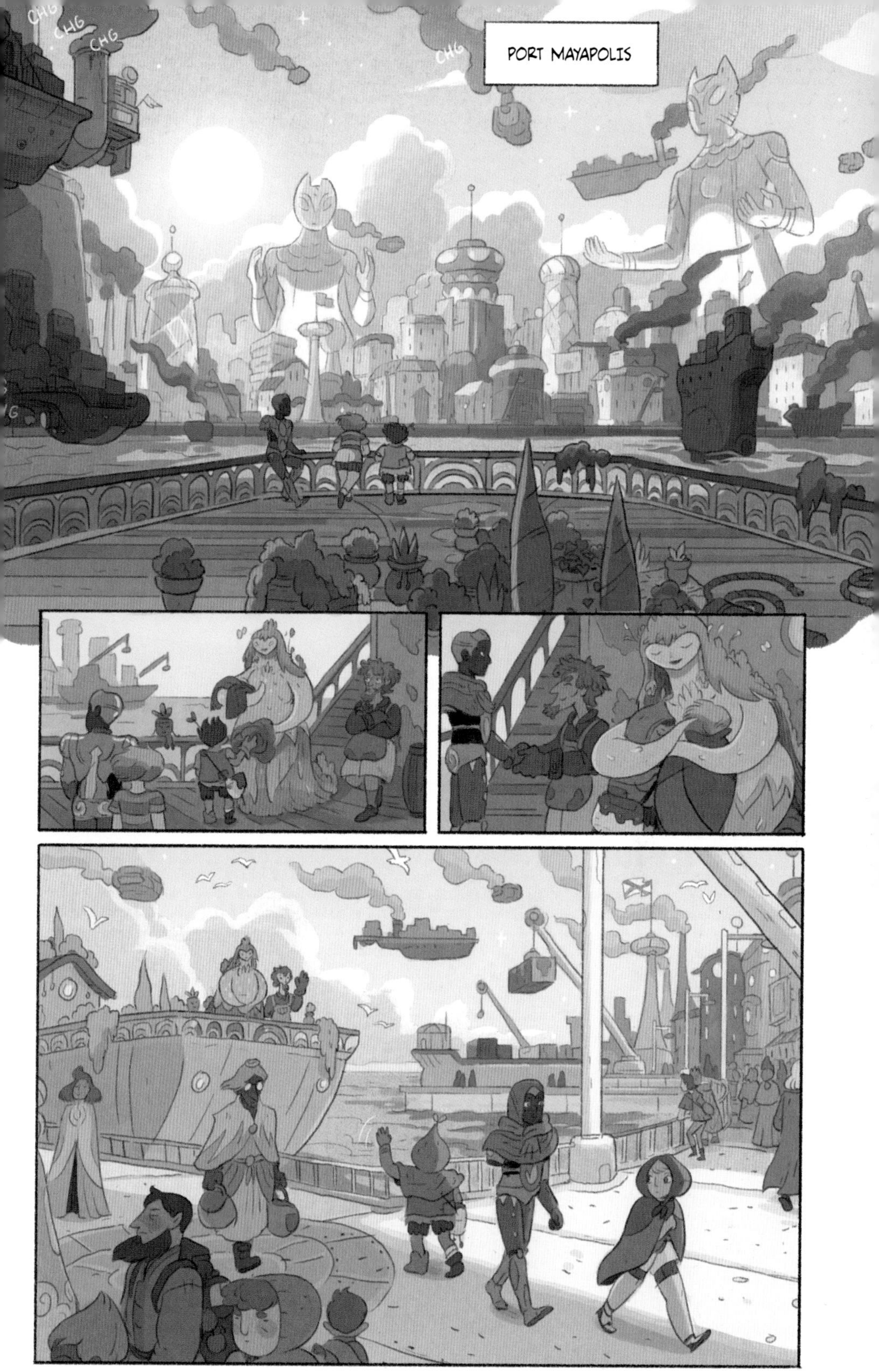
PORT MAYAPOLIS
CHG
CHG
CHG
CHG

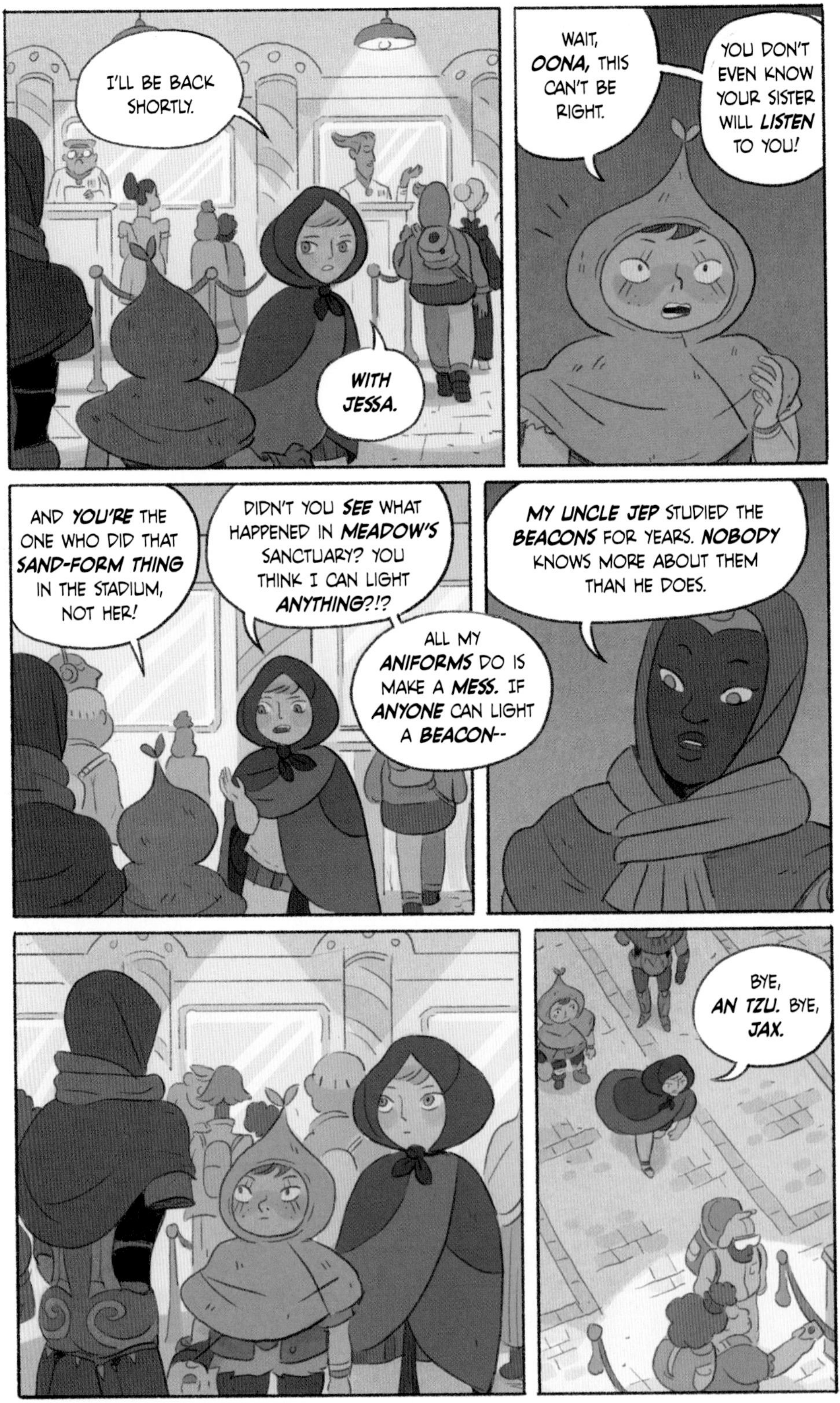
I'LL BE BACK SHORTLY.
WITH JESSA.
WAIT, OONA, THIS CAN'T BE RIGHT.
YOU DON'T EVEN KNOW YOUR SISTER WILL LISTEN TO YOU!
AND YOU'RE THE ONE WHO DID THAT SAND-FORM THING IN THE STADIUM, NOT HER!
DIDN'T YOU SEE WHAT HAPPENED IN MEADOW'S SANCTUARY? YOU THINK I CAN LIGHT ANYTHING?!?
ALL MY ANIFORMS DO IS MAKE A MESS. IF ANYONE CAN LIGHT A BEACON--
MY UNCLE JEP STUDIED THE BEACONS FOR YEARS. NOBODY KNOWS MORE ABOUT THEM THAN HE DOES.
BYE, AN TZU. BYE, JAX.

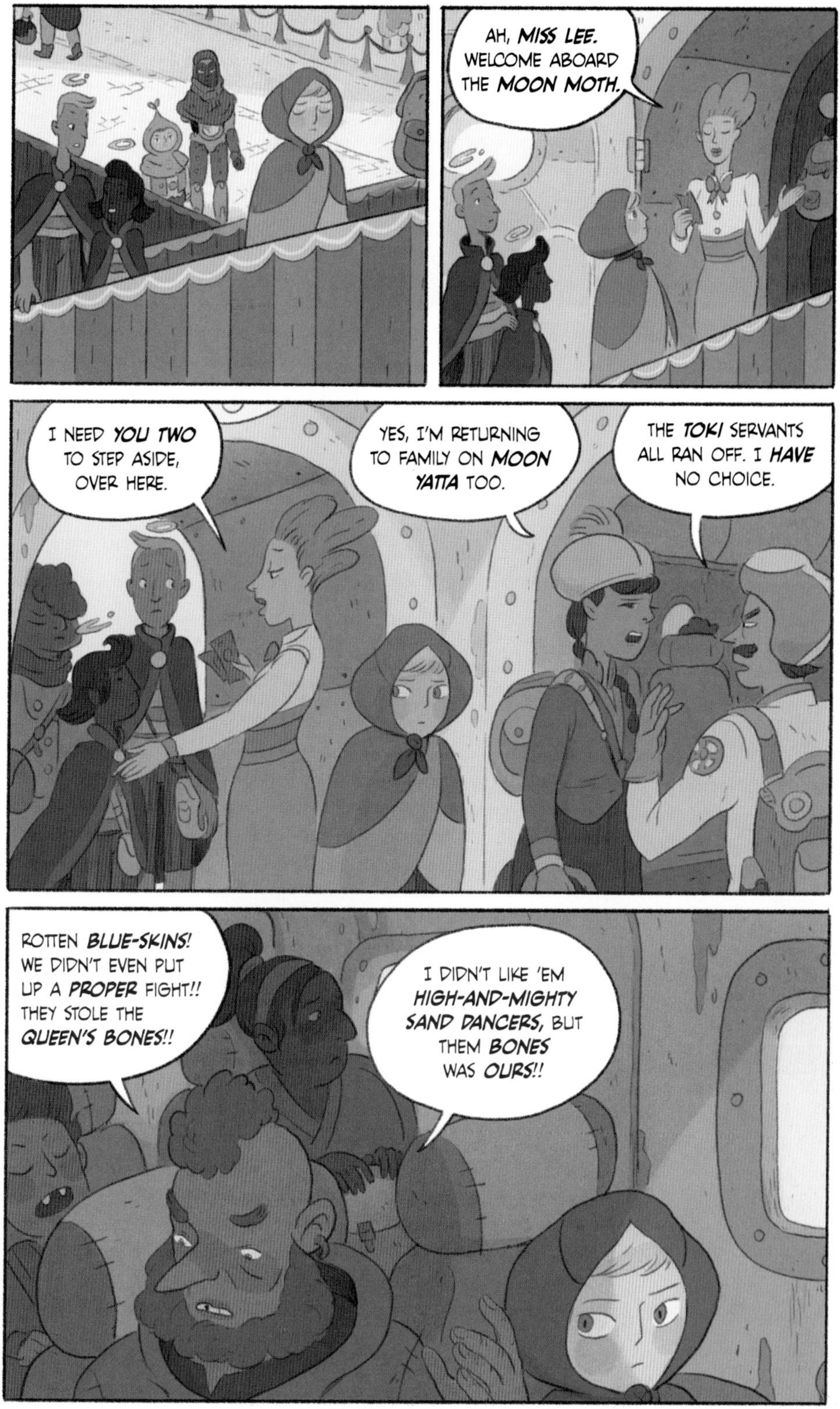
AH, MISS LEE. WELCOME ABOARD THE MOON MOTH.
I NEED YOU TWO TO STEP ASIDE, OVER HERE.
YES, I'M RETURNING TO FAMILY ON MOON YATTA TOO.
THE TOKI SERVANTS ALL RAN OFF. I HAVE NO CHOICE.
ROTTEN BLUE-SKINS! WE DIDN'T EVEN PUT UP A PROPER FIGHT!! THEY STOLE THE QUEEN'S BONES!!
I DIDN'T LIKE 'EM HIGH-AND-MIGHTY SAND DANCERS, BUT THEM BONES WAS OURS!!

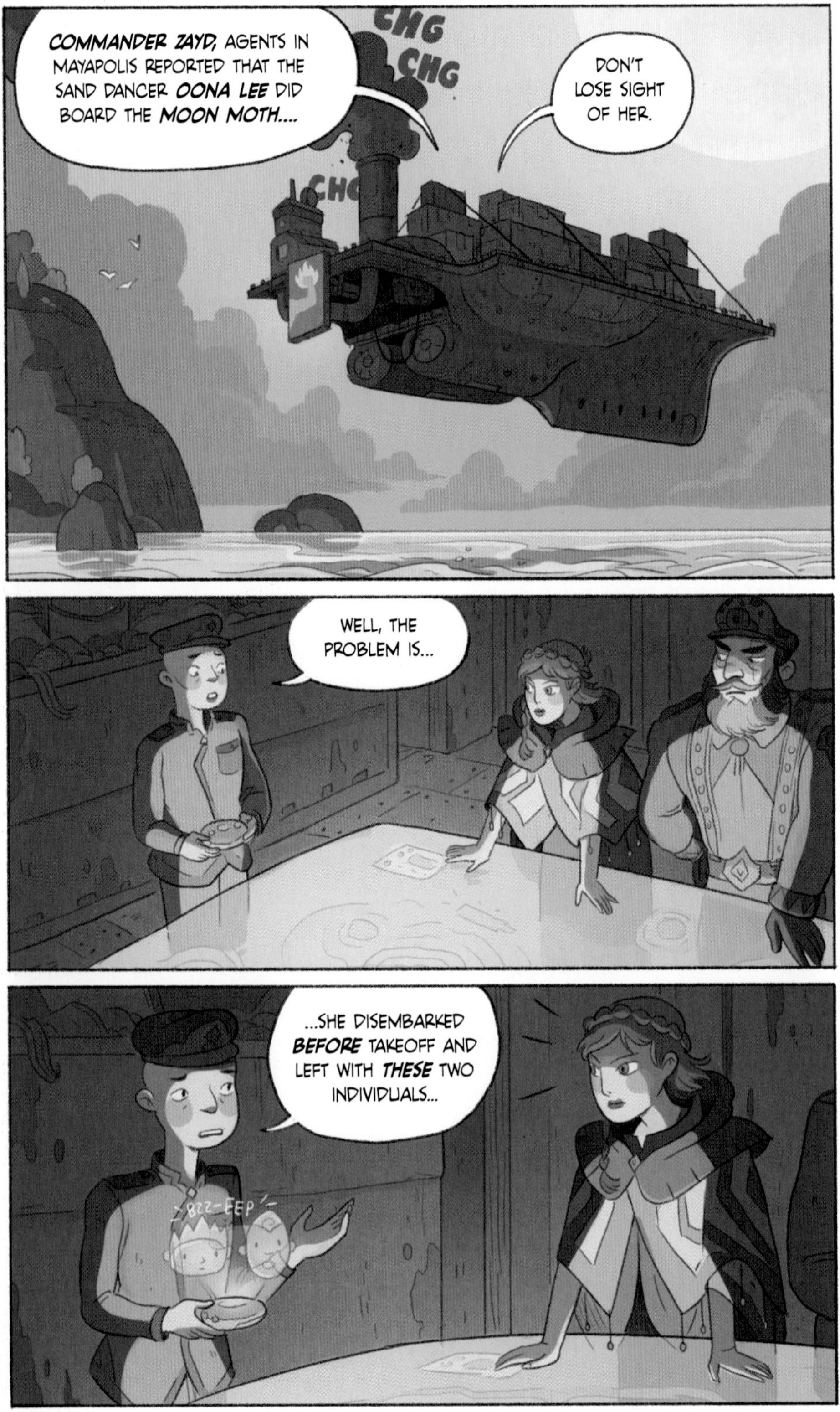
COMMANDER ZAYD, AGENTS IN MAYAPOLIS REPORTED THAT THE SAND DANCER OONA LEE DID BOARD THE MOON MOTH....
CHG
CHG
CHG
DON'T LOSE SIGHT OF HER.
WELL, THE PROBLEM IS...
...SHE DISEMBARKED BEFORE TAKEOFF AND LEFT WITH THESE TWO INDIVIDUALS...
BZZ-EEP

Chapter 8

JED'S NATURAL BOY

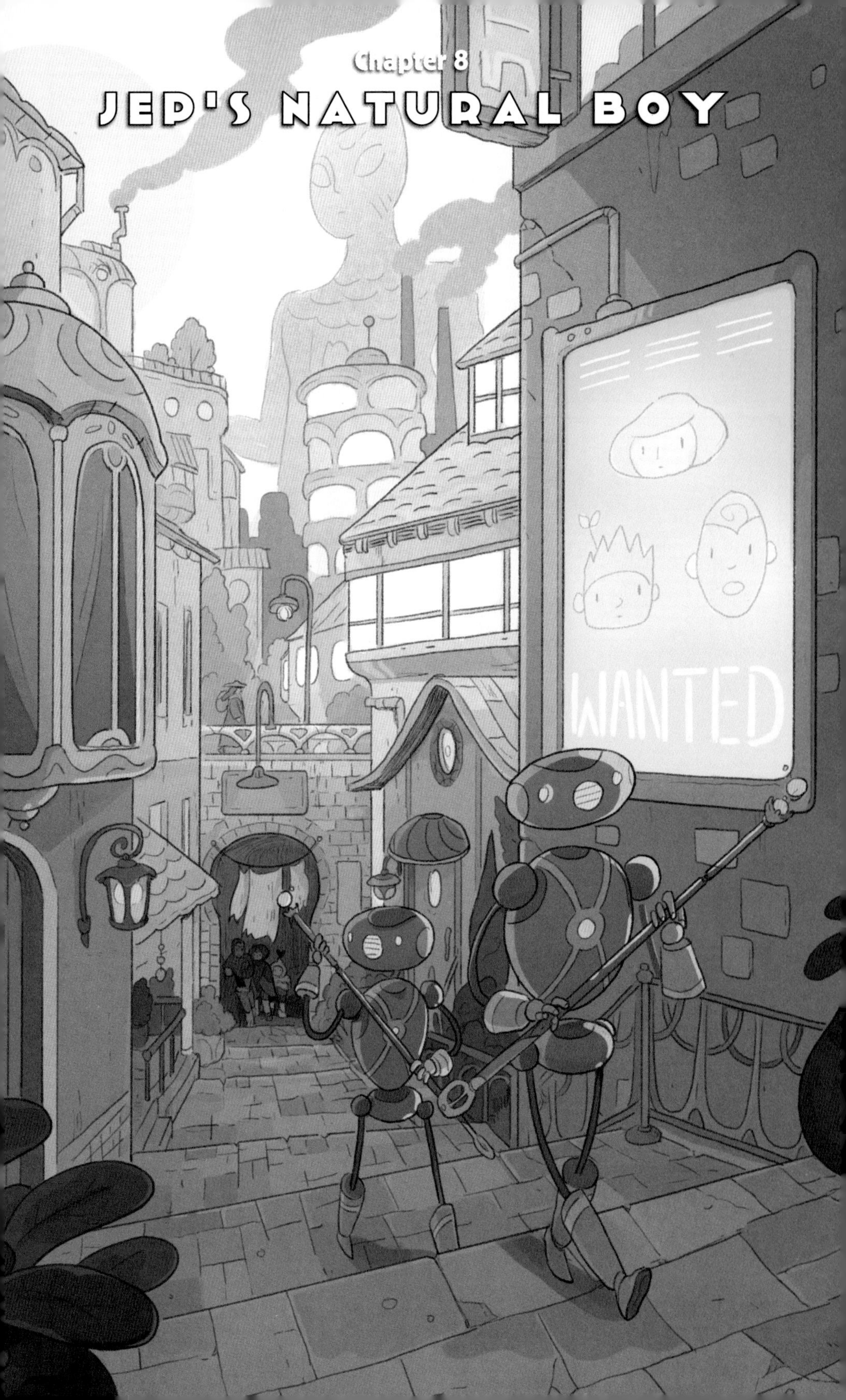
WANTED

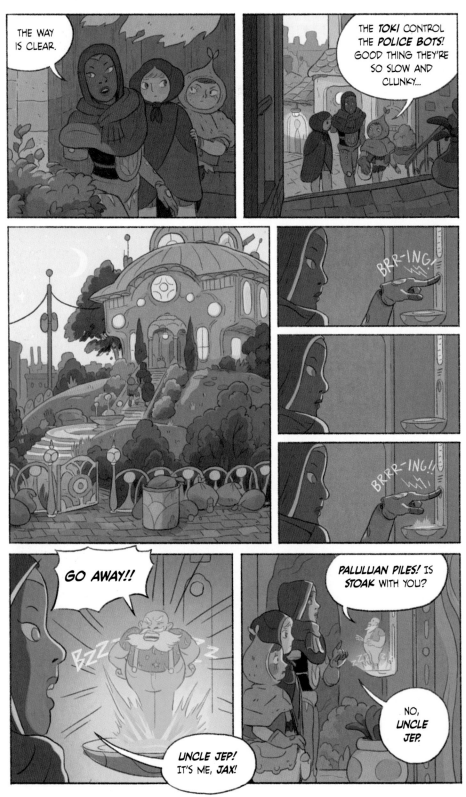

173

IT'S AN *ASTONISHING* DESIGN. WHOEVER THOSE *FELID GODS* WERE, THEY CLEARLY KNEW ABOUT TURNING *MOONS* INTO *PLANETS* AND *PLANETS* INTO *SUNS!*

THE BEACONS WERE MEANT TO *SPEED UP* OR *SLOW DOWN* THE GROWTH OF *ENTIRE WORLDS!* CAN YOU *IMAGINE?* ONLY THEY'VE BEEN *OFF* FOR FAR TOO LONG!

BUT *WHY?*

SO MANY *GREAT SAND DANCERS* HAVE *TRIED* TO LIGHT THEM.

THAT'S WHAT'S GOING TO LIGHT THE *BEACON*, ISN'T IT?

MAYBE THOSE SAND DANCERS WERE MISSING THE *REAL KEY*.

THE LIVING FIRE.

YES! THE *OVERHEATING* OF THE FIVE WORLDS CAN BE REVERSED *AT LAST!*

YOU'RE GOING TO NEED HELP. LET'S GO TO MY LAB.

BUT OUR *FIVE DAYS* ARE ALMOST OVER!

Chapter 9
ALTERATIONS

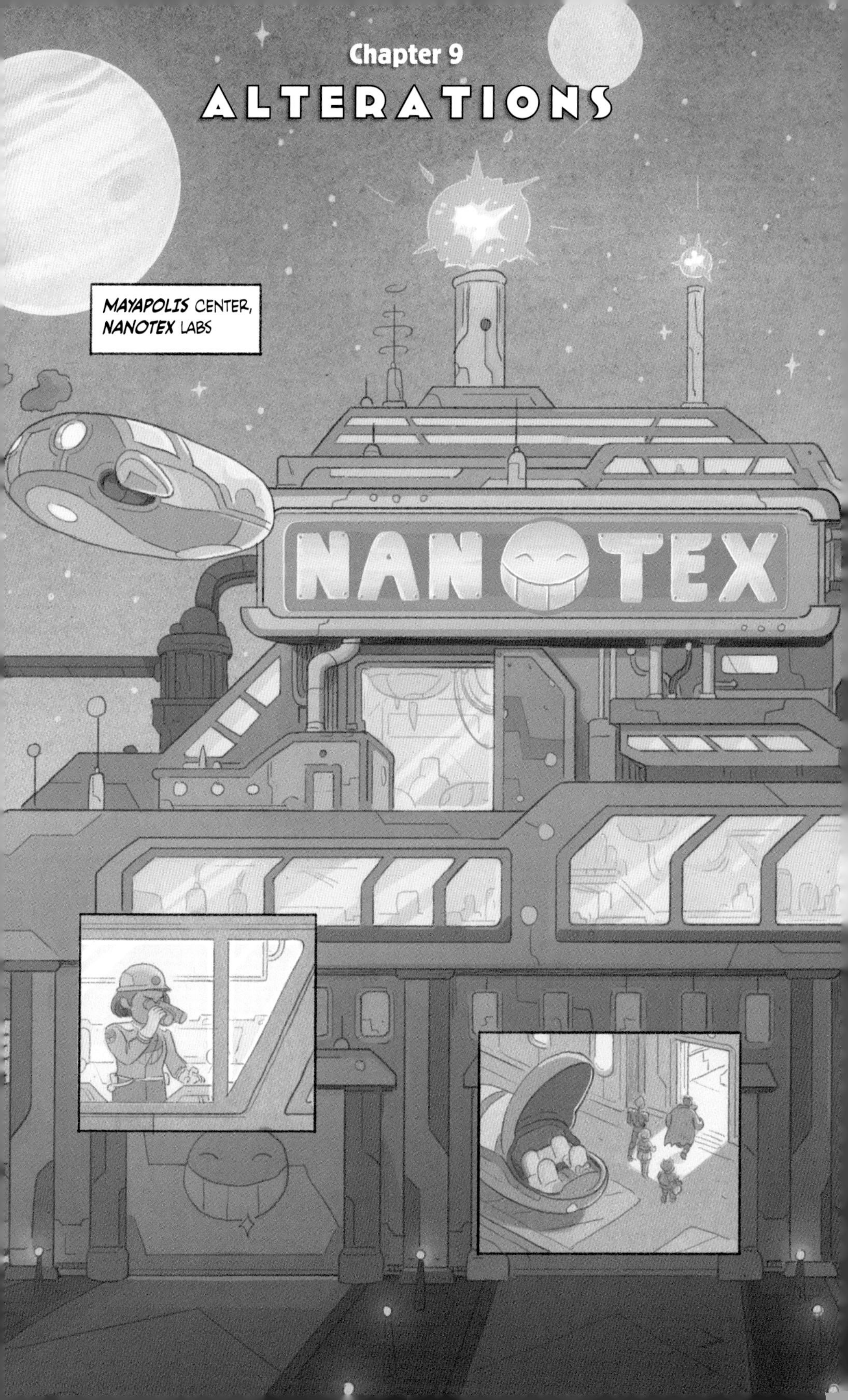

MAYAPOLIS CENTER, *NANOTEX* LABS
NANOTEX

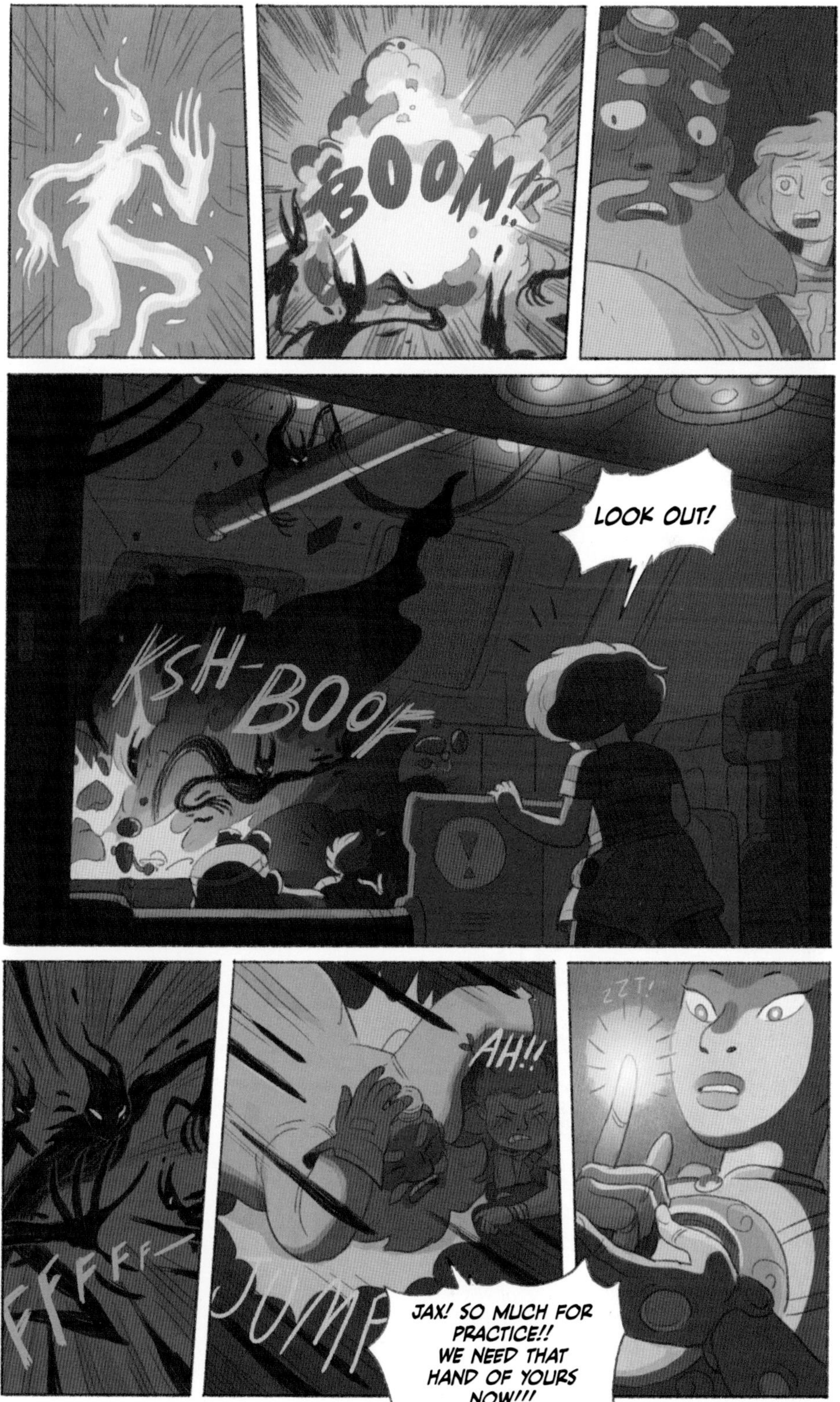
BOOM!!
LOOK OUT!
KSH-BOOF
FFFFf—
AH!!
JUMP
ZZT!
JAX! SO MUCH FOR PRACTICE!! WE NEED THAT HAND OF YOURS NOW!!!

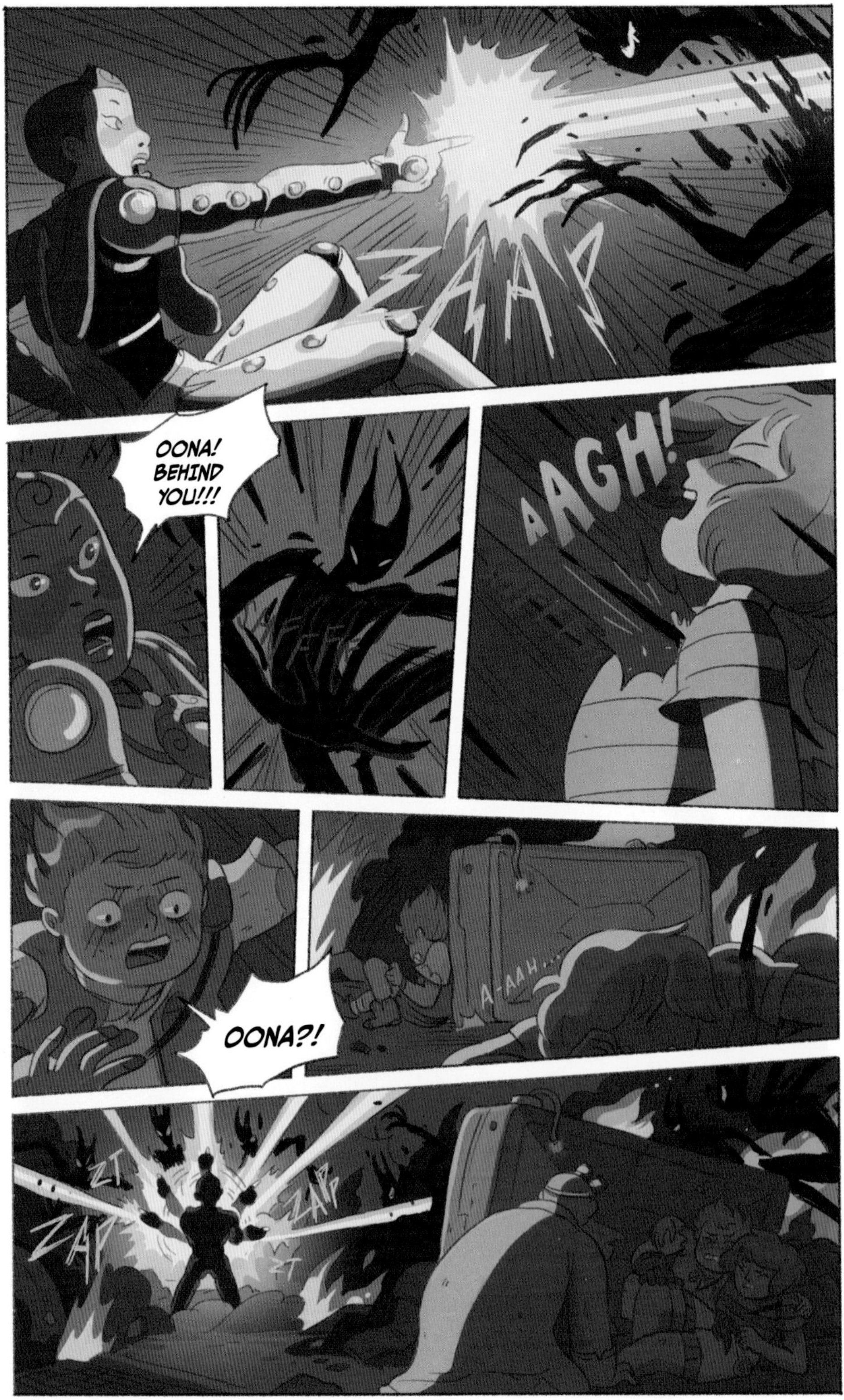
ZAAP
OONA! BEHIND YOU!!!
AAGH!
OONA?!
A-AAH...
ZT
ZAP
ZAPP
ZT

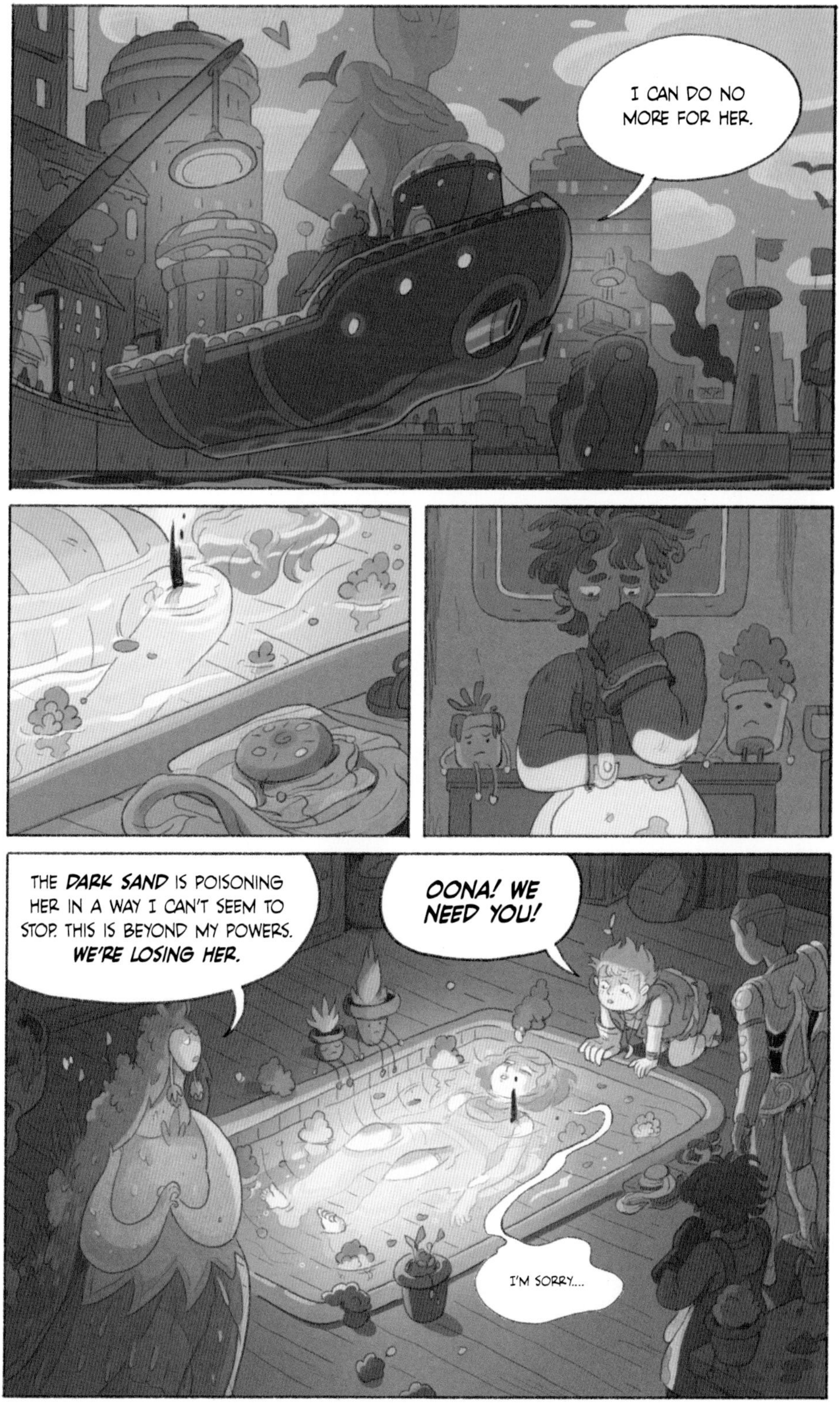
I CAN DO NO MORE FOR HER.
THE DARK SAND IS POISONING HER IN A WAY I CAN'T SEEM TO STOP. THIS IS BEYOND MY POWERS. WE'RE LOSING HER.
OONA! WE NEED YOU!
I'M SORRY....

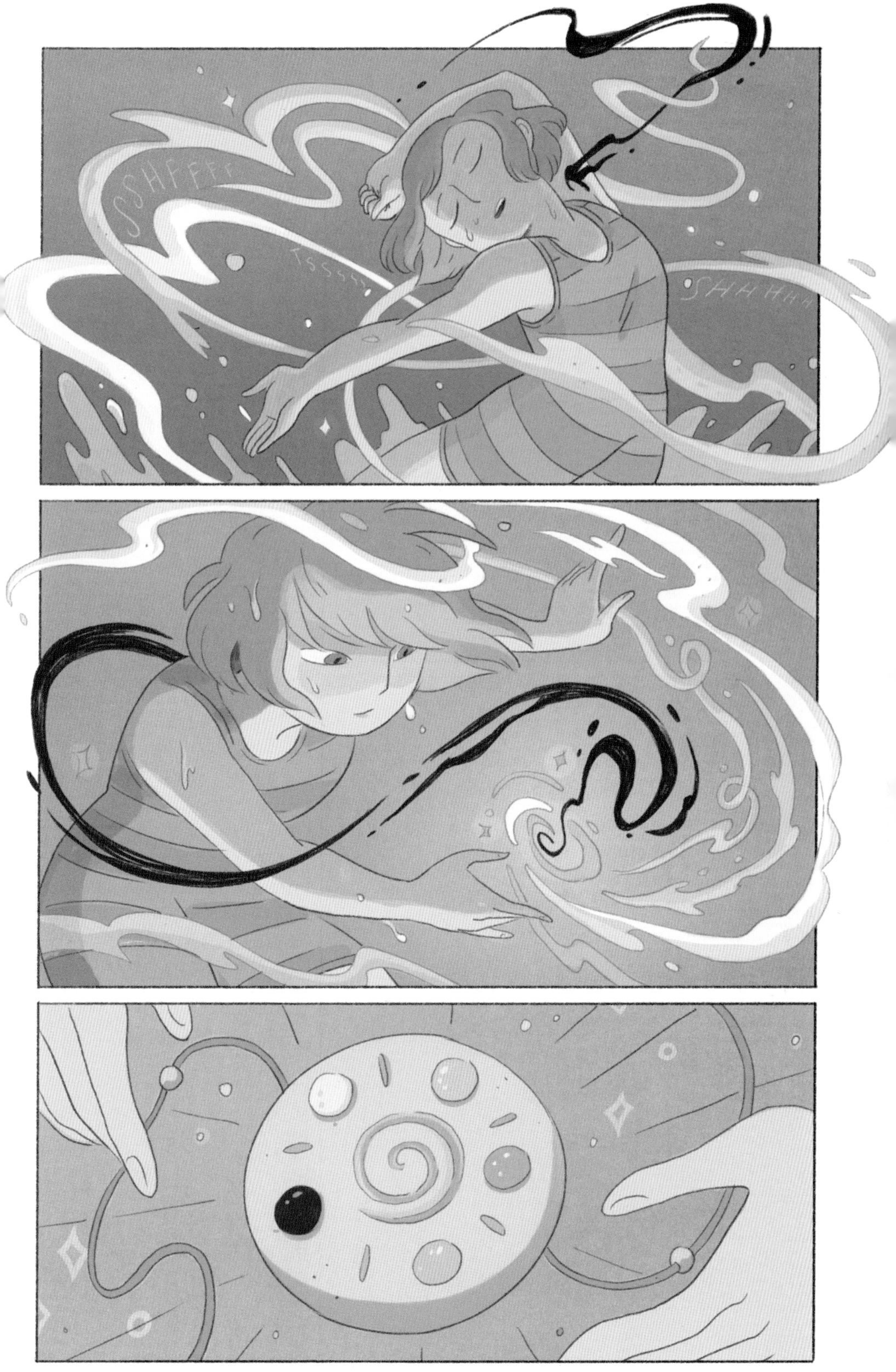
SSHFFFF
TSSSSSS
SHHHHH

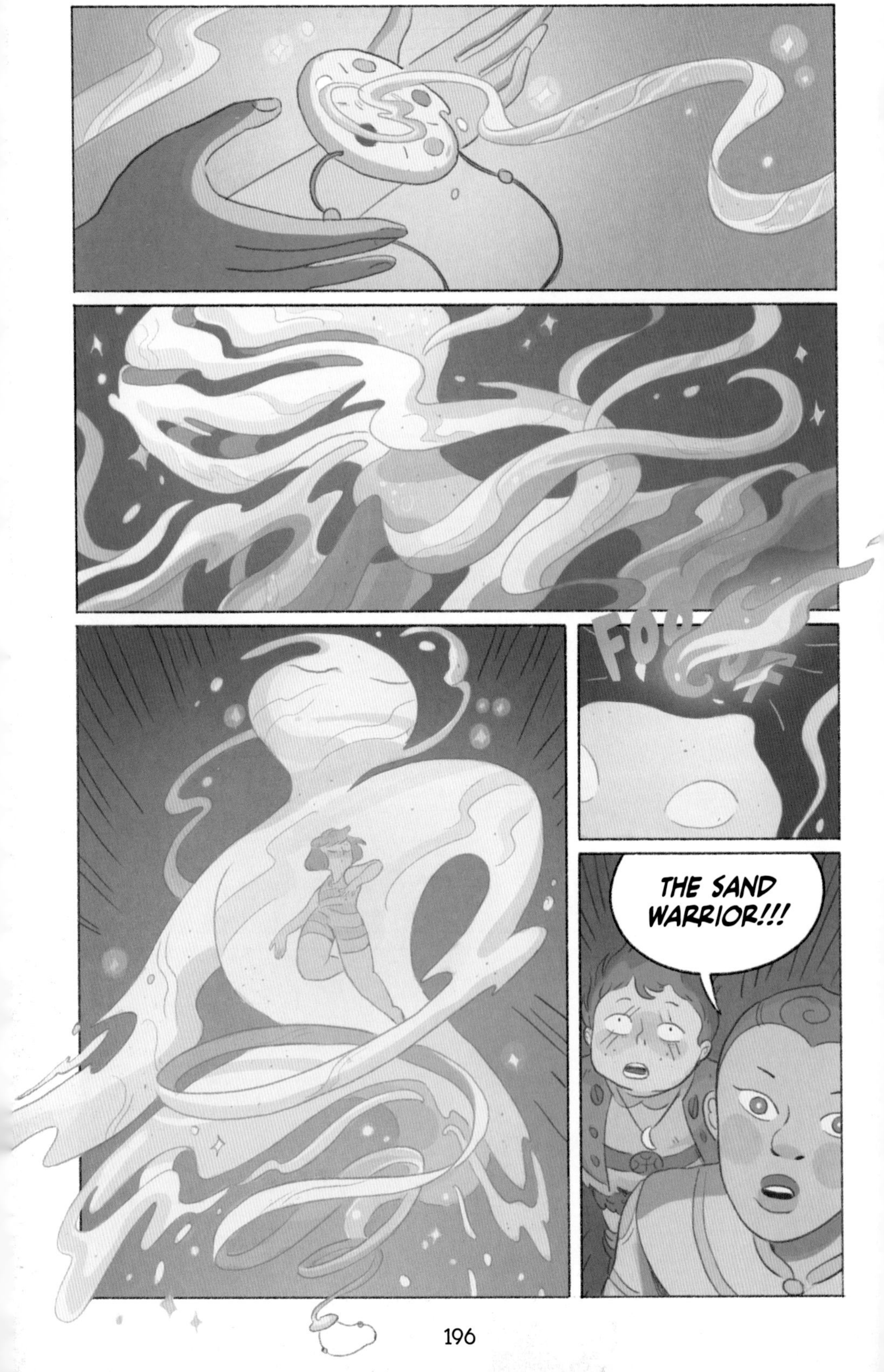
FOOOF
THE SAND WARRIOR!!!

Chapter 10

FIRE & RAIN

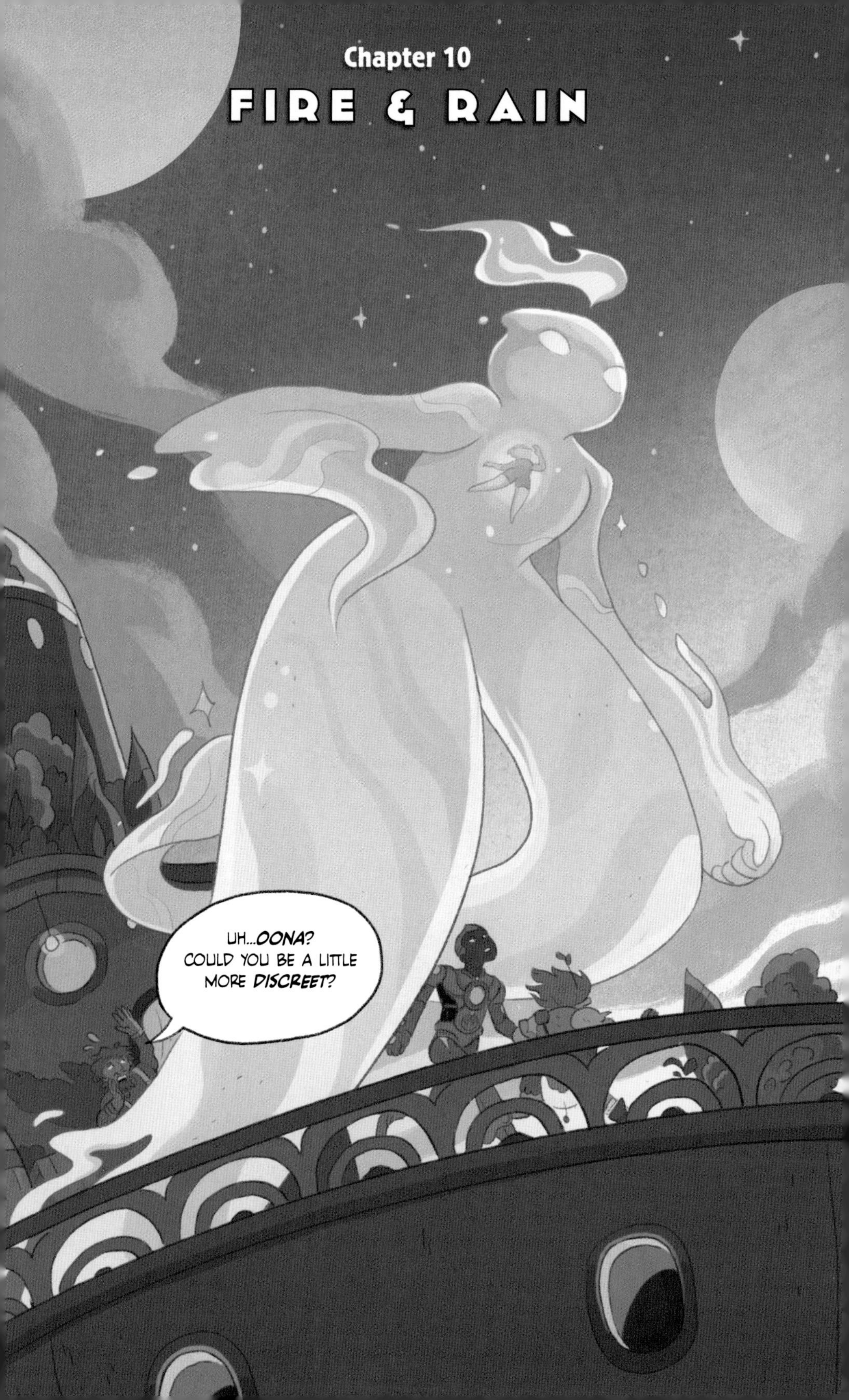

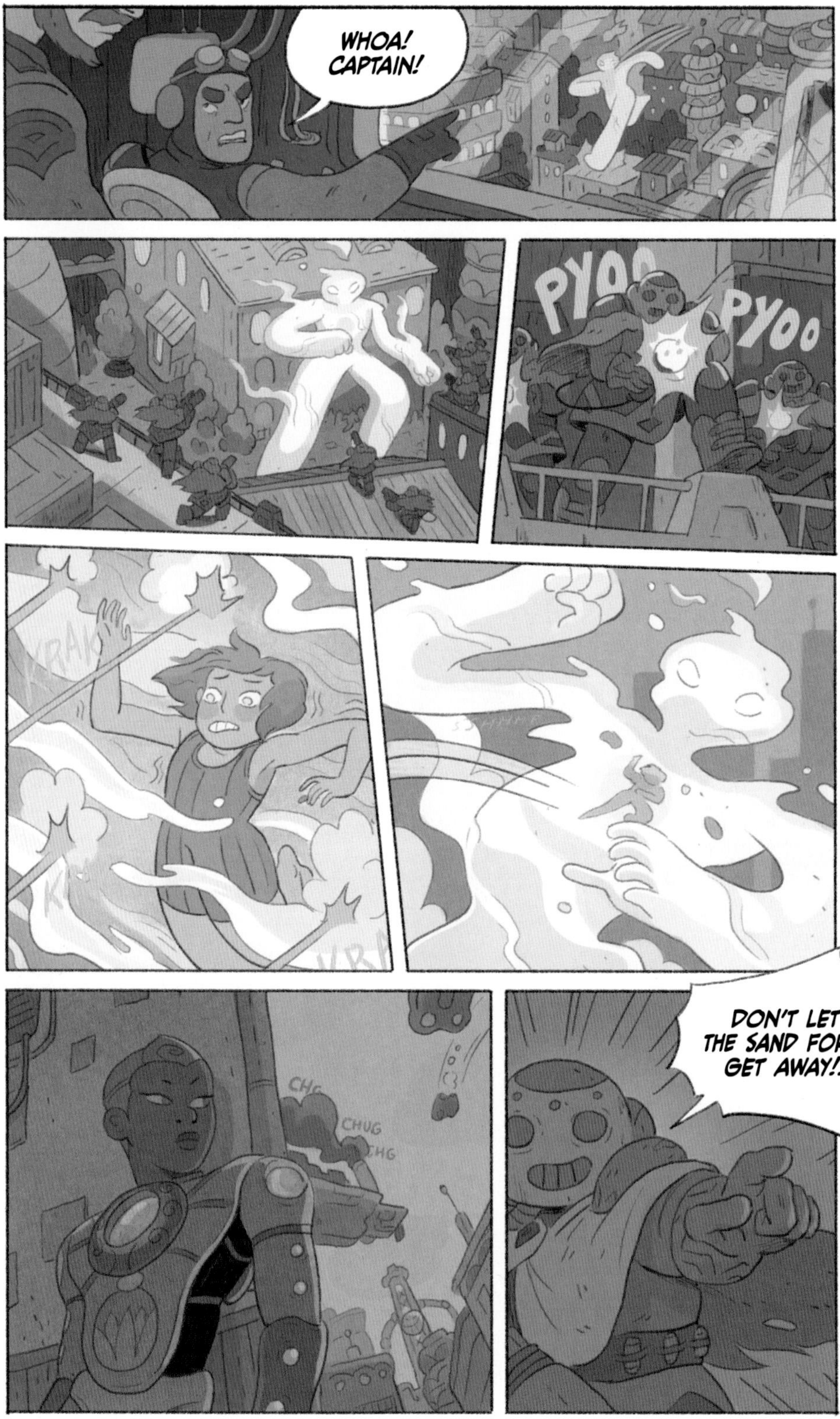
WHOA! CAPTAIN!
PYOO
PYOO
CHUG
DON'T LET THE SAND FORM GET AWAY!!

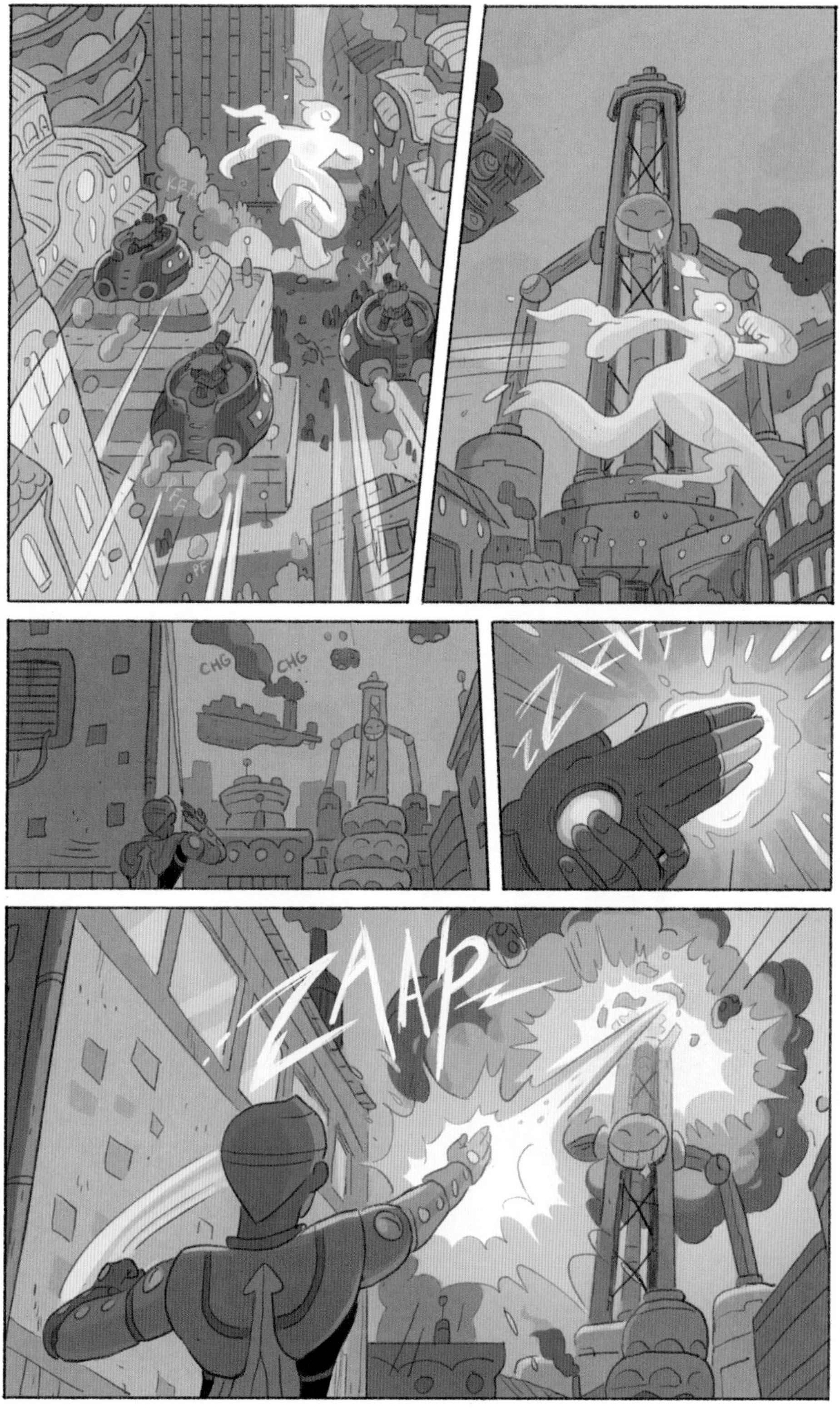
KRAK
PFF
PF
CHG
CHG
ZAAP

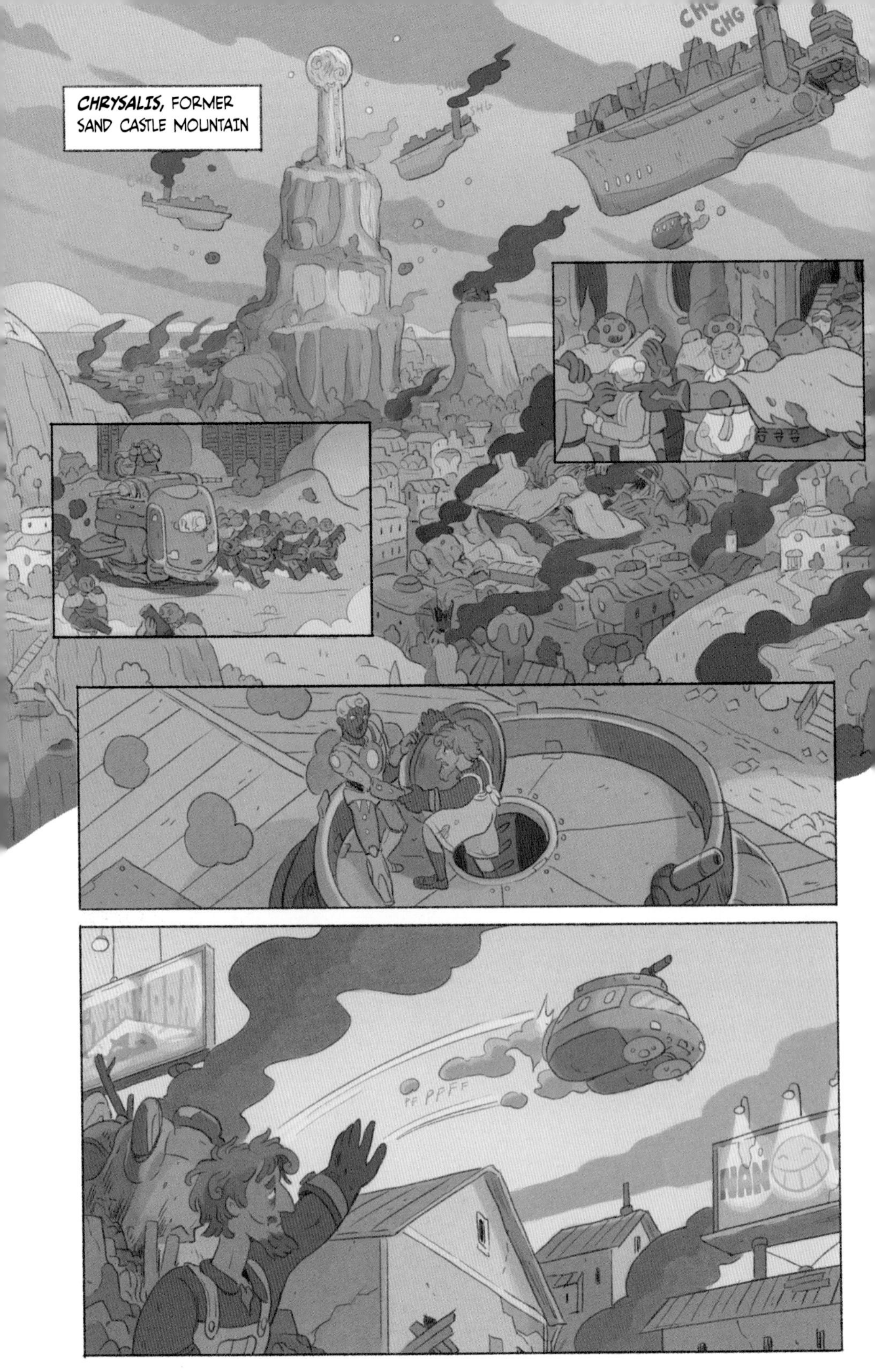
CHRYSALIS, FORMER SAND CASTLE MOUNTAIN
CHG CHG
PF PFFF

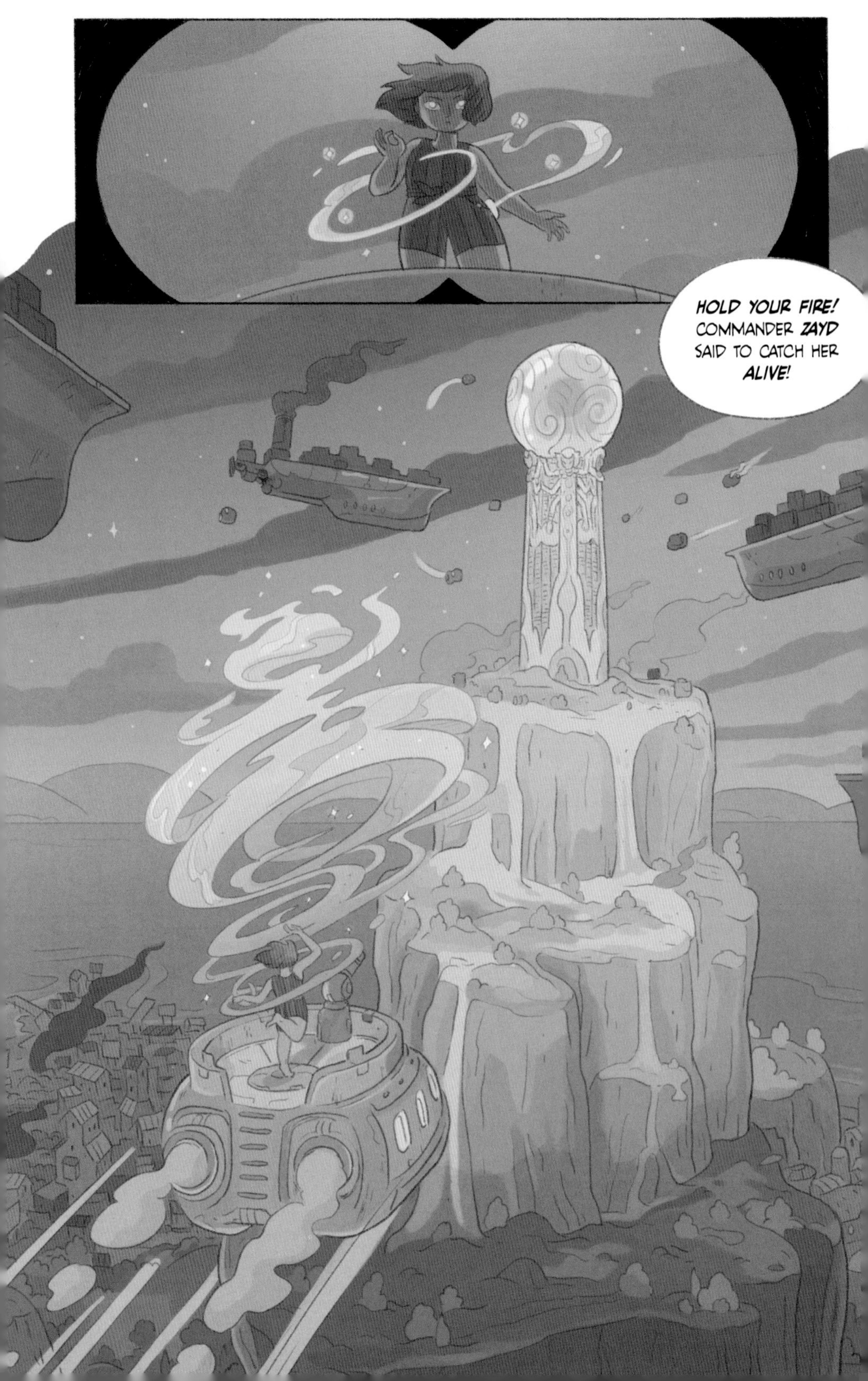
HOLD YOUR FIRE! COMMANDER ZAYD SAID TO CATCH HER ALIVE!

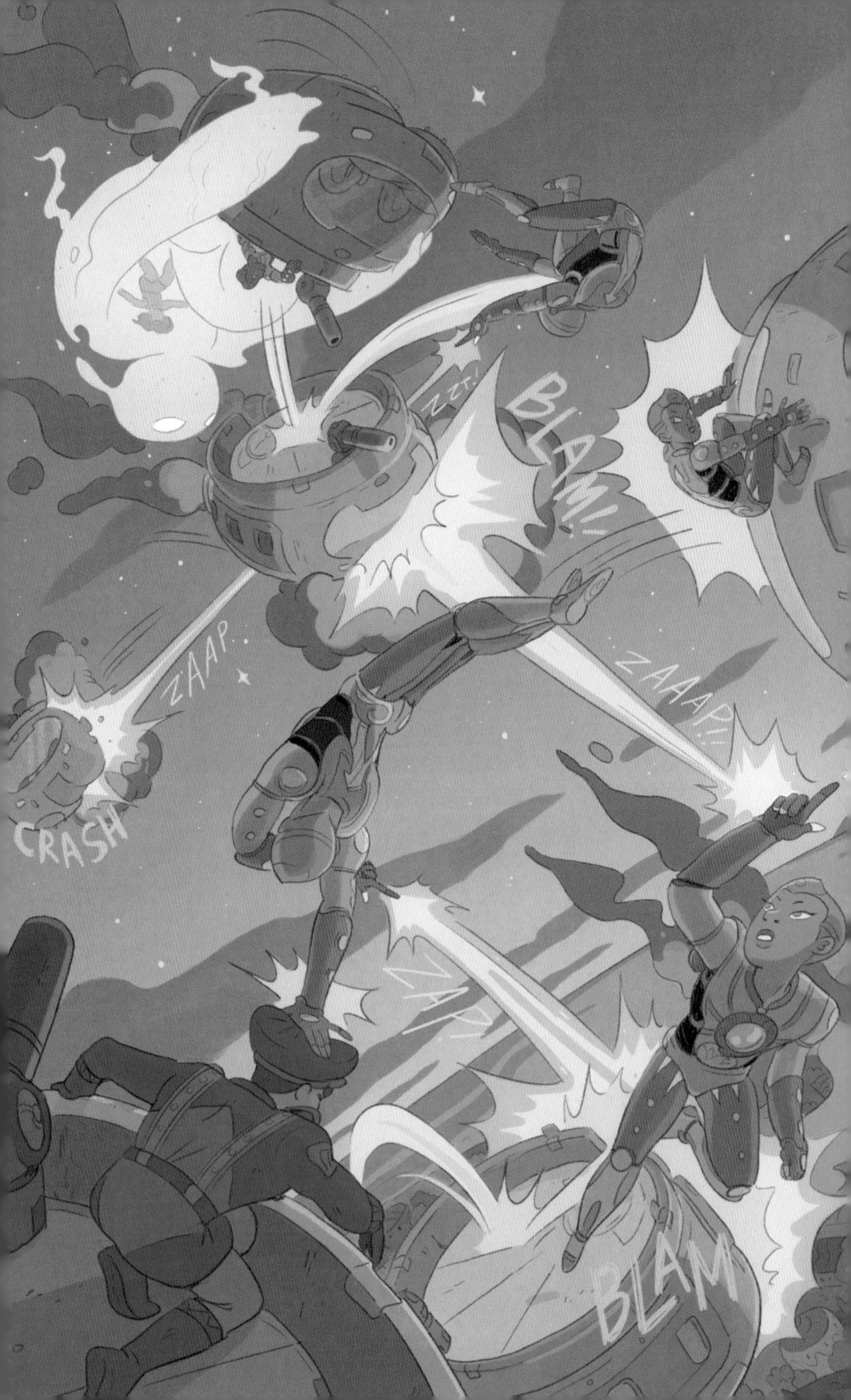
ZZT!
BLAM!!
ZAAP
CRASH
ZAAAP!!!
ZAP!
BLAM

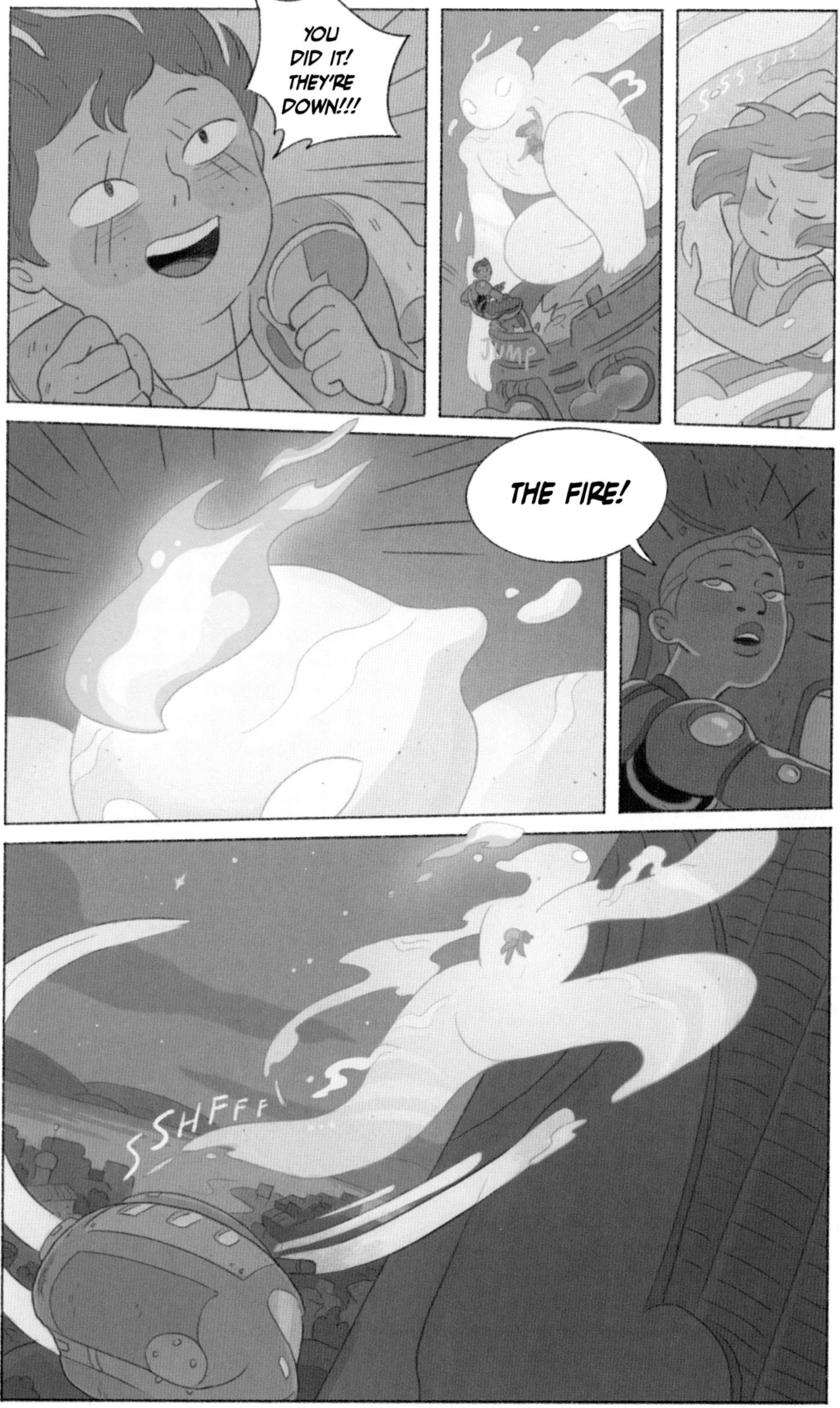
YOU DID IT! THEY'RE DOWN!!!
JUMP
THE FIRE!
SSHFFF

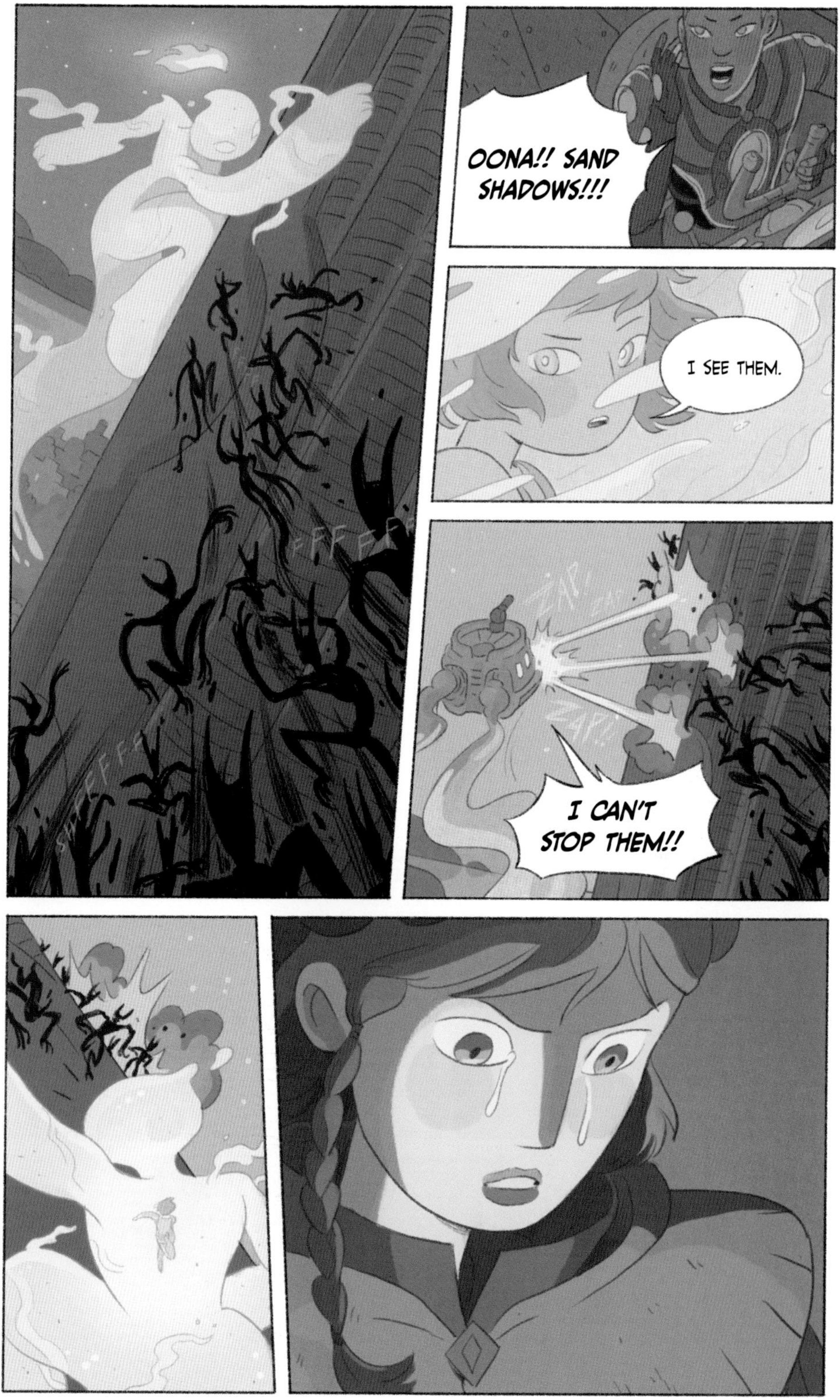
OONA!! SAND SHADOWS!!!
I SEE THEM.
I CAN'T STOP THEM!!

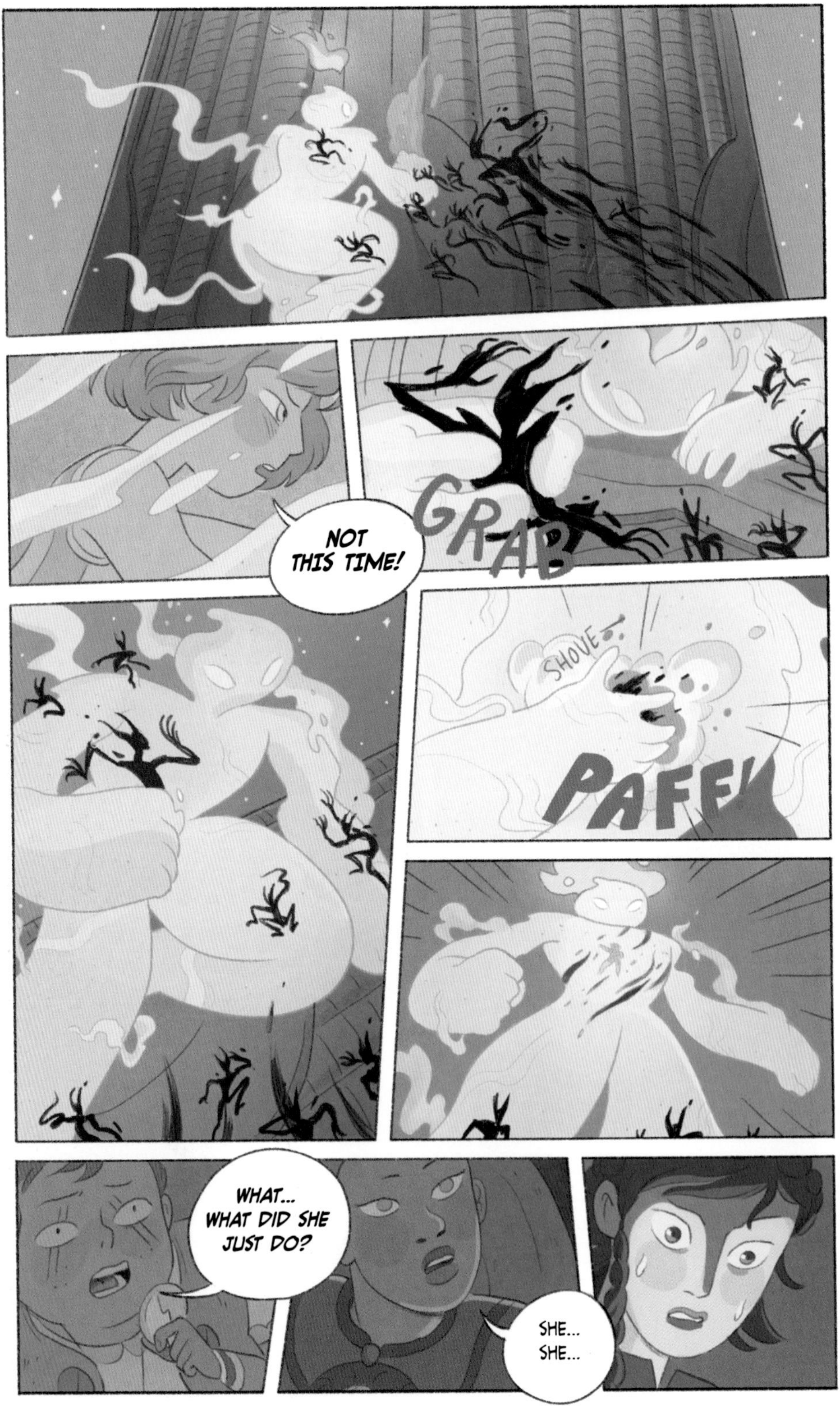
NOT THIS TIME!
GRAB
SHOVE
PAFF!
WHAT... WHAT DID SHE JUST DO?
SHE... SHE...

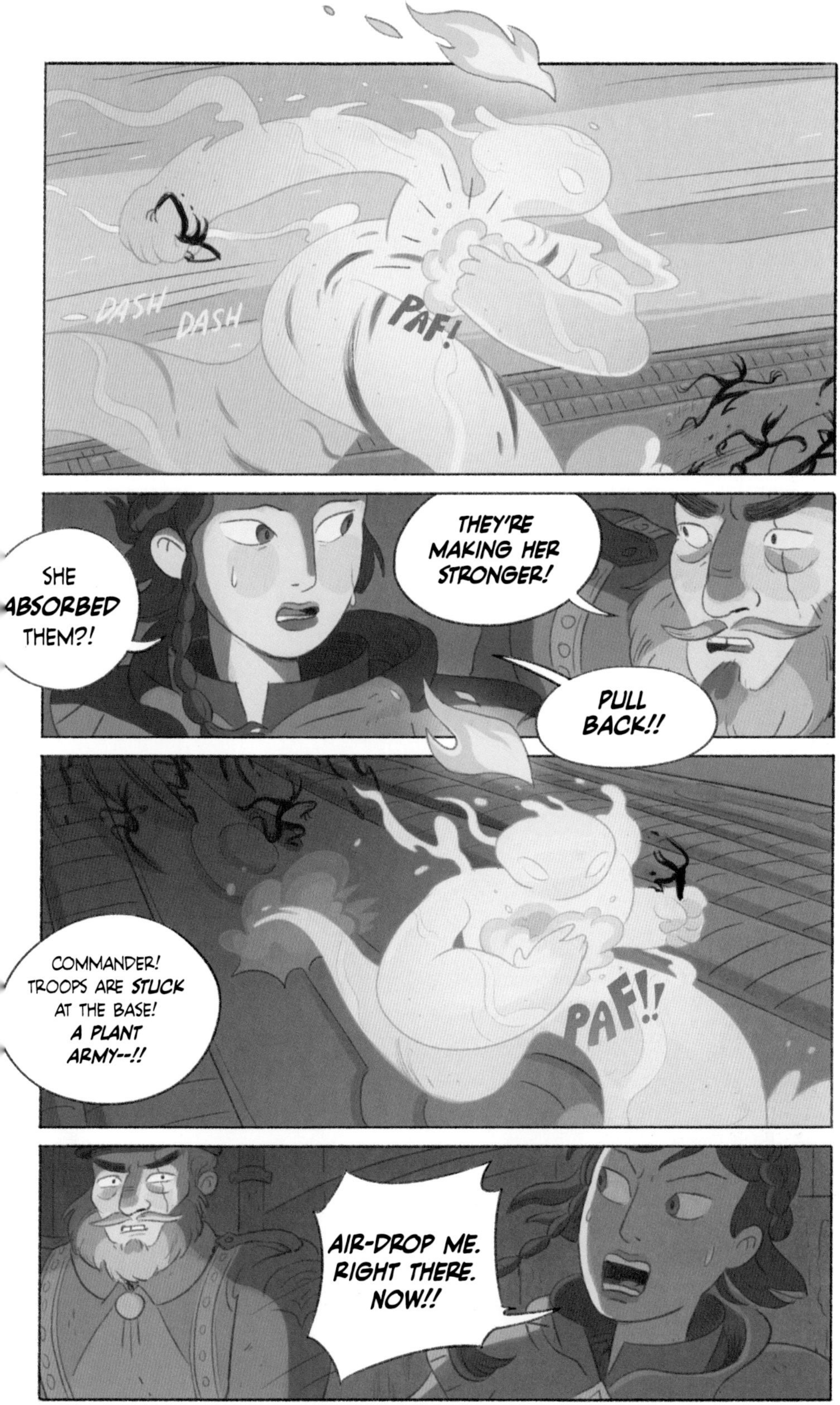
DASH DASH
PAF!
SHE ABSORBED THEM?!
THEY'RE MAKING HER STRONGER!
PULL BACK!!
COMMANDER! TROOPS ARE STUCK AT THE BASE! A PLANT ARMY--!!
PAF!!
AIR-DROP ME. RIGHT THERE. NOW!!

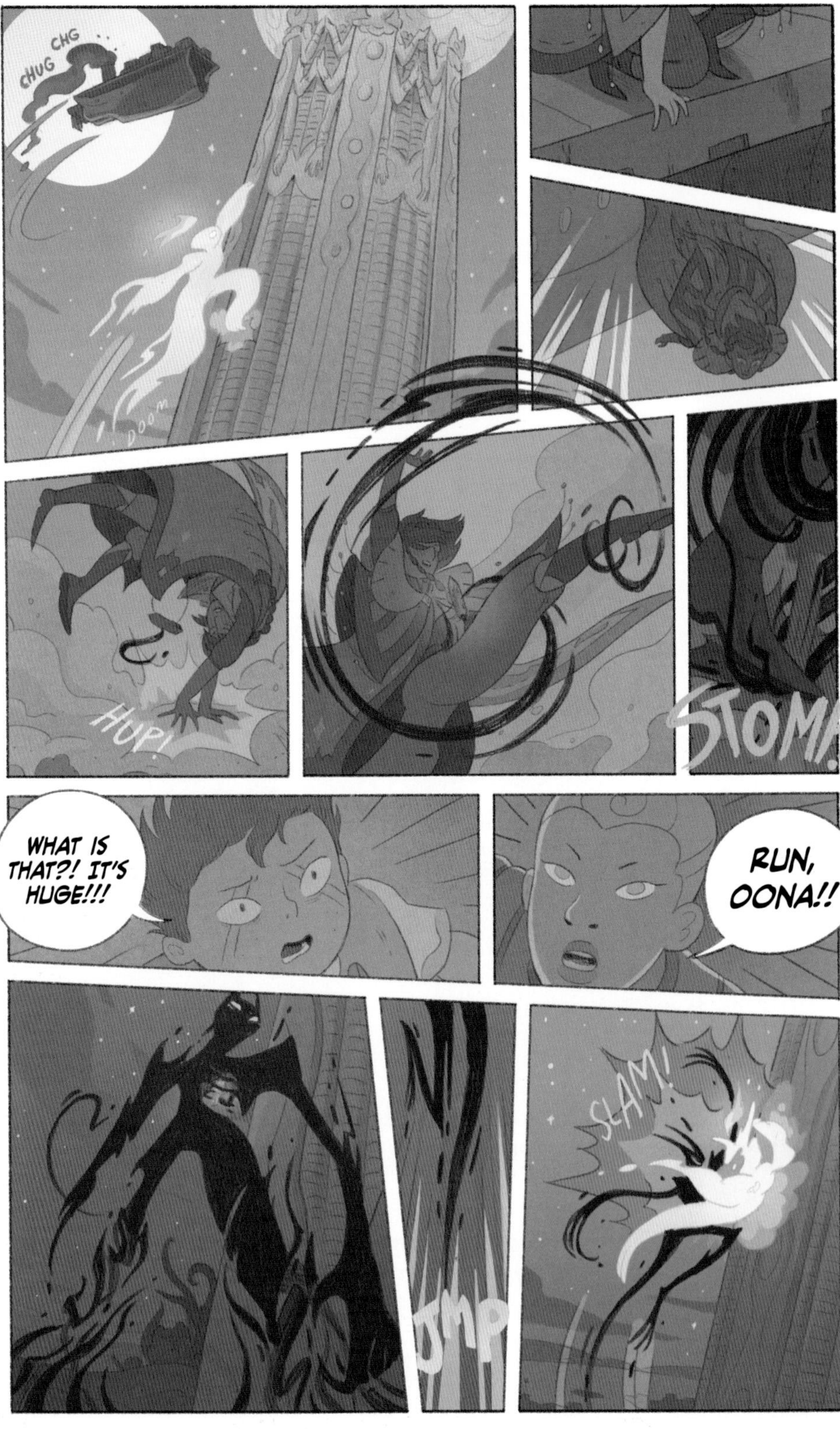
CHUG CHG
DOOM
HUP!
STOMP!
WHAT IS THAT?! IT'S HUGE!!!
RUN, OONA!!
JMP
SLAM!

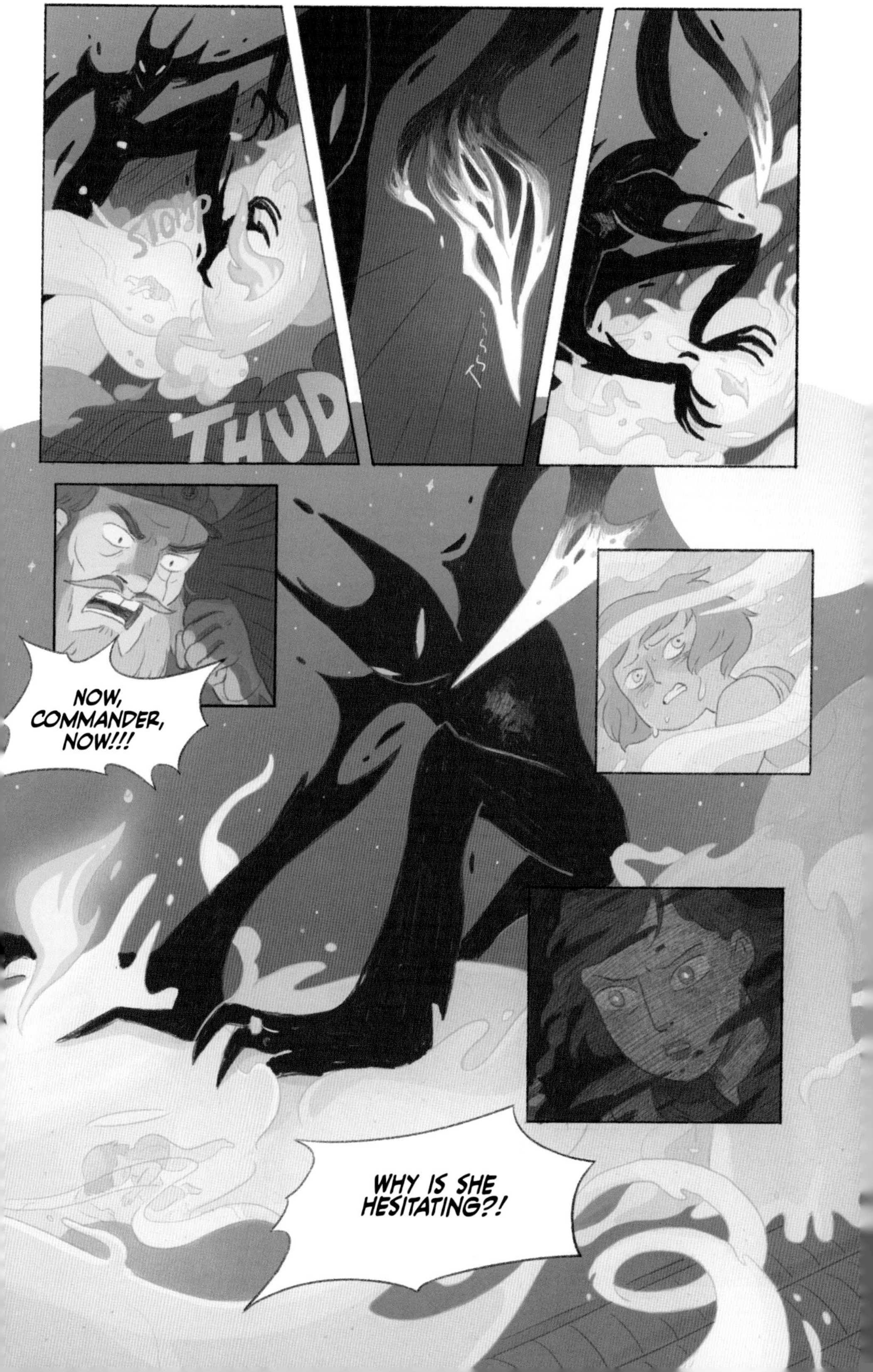
STOMP
THUD
TSSSS
NOW, COMMANDER, NOW!!!
WHY IS SHE HESITATING?!

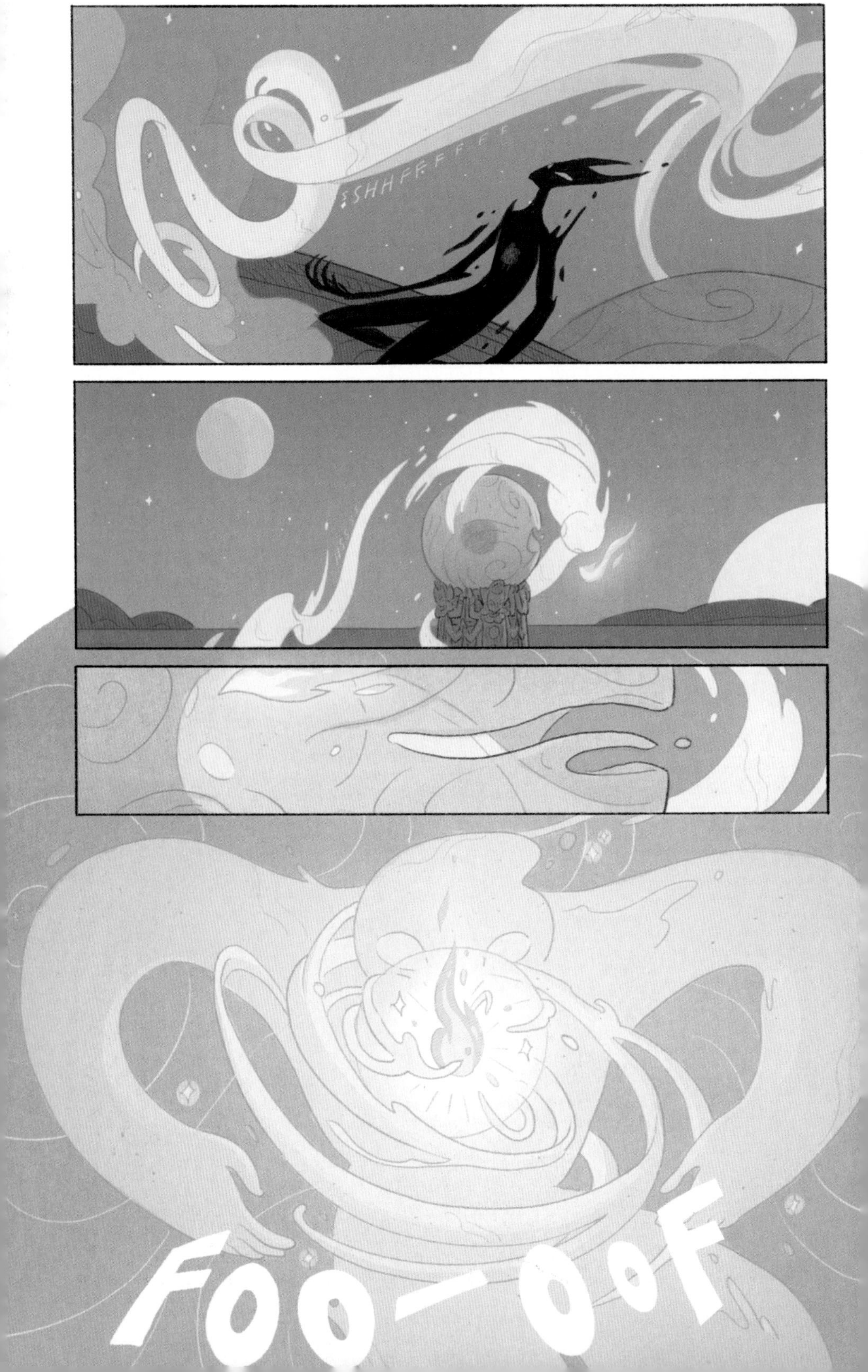
SHHFFFFFF
FOO—OOF

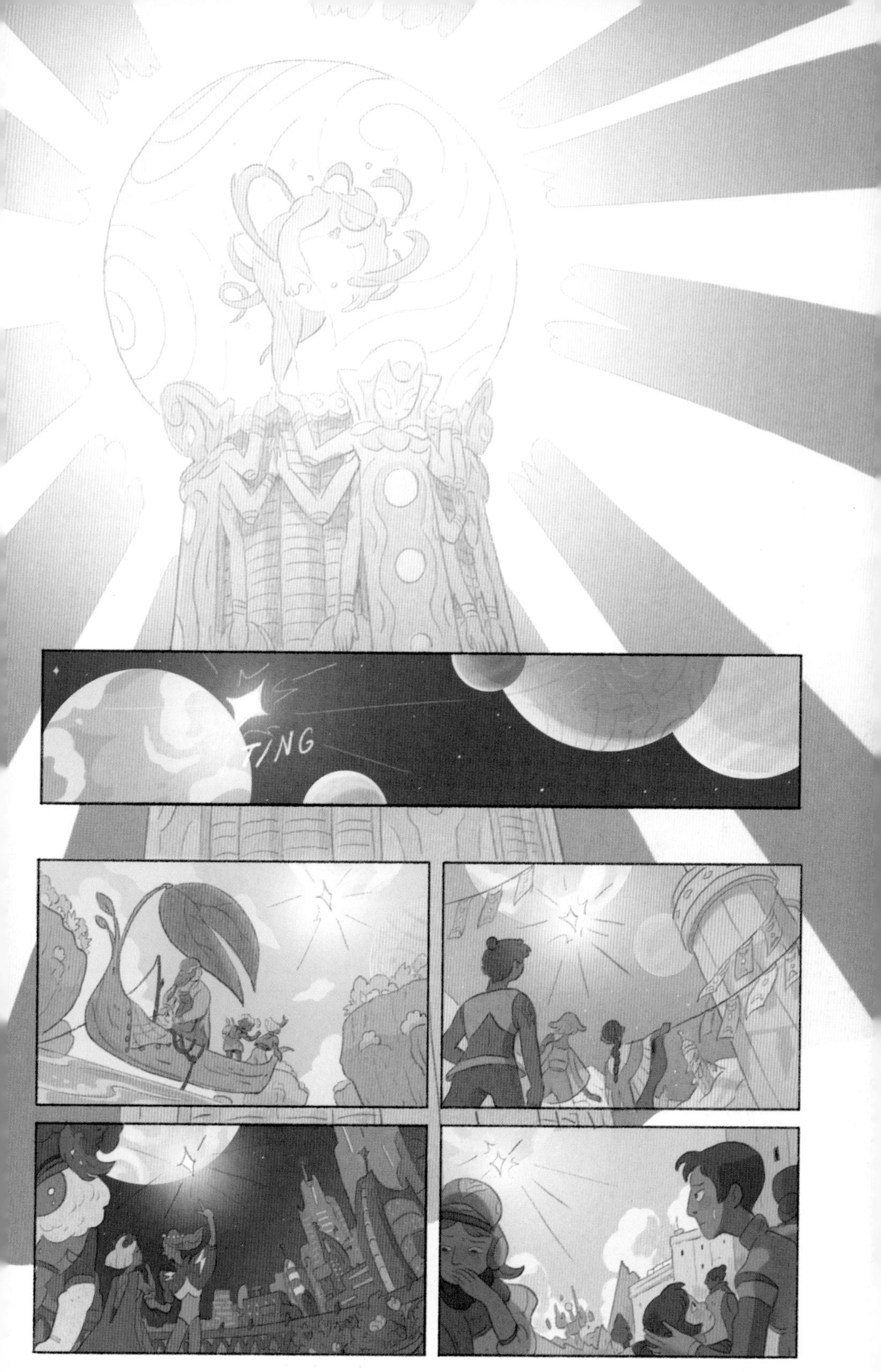
TING

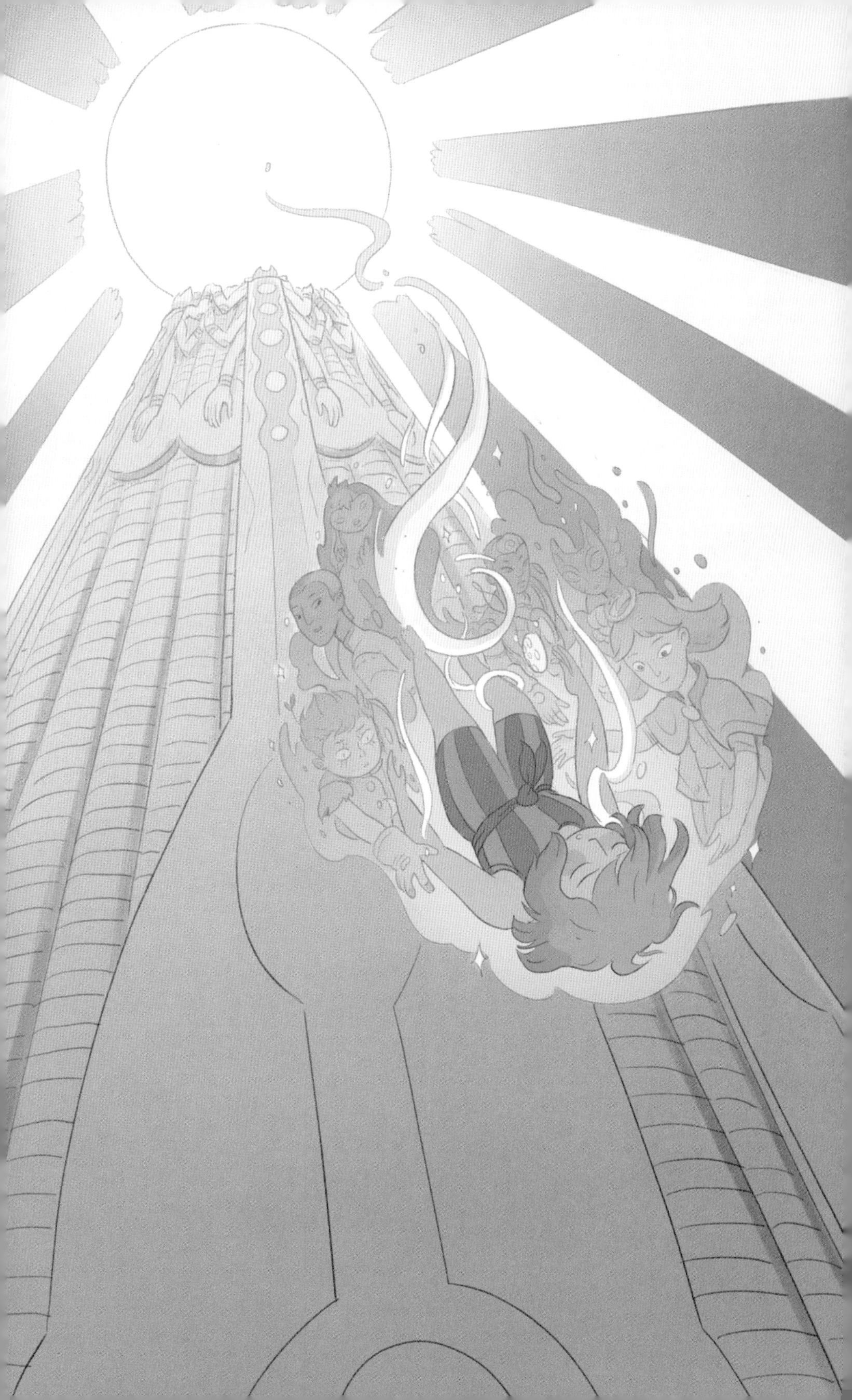

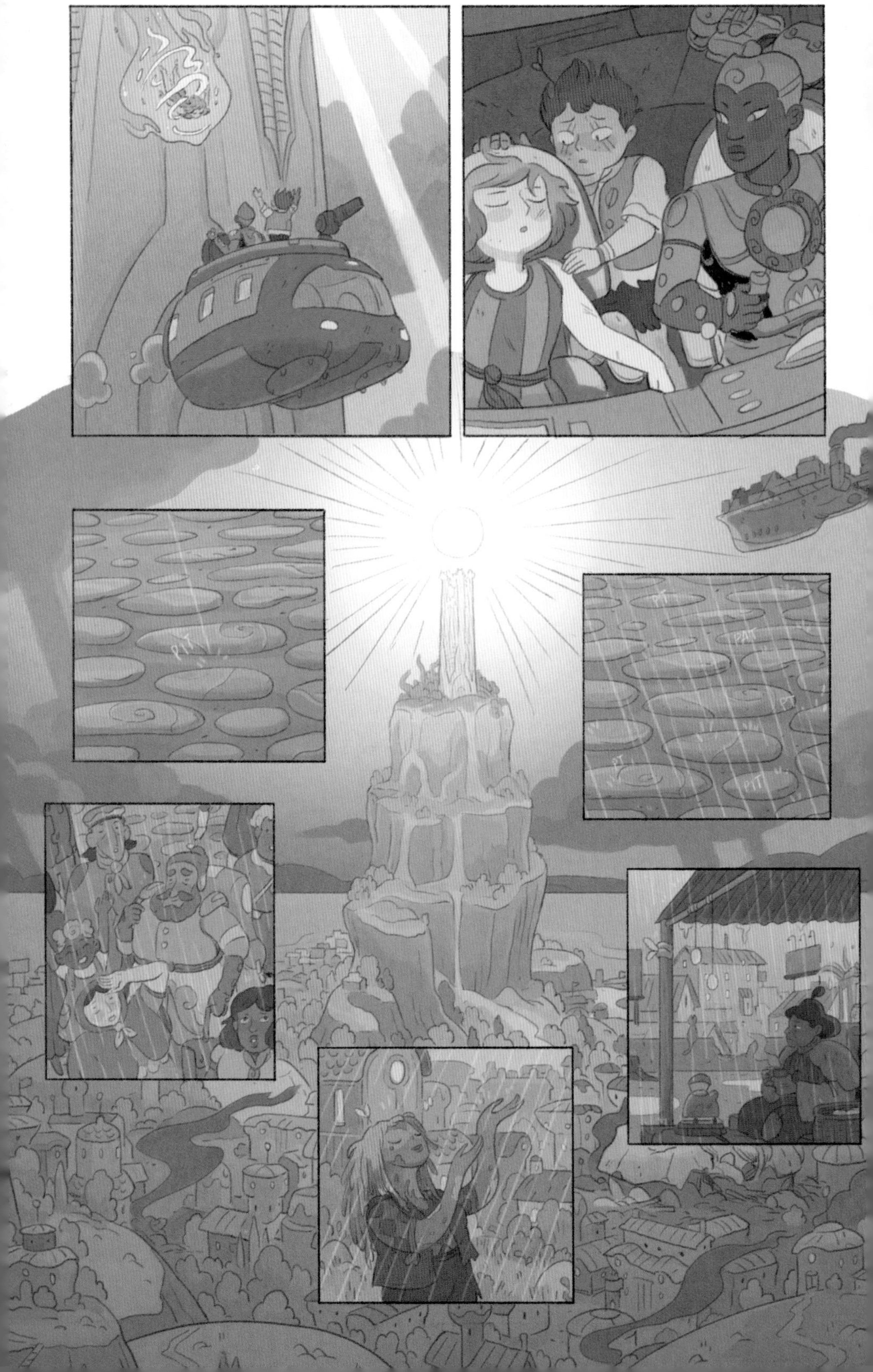
PIT
PT
PAT
PT
PT
PIT

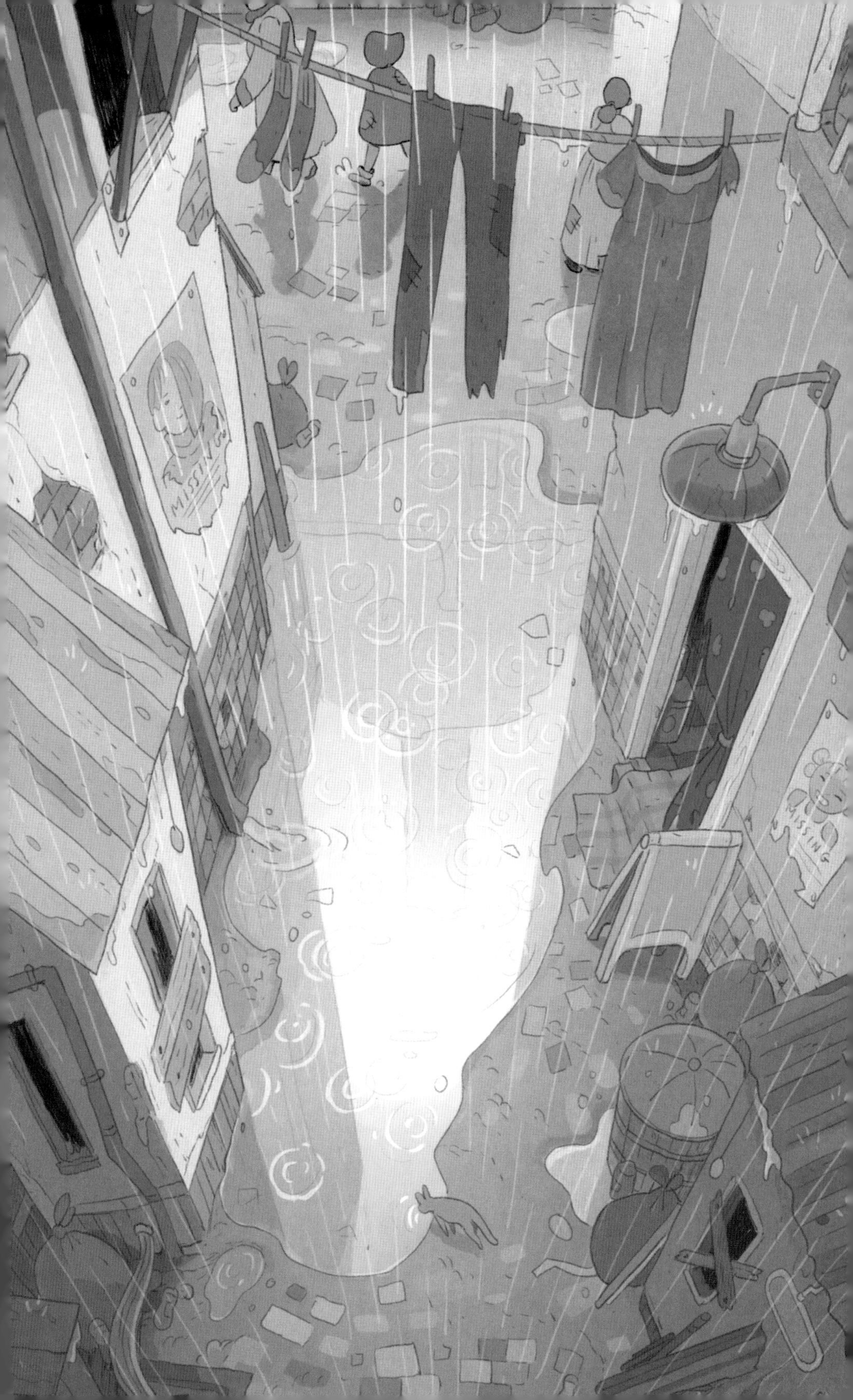
MISSING

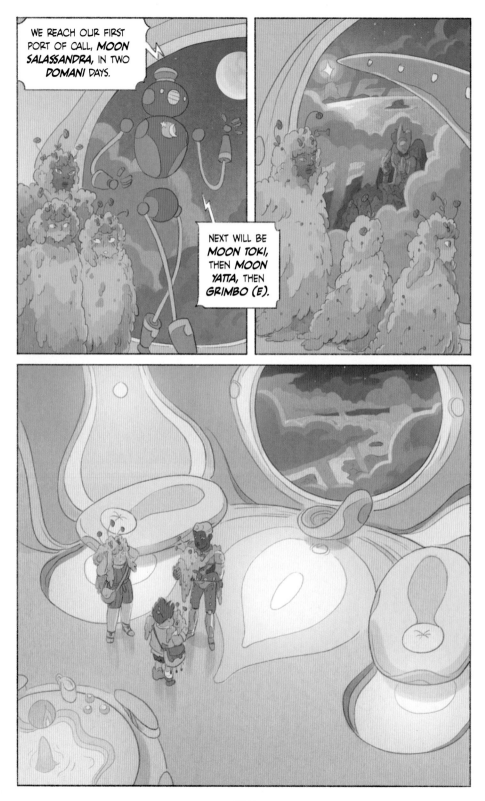

WE REACH OUR FIRST PORT OF CALL, *MOON SALASSANDRA*, IN TWO *DOMANI* DAYS.

NEXT WILL BE *MOON TOKI*, THEN *MOON YATTA*, THEN *GRIMBO (E)*.

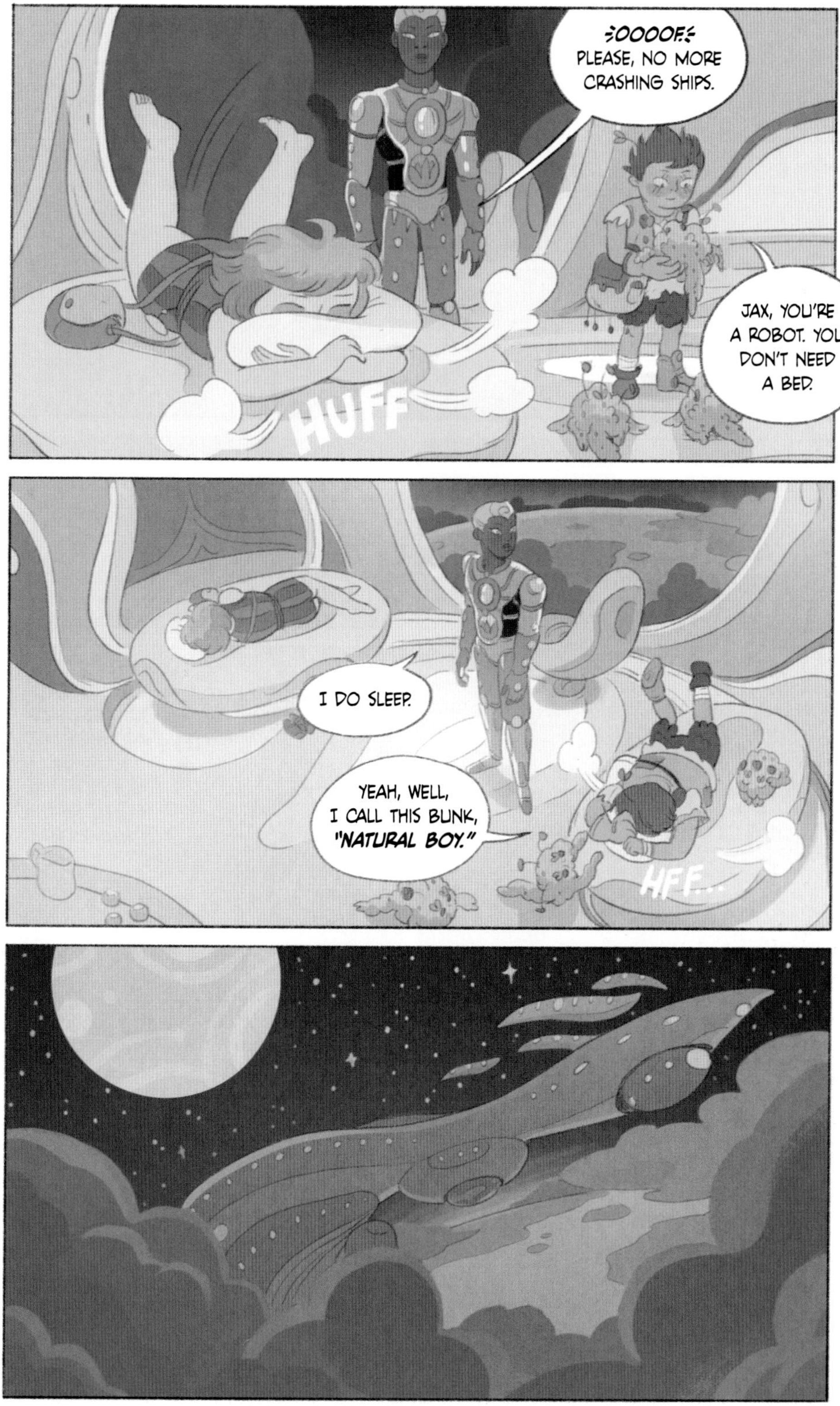

:OOOOF.:
PLEASE, NO MORE CRASHING SHIPS.
JAX, YOU'RE A ROBOT. YOU DON'T NEED A BED.
HUFF
I DO SLEEP.
YEAH, WELL, I CALL THIS BUNK, "NATURAL BOY."
HFF...

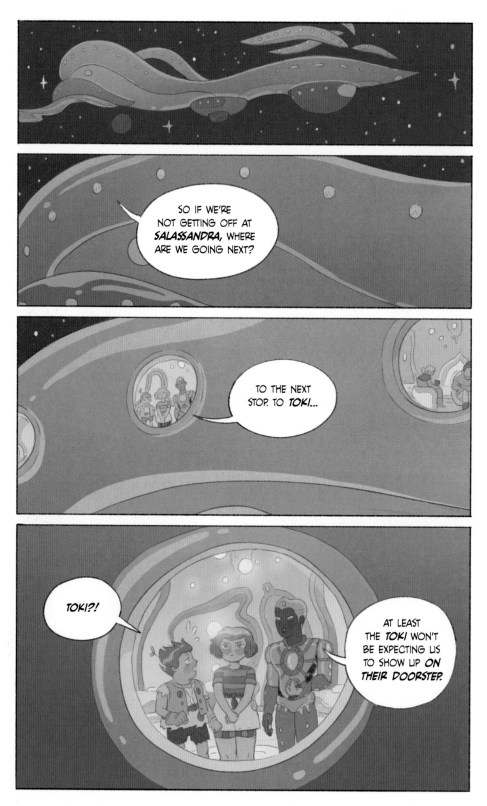

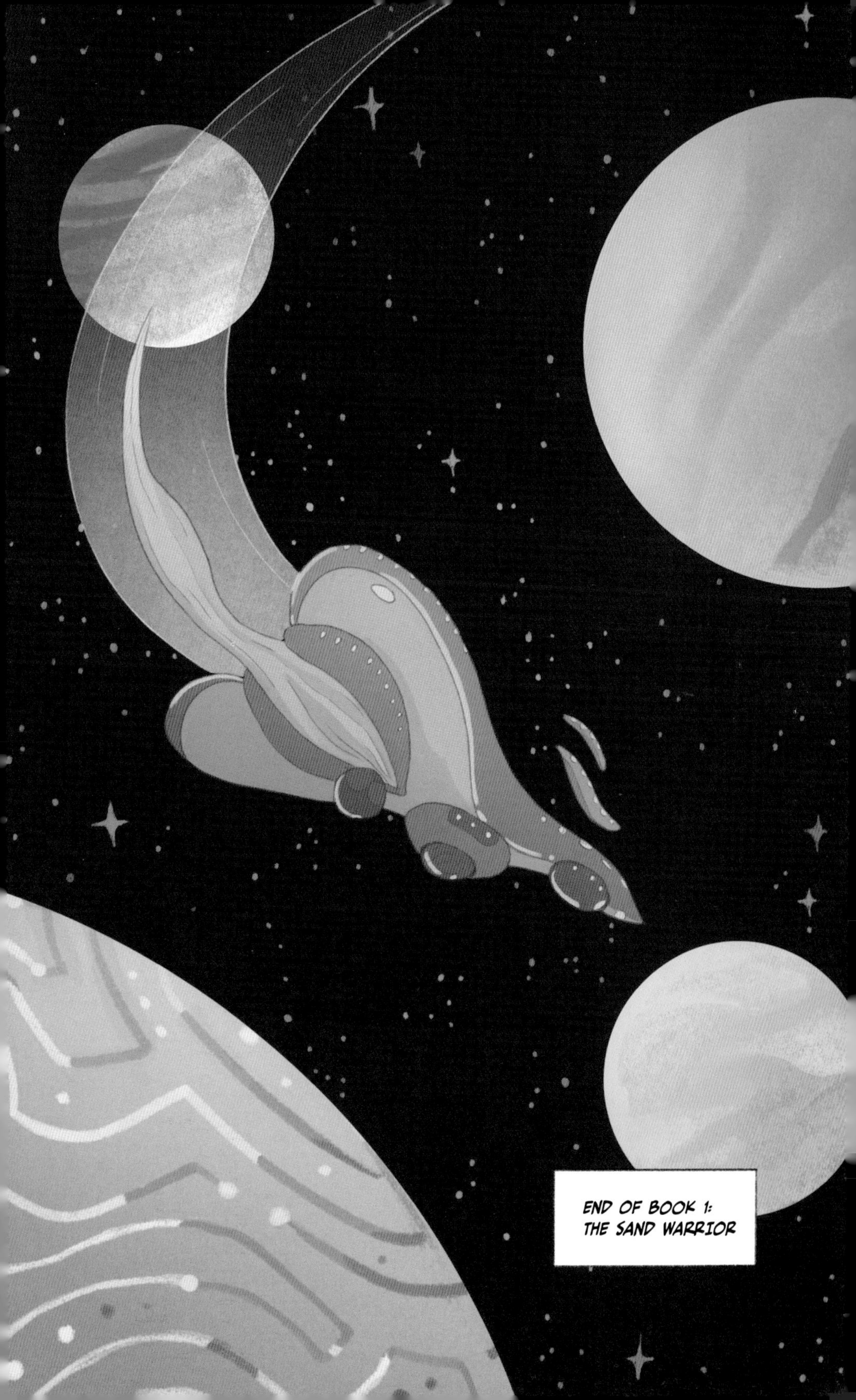
END OF BOOK 1:
THE SAND WARRIOR

To Julien and Clio—MS

To Shudan, Felix, and Elia—AS

To Mom and Pop—XB

To my friends and family—MR

To all my friends—BS

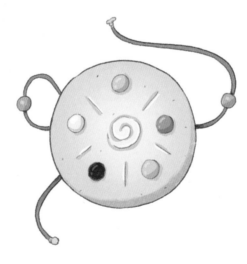

ACKNOWLEDGMENTS

Tanya McKinnon,
for support high and low, above and beyond

Our amazing Random House team:
Michelle Nagler, Chelsea Eberly, Elizabeth Tardiff, Kelly McGauley, Kim Lauber, Alison Kolani,
Dominique Cimina, Aisha Cloud, Lisa Nadel, Adrienne Waintraub, Laura Antonacci, John Adamo,
Joe English, Jocelyn Lange, Mallory Loehr, Barbara Marcus

+ Special thanks for added help, friendship & magic:
Siena Siegel, Sonia Siegel, Macarena Mata, Julie Sandfort, Gene Luen Yang,
Lee Wade, Sam Bosma, Kali Ciesemier, Noelle Stevenson, Carter Goodrich,
Moebius, Ursula K. LeGuin, Doris Lessing, Lois McMaster Bujold

Visit us on the Web! randomhousekids.com

Educators and librarians, for a variety of teaching tools, visit us at RHTeachersLibrarians.com

Library of Congress Cataloging-in-Publication Data is available upon request.
ISBN 978-1-101-93586-6 (trade) — ISBN 978-1-101-93588-0 (pbk.)
ISBN 978-1-101-93587-3 (lib. bdg.) — ISBN 978-1-101-93604-7 (ebook)

MANUFACTURED IN CHINA

10 9 8 7 6 5 4 3 2 1

First Edition

Random House Children's Books supports the
First Amendment and celebrates the right to read.

MARK SIEGEL has written and illustrated several award-winning picture books and graphic novels, including the *New York Times* bestseller **Sailor Twain, or the Mermaid in the Hudson.** He is also the founder and editorial director of First Second Books at Macmillan. He lives with his family in New York.

ALEXIS SIEGEL is a writer and translator based in London, England. He has translated a number of bestselling graphic novels, including Joann Sfar's **The Rabbi's Cat** and Pénélope Bagieu's **Exquisite Corpse** into English and Gene Luen Yang's **American Born Chinese** into French.

XANTHE BOUMA is an illustrator based in Southern California. When not working on picture books, fashion illustration, and comics, Xanthe enjoys soaking up the beachside sun.

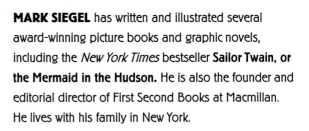

MATT ROCKEFELLER is an illustrator and comic book artist from Tucson, Arizona. His work has appeared in a variety of formats, including book covers, picture books, and animation. Matt lives in New York City.

BOYA SUN is an illustrator and coauthor of the upcoming graphic novel **Chasma Knights.** Originally from China, Boya has traveled from Canada to the United States and now resides in the charming city of Baltimore.

What will Oona, Jax, and An Tzu find on Toki?
The adventure continues in

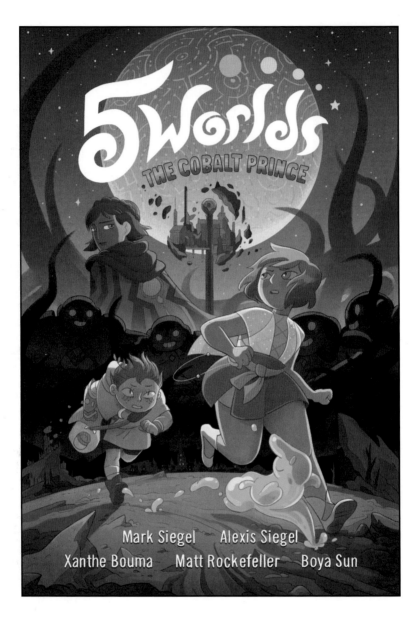

5W2:
THE COBALT PRINCE